In

This edition first published 2017 by Fahrenheit Press

10 9 8 7 6 5 4 3 2 1

www.Fahrenheit-Press.com

Copyright © Jacqueline Chadwick 2017

The right of Jacqueline Chadwick to be identified as the author of this work has been asserted by her in accordance with the Copyright, Designs and Patents Act 1988.

All rights reserved. No part of this publication may be reproduced, stored in a retrieval system, or transmitted in any form, or by any means, electronic, mechanical, photocopying, recording or otherwise, without permission in writing from the publisher.

F 4 E

In The Still

By

Jacqueline Chadwick

Fahrenheit Press

For Simon, Alex and Jamie

*Let conversation cease, let laughter flee.
This is the place where death delights to help the living.*

Giovanni Morgani

PROLOGUE - THE FORSAKEN FLOCK

The unpracticed eye would wonder how they can surrender to sleep. To slumber so soundly, so tranquil, so deep in the midst of what is surely a most despicable place for them to be. The very edge of their own mortality.

Tears parched upon the flush of the cheek, supplication defunct. No muffled begging, pleading, mewling, gasping. Just quiet. Just peace. Exhaustion their liege, in silent acquiescence, overpowered and weakened, they are all finally lulled into the kindness of dreams.

As children – innocent, meek – often our tears are our rafts of egress, our sole means of escape. Under the onion-skin guise of adulthood we dance in denial of danger, of the need for escape. But one should always be wary, always be ready for the descent of our darkness, for we are never truly safe.

Our light is a fiction, the delicate penumbra of which is a mere phantom of hope bathing us in glowing promise, expectations exalting, blithely fluttering on in perpetual disillusionment. But it is unavoidably ephemeral for some whose destiny it is to be clipped at the pinion and curtailed in the briefest of blinks. Out of existence. Hope stripped. The evisceration of purity.

To dispirit is to rule. To make a slave thereof. The ethereal substance that is *spilled hope* is too beautiful, too perfect for this dank world. The essence of it is a palpable, coppery potion that trickles from them all, an invisible trail of sand retracing spent time ever upward, rising higher and higher to become the very firmament, fluffing like cirrus to pelt down again and to percolate through the Haversian conduits of marrow and to fill one with the heady intoxicant that transubstantiates the core of us, vaulting one higher and stronger, metamorphosing one into something new each time. Something purer and more powerful than any seraph or deity was ever bold enough to be.

His quarry is carefully sought out and pursued from afar and then snatched away to rest, at last, in this lair. They are invisible. They are missed not, for they had already been forsaken long before he found them.

The forsaken ones are plentiful. Meandering amongst us. They call to him. Pull him to them. They are sirens in the bleak.

Now they are ready to be shown, to be seen, to manifest revenant. And through them, he too, shall be seen. He shall peek from behind the veil and perhaps take leave of the hide that has served him well as a façade of normality – his fleeced cape. His quiet still.

PART ONE

MONDAY 9TH APRIL

CHAPTER 1 - AN UNEXPECTED PARTNERSHIP

As the kettle took forever to boil in the kitchen, Ali grabbed her dressing gown and pocketed her cell phone, having already sent her husband the obligatory 'good morning' text. She slipped into a pair of her husband's Nikes – gigantic in comparison to her size five feet – to shield her from a spring that was taking forever to wax into being, making this April one reminiscent of Britain's non-existent summers.

The wraparound deck afforded Ali a panoramic view of the Pacific Ocean where it hugged the south-eastern tail of Vancouver Island and meandered north to the Inside Passage. Ali never tired of the view and now that her son and daughter were older – fourteen and eighteen, respectively – Ali could almost enjoy quietude again. *Almost* because typically she found that her rare moments of peace were interrupted in some way – so predictable had the interruptions become they were something of a running joke. Finding the humour in the tortuous mind rot inflicted endlessly upon her over the years had become Ali's salvation. Were it not for her humour, Ali was sure she'd be a raving lunatic by now.

"Who are you fucking kidding?" she mumbled, as she lit her cigarette, sucking as much of the thick, velvety smoke into her mouth as she could. Her enjoyment of this first cigarette of the day was so intense that Ali prolonged the bliss by tricking the smoke into thinking it was free to dissipate into the air, letting it snake out from between her lips before sucking it all back into her lungs, eyes closed in rapture. The nicotine coursed through her blood, penetrating the blood-brain barrier and hitting that sweet spot, triggering all her happy chemicals at once. She exhaled what was left of the smoke and watched as it condensed in the moist air of the drizzly morning.

Many years ago, single and newly qualified in both forensic psychology and pathology, Ali had visited a mall psychic in the Trafford Centre whilst working a case in Manchester. Ali remembered scoffing when the gypsy had prophesied that Ali would not continue in her career but would instead dedicate herself exclusively to her future children, that she would live in a faraway land in a house overlooking the ocean with a soulmate she was yet to meet.

Ali smiled at the memory. With her first fag in hand on her wraparound deck in Mochetsin, refreshed by the settling of the misty drizzle on her cheeks and gazing out over an ocean she was utterly mesmerized by the distant peaks of the mountains of mainland Canada in a life that had metamorphosed into one only vaguely resembling her life in England at the time of that palm reading, Ali had to take back her snort of disbelief and acknowledge the supernatural machinations channelled through the gypsy in the little kiosk between Café Rouge and The Rice Shack.

...

As she trotted to keep up with her beloved Yorkshire terrier, Webster, who was galloping excitedly at the fullest extent of his leash, Marlene McKean cursed the poison pixie immigrant that was her new neighbour.

Until recently, Marlene's access to Alder Beach (a beach Marlene can see from the living room of her house on Alder Beach Road) had always been via the little gate at the end of number 555's lawn. Number 555 was the only house on Marlene's street with direct access to the beach and so she, her neighbours and anyone else in the know had always treated the place as their own private thru-road to the ocean.

For thirty-seven years, Marlene had used the neighbouring drive twice daily to enjoy the shoreline that she felt was an extension of her home. That was until Jean Torrell, the late owner, up and died at the ripe old age of one-hundred-and-two and put a fly in the proverbial ointment. Quickly following their mother's demise, Jean's estranged children had then selfishly decided to rent the place out to what Jean's daughter had described as "a lovely young family" but who turned out to be foreigners with two teenagers, four dogs and – from what Marlene could make out on the day of their move, using her neighbourhood-pod-issued binoculars – a corn snake in a glass tank.

The family's truculent matriarch was a vile little Scottish woman who, although slight in stature, had quite the mouth on her. Marlene had discovered this firsthand when she'd been greeted with a vicious: "What the fuck do you think you're doing?" as she'd headed for her afternoon walk on the beach via 555's steep drive. It had been the last time Marlene had dared to step foot on the property.

Small consolation was that Webster didn't seem to mind the change. In fact the little Yorkie seemed to prefer the beach's alternative entrance, via the treacherous Sitting Lady Falls Trail, even more than Alder Beach itself.

Marlene followed Webster as he happily trotted off down the trail stopping at his usual sites to sniff bushes and mark his territory. The little dog was unfazed as he descended the stepped slope that ran alongside falls and through the haze of mist at the bottom where the waters met the deeps of Alder Lagoon and the thunderous chorus tamed into a peaceful babble.

Two magnificent white swans bobbed happily on the surface just shy of the encircling reeds where the trail was marked by its proximity to the ocean, the mud becoming sandy and the goldfinch's melodic chatter giving way to the seagull's pointed peal. The ocean lay just out of sight around three bends and beyond the pines but no matter how many times Marlene walked the trail, the sight of it was always a gift.

Webster's happy tail disappeared into a nearby hedge and Marlene stopped to inhale the clean, invigorating ozone – her twice daily exorcism of negativity and resentment – but the promise of the shoreline remained elusive thanks to Webster's incessant barking. Alerted like a new mother to her infant's cries, Marlene headed towards the sound of her puppy's yelps, her feet struggling to gain traction in the sandy wet soil underfoot.

Although she had been accused of overreaction before – usually by her husband – Marlene was all too aware of the very real risk of encountering bears and cougars on this trail and had already retrieved her can of bear repellant by the time she reached the hedgerow within which Webster was insistently calling for her. Marlene shrieked in fright as the foliage rustled frantically but much to her relief the little dog's rear end backed out of the bushes.

Hackles up, Webster raised himself saliently on his hind legs, barking furiously and seemingly unaware of Marlene's presence. Following his line of sight and by now convinced that she would have to do battle with a wild beast, Marlene held her bear spray in front of her face as she peered into the shadows of the thick vegetation.

"I see you! Get back!" she lied.

It was not with her eyes that Marlene sensed the threat retreat but with a lightening of the atmosphere. Whatever lay just out of sight within the bushes was so thick with evil that as it backed away, it took with it a cloying dark energy that sucked itself free of each leaf and every atom in the air around Marlene. Feeling it too, Webster ceased barking and stilled, his tail tucked between his back legs.

Suddenly everything seemed to change; sunlight dappled through the tree tops, the goldfinch resumed its song and the not-so-distant surf splashed rhythmically upon the shore. Marlene crouched and scooped Webster into her arms. He thanked her by delving his sandpapery tongue into her nostril. Marlene instinctively recoiled from his loving assault and in doing so lost her balance, letting Webster go and falling back, planting her rear end in the wet soil of the trail's path. From her new vantage point Marlene spied something through the foliage, something white, almost luminescent. Marlene's heart sank with a feeling of foreboding even before she got up to investigate the thicket.

In the umbrage cast by the boughs of centuries old Douglas fir trees, shrouded by fronds of bracken, lay the stark, sallow body of a young woman, a tendril of ivy a macabre lei around her ruined throat.

Cold grey skin, irises bleached by death, dark hair caked with mud and russet leaves. Mouth open and teeth bared in a pleading mask of terror. Pink nipples, the gentle mound of belly, the triangle of dark pubic hair. Thin legs, torn and bruised.

Marlene held back the need to scream with her hand and suppressed her terror with a guttural grunt of abhorrence as she fled, Webster at her heels.

Running as fast as she could, driven faster still by the image of the poor girl's ravaged body. Marlene paid no attention to nature's gifts as trail became beach but set her sights on number 555 with its gate at the end of the lawn.

...

Stubbing out her cigarette and marvelling at the fact she had managed to finish it without even the slightest disturbance, Ali dared to hope for just a few more minutes of peace so that she may enjoy a cup of tea and to catch up on the B.B.C. World News headlines.

It proved to be too much to wish for as she heard the sound of someone calling from the beach. Although Alder Beach was often busy, it was a rare morning when voices could be heard so early. Ali was more concerned, however, by the pitch of the woman's voice – the unmistakable tone of panic.

Ali stepped to the edge of the balcony so she could look along the shore and its juxtaposed picnic area; an insult to the natural beauty of the beach with its public restrooms and mown turf.

Running along the grassed area was a woman, a yappy little dog hot on her heels looking ridiculous in a yellow hat. The woman was heading towards Ali's house but with the clumsy gait and pace unique to someone in late middle age who hasn't found the need to run since childhood.

As the woman neared, Ali recognized the white-on-grey of her bobbed hair and knew – instant depression eradicating all her happy chemicals – that it was the snotty bitch from next door. A local councillor's wife who paraded herself as the unofficial monarch of the municipality, Marlene McKean made it her job to make anyone new to Mochetsin feel as welcome as a shit on a pancake. But Marlene McKean's penchant for bullying didn't fit well with her now desperate need for Ali's attention and it was this contradiction that stirred in Ali a stomach-lurching dread she hadn't felt for years.

Accepting the severity of what must come and cursing the fact that she was wearing her grotty dressing gown and a pair of shoes ten sizes too big for her, Ali hurried down the steps from her deck. The icy dew on the lawn needled her bare ankles as she crossed it, through her garden gate and onto the beach. Marlene stopped twenty feet short of Ali, flush with exertion, panting heavily.

"Oh my God, help…you have to help…"

Not entirely in the present, Ali stared at the woman's rubescent cheeks and took a silent vow to do some cardiovascular training again.

"Please…" Marlene coughed up a meaty glob of phlegm and swallowed it again, "There's a girl…on the trail…bushes…"

"Is she hurt?" said Ali, managing to swallow her distaste for Marlene long enough to step into the present moment.

Marlene shook her head and turned back the way she had

come, gesturing for Ali to follow.

"Dead." Marlene threw the word over her shoulder to Ali.

The word caused Ali's mind to be bombarded with a flood of images from her past. Images she had worked hard to lock away, a slideshow of gore at once came upon her and a tsunami of all the emotions attached to them. The devastating onslaught weakened her knees and caused stinging bile to lick up into her oesophagus. The sudden injection of adrenaline through her system spurred her into a run that belied her shaken equilibrium.

"Call the police Marlene. Where is she?"

"She's just this side of the falls. Across from the reeds."

Knowing that continuing on with them would surely result in physical calamity, Ali kicked her husband's shoes off. It took only two unshod steps for her feet to sport a pair of caked-on mud slippers.

"Wait!" Marlene called. "Wait!"

Ali slowed but didn't stop, she glanced back at Marlene, her face impatient, the same look she had given the woman during their last encounter.

"If I had a phone, don't you think I would have called the cops already?"

Ali delved in her dressing gown pocket, found her phone and carelessly tossed it on the sand between herself and Marlene, wondering as she did, who the hell doesn't have a cell phone these days, even if only to play Candy Crush.

Once in the shadows of the trail proper, the soil sucked at Ali's feet slowing her pace and forcing her to expel what seemed like an inordinate amount of energy. The sound of The Sitting Lady Falls came as a sickening relief – how could she possibly feel relieved to be nearing a dead body? *If* there was a dead body. Ali kept in her mind that Marlene could have been mistaken and was causing a fuss over something simply masquerading as a human cadaver.

But Ali recognized the energy of violent death around her and wondered, in hindsight, if she had been in tune with that same energy all morning. Perhaps that was why random memories, like the visit to the gypsy, had been poking at her in her dreams and since she had awoken. Perhaps the essence of death had slunk its way to her: an experienced witness. Had it penetrated her house as her children and dogs slept? Perhaps that was why she had been treated to rare solitude this morning; maybe her loved ones were in an unnaturally deep slumber forced upon them by a protective subconscious as in tune with the proximity of death as Ali herself.

Drawn to the spot by what felt like psychic magnetism. Like an aging thaumaturge who no longer trusts his once razor-sharp legerdemain, Ali paused and gathered herself in readiness to pull out of her hat procedure and crime scene etiquette desiccated and rusted by time and neglect.

It was imperative that Ali took care not to trample the scene, the moist ground condition an ideal spider's web for footprints and other detritus left by a perpetrator or careless passersby.

She scanned the opposite border of the hedge for an implement she could use. Ali grabbed a long branch nestled amongst the reeds of the marshy swale. She crouched low, peering into the bushes. Parting the plants with the stick, her eyes glimpsed enough of her quarry to know that Marlene had been right.

Hearing Webster's yaps nearing, Ali prepared herself for the dog's arrival and as soon as the pup dashed to her, she scooped him up. Marlene was only seconds behind, Ali noticed that her eyes were puffy, she had been crying on her way back to the scene. Although Ali disliked the uppity bitch, she couldn't help but respect her bravery. As Ali herself knew well, you never forget your first corpse.

"Here, take him and don't let him go," said Ali, thrusting the giddy Yorkie into Marlene's arms. "We have to preserve the scene. You go back down that way a little and I'll stay this side."

Marlene's eyes were wide as she stared at the hedge,

knowing what lay within it. Ali knew that shock was setting in and that if Marlene were allowed to do so, she would spiral into complete futility.

"Hey! Marlene! Look at me. This is serious, do you understand?"

Since Marlene was likely to milk the victim role, it was time for Ali to put her signature asperity to good use.

"Oi! Marlene? Snap the fuck out of it! There's a dead girl there and it's up to us to look after all of this evidence until the police get here. Do you understand? You can't fuck this up, so pull yourself together, stand over there and don't let your dog piss all over her. Got that?"

Marlene snapped back to reality enough to focus again and even managed to look affronted. Ali was almost impressed.

"Okay. Got it." Marlene headed to her designated sentry spot.

"You can't let anyone through," Ali added to make sure Marlene was clear on the rules of the game.

"You'll be good at that," Marlene snapped back.

Now Ali was impressed. Not only had Marlene postponed her PTSD long enough to be a modicum of use, she'd also managed to articulate a bitchy reference to their brief feud regarding beach access.

Ali watched Marlene and Webster disappear around the bend. Once they were at a safe distance, it was imperative that Ali took a closer look at the girl.

CHAPTER 2 - PRESERVING THE SCENE

Cold to the bone, Ali held her position on the trail for what had so far been a very unpleasant forty minutes awaiting the arrival of R.C.M.P. officers. During that time it seemed everyone with a dog and a day off had wanted to walk down the trail.

Her first few encounters with ramblers had been uneventful, people had reluctantly accepted her request not to proceed further and had instead chosen to loiter nearby, eager to witness her promise of the imminent arrival of The Royal Canadian Mounted Police (a great disappointment to Ali's son when the family had landed in Canada and Kenny had realized that they don't actually ride around on horses or wear silly trousers).

As time passed however, the crowd had gathered and gossiped and Ali felt growing paranoia as they stared at her like she was a mad woman. She soon found herself embroiled in several consecutive, heated encounters, one with a brachycephalic nunk of a man – one of the greater-spotted-camouflage-wearing-pick-up-truck-driving-inbred-redneck islanders who decided in his gap-toothed wisdom that *'no chick in 'jamas is telling me what to do'*. Luckily, Marlene had heard the altercation before it had gotten too heated and had shown up from behind Ali, pulled the man aside and in a hushed yet stern manner put him in his place. Ali couldn't hear exactly what was said but did pick out the mention of someone called *Anna* or *Alice*, maybe? No sooner than the name had left Marlene's lips, the man sheepishly turned away from the crowd and headed back up the trail.

Since the beach had been deserted earlier, it seemed unnecessary for Marlene to guard the lower end of the declivity, besides, her pious manner was effective, in a headmistressy way.

With no further hostility to distract her, Ali noticed that her toes were numb and was sure they must have turned blue inside their socks of dirt. Her anxiety was growing too. Would the kids be awake by now? Would they be worried by the absence of their ever-present mother? Perhaps they had called David at the fire hall. Maybe they had even called the police. Or, perhaps more likely, they hadn't even noticed her absence.

As though the thought of him had been a wish whispered into the ear of a genie, Ali's husband, David, appeared on the steps of the falls in his red lieutenant's helmet, 'Mochetsin Fire Service' emblazoned on the front. Ali smiled weakly at him and David almost lost his footing as he approached her through the crowd, so stunned was he to see his pajamaed wife, hair still scare-crowed by sleep, barefoot on the trail, her filthy robe her only protection against the cold, damp air.

"What's going on?" asked David as he draped his heavy tunic over Ali's shoulders.

"You tell me. What was it called in as?"

"Just a first response call. Report of an unconscious person on the trail."

Pulling David aside, Ali explained.

"Unconscious is one way to put it. She's dead, David."

"What? You serious?"

Ali's eyes gave David the only confirmation he needed. He reached for his radio. Ali grabbed his wrist before he could report the information to dispatch.

"David, this is bad. This girl was murdered. They need to get the right people down here, not just a bunch of plod."

Ali saw David absorb the enormity of her words and she

hoped he shared her doubts regarding the capabilities of a small local police force faced with a major crime scene. Car break-ins were a rarity in Mochetsin. Murder was something from books and movies; it simply didn't occur.

David stepped away to make the call. Ali pulled his heavy coat around her. Although the warmth of it was filled with the familiar scent of him, Ali was not comforted. Things inside her had been brought back to life: her skills, her instincts, her brain, all honed by decades of experience but, until now, suppressed into silent submission for her to function in a world where she could be nothing more or less than 'Mum'.

There was no going back now. There was no un-reading of the scene, no erasing her analysis. Ali had seen enough to have a sense of what lay in wait for them and it thrilled her as much as it scared her.

CHAPTER 3 - VIIMIS

In the carpark of St. Margaret's church, perched on the edge of his open trunk, Inspector Rey Cuzzocrea pulled his Tyvek bootees over his shoes and zipped up his coverall. As he slammed down the lid of his trunk, his cell phone pinged from inside his VIIMIS wind cheater.

Cuzzocrea huffed as he unzipped his crime-scene onesie and retrieved the phone. The text message was from his commanding officer, Superintendent Doug Shaw.

<Eta 3 hrs. Munro within the hour. Take command.>

As a white van pulled away from the carpark and headed south on the Mochetsin Road, Cuzzocrea shook his head in dismay. He hated working major cases in small towns. Small-town people tended to have small-town minds and, he knew from experience, that not much better could be said for most small-town cops.

At the entrance to a wooded trail marked by a sign for Sitting Lady Falls, Cuzzocrea was disheartened further by the sight of a gathering of onlookers peppering the trail's stepped slope.

It was unnecessary for Cuzzocrea to push himself through the throng as the crowd parted for him, their collective gossip ceasing temporarily in reaction to his attire. Once he was through the group, Cuzzocrea heard the excited yet whispered mumbling resume as he approached a pair of uniformed R.C.M.P. officers.

Cuzzocrea held up his I.D. in a cursory fashion and addressed the ranking officer: "Inspector Cuzzocrea, Vancouver Island Integrated Major Incident Squad. Where is my M.D.?"

"He needed to get back to his surgery, downtown," said one of the officers, holding out his hand to Cuzzocrea, "Sergeant Hewer…"

Inspector Cuzzocrea held his surgical-gloved hands up in lieu of the offered handshake. He pointed at the officers' boots, "You two went in there?"

Hewer appeared to be offended by Cuzzocrea's tone of voice. "Yes. She's down there a ways."

"And you sent the attending M.D. away?" Cuzzocrea asked. Hewer nodded. Cuzzocrea sniffed and turned to Hewer's partner who he assumed to be a rookie trainee on account of his acne and wide-eyed naïveté. "You are?"

"Burton, Sir. Constable Burton."

Cuzzocrea nodded. "Where's my cordon?" Hewer began to answer but Cuzzocrea continued over him, "Witness statements? An inventory of all of the vehicles in the immediate area? I've been here less than five minutes and I saw already saw one vehicle leaving the carpark up there."

Hewer cleared his throat and straightened. Cuzzocrea saw the sergeant flash a glance towards his subordinate before he replied, "Get the tape, Burton."

Cuzzocrea stopped Burton from passing him and continued: "I can see by your reaction, Sergeant, that none of the aforementioned tasks have been implemented. Need I ask if you initiated a crime scene entry log yet?" Cuzzocrea watched as Hewer considered a response but then simply shook his head. Cuzzocrea sucked his lips, "Officers, this is an official VIIMIS case and as such I am assuming command of the scene. Forensics have been delayed up-island and so, in the interim, I need you both to try your very best to recall everything you were taught in basic training. You can start by stepping out of your boots. Then I want the area from the entrance to the carpark, all the way down to the end of this trail in the other direction, cordoned off. Sergeant Hewer, call in three additional units, I want officers posted on sentry duty at the cordon, I want all of these people here documented and statements taken. I want to speak to the witness who found the body."

Sergeant Hewer and Constable Burton exchanged a glance.

"We sent them home, sir," said Burton.

Cuzzocrea frowned. "You sent them home?"

Burton answered: "Yes, sir. They'd been here a while and we…"

Hewer interrupted Burton, "Marlene McKean – I know the witness well. I know where she lives. It's all in hand, Inspector Canzererra."

"Cuzzocrea," the inspector corrected him, "You'll get to know my name because it'll be on all of the official complaints I'll be lodging against you. Hewer, do you have any idea the extreme to which you have already compromised this investigation?" Cuzzocrea turned to a now blushing Constable Burton. "You said you sent *them* home?"

Burton looked at Hewer.

"Don't look at him. Look at me," said Cuzzocrea.

Burton swallowed. "There were two ladies here. Mrs McKean and another woman. She was the one who was keeping everyone back. She said we should have taped off up there but…"

Hewer glared at Burton.

"At least someone in Mochetsin was thinking today, a pity that wasn't either of you guys. So, who was this woman?" Cuzzocrea asked but was met with silence. "Please. Don't tell me…"

"She was, from what we could tell, just a tourist. Not from round here. Irish, I think," said Hewer.

Cuzzocrea pinched the bridge of his nose. "You I.D.ed her? You took her contact information?"

"No, but Marlene'll know for sure who she was," Hewer

said.

"Jesus Christ. This is a total shit show. I'm embarrassed for you," said Cuzzocrea. "Get on with my orders and then you, Hewer, are going to remedy that monumental fuck up before Superintendent Shaw gets here. You know he's going to tear you a new one for this."

Hewer began to step past Cuzzocrea.

"Woah! Boots!" Cuzzocrea snapped.

"But...?" Hewer looked at the ground beneath them.

"You think I give a shit about your socks getting wet? You know, you're lucky that I was the first one here because if Trina Walsh had been, you'd be breathing through a straw right now. Boots off. Tape. Make sure none of those people leave until you've taken statements. Burton, step out of those boots but I want you up there, speak with them and make it clear that you need to keep them for a while. Hewer, get on with it and I need those additional units, now."

Cuzzocrea dialled Shaw and spoke as he carefully stepped along the outer edge of the path towards the thicket of bushes across from a softly swaying swale.

Shaw answered and Cuzzocrea spoke: "Sir, this is bad. Trina's going to pitch a fit. We got some real Keystones here."

"Shit. Munro with you yet?" Shaw said.

"Not yet. I'm setting up a cordon and an entry log."

"What! They didn't even cordon the scene off?"

"No sir." Cuzzocrea surveyed the ground beneath him, "It's a mess. No statements either and the two women who were here, one of whom made the discovery, were sent home. As was the M.D."

"On whose authority?" Shaw barked.

"A Sergeant Hewer? I'm assuming he's Glandford R.C.M.P.. They cover Mochetsin, right?"

"Asshole. I'm on it. Listen, Rey, we hit traffic out of Park Vale, we're not even near the Malahat Pass. You have eyes on the D.B.?"

"Just looking at her now, sir." Cuzzocrea crouched down

in front of the bushes and parted the foliage. "I see her. Female. Late teens, early twenties, maybe. Naked. Sections of her skin have been removed. No sign of blood on her or in the immediate area. She was cleaned."

On the other end of the line, Shaw was silent.

Cuzzocrea stood and continued, "Sir, this is a display. She was put here. For us."

"Okay. Preserve the scene. Did you call for additional units?"

"En route," said Cuzzocrea.

"Good. Stay in touch. Fuck." Shaw ended the call.

Cuzzocrea took note of the footprints on the trail: walking shoes, small, probably a woman's; a small dog; boot prints, numerous, R.C.M.P. officers?; the final distinctive set of prints intrigued Cuzzocrea the most; they had been made by a very small person, a person with bare feet.

CHAPTER 4 - FUCK HOUSEWORK

Ali accepted that it would be fair to describe her as a bit of a curmudgeon, even, at times, a total bitch. It was something inextricably linked to her habitual truthfulness. Her veracity had come about thanks to her formidable mother who treated lies – even harmless white ones – as mortal sins, a lie would beget the bearer a swift, sharp skelp across the back of the 'heid'.

And so it was, Ali Dalglish could not tell a lie. Although deceitful thoughts could flit and flirt within her mind, her lips were impervious to them, her teeth an impenetrable portcullis guarding against even the kindest of fibs.

So, as she stood face to face with her husband Ali literally bit her lip to curb the vile triumvirate of her personality; her grouchy manner, her savage candour and her vicious temper. Ali's wrath skulked within her like a warty troll beneath a bridge, barely tethered in restraint by her desire for peace, fomented by the merest confrontation or the threat thereof.

David had come home to find Ali still dressed in her pyjamas, hair still a ravel of sleep, at her computer in trance-like concentration. The hour had gotten away from her but she had, at least, managed to wash her feet and don her favourite pair of purple and white striped bed socks. Ali had detected a distinct look of near revulsion in David's eyes when he'd glanced at them.

"What are you doing?" he said.
"Nothing."

"Well, obviously." His subtext was vocalized by a sweeping gesture of the arms that brought to attention the untidiness of the large, open-plan living area that incorporated the T.V. lounge, dining area and Ali's desk.

The troll began to scratch. Ali suppressed it with a roll of her neck (stiffened by hours of study) and by doing so denied herself the pleasure of an acerbic bon mot in response. She watched as David took his work trousers off and draped them over a dining chair before entering the kitchen – clearly *his* mess was perfectly acceptable.

Her ulcerated hobgoblin gathered strength when David called through the kitchen hatch, an architectural installation consisting of a framed rectangular hole in the wall that would otherwise separate the kitchen and dining area, designed to make the 1950s housewife's life so much easier as she toiled to get a hot meal on the table upon the return of her hard-working husband.

"What's for tea?"

"Whatever's in the fridge," said Ali, blowing out a long-held breath.

And then he did it. He mumbled it under his breath but Ali heard his comment nonetheless: "*For Fuck's sake.*"

Ali joined him in the kitchen. She slid closed the hatch doors (because sometimes housewives should be careful not let their kitchen noise disturb the rest of the house) so the kids wouldn't hear what would inevitably follow.

"What's been going on all day?" he said but it was husband speak for *'Where's the food you should have been making for me and why haven't you cleaned up the house so it feels nice?'*

"Well, *David*," she couldn't help but over-enunciate his name – a warning sign that the demon was about to take full possession of her, "I've been busy."

"Busy? Doing what? Where are the kids? You haven't even showered, Ali."

That was it. Portcullis: gone. Troll: free to destroy.

"Fuck you!" Ali said.

"Don't speak to me like that please. I've been at work all

day," said David, adopting the guise of the hard-done-by innocent.

"Fuck off, David!" spat Ali. "What? Is your dinner not ready? Poor you! Here's a novel idea, make it your-fucking-self and then, when you're done, you can tidy up and do the laundry and hoover and mop and scrape that stubborn piece of shit off the toilet bowl in the guest bathroom – which, by the way, I'm pretty sure, came out of your fucking arse. You know why, David? Because I have more important things to do."

"Like what?"

"Like, oh, I don't know...let me see? What was it that happened today? There was something...wait, it's on the tip of my tongue...Oh yes! That's it! I found a dead body in a bush this morning."

"So?"

"So?" Ali was momentarily dumbfounded by his indifference. "David, I think that is slightly more important than my duties as your fucking house elf, okay?"

"Ali, that's not your problem. It has nothing to do with you."

"You mean I should just sit back and let the farce that was going on down there – a farce that you were part of, by the way – handle it?"

"Yes! That's exactly what you should do. You're just Joe Public here, Ali. Just a witness. You gave a statement, they'll handle it. It's not your problem."

"First off, I haven't given a statement because the acned fucking twelve-year-old constable in charge of the scene sent me away. Secondly, it is my problem, David, and it's yours and it's everyone else's around here because that shit down there was not a one off. Not an accident and definitely not a rookie killing."

David didn't reply, Ali's words had taken the wind from his sails, giving her a second of respite enough to rein in her temper, knowing full well that her bulging forehead vein was never a good look on her.

"Look, I know it's not my job anymore, David, but I picked up on some very worrying stuff down there and I have to do something about it. I'd never forgive myself if something else…"

"Okay, okay. I get it," David said, husband speak for *'Okay little lady, don't you be getting yourself in a tizz now.'*

He continued, "Look, I'll get something together for us to eat, you do your thing."

This was another maddening quality in David – almost as infuriating as his passive-aggressive dominance – his ability to efface his part in an argument and elude responsibility by suddenly placating Ali and being cloyingly accepting of her point of view. Now Ali's sails were a saggy, windless void like the baggy skin of a spent blister.

"And then I'll have to get out of here," he added as he washed his hands.

"Why?" Ali asked.

"There's a meeting at The Pioneer House. At seven tonight."

"About the body?"

"Yes."

"Well, how was I supposed to know about that?" said Ali. "How do you know?"

"E-mail, Ali. We live in a country with neighbourhood pods now, remember? Anyway, you don't need to go."

Ali glared at him.

"I'll let you know if there's anything you need to know," he added.

Ali left David as he inspected the freezer, as dads do when they are charged with the task of meal-making.

CHAPTER 5 - CULTURE SHOCK

Culture shock is an actual thing. Ali had discovered the ravages of the phenomenon shortly after her immigration to Canada from the U.K. in 2008. It is a poisonous sediment consumed unconsciously every time a denizen of one's new country makes one feel like a most unpleasant blot on their landscape.

So frequent are encounters with xenophobic Canadians that eventually the sediment hardens and crusts and acts as the mortar between the bricks that become your internal battlement against them. Void even of loopholes through which an arrow of friendship may pass, Ali's protective fortress had become to her a place of refuge, a labyrinth within which she could sequester herself safely away from the madding crowd.

Although her culture shock had resulted in the blackest depression of her life — a first-prize ribbon hard won in consideration of her near lifelong battle with the illness — and a deepening of her hermitic tendencies, her love for the country itself had only intensified. The physical landscape, the abundant and glorious wildlife and the largely barren, untouched freshness of the place had become her true home. Ali's spirit sat comfortably nestled here in meditative tranquillity on the shores of the Pacific Ocean, in the shade of myriad Douglas firs, and didn't seem to mind one bit that the Juan De Fuca Plate was subducting the North American Plate below them and that the region was likely, therefore, to experience 'the big one' at some point – the earthquake of all earthquakes and the reason Mochetsin residents are obsessed with disaster preparedness and neighbourhood pods.

The epicentre of Mochetsin consists of a cluster of five buildings: the municipal hall, where the mayor and his merry band of councillors rob to give to God-knows-who since Mochetsin is the only local council Ali had ever encountered that was $7,000,000 in profit; Mochetsin fire hall, her husband and the Chief being the only two full-time paid employees there, the rest of the manpower was generated on a voluntary basis; Mochetsin Country Store, the only grocery store that isn't a twenty-minute drive away and so consequently, a loaf of bread will set you back a full seven dollars; Mochetsin Café, serving platters of food big enough to satisfy the heartiest of appetites and also home to Mochetsin Ice-Cream Parlour and Mochetsin Pizza, a hive of activity day and night to Mochetsinites and out-of-towners alike; and Pioneer House, a renovated version of the house built and lived in by the first Mochetsinites ever.

The existence of Pioneer House really pissed Ali off. It struck her as curious that locals seem to have a strange knack of forgetting the very existence of the continent's aboriginal people who they prefer to keep hidden away on reservations, drug and booze addled as a result of years of unrelenting disenfranchisement and alienation (a mere taste of which had sent Ali scuttling into her own internal reserve).

As soon as she stepped through the front door of Pioneer House, Ali was rooted to the spot atop the rag-rug welcome mat. Two tall, oak display cabinets flanked the doorway and exuded the exact scent of her primary school headmaster's study. From Ali's vantage point she couldn't see what was housed within the glass-fronted cabinets beside her but, judging by the cacophony she caused when she steadied herself against an inebriating swell of anxiety by leaning on one, she guessed a farrago of porcelain and earthenware. As the crockery heralded her arrival the convocation within the musty room – predominantly consisting of octogenarians —seemed to turn as one, forever rendering the phrase 'fifty shades of grey', anything but sexy.

As if in denial of the morning's macabre trove, April had donned a stiff-upper-lip by finally allowing spring to bloom forth. As the sun lowered in the western sky it cast long columns of tangerine light through the rectangular, mullioned windows along the left side of the large room. Although the ceiling was vaulted — an effort to celebrate the raw craftsmanship of the original beams and trusses — and the square footage of the place was ample enough to comfortably house more than the sixty-plus people in attendance, to Ali it felt claustrophobic. Panic attacks were not entirely alien to her and the thought of suffering one in a public place scared her enough to almost induce one.

Ali needed to take a deep breath as she headed for the back row of chairs in the darker end of the room. Aware of the millions of dust motes undulating in the last light of the day throughout the space, conjuring thoughts of skin flakes, mould spores and dander forced Ali to make do with what little oxygen there was in the space by sucking deeply of it through her nostrils.

The front row was made up of a line of older women, including Marlene, who were all huddled together, probably gossiping, and Ali brushed her paranoia aside long enough to reassure herself that they probably had better things to talk about than her.

The social antithesis of Ali, David was on form at the front of the room. A frenetic, ass-kissing moth, the mayor (who was failing to squeeze his expectant gut under his waistband) his flame.

David seemed to be the flavour of the month in Mochetsin, and Ali wondered if he'd ever been asked, "Why is your wife such a weirdo?" She suspected his answer to that would cut her to the quick. Whenever Ali confronted David about his unabashed propitiation, his justification always implied that the responsibility lay with her and their children — something about 'survival' or everything he does being 'for you guys'.

Ali chided herself. Her lack of gratitude for David always filled her with sickening compunction. She hated thinking of him in that manner – *seeing* him in that manner – but sometimes, no matter how long she was married to him, she just wanted to smack him in the middle of his Romanesque nose and splatter it right across his face.

As if on cue, David found her face through the crowd and gestured for her to join him and the mayor at the foot of the improvised stage area. Eyes wide with alarm, Ali's mind was a tennis ball, bandied back and forth between two options: the horror of shaking her head, further cementing public opinion of *'poor David has a very rude wife'*, or the terror of smiling agreeably, walking her green mile to the front of the room only to, no doubt, say something crass and highly inappropriate, therefore achieving precisely the same end.

Luckily, Christine Labreque (the self-appointed leader of the Mochetsin Neighbourhood Pod) chose that moment to call the room to attention. Ali thanked God for the woman, accidentally giving her thanks out loud which snared the piercing attention of a little blonde girl seated in front of her. The girl was no more than four years old yet studied Ali with the cold gaze of a harridan whilst sucking on the four pudgy fingers of her left hand. The girl seemed to disapprove not only of Ali's very presence in the room but also of her less-than-perfect pedicure, bared for all to see in a pair of green, open-toed sandals Ali had grabbed from the closet in her last-minute rush to get to the town meeting.

Ali smiled a strained counterfeit of maternal kindness at the cherubic fiend as she pulled her feet as far back under her chair as she could without risking the blood supply to her lower limbs. Ali cursed herself for ever having thought it was prudent to buy footwear in the Real Canadian Superstore in Glandford; anyone who buys their clothing where they also buy their butter has lost their raison d'être. As Ali resolved to burn all her ugly shoes immediately upon her return home, Christine Labreque welcomed the gathered crowd.

"Good evening everyone. Hi. Hello." Christine paid particular attention to the front row, clearly these were the premier members of the congregation. "We are going to get the mic up and running but firstly I just want to thank you all for coming tonight, it makes it a whole lot easier, I think, if we are all singing from the same song sheet...or...so to speak..."

Christine's attention was required in the front row, she scooted off to her coven and Ali marvelled at how the woman had given herself a starring role in what was becoming a tasteless display of indulgence. Marlene, it would seem, had been demoted to a supporting role but was managing to wring every drop of attention left of her relevance in the front row, dabbing her eyes clear of what Ali suspected to be imaginary tears.

Of course the mayor was the behind-the-scenes genius of the piece and was currently providing Christine with directorial instructions while Dr Labreque (Christine's husband) enjoyed his moment centre stage setting up Christine's microphone.

Dr Robert Labreque was local G.P. to everyone in Mochetsin except, of course, Ali and her two children (for whom there was simply no space on the patient roster). David, however, had been welcomed with open arms into the care of Labreque, the justification for which was his job at the fire hall. Ali and the kids were forever destined, it seemed, to join the hordes of the moderately sick who pack the walk-in clinics of Victoria, clutching a paper number in hand as if waiting for a bag of sliced ham at the deli, only to be misdiagnosed by any one of a number of jaded, semi-retired doctors with no hope of ever owning a private practice and who, evidently, neglected to read any up-to-date medical findings or guidelines since their graduation from college sometime during the 1960s.

Mochetsin's Dr Labreque reeked of self-adoration, his blow-dried hair something straight from a box of Just For

Men was reminiscent of Tom Selleck's 'Magnum P.I.', the red dick-on-wheels he revved morning and evening along Alder Beach Road, further evidence of the doctor's desire to emulate the 80s heartthrob.

Ali watched Labreque as he adjusted the mic stand and was sure she hadn't imagined either the glint of sunlight off a chain around his neck (at the end of which, nestled in a copse of salt-and-pepper chest pubes, she imagined dangled a tacky medallion of some sort) or the lecherous wink he sent in the direction of a girl, no older than Ali's daughter, who pooned on the sunny side of the room in a manner entirely at odds with the chubby roll that girded her middle and was pinched out of existence inside a pair of size zero skinny jeans.

Scribbling a note on a cue card she had been handed by an old lady in a crocheted shawl of subtle pastels and creams, (who had been helped into her seat by none other than the ignorant redneck Ali had argued with on the trail that morning) Christine returned to centre stage and, noticing the microphone in place, thanked her husband in a gratuitously flirtatious manner that instigated a wave of appreciative giggles throughout the audience and a wave of bile in Ali's throat.

The doctor retreated to a windowsill positioned directly opposite to the one his pooning Lolita had shuffled her humpty-dumptyesque silhouette onto. Ali envied the girl's naïve over-confidence fuelled by hormones and blindly ignorant of a world intent upon crushing women into impossible moulds.

The P.A. system spoke for Ali when Christine piggishly cleared mucus from her gullet by keening a squeal of threnodic feedback in lament of its unfulfilled potential gathering dust in The Pioneer House filled with old farts who have nothing of importance to say to the public, ever.

"Get the fuck on with it, you daft cow." Ali wondered if she had said it out loud and received affirmation when the mother of the little blonde demon looked askance at her.

Noticing a cluster of meaty skin-tags on the woman's neck, Ali felt altogether better about her poor toenail care.

"Okay, so thanks for coming, same song sheet...da da da da, let's see." Christine checked her cue card and continued. "The mayor has requested the presence of local R.C.M.P. officers. I'm told *heads* of the investigation, no less. They should be along shortly, that being said, yes, tonight is about communication but what we don't want is to hijack the matter in hand with any sort of rant or debate on local policing in general – I know, I know, many of you are concerned about the rash of vehicular break-ins of late and the graffiti on Jim Deveer's headstone but please, please, please hold off on any questions that don't relate to this morning's incident. In fact, Mr Mayor just suggested that it may be for the best if we were to hold off on any questions at all. We know the R.C.M.P. are on it, they are working hard doing what they do and so we, as always, thank them for their service..."

Ali was disquieted by a spontaneous round of applause which shuffled through the room.

"Ooh, talk of the devil, and he's presently at your elbow...here is the sergeant now."

Ali, along with everyone else in the room, turned to see that the pubescent constable she had encountered at the crime scene had entered the hall with, what Ali assumed to be, his superior by his side.

Ali hoped there had been some mistake and this man was not who Christine had referred to as *'head of the investigation'*. Yes, Ali had been known to make quick assumptions about people based on their appearance but her first impressions were rarely wrong. Ali deduced from the man's severe underbite and weak mandible that he was not only the product of inferior genetics but, since there was no sign of the splayed, goofy incisors that are the twin of that particular flaw, he had evidently invested in a set of perfectly straight, white porcelain veneers. Since neither trait was indicative of high intellect, Ali felt fearful that justice and the pursuit thereof lay in his hands.

David caught Ali's eye from across the room and, seeming to accurately read her thoughts, pleaded silently for her patient restraint – something that Ali had noticed her husband required from her at an ever-increasing rate.

"So, I will hand over to you in a tiny sec, Sergeant Hewer…"

Ali wondered if she had hallucinated it but felt sure that Christine had curtsied at the policeman.

"…but first, just a reminder that Thursday's pod meeting will be at six, not seven, at my house and please consult the potluck list on my website, w w w dot chrissy l dot com, before you prepare anything to bring along, *jeez* we do not need three potato salads again! Thank you."

As another, more enthusiastic than the last, round of applause erupted, Christine exited stage right. Ali was agape with bewilderment. Was she missing something? What was going on here? These people seemed to her to be of the weirdest wicker-man variety. Potlucks and no questions during a town meeting called because a young woman had been murdered and her body dumped in one of the municipality's most picturesque spots?

Dressed too casually for Ali's liking in a bomber jacket hitched up over his gun, Sergeant Hewer took the stage, his spotty sidekick a diminutive shadow.

"Thank you, Christine," the officer began. "Okey dokey, let's cut to the chase here. The body of a young woman was discovered along The Sitting Lady Falls Trail this morning at approximately seven forty-five a.m. by our friend, Marlene McKean, efforts to preserve the scene of crime were undertaken by Mrs McKean and I commend her for her mindfulness under such circumstances.

"Now, before I go any further into the whys and the wherefores, I have to remind you that I am not a coroner and so I don't come bearing all the answers – this isn't C.S.I.: Mochetsin. Stuff doesn't quite happen in the real world the way many of you might think it does but what I can say is that early indications do, unfortunately, point towards homicide. We do not, as yet, know the identity of the deceased nor have I received confirmation of the exact cause of death.

"Now, I know many of you were around and about the trail this morning, maybe last night? Yesterday at all? Anyhow, Constable Burton here will be taking statements from you and, if it turns out your statement is of importance to the ensuing investigation, you may be asked to come into the local station, down the road there in Glandford, to help us fill in a few blanks. If at any point you do feel you have information that could advance our efforts in any way then, obviously, you shouldn't hesitate to contact either Constable Burton or myself without delay. If anybody does have a question, I would be happy to listen, otherwise Constable Burton will be taking statements…ah…somewhere in this room? Christine?"

"We set you up in the annexe, Greg, just through the doors to your left, behind you."

"Awesome. Thank you again, Christine. So. Do any of you have a question?"

With a short-sighted squint, Sergeant Hewer scanned the room for hands.

"Nope?"

At the risk of putting herself in the social equivalent of the village stocks, Ali raised her hand. Sergeant Hewer pointed towards her.

"Yes, lady at the back?"

Ali rose to her feet somewhat reluctantly but driven up by an overwhelming sense of responsibility.

"Do you have any persons of interest at present?"

"Woah. It's early days for all of that. First things first is seeing what it is we're dealing with here."

"So, is that a no? You have no clue as to who might have done this? Furthermore, you aren't at this time even looking into that factor? Is that what you're saying?"

"Yes. No. It's really not as simple as that. I sure wish it

were but like I said this isn't some T.V. show. Real police work happens a little differently."

"I didn't say anything about T.V. shows, Sergeant, so I suggest you drop that little fixation of yours. Are you looking for the perpetrator of this crime or not?"

Like a child for whom any attention is good attention, Marlene jumped up and added to the conversation.

"So, Greg," Marlene inserted a perfectly timed sniffle, "are we safe? Or should we start locking our doors at night?"

"No. No, there's no raving lunatic prowling our streets, people. There's no need for any sort of panic."

Ali's troll was churning and turning, irises white, like Bruce Banner's Hulk. "Wait a bloody minute. Who *are* you?"

"Excuse me?" The R.C.M.P. officer, it was clear, didn't take kindly to being confronted in this way. Ali felt hated but found that she was loving every single second of it.

"You heard me. Who are you?"

"I'm Sergeant Hewer, ma'am, I'm assigned to this case –"

"Do you…have you ever worked a murder case before, Sergeant Hewer?"

"Ma'am, I can assure you that this investigation is in good hands and procedures are in place…"

"Please tell me you are not going to be running this investigation because the words 'piss-up' and 'brewery' spring to mind – as in, you couldn't organize a piss up in a brewery. Jesus! Now, I imagine you probably don't get your fair share of murders here in Mochetsin but you, Sergeant Hewer, just stood in this room and admitted that you haven't even started looking for a suspect, you don't know the cause of death, you haven't I.D.ed the victim then you just said that people don't need to panic, that locking doors is panic? Are you on glue?"

"I'm not sure I appreciate your tone Miss…?"

"*Mrs* Dalglish. And you, Sergeant frigging Hewer, can suck my tone's dick."

PART TWO

TUESDAY 10TH APRIL

CHAPTER 6 - MORNING BLUES

The light fixture came with the house. Frosted glass boxed in teak and stamped with a gilt sunburst. At its centre, an octagonal filial of nine-carat plastic defines the piece as a relic of the 1970s in the centre of a ceiling spattered with tiny plaster stalactites. The light stared back at Ali and asked her, "Who are you? Why are you here?" Then it finished with a cold, "You don't belong."

Some mornings, most mornings, it was just a light in the bedroom, barely noticeable and rarely illuminated so as not to highlight her failings as a domestic goddess by casting the shadows of the dusty carcasses of moths and flies entombed within it onto the quilt. Only on the days when the cloven-hoofed Chimera of depression stepped forward, three sets of venomous fangs opening to permit its roaring call to arms, did it loom above her and hate her.

As Ali sat up a wave of electricity juddered her spinal cord. Accepting that to not get up – to just cover her head with the quilt and stay there until starvation and dehydration caused her to wither and expire enveloped by the musky scent of David – was an option no sane mother would choose. So the desire to appear to have a pinch of sanity left had her slipping her feet into her purple and white striped bed socks and her arms into the cosy pilled cardigan she always wore when the Chimera was skulking. That and the incessant machine-gun-bursts of laughter she could hear in the kitchen – only emphasizing the loneliness of her joyless state.

In the kitchen her daughter, Sandy, was preparing a bowl of Rice Krispies for her brother who was in the midst of a joke, the subject of which was Bill Cosby and the rape allegations surrounding the man.

Kenny (named after David's all-time favourite Liverpool F.C. player) had always been an excellent mimic with the timing of a seasoned stand-up comedian, always chose subject matter for his endless jokes that danced the thin line between humour and offensiveness. At the denouement of Kenny's performance, his sister's triplicate peal of laughter speared Ali's medulla and left a pulsing headache in its wake.

"Kenny," Ali warned. It only ever took a word or two for her essentially good kids to recalibrate their behaviour whenever they veered off course. Ali had never allowed the kids enough rope with which to hang themselves and had nipped bad behaviour in the bud. Ali's style of parenting was mindful of a world capable of ripping her kids up for arse paper if she allowed them to grow into socially inept adults, inconsiderate of their environments and ignorant of social graces and etiquette. Okay, okay, that could seem a little rich coming from a woman who just told a police officer to suck her tone's dick but as far as Ali was concerned, it was a case of 'do as I say, not as I do'.

David's parenting was polarized into two distinct styles: infantile 'fun dad'; and stiff 'Victorian father', known to spout clichés such as "manners maketh man" and "you don't know you're born" as well as the torturous punishment of lengthy lectures earning him the secret nickname Hannibal Lecture.

"Morning babies, what are you up to today?" Ali jiggled her bum cheeks (the only effective way to hold in a pee post forty) as she filled and boiled the kettle.

"I have a shift 'til four and then I have to go to TD bank and pay in," said Sandy who had inherited her father's obsession with the minutiae of personal finances.

"And what about you, Kenny? What are your plans for

today?"

Shovelling a heaped spoonful of the snap-crackle-popping cereal into his mouth, he answered with a dribble of milk down a chin Ali still saw as babyish.

"Revision." Kenny rolled his eyes and hunched his shoulders, a tell-tale sign that he wanted to find a way to wriggle out of the task.

Not one to fall for his tricks, Ali persisted regardless of her son's demeanour. "Of?"

Ali squinted her eyes as if the act would help her decipher her son's inaudible response through his mush of breakfast. It did. "History?" Kenny nodded and swallowed then filled his mouth again.

"Ready for the mock test on Friday?"

Ali saw her son's eyes widen in horror, he shook his head an emphatic 'no'. Kenny preferred to procrastinate and had been known to enter into lengthy debates regarding the usefulness of education. He was of the mind that 'scholastic training lacked purpose and was a system invented to manipulate and brainwash young minds so that their thoughts and beliefs may be cultivated and pruned, creating an adult population of conformists easily controlled and manipulated by totalitarian western governments who disguise themselves as democracies.' Ali had pointed out that it was only because of a quality education that he was even able to create such a bullshit argument in the first place.

Ali wasn't just mum to her kids, she was also their teacher. She had decided, when her daughter was four and her son was born that she would home school her children. A decision she rarely regretted except when spending twenty-four-seven with them became a little too much or when she second-guessed her decision all those years ago (governed largely by reports of overcrowded classrooms, lack of funding for local schools and a burning, nurturing instinct magnified by a massive pair of pulsating, lactating breasts) to opt-out at the peak of an astonishing career.

In the workplace, Ali had defied all the limitations

imposed upon her by a naturally misogynistic environment and had shattered her glass ceiling, not only gaining equal pay to her male counterparts but surpassing them and procuring the highest-paid contract in her field by the time she was twenty-five years old.

Ali let her teabag steep as her lungs ached for a fag.

"Well, let's do your mock exam on Friday morning and then, depending on your grade, you'll have two or three weeks of targeted revision ready for your actual G.C.S.E."

Kenny was about to interject – probably with another David-like diatribe about the merits of qualifications, or the lack thereof – when Ali allowed her mood, and her need for nicotine, to snap him into the acceptance of their teacher-pupil dynamic.

"Look Kenny, you have to do the test so you're just going to have to knuckle down and do the bloody work. If you're efficient, you might be able to start your summer holidays sooner. Okay?"

Kenny almost brightened only to sulk into melancholy, stabbing at his breakfast realizing that targeted revision was the bridge over a crevasse of mock exams that lay between him and an extended summer.

...

The gently undulating surface of the ocean was a quivering reflection of a Magritte sky. As Ali inhaled, the smoke had a catalytic effect upon her olfactory senses and she found it hard to believe that it had been a little over twenty-four hours since Marlene had come running along the beach in search of her. Ali supposed it would have taken no less than death itself for Marlene to ask for her help although, now she thought about it (with a stomach plummeting wave of shame), Marlene had seemed nothing less than in full support of Ali last night at the culmination of her tirade at the goofy copper.

Her tirade – the likes of which the folks of Mochetsin

had never seen, evidenced by the old lady in the crocheted shawl who had swooned as Ali peppered the air with hues of blue – not only infuriated David but the entire event had been captured on the iPhone of the tubby teen who fancied herself as much as she did Dr Labreque.

Ali hoped that the video hadn't been uploaded to YouTube – censoring bleeps would only make her look worse. She didn't even want to imagine the effect that such a video might have on an already embarrassed David who, Ali assumed, had spent two hours attempting redemptive damage control on her (his) behalf since that was the time it took between Ali storming out of Pioneer House and David returning home. He had come in, stroked the dogs, rubbed each kid on the head then draped his trousers over a chair and done his own bit of storming off into the bedroom. When Ali had joined him a few hours and two glasses of red wine later he'd built a barricade of pillows between himself and her empty side of the bed.

Feeling shit, Ali considered texting him an apology, but she was so stubbornly defensive that she knew there was no chance of that happening before noon, for, as she read in a Dean Koontz novel last night in their bed of awkward stillness, one eye clenched to marginally improve her red-wine-diminished focus, *We are not strangers to ourselves, we only try to be.*

Suddenly a thought descended upon Ali that lightened her spirits somewhat: maybe that YouTube video would be a boon.

Throwing the remainder of her cigarette over the deck rail, Ali said, "Fuck it." Arrogant she may be but Ali's arrogance was rooted in brilliance and she knew then that she wasn't in the throes of a persecution complex, she wasn't being paranoid. Ali *was* being treated like a stay-at-home mother, a jobless housewife, a television watching, dish washing, barefoot, badly-pedicured, filthy-mouthed nothing because that is all she had allowed herself to be since her kids were little.

There was no clearer sign: Ali had to dust off her smarts and be who she was, always has been and, most importantly, who she *is*.

Ali had to get to work – actually, first she had to pee, then she would get to work.

CHAPTER 7 - THE GINGER-TOOTHED GATEKEEPER

Your fanny is your bum, a bum has no home; if you make a spelling mistake ask for an eraser, not a rubber; courgettes are zucchinis, swedes are rutabaga, rocket – arugula, coriander – cilantro, a vest is a tank top, an undershirt – a vest, a jumper is a baby-grow, diagonal is kitty-corner, woolly hats are toques, chips are crisps and fries are chips; flip-flops are thongs and thongs are, well, unusual judging by the visible panty lines in the ever popular yoga-pant-wearing population consisting predominantly of turgid, harried housewives who, quite clearly, have never even so much as smelled a yoga mat.

But some things in Canada are exactly the same as they are in Britain like haughty receptionists whose life goal it is to prevent one from seeing the person they wish to. Although a ubiquitous feature in schools and doctors' offices on both sides of the pond, Ali was surprised to encounter one of the defiers of all that is convenient in Glandford's R.C.M.P. station. Back home, only police officers worked in local police stations.

Dealing with the hawk-nosed receptionist (her halitosis was rotten and permeated the glass barrier separating the foyer from the rest of the building) was the equivalent of asking a library's resident plumber where the classics section was.

Sometimes people need a good kick up the arse and as Ali drummed her fingertips impatiently on the counter, she slipped into a charming reverie of firmly planting the toe of her boot right up the R.C.M.P. receptionist's fat jacksie.

"Fill this in." The pompous secretary slid a white form into the steel basin that guttered the partition between them.

"What is it?" Asked Ali.

"A request form. Fill in your details at the top, the case number below that, the name of the officer assigned and then, the nature of your request."

Bemused, Ali briefly glanced at the paper before slipping it back the way it had come, much to the annoyance of the woman, who seemed unaware of the white globules of spit at the corners of her mouth.

Ali gave reasonable communication another go. "Look, the very reason I'm here is because I don't know who is in charge of the case, I only know that it has been handed over to VIIMIS, so, you see, I couldn't even fill in that bullshit form of yours if I wanted to."

"Excuse me?"

"Right. I can see where this is going so let's just save ourselves some pointless back and forth, shall we? I'd like to see an actual police officer please."

Sucking in her cheeks – causing the white spit to bubble – and twisting her mouth in a spittle-squishing grimace, the woman calmly passed the same form back into the steel basin.

Ali took a calming breath and even managed a bit of a smile. "Okay, lady." Ali made a show of taking the form and filling it in with the chained-to-the-counter pen next to her (maybe biro thievery was rife in Glandford). "I am going to put my details on your little form and while I waste my time and your ink doing that, you are going to find one of the officers on that crime unit dealing with the dead body found on Alder Beach Trail yesterday. Now, I don't care if they're somewhere in this building or next door at Boston Pizza or even in Tim Horton's, wherever it is that you've squirrelled them away, I want you to ferret them out," Ali slipped the form back to the receptionist, "and have them come see me here. Now, if you don't do that, I swear to the good lord above that I will see to it that you are charged with impeding an investigation, or whatever the most similar charge is here, and I would *hate* to see you arrested by the very people you work with. I mean, that would be *super* embarrassing for you, and I for one would not find that hilarious *at all*. Do we understand each other?"

Décolletage flushed, grey eyes twitching, the jumped-up gatekeeper was a worthy opponent, "I'm afraid there's no-one available right now…"

"…Okay. So you are stupid, like actually bloody stupid." In a manner favoured by her mother-in-law whenever speaking to the elderly or anyone who isn't Caucasian, Ali deliberately over-articulated her words. "Go-and-get-a-police-officer-for-me-to-speak-to-right-now or I might just do something that'll require one. Got it?"

No denying the impasse, Ali could see the receptionist silently wish a painful death upon her as she snatched the form back and headed through a door in her sanctum, to the police station proper.

…

It had taken the bitch from forty-three minutes past eleven until a minute before noon to return. "Someone will be right with you. Feel free to take a seat."

Ali sensed she may have shot herself in the foot by making an enemy of Ginger Vitus – the nickname she'd happily bestowed upon spittle lady in the sixteen minutes she'd left Ali waiting – and so settled herself in readiness for a long wait in one of the less-than-comfortable chairs along the brick wall of the superfluously large reception area.

Ali tried to imagine all the possible scenarios that may have warranted the architectural design of such a massive public area. Maybe an uprising of some sort, a revolution where anarchists run riot and the square footage would teem with pitch-fork-wielding locals baying for the blood of civil servants.

...

Fifty-two minutes later, Ali heard her name called through the – what she assumed to be – bulletproof barrier designed to protect law enforcement from a surging throng of miscreants and rebels.

The non-uniformed police officer behind the voice had a pheromone-inducing presence in the room. If Ali had a *type*, then the officer before her would certainly be it. He was muscular yet not meaty, dark haired and tall. Handsome in a way that was simultaneously pleasing and intimidating. He carried himself with a confidence that betrayed a knowledge of his own appeal. Scientifically speaking, he was certainly the by-product of good genes and his symmetrical face would certainly sit comfortably somewhere on the Fibonacci Spiral.

Feeling uncharacteristically self-conscious, Ali clumsily bundled her laptop, jacket, notepad and pen against her chest as she heard a dull buzz and the satisfying scrape of a heavy metal lock withdrawing from the snug fit of its mate. The door adjacent to the reception fort opened for the policeman who headed towards Ali in the foyer. The action was ambiguous, did it denote trust or was it quietly aggressive?

Ali half smiled at him as he approached her and felt intimidated enough to ponder the gun on his hip. Ali estimated his height an easy six-two, his walk was a contradiction, at once butch and yet gliding. If this were a bar, a younger, single Ali would have to ask him if he was straight and as quickly as the thought entered her head, so did a covenant – more a beseeching plea to herself – *not* to ask that question.

"Mrs Dalglish."

Ali found the offer of a handshake surprising and found it difficult to even find her right hand in her muddle of paraphernalia to place it in his.

"I'm Inspector Cuzzocrea. I understand you have information regarding the incident on Alder Beach Trail yesterday?"

"Yes. I do. I, um, well, I think I can be of assistance." The inspector cocked his head slightly to the left. Ali ignored his silent condescension and continued: "I was there and I noticed some things. Nobody has even taken my statement, Inspector. I did write one down, in the end. I gave it to your Sergeant Hewer last night, at the meeting."

"There was a meeting?"

"At Pioneer House in Mochetsin. It was a public meeting."

"I see." He puffed up his chest and seemed to be assessing whether Ali was unhinged in some way. Ali did her best to look as sane as possible which caused her eyelid to twitch furiously, making vain her attempt.

"Why don't you come through?"

"Okay."

Ali followed Cuzzocrea's lead. Ginger seethed with contempt as she buzzed them through to her realm. The lock uncoupled and Ali couldn't resist throwing a smug thank you at her, as well as a cheeky glance at the inspector's gravity-defying buttocks which, she could not deny, were simply marvellous.

CHAPTER 8 - PERFECTION

When the destination is perfection, the road to it is arduous, pitted and steep. Serpentine meanderings torment the will and stab a thousand cuts upon patience. But, at the last it is achieved and the onerous journey – a means to that end – fades into memory. Mistakes made were lessons learned and follies became the building blocks of a pedestal upon which genius may revel.

The delicate sweep of a neck from lobe to shoulder lays bare the lady. Even when fully clothed, a woman is naked to all who view her exposed throat. Perfection lies in the length of the sweep and of the glance as it covers the gentle scoop. From behind, a bared nape teases the peruser with the whisper of lanugo; baby-hair fuzz, a tattoo of innocence retained.

Through the cover of skin ticks the rhythm of the jugular and, deeper still, the thump of the carotid artery. When they face their fear made manifest, when they are most terrified, the heart pumps pint after pint after pint, faster and faster still and the arterial canals and veinous tubes pulsate ever thicker and the neck becomes a red flag to the bull, a beacon to those lost at sea and a babbling fount for the nixie. The mesmeric cadence is the charmer's mellifluous flute, capturing the serpent spellbound.

Transforming the cygnet into the swan takes no less than seven hundred and thirty days, even one day less is too short. Eagerness to condense the process must be thwarted for it is vital to remain respectful of the might against which one acts, after all, to force the hand of nature is to alter the natural bearing of a thing. Subtlety is key, tricking nature into blindness, actions so slow and slight that nature looks away and she forgets to resist.

The harvest is bountiful now and reaping the fruits of careful labour is divine. To sup and to pierce, to flay, to explore and to ultimately extinguish is tantamount to heavenly rapture, a reward of the finest reserved for only the most zealous of nurturers, the ardent cultivators of perfection.

The turn of each carefully fashioned coil marked the journey towards it and the unwinding of it is the unwrapping of a gift so unique, so ideal that nature opens her eyes and looks with envy upon the yield.

And the mellifluous flute whistles its undulating sonata that will soon become a requiem. And she, as white and bare as she has ever been, is beholden to him, the sculptor.

CHAPTER 9 - INSPECTOR CUZZOCREA

"It's not the best coffee but it's brown and it's wet." Inspector Cuzzocrea placed two steaming cups on his desk.

"That's okay, I'm a gourmand of instant coffee and fast food."

"Really?"

As the police man sat, Ali took the seat at the side of his desk. The many-windowed office was home to twenty desks like his but only three of them, including Cuzzocrea's, were being utilized at present.

"No, well, sort of. Instant coffee, yes, but I actually like good food…it's a British thing, self-deprecation, for some reason we imagine it makes us more likeable. My theory is that it's one of the many ways in which we salve our subconscious guilt and apologize for the empire."

Cuzzocrea's expression was blank as he stirred his coffee. Ali waved his confusion away.

"Never mind, really, you don't have time for me to explain all of the nuances and subtle variances between Brits and Canadians. For instance, here we are in a police station but if you were to ask me how I am, I might reply with, 'Oh my God, my husband's doing my head in, I swear I'm going to murder him', *you* might not laugh."

Cuzzocrea eyed her over the rim of his coffee cup.

"I don't get out much." Ali sipped her coffee and noticed a hint of a smile on the inspector's face. She noticed that he had very dark, thick eyelashes. Was he wearing mascara?

Don't say it, Ali, she warned herself.

"So," said Cuzzocrea, "Do you happen to have a copy of that statement you mentioned?"

"The one I gave to Hewer?"

"He didn't submit it yet. Actually, between you and I, he'd be in hot water if he did. We took over the investigation hours before that town meeting you told me about."

"Really? Oops. Well, he didn't strike me as the sharpest tool in the box."

"I'm saying nothing."

"Here." Ali pulled the enveloped copy from her bag and slid it across the desk to Cuzzocrea who began to skim it. "So, then, I'm assuming you have your own forensic team?"

"Yes. Are you familiar with VIIMIS?" Cuzzocrea asked.

"Vancouver Island Integrated Major Incident Squad. That's about it."

"Okay, in a nutshell, we specialize in the investigation of major crimes so we have a team of detectives, a special victims officer, a dedicated missing persons officer, forensic services and IDENT (forensic identification)."

"So are you R.C.M.P.?"

"Some of us, I am, some are Victoria P.D. – they're the ones with the cool cars downtown – and we have outside experts too but we're from all over the island. Basically, when a case becomes a VIIMIS case we get the call and we drop everything and run. Our forensic team was working the scene on Alder Beach Trail by midday yesterday."

"Thank God for that," said Ali, "I barely slept last night worrying about the evidence that could be missed or overlooked."

"I don't in any way wish to offend you by this..." Cuzzocrea rested his elbows on his thighs and looked Ali directly in her eyes making her feel like a naughty child, as only those with the power to arrest can, "...but you seem to be of the opinion that you can help us, vital evidence? Do you have an interest in this type of thing?"

"Oh, God. Of course, I suppose I do look like some

nosey bitch to you. No, I used to do this, many moons ago. This was my job. I'm sorry, I should have clarified."

"Law enforcement?"

"God, no! No offence. Private sector but I worked alongside various police forces in the U.K."

"I see. Forensics?"

"Primarily criminal psychology but forensic pathology is, ah, my hobby? for want of a better term. Although you should know, I'm a qualified enthusiast – self-deprecation, again." Ali shrugged and elaborated: "I find that in the course of an investigation, things go faster when forensics works hand in hand with criminology and victimology, so I qualified in both fields simultaneously."

"Ah." Cuzzocrea was making a note on the back of the envelope Ali had handed him. "And Dalglish is your married name?"

"Yes. Ali McFee is who you want to check up on – I assume that's what you'll be doing with that information, Inspector?"

Cuzzocrea smiled. "Just making sure you're not a fantasist. Okay, so I have your information, I have your statement but when I first met you, you said that you had 'noticed some things'. Were those things from a forensic point of view or with regards to a possible perpetrator?"

"Both, but I'm sure your VIIMIS team are more than capable. Look, yesterday I saw Hewer and his little monkey and I wrongly assumed that they were in charge of the investigation and for that, I apologize. It would be inappropriate for me to interject with my assessment now."

"Fair enough." Cuzzocrea sat back and smiled at Ali. "I specialize in criminal analysis too so, naturally, I'm curious as to what you picked up on."

Ali huffed. The forensic pathologist in her was reluctant to step on toes, but the criminal psychologist itched to ensure that the investigation steered itself in the right direction.

"Obviously you know she was moved, post mortem."

Cuzzocrea nodded.

"Now, I can't say for sure because this is based on my looking at the deceased in situ and not a full examination, but the lividity suggests that at the time of death and for a minimum of twenty to a maximum of twenty-six hours post mortem the victim's body was hyperextended, opisthotonus in a manner indicative of infection with the bacterium clostridium tetani."

"Tetanus?"

"Now, that begins to frame a profile that is worrying, to say the least."

"Go on," said Cuzzocrea.

"Let's assume the infection was contracted via the wounds inflicted upon her by the killer, so her death may have occurred prematurely – the wounds inflicted upon her may have been part of a longer, more tortuous ordeal from which the bacterium, by killing her, essentially rescued her. Now, since generalized tetanus takes a mean average of seven days to fully develop, and, again, assuming that she contracted the infection because of the open wounds caused by the killer, then we can also assume that the time the killer takes to torture his or her victims is much longer than that."

Cuzzocrea raised his eyebrows, "Okay. That's something."

"But, the real concern I have was the unnatural length of the victim's neck, the discolouration on parts of the skin of the neck, indentations on either side of the centre-most point of the clavicle and the angle of the upper ribs and clavicle. I do have a theory regarding this but I'd rather keep schtum for now because I'm a bit out of practice and, well, I don't want to make a fool of myself. I'm sure your forensic team is already way ahead of this but what I will say is that, in my professional opinion, you are dealing with a very patient, careful, diligent killer who is highly intelligent and bold. Skilled to a degree that suggests practice, even expertise, and I therefore think that your victim is one of many. The most worrying aspect, if my theory about the length of her neck is correct, the killer keeps the victims, stores them up, if you will – alive – before he or she kills them. Perhaps for years."

Cuzzocrea stared at Ali. Finally, he spoke: "One of many? What makes you think this isn't an isolated incident?"

"Hmm. How do I explain this? Okay, it's like soufflés – chances are your first one will be a bag of shit so you put six in the oven and hope for the best. Now, if each batch of soufflé batter took years to prepare, you'd probably overlap the making of batches, starting a new one while half a dozen are rising in the oven. Then failure isn't an ending but rather an opportunity to do better; failure becomes an exciting development and a step closer to success. That's what your killer is doing. He or she is perfecting the recipe."

Cuzzocrea was silent, Ali hoped he was merely pondering her theories but began to feel disconcerted by his lack of response. To ease her discomfort, Ali blurted, "Are you wearing mascara?"

Cuzzocrea snapped out of his catatonia. "Excuse me?"

"I'm sure you don't but you have really good eyelashes." Ali's inner awkwardness was emphasized by an involuntary tightening of her vagina.

"No, no mascara."

"Okay. Thought so. Anyway, I've taken up enough of your time. I'll be heading home now."

"Thank you for your insight, Mrs Dalglish."

"No problem. My pleasure. Thank you. Bye."

As Ali crossed the expanse of grey, industrial carpet it was truly beyond her to imagine what impression she had managed to make upon the man. She spoke to her reflection in the silver elevator doors.

"You really need to get out more."

CHAPTER 10 - BRIDGING THE ABYSS

Ali dropped into third knowing that her Porsche would enjoy the throaty power of the gear through the upcoming double bends. She flagrantly ignored the sign post that read 'MAX 30' and gunned the curves at a smooth and weighty fifty-five. Daisy Farm Road always put her in a good mood. The five-mile stretch of relatively smooth concrete ran from Glandford to Mochetsin and exemplified the varied landscapes of the area. It was a true treat for anyone lucky enough to call themselves a resident.

Once free of the worker bee traffic around the strip-mall hive that is Glandford, the road takes you through bend after silky bend, the dipping sun throwing the many rocky hills and outcroppings into relief. Every few metres or so a steep driveway cuts itself up out of the road to disappear into the dense woods indicative of the island's untouched, robust beauty. Through the trees, glimpsed only briefly in passing are often humble but sometimes magnificent homes.

Ali shifted into fourth out of the bend with a burst of acceleration, her head pushed against the leather headrest embossed with the famous Stuttgart logo. She eased off the gas and slipped into fifth, sixth, allowing momentum to carry her over the humpback bridge and down the avenue of cloud-scraping trees. With the roof down, the engine's grumble seemed the only disturbance for miles and the warm breeze played with the back of her hair, scooping it up and laying gentle kisses on her nape.

"Life is good," Ali exhaled. She was almost content. It was an alien feeling but one she wished to prolong. Ali ran through the things she was grateful for: two kids, a devoted husband who had stuck by her through some troubled times…she drummed her fingertips on the steering wheel, thinking hard…her dogs? Actually, Ali was a reluctant pet owner, she'd only agreed to buying one dog for David and the other three had come as a result of the kids' nagging her relentlessly.

Ali felt her euphoria slipping momentarily before she allowed herself to remember how exhilarating it had felt to convey her findings to a fellow criminalist; just like the old days. The thought made her stomach flutter with hope and she realized then that hope was the very thing she had been bereft of for so long. With that realization came another: her moment with Inspector Cuzzocrea, however exciting and reminiscent of her past career it had been, regardless of the fresh hope that had bloomed within her at the time, had been just a moment and that moment was gone. Ali felt her hope recede into a cloud of reality. Ali was a tiny rowing boat – a tempestuous sea of chop and maelstroms loomed at the very edge of her calm waters.

…

Outside the fire hall, David was working on Engine 4. He stopped and turned, sensing her approach as only the truly married can. Ali pulled up alongside him and beckoned him to her.

"Hi." David dipped his head into the open-topped car and kissed Ali's head.

"Hey. How's it going?" Ali smiled.

"Where've you been?"

"I went to the cop shop…"

David was about to protest but Ali stopped him.

"I was just handing in my statement and I picked up a bottle of red for tonight."

"Good for you. I've got practice tonight."

"I know."

"Engine four's water pump is fucked so I won't even get home for tea before training."

"That's crap."

David shrugged. "Whatever. Go home and crack open that bottle of wine. I'll be late back."

"Okay. You want me to wait up for you?"

"No. No point."

"Okay. Love you."

"Love you too."

Ali waved her hand above her head as she drove away, she heard the distant call of David telling her to be careful.

...

Freewheeling down the escarpment that cut between the fecund foliage at the entrance to her home, Ali heard the swish of the shore and the crackle of dead branches under her tyres. The peek-a-boo blue of ocean beyond the house unfurled into sweeping magnificence as she swung the Porsche into the crunching gravel of the parking circle.

Waiting for Ali, sitting at the foot of the stairs that led to her front door, was the maelstrom herself, Marlene McKean. Ali killed the engine, the cooling motor tick-tocked as she retrieved her belongings and the brown paper liquor store bag.

"Hi Marlene. Don't tell me you found another corpse."

"No." Marlene held up a matching brown paper bag, the burgundy foil of a bottle of wine peeked out from inside, "Fancy a glass of wine?"

Ali held up her booze with a smile. "I fancy more than one."

...

The initial attack of slobbery love and infernal barking of

Ali's four attention-starved dogs had left Marlene reeling. Ali was mortified when Marlene was making small talk with Kenny and Oscar, her Newfoundland, decided that the woman's crotch needed some intense investigation, leaving a fat, shimmering web of saliva on Marlene's thigh. Ali was most relieved when the dogs finally, one by one, found better things to do even if those better things involved the concentrated licking of testicles. Ali handed some kitchen towel to Marlene so she could clean herself off.

"Let's go and sit out, away from these guys and make the most of the end of the day," Ali suggested.

...

"I bet you wish you'd stayed at home," said Ali as she watched Marlene trying to position her arse into one of the two blue hammock chairs that hung from the maple on the edge of the property, overlooking the ocean.

"Why can't you just have a patio set like a normal person?"

"You'll see."

Once her butt was finally placed, Marlene gingerly shifted her weight from her feet, glancing at the branch from which they were suspended.

"It's okay," Ali reassured her. "That one's David's and he's way heavier than you."

Marlene startled like a newborn when her feet finally untethered themselves from the earth beneath them. Ali reached over from her hammock chair to steady the swing of Marlene's chair as it adjusted to the weight of her trust. Once steadied, Ali handed Marlene her glass of wine.

"There, see?"

Ali watched as Marlene surrendered control and relented to the free swaying of the chair, taking in the expanse of ocean before her and swallowing her first mouthful of Merlot. Ali could see then that Marlene had become a fan of the hammock chair she had despised only moments before.

"Oh, that takes some beating, doesn't it?"

The women chinked their glasses together.

"Indeed," said Ali, increasingly intrigued by her companion. Ali smiled. The day before yesterday she would have chosen to stick hot knitting needles through her armpits before spending time with Marlene McKean, but she found herself savouring not only the wine and the view, but also the company. Ali couldn't remember the last time she had enjoyed the presence of a female friend. She supposed that *friend* was presumptuous and so armed herself against yet another social disappointment but, in the spirit of the afternoon thus far, decided to embrace the calm while it lasted.

"So, Marlene, to what do I owe the pleasure of your visit?"

Marlene let out a tired sigh. "I don't know…maybe I *am* too sensitive."

Ali understood, immediately. "Yep. I got the same lecture from David."

"You did?"

"Oh, I get so sick of being told how I should react all the time. You know, what happened to us yesterday is disturbing and, yes, I want to talk about it…God, it's the only thing I can think about."

"Me too. It was so…I don't mind telling you, I was scared."

"You wouldn't be human if you weren't. It's a disturbing bloody thing and yet it's like everyone around us is kind of enjoying it…or, not enjoying it but…"

"Like they've taken it over…taken it away from us?"

"Yes. Last night? That meeting was a joke."

"I totally agree," said Marlene.

"Wasn't it? I mean, I know I overreacted…"

"I don't think you did at all."

"Really? Wow, I did not expect that from you. David was mad."

"Oh! Men! They're shits."

Ali snorted a laugh, "Cheers to that."

There was something intrinsically hilarious about Marlene swearing. Glasses chinked over common ground.

"It's worse for me, Ali."

"Oh? Why's that?"

"I'm married to none other than Councillor Peter McKean, Deputy Mayor of Mochetsin, thank you very much. Honestly, that man, God love him, takes himself very seriously. Do you know, I've caught him practising his speeches in the bathroom mirror, saggy old tighty-used-to-be-whities with his belly just hanging there, pontificating away to himself. Bless."

"That's cute."

"Ali, honey, there are many words I could use to describe Peter McKean but *cute* is not one of them. Your husband, on the other hand, is not too hard to look at."

"I'll give you that, but he's not the saint everyone makes him out to be either. People round here seem to think the sun shines out of his arse."

"Yes, he has settled in very well. But you will too. You know, it's harder for us, it takes longer. Especially somewhere like this, I know, I was an outsider once too *and* I was a lot younger than you are now."

"So you weren't born and bred here then?"

"No. We moved from Saskatchewan when we first married. Peter had work here but I had nothing – no friends, no family, nothing. I remember seeing him getting on with it, happy as a dirty pig and I remember hating him for it. Oh, would I pick fights with him. But it was just jealousy, loneliness, insecurity *and* I was *convinced* he was having an affair."

"Was he?"

"Nooo, he wouldn't dare but there was this one woman he worked with – she was a single mother, quite the scandal back then – and I was sure she wanted to get her hooks into my man, of course this is pre hair-loss, dentures and the thirty extra pounds. Peter was quite the looker at the time."

"I can imagine."

"Hmmm. Anyway, it turned out that she was playing for the other team all along."

"She was gay?"

"No, a lesbian. She still lives here with her partner, I'll point her out to you."

"Scandalous."

"Oh, that's nothing. We're no strangers to scandal here." Marlene eyed Ali suspiciously, "Can you keep a secret?"

"Yes. And, also, nobody speaks to me here anyway."

"Honey, that will change. I told you, it just takes time for them to accept someone new, that's all."

"So, what's the secret?"

"To them accepting you?"

"No, you asked if I can keep a secret."

"Oh, yes." Marlene held her glass out to be topped up. Ali filled it just shy of the brim. "Now, be warned, I get drunk very easily so if I start with the giggles then you'd better send me home."

"You're kidding, that's when I'll open the other bottle."

"And don't let me near your son's trampoline. I was at a great niece's christening last summer and I'd had a few too many of those silly jello shots they do and well, I got on that bouncer of theirs and I nearly broke my neck but not before I peed myself."

"Oh shit! You did?"

"Yup, and not just a dribble."

"Oh my God, how embarrassing."

"Oh, nobody knew." Marlene dropped her voice to a whisper and mouthed the words, "I was wearing a Depends."

Ali laughed. "I'm not far off those myself."

"Ah, the joys of having turned your innards the wrong way around, pushing out offspring, eh?"

Ali and Marlene chinked their glasses as they giggled together. A woodpecker applauded with its staccato against nearby bark.

"You know, Marlene," Ali sniffed and swung, "you are nothing like I thought you were."

"Ali, nobody is. Really, I think sometimes I just, *we all* just get stuck in the habit of being rude to one another. Or, at least, not even noticing how we are being perceived anymore, you know?"

"I get that. I show myself up – and poor David – all the time. I did it today at the police station."

"You went to the police station?"

"Yes. I just couldn't bear to think of that poor girl…if her case were to be mishandled, well, I don't know…"

"I feel exactly the same. Maybe it's because we found her. You know, she's someone's daughter. We're both mothers, can you imagine?"

"I know. So, anyway, I had to do something. I popped in to meet whoever was in charge, hoping that Sergeant Hewer was as far away from the case as he can be."

"Ah, Greg Hewer means well, he's just a bit of a puppet to the mayor. So, what did you find out?"

"Well, VIIMIS – this team of specialists from all over the island – are handling it and so, at least, she's in good hands."

"Who did you speak to?"

"Cuzzocrea?"

Marlene shook her head to indicate that she'd never heard of him.

"He's a detective, no, an inspector. He was nice. He listened to my ideas."

"Well, so he should."

"Why?"

"Ali, honey, this is a very small community in the middle of a very big drama, a murder mystery the likes of which you only see on *Forensic Files*. Lips are loose. Besides, your husband never shuts up about you and how amazing you are. Anyway, he mentioned to the mayor last night that you'd only gone off on Hewer because you used to be a big cheese in charge of murder investigations in England."

"I don't know about *big cheese*."

"Don't be pedantic, big cheese, shmig shweese."

"Okay. Well, maybe I was a 'shmig shweese' but David's right, it's none of my business."

"It is your business, it's our business and I for one am not going to apologize for giving a hoot about that poor girl. What would be the harm, say, in the two of us – nobody needs to know – having a little look into it ourselves?"

"Us? You and I?"

"Why not?"

Ali lit a cigarette, only her second of the day thanks to an unnecessarily long sojourn at the local police station. Marlene gasped as Ali took a long drag.

Ali recognized the all too familiar reaction to the heinous act of tobacco smoking these days.

"I know, I will give up one day."

"Please can I have one?" Marlene begged.

"Sure. Here."

Marlene held the cigarette awkwardly against her lips as Ali lit the end for her. She inhaled, spluttered a cough then sucked back a lung full. Ali knew well the dizzying feeling of the first fag in a while.

"I haven't had one of these since New Year's Eve nineteen eighty-four." Exhaling, Marlene kicked a toe off the grass below her, the hammock chair swung languidly. "I don't know why I ever gave up."

"I know, right?"

"Ali, do you know, tonight reminds me of when I actually used to have fun."

"Me too."

"So, what do you think, girl? Shall we do some digging of our own? I mean, with your background and me? Well, I know just about everyone and I can get us just about everywhere. In fact, I bet you had one hell of a time getting to speak to that inspector of yours today."

"Oh my God, there was this horrible receptionist."

"Alice Luckinuk."

"She was vile."

"Very abrasive character. You know, they only keep her on there because her dad was a cop and he was killed in the line of duty back in the seventies. I think he was shot, maybe he was stabbed, anyway, he died. Everybody hates her."

"You know what, Marlene? I'm up for it."

"You are?"

"Fuck it, why not?"

"Yes!" Marlene chinked her glass against Ali's. "Fuck it!"

The unlikely friends laughed together as a shining white cruise ship slowly drifted on the horizon and the sun cast an orange spotlight on the spit of land called Witch's Landing where Alder Bay nodded a welcome to all aboard.

"So, Marlene, what was that secret?"

"Huh?" Marlene stepped on the butt of her cigarette. "Secret?"

"Yes."

"Ooh! I forgot. Okay, so have you met Christine yet?"

"Pod lady? Yes."

"And Dr Labreque, her husband?"

"No, apparently there's no room at the inn for me and mine."

"Oh honey, you won't mind a bit when I tell you this…"

"What?"

"They are slingers." Marlene swung smugly, awaiting Ali's reaction with impish glee twinkling in her eyes.

"Slingers?" Ali was at a loss.

"You know, they have orgies and slinger parties – at that house over there."

"You mean, *swingers?*"

"Whatever you call them."

"Oh. Wow. That explains a lot. How do you know?"

"Well that's another funny thing because, honestly, I didn't think that was a thing so I was completely naïve to it but I did notice that they were very, *very* friendly, you know, touchy-feely? Anyhoo, this one year, they invited Peter and I to one of their parties. Now, we just thought it was one of their usual ones, you know, a potluck…"

Ali and Marlene caught a fit of the giggles.

"So, anyway, we're at this party and there's some very strong punch going around and I notice that everyone is *super* friendly, there was even a man over by the buffet with his shirt open and a woman – not his wife, the woman *next* to his wife – was rubbing his chest. Of course Peter was in his usual 'networking' mode and completely oblivious to it all. Well, it hit me, this was some sort of group sex thing, like in that Kubrick film with Tom Cruise except with a lot more flesh and a lot less Cruise…anyway, I couldn't get out of there fast enough."

"What did Peter say when you got home?"

Marlene began to laugh, head back, clasping between her thighs in desperate need of a pair of Depends.

"That's the funny bit. I told Peter that I had a headache and that I had to go home but that he should stay because he could make some valuable connections."

"You left him?" Ali laughed along with Marlene.

"Yes! He came stomping in about an hour later, blushing like a boy. I pretended I'd just woken up, but then I heard him crashing and banging about the bathroom, mumbling to himself and then he tossed and turned all night. The next morning, I brought him a cup of coffee in bed and I asked him, 'Did I miss much at the party?' to which he replied, 'Yes, Marlene, you missed a hot tub full of things and that's the last I'll speak of it!' To this day, he thinks I am unaware of it all. It's his way of protecting me, I suppose, maybe he thinks I'd have a heart attack if I knew what was going on across the road."

"Marlene, you are fucking hilarious."

"You really do have a filthy mouth."

"I know, it's a Scottish thing."

"Okay, so what do you say to getting a little drunk together tonight and then tomorrow, say tenish? We sit down at your table and we see what we can do together for that girl?"

"Well, Marlene, I say – why the fuck not?" Ali raised her

glass.

"Oh dear." Marlene raised hers too.

And they both made the toast together: "Why the fuck not?"

CHAPTER 11 - THE NUTRIMENT OF LOVE

When the thing that others call love is alien, something only others speak of, something others feel but that is entirely absent within, it becomes an intriguing enigma, an elusive sentiment.

Much is labelled love that is not love. The word is used when the true feeling exists not. Do they really love? Or do they manufacture a pretence of love to fit within the ideals of our species?

Love is rammed down our throats by the media, sickening romantic notions and themes in films and art and music and on the bastardization of culture that is T.V. Sickly advertisements, mall posters for clothing companies, perfumes and cars. We are supposed to feel love, be *in* love. The subliminal message therein is that we are not truly alive without love, the underlying message addressed to the unloved is: YOU DON'T MATTER.

But love is adaptable. It is subjective. What may be love for one is not for another. How we love is up to us and it may not resemble those windswept couples in expensive knits and torn jeans, asleep in each other's embrace on a generic beach, but it might be love, all the same.

To nourish is to love. A dependant, unable to feed themselves, would perish were it not for the one individual, their caretaker, the provider of the nutriment required to sustain life – *that* is love.

There is a state of being conducive to this act of love. It is a familiar friend and the vessel through which true love is conducted. For the reciprocation of love to take place, to ensure that entitlement and churlishness are eradicated, the fed must be sedate. They must be at peace, their thoughts gliding, soaring like the scissor-tailed kite on a thermal.

To keep them in their sedentary state is kindness indeed for it is to preserve their lives. Love is not present in futile pleads and tears. Love is not present in the thrashes, the kicked over stench of their piss and their shit – fury lives there; agitation is in that; puking, vomiting hatred spills with it.

Love blooms after the imbibition, once the swallowing is done, once the velveteen opiates engulf them. Only then can tender care be taken: nourishment of the body; they must be cleaned so that they remain healthy and more fragrant than once they were; movement is vital, the manipulation of their limbs, their muscles must be exercised. Finally cleaned and fed and riding the thermal, they become alive and excited sexually because that is an inextricable facet of love and it is how they thank him for his.

PART THREE

WEDNESDAY 11TH APRIL

CHAPTER 12 - THE PROFILE

"First things first, I need you to compile a list of all the men who were present at the crime scene and at The Pioneer House meeting the other night."

Marlene nodded and sat up straighter in her chair at the end of Ali's dining room table. She had arrived at Ali's door at nine fifty-eight a.m. toting an ancient laptop, snacks, notebooks for each of them and an assortment of pens in a mug that read 'World's Best Dad'.

"So it's a man then?" Marlene popped the end of a strawberry lace in her mouth and let the remaining six inches of the confection dangle down below her chin.

"We have to narrow our investigation and work with several assumptions, yes. Male fits the profile."

"This profile? Do I get to see it?"

"I'll get to that in a bit. First, you think back and make a note of everyone you remember there."

"Yes, ma'am."

...

Superintendent Doug Shaw somehow managed to appear superior and command respect in VIIMIS's makeshift squad room despite his attire. A passionate marathon runner, Doug Shaw rarely missed his early morning ten-kilometre run to warm up his body and mind. Standing at the front of the room in his form-fitting Under Armour leggings and high-visibility green top, iPhone still in a holster on his upper left arm, Shaw briefed his team.

"I'm still awaiting a full report from the Medical Examiner and he's refusing to tell me much of anything until he can find a conclusive C.O.D."

Cuzzocrea wondered if he dared suggest tetanus.

"Was there any evidence of sexual assault?" Sergeant Eden Harrington, the team's special victims officer, seemed eager to know how crucial her role in the case would be.

"Still waiting for that. Tox-screen isn't back yet either. Crime scene analysis, Trina? Where are we?" Shaw asked the team's forensic officer.

"Fibres collected from the body, fingernail scrapings, hopefully we have some D.N.A. but what we did collect from the surrounding area is going to be a mess since it's a populated public trail. I've requested hair sampling to give us a picture of at least recent history but that is done off site and so it will take some time. Everything is tagged and bagged and on its way to Regina." Trina Walsh, when not working VIIMIS forensics, was a no-nonsense ball-breaker according to her male counterparts in her home town of Cedar River.

"You going with?" Doug Shaw enquired.

"At this stage I'd rather stay here. I'm liaising closely with the lab but I want to see what we get back from the M.E."

"How close are we to an I.D. on the victim?" Shaw addressed the newest member of the team, Corporal Paul Abbott, a dedicated missing person's officer who was recruited only six weeks prior and as such, seemed intimidated by Shaw's attention. He answered nervously.

"I have nothing yet, sir. I'm cross referencing the description of her and that of the tattoo on the small of her back – it's pretty generic though, a butterfly – with the N.C.M.P.U.R. database – the National Centre for Missing Persons and Unidentified Remains –"

"I know what N.C.M.P.U.R. is, Corporal." Shaw was impatient.

"Yes, sir. Of course."

"That's it?" Superintendent Shaw ripped the velcro securing his phone holster to his arm and dropped the phone onto a desk, a sign that he had grown impatient and was newly focused on showering.

"Sir." Paul Abbott reddened.

"Not good enough." Shaw fixed Abbott in his sights, "I want something by tonight, find out who she is, it's your job."

"Sir." Abbott loosened his tie and swallowed the order.

...

"I think that's everyone." Marlene turned her laptop away from her to face Ali who had removed a large canvas and several framed photographs from the wall that ran alongside the dining table.

"Later," said Ali as she pinned a rough sketch of the victim on the left of the otherwise bare wall. "Okay, victimology is key, Marlene. If we know our victim, we get to know our killer. Now, it's my theory – understand this is a *theory* – that the C.O.D. –"

"C.O.D.?" asked Marlene.

"Cause of death."

"Right, C.O.D." Marlene made a note of the acronym in her new notebook.

"I have reason to believe that she died as a result of a tetanus infection."

"But she was murdered. You saw her throat." Marlene saw that the drawn girl on the wall sported a gash of red ink on her throat.

"Yes, she died as a result of her injuries for sure. She probably contracted the infection through the open wounds on her neck. Here's why this theory works for us: one, it tells us something about the location in which she died; two, it tells us that the victim wasn't immunized against tetanus."

"Okey dokey, but how did you come up with this theory?

This C.O.D.? Is that what the police say?"

Ali explained, "I've no idea what the police have discovered yet but, look, in layman's terms…when we die several key changes happen to a body and these changes happen in the same order with everyone but they can be effected by environmental conditions or external influences. It's by observing these changes and any irregularities in them that investigators can determine things like time of death, cause of death, whether the body was moved and if so how long after death that may have happened, etcetera. Now, the live body also reacts to stress, injury and infection and leaves evidence of this – anti-mortem changes or necrosis – on the body, so an expert can evaluate markings on the surface of the body and on the internal organs and determine not only what happened at the point of death and soon after but also prior to it."

"So?"

"So, clostridium tetani – that's the bacterium which causes the infection we know as tetanus – which, by the way, is second only to botulinum as the deadliest toxin in the world…basically, don't get Botox, Marlene."

"Too late." Marlene shrugged. "I only get it in my armpits. It stops sweating."

"Okay, so it takes between four and fourteen days from exposure to the bacteria for the infection to become generalized tetanus. Now, in the early stages of the infection – contracted through exposure to soil, dust or manure within which the spores lie dormant – there would be red streaks on the skin running from the site of the open wound toward the centre of the body. It's called lymphangitis, some people confuse it with blood poisoning but it's not. Anyway, the girl we found displayed evidence of lymphangitis as well as necrosis in the tissue immediately surrounding the wound on her neck."

"Kind of with you so far, although your idea of layman's terms is a little different to mine." Marlene popped another strawberry lace in her mouth. "Go on."

"You've heard the term rigor mortis, right?"

"Yeah, that's why they're called 'stiffs', right. But, you know, she didn't look stiff, she looked floppy, like someone sleeping."

"Well, rigor sets in between two to six hours post mortem and, depending on the external environmental temperature, the stiffening process lasts for about twelve hours and then the body is typically in a rigid state for about eighteen hours after that."

"So, she was dead for a long time before we found her."

"Yes."

"Do you think she was killed there? In the bushes?"

"No, I know she wasn't. She was placed there. Displayed there. Once generalized tetanus sets in, the patient experiences several specific symptoms." Ali counted them off on her fingers as she listed them for Marlene: "Torpor, so, kind of lethargic, inactive; inability to prehend food; dysphasia, difficulty swallowing food and water; then stiffening of the muscles particularly trismus – or lockjaw; then into opisthotonus spasms, which is where the muscles contract causing severe hypertension; death would occur soon after most commonly because the contracting muscles make it impossible to breathe but also due to cardiac failure or as a result of status epilepticcus, a state of prolonged or even constant seizure.

"The severe hypertension, the opisthotonus spasming – the term comes from the Greek word meaning *drawn backwards* – so the head, neck, the whole spinal column bridges up into a severe arched position. It is very extreme and specific to generalized tetanus. Now, before rigor sets in there is algor mortis – that's the cooling of the body – then comes livor mortis, that's when the blood congeals in the capillaries and settles in response to gravity so, for instance, if I die face down, flat on my stomach –"

"– your blood would fall down into your stomach?"

"Well, it would settle towards my stomach but not in any area in direct contact with the ground or another object because the pressure of the ground or an object – even my own arm, say – compresses the capillaries, restricting access to the gravity-responsive blood through them. So, the area of my front that was in contact with the floor would look white and if I died with my arm underneath me, there would also remain a perfect outline of that arm. Both of the white, indented areas would be surrounded by the darker purplish, burgundy of the gravity-pulled blood."

"I see, sooo?"

"On our girl, lividity – the markings I just described – was consistent with a hyperextended bridging of the spinal column prior to death and the muscle spasms were so severe and of such spasticity that her body remained in that position – in cadaveric spasm – throughout the three initial stages of mortis. Taking that into account along with the lymphangitis, my theoretical conclusion is that the cause of death was a direct result of generalized tetanus."

"Ali, honey." Marlene huffed as her brain digested the information. "That's all very impressive but all I'm hearing is an argument that a defence lawyer would use to get the killer off."

"What do you mean?"

"Well, you're saying that the C.O.D., as you put it, was tetanus, not murder."

"Marlene, nobody dies of murder. It's not a cause of death. She died because someone victimized and brutalized her. Tetanus is just the infection that led to her scientific cause of death, the same as a stabbing victim doesn't die of stabbing, they die as a result of exsanguination, blood loss."

"Okay, but how does your tetanus theory help us? It's not like we can now go out and find someone because of it."

"No, but it will take us closer through victimology. We can narrow down our list of suspects based on the definable group in which the victim belongs. It also tells us a lot about the site of the murder."

"How?"

"Who isn't immunized? What group or groups of people

in Canada are likely not to have received the vaccination?"

"Well, when your kids are little you get them immunized, you have a little blue card and everything."

"What if you don't have parents? Or at least ones who give a shit about you?"

"Hang on, it's given to every kid in grade…what was it? Eight or nine, I can't remember. So, either she wasn't at school or maybe in a different country?"

"Or, she was immunized but never received a booster. To be protected against tetanus you need the initial vaccine early on and then a booster shot every ten years, sooner if you're involved in an accident and suffer a traumatic injury. So, what group of people doesn't take care of that stuff?"

"Well, dumbasses, um, maybe if they don't know any better so…mentally ill people? What about drug addicts? The homeless?"

"Exactly."

...

"Cuzzocrea? Where are you and Detective Munro on Patterson?"

Cuzzocrea nodded to his investigative partner. Munro brought up the mugshot of Patterson on his laptop and shared it with the interactive whiteboard behind the superintendent so the whole team could look at the fugitive.

Cuzzocrea cleared his throat and addressed the group. "James Henry Patterson. Fifty-two years old. Two hundred and twelve pounds. Five feet, ten inches tall. Escaped from the minimum security Mochetsin Institute on the night of the eighth of April, some three nights ago. Convicted in nineteen seventy-eight of first-degree murder. Transferred to the Mochetsin Institute last year awaiting his upcoming release due in November. He was initially sentenced to a minimum of twenty-five years but had incurred additional sentencing as a result of crimes committed during his incarceration in the Kent Institute, Agassiz, B.C. Patterson was originally convicted for the kidnap, murder and dismemberment of the president of the Nanaimo chapter of The Devil's Fang outlaw motorcycle gang. A nationwide BOLO has been issued."

"What do we think, Rey? Does he fit the profile?"

Cuzzocrea paused, it was the first time that his boss had ever used his first name, an honour everyone under Shaw awaits for years and often never gets.

"No, sir. No history of sexual assault, no crimes against women, not even domestic abuse charges. His record is littered with the typical outlaw gang related charges – battery, assault, a weapons charge, an extortion charge that was later dropped. The murder he committed was rumoured to be a revenge attack in response to an earlier alleged sexual assault of a fifteen-year-old Nanaimo girl. The girl was Patterson's niece."

"Any physical evidence linking him to the crime?"

Trina Walsh shook her head, "Sir, not at this time. I can rule him out when I get the results back from Regina but it doesn't fit for me either; it's not his M.O."

"Well, he still has to be our prime suspect. A prisoner escapes from the local minimum security facility and the body of a girl is found in an otherwise peaceful community just a few hours later…I have to anticipate public perception on this one, once the public hear about the escape and it becomes common knowledge and, in a community like Mochetsin that won't take long, a fugitive on the run will pull focus and if the general public think we're doing nothing about it, there will be outrage."

Cuzzocrea realized that he and the rest of the team were about to be tasked with the hunt for Patterson regardless of the lack of evidence linking the man to the murder.

"Sir, I'd like to start compiling a criminal analysis based on another unknown offender."

"We are focusing our combined efforts on finding Patterson."

"I think my skills as an analyst are better utilized –"

"Listen, Cuzzocrea, I don't need your résumé, I picked you, remember? I'll decide how your skills are best used, thank you."

The use of his last name told Cuzzocrea that by questioning his superior's orders, he'd slid down the back of a python on Shaw's game of VIIMIS snakes and ladders. Regardless of this and running the risk of inciting Shaw's wrath further, Cuzzocrea felt compelled to plead his case.

"Sir, I might have something to go on in terms of profile – I'd need Trina's opinion on a theory – but it could be something."

"Your theory?" Shaw pulled the crotch of his leggings away from what Cuzzocrea imagined must be a very sweaty pair of testicles.

"Not exactly, sir. One of the witnesses at the scene of the crime has a history in forensic science and she made me aware of her observations. I feel like there might be something there."

Everyone in the room was silent. Shaw poked at one of his back teeth with his tongue. Trina Walsh crossed her legs and Cuzzocrea took the bobbing of her upper foot as an indication of potential aggression.

"Well, Rey, you just managed to insult Trina by insinuating that random witnesses can do her job better than she can. Good luck getting that opinion you needed."

"No offence intended, Trina." Although it was a sincere apology, Cuzzocrea didn't dare to make eye contact with the woman.

"None taken, Rey," Trina lied. "I'm just going to the mall to ask if any of the store clerks there have investigative tips for you."

Shaw snorted his appreciation of Trina's retort. "Focus on Patterson, Rey. You and Munro head down to the prison. Against my better judgement I'll let you put together a brief – and I mean brief – in your own time, outlining this theory. Trina and I will look it over to see if it has teeth."

"Sir." Cuzzocrea was happy with the compromise and the

reintroduction of his first name.

...

Marlene put her hands against the lumbar region of her back and arched with a grunt. She and Ali had decided to get some fresh air (and nicotine) and continue their meeting on the deck.

"Takes some maintenance, doesn't it?" said Marlene.

"What does?"

"Ten acres."

"How do you know it's ten acres?"

Marlene turned to Ali and explained, "All of the parcels of land in Mochetsin are ten acres, apart from the farm plots because they've been handed down through generations and there's different zoning for arable land. But residential plots are all ten acres."

"Yeah, the property is big, it goes all the way back, almost to the Mochetsin Road. I don't do anything with that section at the back because it's mostly brambles and apple trees. I just cut the grass here on the ocean side."

"You cut it?"

"Who else do you think would?"

"David. I refuse to do any house maintenance and so Peter just employs other people to do it."

"That's not a luxury we can afford, besides, I've always been handy. I put up shelves, I paint, I tile, I repair the plumbing."

"Wow. I'm very impressed, Ali."

Ali shrugged in response to the compliment. "Now, shall we get on with what's what? I think she was held in a cellar or an unfinished basement, maybe an outbuilding or shed of some sort."

"Well, needle in a haystack then. Like we were just saying, everyone has a minimum of ten acres. You can put a lot of barns and outhouses and workshops on ten acres. And if we're looking for somewhere where there's soil or dust or animal droppings then, we've got one hell of a search ahead because this place is mostly farmland."

"I know but it had to have been an extremely private space. I think he kept her there for a long time. As a prisoner."

"Why do you think that?"

"She appeared to be undernourished, if not malnourished."

"Really? She was slim for sure but she had a little belly. She didn't seem like she was starved."

"Her belly would have been due to putrefaction, the bacteria in the body breaks us down after death and as we decompose, gasses are produced –"

"Nope!" Marlene held her hand up as she passed Ali, opened the patio door and reentered the house. "No slime or gasses please, I draw the line there."

Ali stubbed out her cigarette and joined Marlene back at the table.

"Okay, well, she appeared to be undernourished and there was evidence of muscle wastage – the kind of thing you see when someone is in a non-ambulatory state for prolonged periods, you see it on people who are in a coma or if you look at the legs of someone who is wheelchair bound. Also, I noticed discolouration on the underside of her jaw and the region of her neck where the skin remained intact. I initially thought it was bruising but on closer inspection I determined that it was in fact a patina – verdigris, to be exact."

"Verdigris? Like on the roof of The Empress Hotel downtown?"

Ali couldn't help but smile, "Marlene! You are better at this stuff than I thought you might be."

"Why, thank you."

"Okay, here's a test for you."

"Shoot."

"Why is there verdigris on the roof of The Empress?"

"Easy, because of the copper spires, they age and turn

green. Something to do with our proximity to the ocean."

"You get a gold star, Marlene. Fucking awesome."

"Not just a pretty face. But why was there verdigris on her neck and jaw?"

"Our victim's neck was patinated with verdigris because…"

"She had on a copper collar." Marlene jumped up and clapped her hands together in triumph.

"Precisely."

"Oh dear." Marlene's triumph disappeared along with her smile as the ramifications of a girl in a collar began to sink in.

"A neck cuff of some sort, for a long time. Long enough for the copper to oxidize."

…

Cuzzocrea gathered his paperwork up and stuffed the files into his laptop bag. At the end of the briefing Superintendent Shaw had announced he was going for his shower but hadn't yet managed to prise himself away from Trina Walsh who seemed to have the man cornered.

Cuzzocrea's partner, Munro, whispered in Cuzzocrea's ear with a faint whiff of old coffee on a furry tongue, "You think they're screwing?"

"I don't know buddy, and I don't care," said Cuzzocrea as he made his way out of the squad room.

Munro caught up with him. "I'd put money on it."

"Shaw's married."

"So's she. Maybe they see these VIIMIS cases as a good excuse, you know, they're both away from home.'

"Whatever." Cuzzocrea liked to avoid gossip as much as he could, especially about people he might need a recommendation from one day. He pressed the button to call the elevator.

"Maybe he's not sweaty every morning because he runs but because he's been…" Munro slipped an index finger back and forth through a circle formed by the other hand.

Cuzzocrea didn't think he could like Munro less but somehow the man always managed to sink to new lows.

"This is bullshit," said Cuzzocrea.

"Hey, buddy. What's with you today?" Munro asked.

Cuzzocrea stopped and turned to him. "Wasting our time on this manhunt when we should be investigating the homicide."

"You heard Shaw, and he's right. We have to at least be seen to be looking for Patterson. Just because he doesn't fit your analysis, we can't just presume him to be innocent."

"He didn't do it."

"Orders are orders, Rey."

"It's still bullshit."

Munro shrugged as he headed down the stairs, most probably to catch a smoke before their drive out to the prison. Cuzzocrea decided he'd rather wait for the elevator. He felt the familiar twist in his bowels, the feeling he always got when a case was losing its way. The way he felt last year when a similar case went cold on another Jane Doe, decapitated, who had washed up on the shore in Sooke.

Upon his promotion to VIIMIS Cuzzocrea had naïvely imagined that his time in the unit would have plumped up his already impressive résumé with a series of high-profile cases for which he could share the credit of solving, not a depressing list of failures.

...

"Right, so she was a prisoner. A sex slave? I watched a documentary not so long ago about how the West Coast is a hotspot for human trafficking." Marlene was studying the screen of her laptop intently. "I'll find the link and send it to you."

"I don't know if the crime was sexually motivated; I only looked at her. I'd need to have examined her to know for sure."

"But it feels like it, doesn't it? Isn't this type of thing

usually sexually motivated?"

"All we can do is work on assumptions based on what we observed *and* the profile."

"So? This profile?" Marlene suggested.

Ali carefully laid several sheets of paper on the table as she spoke, "If we are really doing this, and it looks like we are, then we have to follow the profile and trust it to be true. Now, I've built this on limited knowledge of the case and a profile is a series of guesses *but* they are highly educated guesses. Profilers follow tried and tested methods so more often than not they tend to be quite accurate but there will be mistakes too however, as we learn more from the police, crucial evidence and such, then we can refine it as we go."

"Got it." Marlene folded her arms and adopted a look of intense concentration.

"We are looking for a male, caucasian, aged between thirty and forty-five – probably on the older end of that scale. He is most likely married or, at least, in a significant relationship with a woman.

"He lives and works in the area and is familiar and comfortable with the outdoors. His occupation is menial, mundane, routine. It requires the use of a vehicle. His vehicle will have high mileage and it will be usual for him to spend a lot of time driving. It will probably be a trade vehicle with a covered cargo section at the rear. This cargo section will be kept in an overly neat and organized condition.

"He will have been educated formally no higher than a high-school level but he will have continued to educate himself after graduation. He is above average intelligence and may even have an I.Q. of one sixty or above.

"He will have a juvenile criminal record of arson and probably breaking and entering although he will have committed other criminal acts as a juvenile which will have gone unnoticed or unpunished. He will have endeavoured to have his juvenile record sealed and will most probably have achieved that by the dogged manipulation of the person or persons in charge of monitoring and evaluating him.

"He will have found a way to navigate a world within which he doesn't feel he belongs. His outward appearance and all details of his manufactured life are an illusion designed to mask his true personality. It would be a rarity for him to let the act slip but if he did it would result in a brief, aggressive outburst that would seem out of character to the people closest to him.

"His family background was highly dysfunctional. As a child, he would have experienced neglect and abuse including sexual abuse. An absent father as a result of divorce, death or incarceration.

"He has a history of mental illness and is probably in treatment at present.

"He is taunting a community he feels has taunted and rejected him. He was probably made to feel dirty and dangerous before his crimes, perhaps by the community or by a significant other, probably his mother. He will have experienced being shut away and even tortured.

"If the crimes are indeed sexual in nature, rape will be a factor but will *not* have happened post mortem. He will have a collection of s&m equipment and pornography. He is sexually dysfunctional. Probably impotent.

"He believes himself to be superior to the authorities but he will also be obsessed with the police and their investigation of the case. The way in which he disposed of the body was in a manner designed to taunt the police so it is likely that the police were, at one time, investigating another of his kills but the case remains unsolved. This will have frustrated him, not because he wishes to be caught but because he feels the police are incompetent and he would have taken it as an insult for them to give up on the hunt for him, to not have taken him seriously. With this body, he is making it easy for them. He enjoys the attention. He enjoys the chase.

"The police will already have spoken to him, in fact he will be known to them. He may have tried to befriend police officers and would even go as far as to frequent establishments where they are known to hang out. He will have applied for a job as a police officer but his application will have been denied. He may also have similar obsessions with other first-responder personnel such as those in the fire service and paramedics. He may also have applied for jobs within these vocations.

"He will return to the scene of the crime, the site where the body was discovered and will, most definitely, attend memorials, funerals or visit graves.

"He is driven by domination, manipulation and control. His modus operandi is kidnap, torture, perhaps rape and murder. His signature is neck lengthening with the use of a copper cuff or piping coiled around the victim's neck. His paraphilia is odaxelagnia; he experiences sexual arousal through biting. He relishes schadenfreude and so inflicts as much pain and discomfort upon his victims as he can prior to their death.

"He hunts and stalks his prey from a definable group – specifically young, homeless women in and around the Victoria region. It is likely that he is a familiar face to them, perhaps he volunteers at a shelter or a soup kitchen in the area? He lures them, charms them, perhaps he offers them something before he overpowers them with the use of either physical force or possibly narcotics.

"The property on which he keeps his victims prior to death is large and there will be outbuildings situated some distance from the main house. He wishes to be undisturbed here and so has allowed nature to obscure this area in some way and may even have planted bushes and trees in recent years. The building itself will have been adapted for its purpose and, unless it has a below-grade cellar, will be soundproofed. He will have made all alterations himself and so he is competent with tools and probably frequents stores like Rona, Canadian Tire and Home Depot.

"And then I have some recommendations regarding interrogation techniques in the event of his capture because he wouldn't keep a diary of his projects. At most he may have taken pictures or filmed encounters with his victims for later gratification. The police would most likely need a confession to secure a worthy conviction."

Ali looked at Marlene, took a deep breath and exhaled.

"Wow. How on earth did you come up with all of that, missy, just from looking at that girl?"

Ali shrugged. "It's what I do. It's what I'm good at."

"Are you going to give this to Inspector Guzzo…what's his name?"

"Cuzzocrea? I don't know. What do you think?"

"Hell yeah. You're like a real-life Columbo but without the funny eye and the raincoat."

"Like I said though, this isn't one hundred per cent, and I'm a little out of practice. Some of it might be right, some of it could be embarrassingly wrong."

"Well." Marlene got up and walked round the table, she placed her hands on Ali's shoulders. "This is what you do, this is what you're good at. All we need is more right than wrong and we catch the dirty sonofabitch."

As Marlene hugged her and Ali felt pride swell within her. The feeling was akin to finding something precious, once lost. Ali suddenly felt an authenticity that had been lacking during her time dedicated purely to her family.

CHAPTER 13 - THE MOCHETSIN INSTITUTE

Whether you're an overworked venture capitalist with your own helipad or a former bra-burning hippy whose metier is the agronomical development of the perfect soil within which to spawn champion squash. Perhaps you're a seclusion-loving, pot-growing, still-bubbling, meth-cooking distributor? Mochetsin is the perfect hidey hole for all those who crave privacy and anonymity; a Canadian paradise kept secret and protected from all those who covet her.

You don't have to be a conspiracy theorist to pick up on the surreptitious atmosphere of the region. It's evidenced in the myopic study of your number plate as you park near the elderly couple on a midday stroll or the pointed and loaded, "Just passing through?" from the waitress serving coffee in the Mochetsin Café.

Cuzzocrea wound down the passenger window of Munro's ancient Toyota Corolla for a much-needed change in the breakfast-biscuit, old-socks-fermenting-in-the-trunk atmosphere of the car. Cuzzocrea rested his elbow in the new opening and felt the cool breeze drying the sweat of his armpit hair. Since they'd left the cafe, Munro's thumb had been on a mission to dislodge a stubborn bogey from his right nostril. Cuzzocrea watched from the corner of his eye as his partner finally snared the semi-viscous fleck of sticky mucus, its dry, spiked tail dangled as Munro studied it briefly before rolling it between thumb and forefinger then wiping it onto the side of the driver's seat. Cuzzocrea scanned the passenger side of the vehicle where he sat for evidence of any older boogers and wondered what a forensic swab test of the car would come back with. As Munro pulled into a parking space, Cuzzocrea hoped there was a bottle of hand sanitizer available at the Mochetsin Institute.

The external structure belied the purpose of the minimum-security facility as well as the intended prisoner experience nurtured within. Sure, there was high, steel fencing with rolls of razor wire along its top and, yes, the main building appeared battlement like – a seemingly impenetrable fortress – but anyone with any experience in correctional facilities could deduce that those gimmicks were a façade of immurement, a token gesture in place to placate the locals and prevent hysteria born of the average human's atavistic aversion to the criminal element of our species.

Munro pulled himself out of his sweaty Corolla, relieving his stiff back with a grimace and a crackling stretch and increasing the comfort level of his nether regions with an unapologetic positional adjustment of his gonads.

"Do me a favour, Rey," said Munro as he looked at the prison. "If I'm ever sent away for something, pull a few strings and make sure I'm sent here."

Mochetsin had no shortage of jaw-dropping real estate but the half-mile stretch of secluded beach that shouldered Peddar Inlet – the site of the Mochetsin Institute – left nothing to be desired.

"Yup," replied Cuzzocrea, "it makes you want to get a double life sentence, huh?"

Cuzzocrea shut the passenger side door and walked to the front of the vehicle where Munro was lighting a cigarette.

"Seems kinda chilled considering there was an escape." Munro sat on the hood of his car.

"Why d'you think there was an escape in the first place? It's a spa retreat. Patterson probably just walked right out in a robe and slippers."

"You been here before?" asked Munro.

"Yeah, for an escape in two thousand twelve."

Munro exhaled a smoky, "Jeez."

"Well, it was officially documented as an escape, technically it was but the truth was covered up." Cuzzocrea tidied his tie.

"Go on."

"See just out there, past those three houses?" Cuzzocrea pointed beyond the façade turret of the main entry to the sea beyond three detached adobe red bricked homes.

"Yah? What are they? Houses for the guards?" Munro flicked the ash off the top of his cigarette.

"Buddy, those houses are where the inmates live," replied Cuzzocrea.

"You're shitting me."

Cuzzocrea explained: "In the main building there's a regular cell block for newer inmates who are transitioning from max or medium security prisons. They're there for about six months while they adjust, then they're given a house. They share it with three other inmates; their pod. Apart from a bedtime curfew and work duty, they live here like regular people."

"What the fuck?" Munro looked quizzically at Cuzzocrea, disbelieving.

"I know, right? This place is the over-funded poster child for Canada's Correctional Service. It's all about reintegration, teaching them how to live in a normal society again. They get vocational training, do their G.H.D.'s and shit, hell, they even get jobs outside the prison while they're here."

"So, what are we talking here? These must be guys with minor infractions, short-termers?"

"The antithesis, in fact. The guys in here are *only* life-termers who fall into the category of institutionalized – in for so long that they've forgotten how to be a law-abiding citizen, how to function naturally outside. They've been told what to do for decades, when to eat, what to eat, when to shower, shit and shave. Every decision has been made for them for so long that making one for themselves scares the crap out of them and by the time they're ready for release they break down."

Munro crunched his cigarette butt into the gravel of the car park. "I don't feel sorry for them. Boo-fricking-hoo. They come here, live in a big house overlooking the fricking ocean for free? Damn right they don't know what the real world is like. So if these guys have spent so long inside, then there are some twisted fucks in here who just come and go as they please?"

"Yep. The theory is that you *can* pay your debt to society. That, by serving your time, you are rehabilitated and ready to be a productive member of the community again."

"Bullshit. How rare is it for us to arrest a first-time offender?"

Cuzzocrea replied, "Well, if we, as a society, don't foster that belief then, what? Kill all the criminals? Because they're only going to offend again?"

"Now you're getting political on my ass. Come on."

Munro pressed a button on his key fob and the car doors clunked in unison bereft of the accompanying bleep of cars manufactured post-2000.

As the two officers arrived at the facility's outer gate the sun's heat quivered the ground-floor levels of the brick houses beyond. Cuzzocrea pressed the button on the intercom and held his identification up towards the overhead security camera. With a smile, he muttered: "This is a gigantic waste of my fucking talent."

CHAPTER 14 - THE PSYCHOPATH

Marlene and Ali unintentionally mirrored each other as they leaned side by side against the dining room table, arms folded, lips pursed, perusing the 'wall of death', as Marlene had begun to call it.

The new macabre interior design of Ali's signature wall was separated into three sections by two vertical strips of green painter's tape. The left was the 'victim section'. Ali's diagram of the dead girl was surrounded by half a dozen post-it notes containing any information from the profile specifically relating to victimology.

On the far right of the wall was a similar section in the centre of which was a print of a generic, male silhouette upon which Ali had drawn a large, red question mark with a Sharpie marker from Marlene's 'Worlds Best Dad' mug of pens. Running in concentric circles around the silhouette of the elusive mystery man was a ripple of multicoloured post-its inscribed with every detail from the profile regarding the suspected perpetrator of the murder.

In the centre of the wall, Ali had pinned up a map of Mochetsin – Marlene had stolen it from a dusty collection of ordinance survey maps on the top shelf in her husband's study when she'd popped home to quickly feed Webster. A red 'x' marked the spot on the map where Webster had sniffed out the decaying flesh of the dead girl on Monday morning.

Below the map were two lists of names: all the men

present at the scene of the crime and all the men present at the Pioneer House meeting on Monday evening. Highlighted in luminous pink were the names of men present at both locations.

"Would you mind explaining a couple of things on here?" said Marlene.

"Not at all, hit me." Ali shuffled back onto the table, sitting with her feet dangling free.

Marlene crossed to the right side of the 'wall of death' and studied the perpetrator-related post-its.

"So, I'll work from the inside out. You said he was thirty to forty-five, probably on the older end of that scale. How would you know that?"

"I don't *know* that but there's evidence to support it. Okay, this profile is based largely on the fact that we are dealing with an organized killer – it's the foundation of any profile, organized or disorganized. So someone who suffers from schizophrenia or someone who just flies off the handle and kills in the moment of passion or rage would be classed as a disorganized killer. Our killer was very careful with his victim, he didn't bash her brains in. The kill lacked passion, it was emotionless, methodical and careful. These types of organized killers fall into a specific bracket. The placement of the body was thought-out, considered – not dumped. That's why I think we have an organized killer, he isn't driven by emotion, he appears to be practiced. He displayed the body carefully, almost beautifully. It's indicative of an older killer. An organized, mindful killer."

"Okay, makes sense." Marlene picked out another post-it and read, "Lives and works in the area and likes the outdoors."

"Placement of the body on the trail. He hid it well in a place that is largely unknown except by locals and people who are familiar with Mochetsin. It's also why I believe the police failed to solve a previous murder of his. He could have dumped her in the ocean or buried her on his ten acres. He wanted her to be found. He showed her off."

"So his job, his vehicle, all very specific. Just guesses or based on what? Past cases?"

"Based on the typical traits and habits of organized killers. I hate labelling mental illnesses, dysfunctions or disorders because, actually, the labels assigned to these things aren't recognized by science but are actually only in existence because of the law, as a means to argue a defence or to justify a forced certification and resulting incarceration. Also, these titles and labels are usually in vogue for a short time before being reclassified by a new ruling or precedent following a successful mental evaluation resulting in a conviction or the avoidance of one, *but*…if I had to label our organized killer, I would say he is a psychopath – in the truest sense of the definition."

"Like *Psycho*? Norman Bates?" asked Marlene.

Ali huffed. "If you start allowing Hollywood to dictate classifications of mental disorders, you're in muddy waters. The diagnosis 'psychopath' doesn't exist but there are psychopathic characteristics – again, used in criminal justice *not* in science. Basically, a psychopath is anti-social, lacks empathy or remorse, is disinhibited and bold. It's a form of brain damage thought to be caused as the foetus develops in the womb due to viral exposures in-utero – hypoxia, infection, even stress or malnutrition cause the unborn child's brain to develop abnormally resulting in irregularities in the prefrontal cortex and the…" Ali stopped herself, "Are you sure you want a biology lesson right now, Marlene?"

"One hundred per cent," Marlene said. "Go on."

"Okay, where was I?"

"Irregularities in the pre…something something."

"The prefrontal cortex and the amygdala regions of the brain associated with social and moral reasoning."

"So what's the difference between a psychopath and a sociopath, then?"

"Sociopathy is a Hollywood creation but if we apply it to actual personality disorders: a psychopath is born; a sociopath is made. Basically a sociopath is created by his or her environment; it's not a genetic or biological deformity and if our killer was a sociopath he wouldn't have had the detached coldness of our killer. He would have made crucial mistakes and our job of finding him would probably be over already. Our psychopath was born – in fact many are. You wouldn't know a psychopath if you were married to one but a sociopathic husband would be an absolute shit to live with."

"And how would a psychopath be?"

"A psychopath takes great enjoyment in manipulating the world around him. He learnt from a very early age that he was fundamentally different to other people. This wouldn't have made him feel bad because psychopaths are incapable of feeling emotions. It would, instead, have confirmed his own superiority over other humans who are preoccupied by all the minutiae and stresses caused by emotions. However, he will have realized that to manipulate his environment efficiently he would have had to appear to be 'normal'. Psychopaths are the actors of our species, they play a part, they fake emotions, they know how one looks when one feels an emotion and they mimic emotions, they mimic compassion and empathy. A true psychopath is incapable of love – of even seeing other people as anything other than vaguely interesting ant-like creatures, at best – yet, they will invariably be married, have children, be the most charismatic members of a community, they are often successful, rich, they are leaders, surgeons, judges, professors – they are extraordinary."

"Oh my, it makes you wonder."

"It makes you take another look around, for sure. Crucially though, for a psychopath to become a murderous one, their psychopathy needs a couple of friends: narcissism and Machiavellianism; it's known as the dark triad. Without the dark triad, a psychopath isn't necessarily dangerous – just another type of human being. However, if we take someone who has the biological dysfunction in the brain – so someone who was born a psychopath – but who also experienced an upbringing that allowed narcissism to flower twinned with the intellectual capacity to open the door to Machiavellianism *plus* a predilection toward sadism, then you have not only the dark *triad* but the dark *tetrad*. And that, my friend, creates a very dangerous monster."

"So all of the things you said about his childhood, the treatment, the abuse, that's what? The difference between a good psychopath and a bad one?"

"Except there is no good or bad for a psychopath. There is no moral right or wrong. There is only manipulation, domination and control."

Marlene stood silent for a moment, Ali watched as she chewed the notions over in her mind and then turned again to the wall.

"So, the menial job and the truck?"

"Organized thinking. Hiding behind an illusion of normalcy. Also, the truck is practical. He transports his victims in it, hidden away, in a vehicle that doesn't stand out, no matter where it's parked."

"What about rape?"

"Good question. I believe a true psychopath cannot be motivated by sex as we know it, in the sense of love or attraction. Again, a psychopath is incapable of love. However, I wouldn't rule rape out as it is an efficient form of torture. Rape is often misinterpreted, by those of us who do not rape as being connected to sex. It isn't. Rape is power. Rape is domination. If our killer raped, it would be in a sadistic manner – to cause pain and suffering; to control. Also, psychopaths would never rape post mortem – this only happens when someone is embarrassed by their sexuality. They want to have sex with the victim privately, even away from the owner of the orifice themselves. They are usually young offenders, disorganized killers, and they also tend to place foreign objects in the dead victim's sexual orifices. Anyway, there would be no point in a psychopathic killer having intercourse with a corpse because corpses don't cry, they don't suffer, plead or react to pain. It would be an utterly pointless act."

"But if he doesn't feel emotion, why would he visit graves or memorial services? You said he would certainly do that."

"The same reason he will attempt to involve himself in the police investigation. Arrogance, narcissism, superiority – he is the conductor of his own orchestra, the police force is the string section, the mourners are the flautists. If you really get into his mind, you would ask yourself why he would ever miss a funeral or a statement to the press. He's his own biggest fan."

"My God, he really is a monster." Marlene looked wan.

"The most awesome kind of monster and very, very rare. It's unusual to find one, to hunt a true psychopathic murderer. It's once-in-a-lifetime stuff for people like me and for the VIIMIS team. It's likely he'll never be caught. He might just be too clever."

"Right. So this is what is really confusing me. The whole biting thing doesn't make sense. I saw her, she didn't have teeth marks on her but it says here…." Marlene pulled a pink post-it off the wall and read the words out to Ali, "His paraphilia is odax-ela-…"

"…odaxelagnia. Biting brings with it sexual gratification, for him. Think about it, if anything turns our killer on, it's sadistic in nature, it allows him to dominate, it causes suffering."

"But why biting? I don't mean him, I mean how did you come to that conclusion? Like I said, there weren't any bite marks on her."

"The neck lengthening and the careful excoriation of the skin on her neck. She wasn't sliced. A full rectangular segment of her neck skin had been removed and very carefully too – straight lines, corners. Our killer removed the portion of skin bearing indentations made by his teeth. It's delectable to him, so much so that he needs more – more neck – to enjoy. He carefully prepares the area, quite literally making the most of his favourite part of the body to bite."

"He's a vampire?"

"What? A vampire?" Ali laughed, "Like, I vant to drink your blaad?"

"Yes, exactly like that. Except without the terrible accent."

"I don't believe in vampires, no matter how popular they are – and before you ask, a psychopath is beyond being inspired by pop culture, it would be beneath him. But I do understand paraphilia and biting, tearing, ripping with his teeth is how he gets off. If he were vampiric – if there is such a bloody thing – he would want to drink blood, right? So he would have to puncture the jugular or the carotid artery, very hard things to find even if you're familiar with the circulatory system and then if he did puncture the – let's assume it's the jugular because the carotid is tucked away and protected by other structures in the throat so even if he did find it he'd have to bite a huge chunk out of her neck to get to it – so yes, he finds the jugular, he pierces it. She'd bleed out very quickly and if that happened she wouldn't be alive for the four to fourteen days it takes for –"

"A tetanus infection to become generalized tetanus!" Marlene stood erect, breath bated waiting for Ali's validation.

"Exactly! Marlene! I feel like Mr Fucking Miyagi. You're my Daniel-son and you are waxing off and waxing on like a frigging genius!"

Marlene shook her head. "I have no idea to what or to whom you refer, but thanks?"

"Never mind. Anyway, he enjoyed her neck, he finds the area delectable and he takes time to prepare it. By my estimations the process takes a couple of years, maybe, to lengthen it. And then, once it's ready, he enjoys her in bits. A bite here, a nibble there, a tear of the skin is left to dangle, to harden and pull off tomorrow, the day after, in a week maybe. Open wounds, dirty cellar or barn or outbuilding, soil, bacteria and, voilà! Tetanus."

Marlene studied the perpetrator's side of the wall of death, then the victimology portion and finally her eyes settled on the centre, on the map of Mochetsin and the lists of names underneath.

"Shit. Ali? I need a drink."

"Tea or coffee?" asked Ali.

"Something way stronger please. My once bright world just became a very dark place and I feel very...sad."

"Well then," Ali said as she slid off the table to her feet, "at least we know you're not a psychopath. Wine?"

CHAPTER 15 - CLUB FED

Warden Chris Maedel was a short, blocky man in his fifties with pan-scourer red hair, thinning on top but fizzing out above his ears, giving him the look of a clown past his prime. Maedel greeted Cuzzocrea and Munro in the prison's strangely welcoming reception area, exhaustion pulling at his jowls. A thatch of ginger lashes umbrellaed scleras webbed with the red threads of unrested eyes. Patches of gorse-like stubble poked angrily from his folliculated, pockmarked cheeks and chin. His chewing-gum-white shirt sported the tell-tale creases of one worn in lieu of pyjamas.

The warden held out a pudgy, pink hand to Cuzzocrea and his partner.

"Inspector Cuzzocrea. Detective Munro? I'm Chris Maedel, I'm the warden here at the Mochetsin Institute. I hope you managed to find us okay."

"Actually, I've been here before," said Cuzzocrea.

"Oh?" said Warden Maedel.

"In two thousand twelve."

"Ah, Warden Philips, then. The Kessler escape?" said Maedel.

"That's correct."

Warden Maedel looked crestfallen, realizing that the peroration of his predecessor's story was about to befall him. When it comes to escaped prisoners, shit tends to roll uphill, instigates an overhaul of practices, policies and procedure and invites the microscopic evaluation of all staff members but ultimately results in the deposition of the warden. Maedel's days were numbered.

Cuzzocrea and Munro placed their belongings, including their sidearms, in the pigeonhole lockers to the right of the reception area and followed Maedel's lead through the single metal detector and down a narrow, windowless corridor of closed office doors.

"So where are we with this?" The warden glanced over his shoulder as he spoke, greying pouches cupping his eyes.

"You tell us." Munro grunted. "Surely everything's going through you."

"The only thing going through me right now is last night's pad thai. My priorities remain in-house, the search for Patterson is out of my hands. I couldn't help out even if I wanted to. Glandford R.C.M.P. is in charge of the manhunt." Maedel stopped at a water cooler and looked at the men. "You're not with R.C.M.P.?"

"We're working on another case," explained Cuzzocrea, "but, due to the geographical and chronological proximity of our case and Patterson's escape, we've been tasked with expediting his recapture, if only to rule him out as a suspect in our case."

"That's all I need." Maedel filled a paper cone with water from the burping dispenser, swallowed it back, scrunched the cup in his fist and discarded it in the neighbouring recycling receptacle. As he left it, the warden lay an affectionate hand on the inverted water bottle as though wishing a trusty friend a fond farewell and entered his office. Cuzzocrea and Munro shared a 'he's losing it' look and followed him into the beige, nondescript office, the stodgy air still thick with fretful sleep.

Munro began, "Here's what I'd like to know: why would Patterson want to escape in the first place? He spent decades at Kent then he qualifies for relocation to this, let's face it, paradise. He's coming up for release. I don't get it."

Warden Maedel huffed into his desk chair. "Institutionalization one-oh-one. Some long-term-lifers don't want to be released. In fact, some of them will do some heinous stuff to stay in. We're lucky he escaped instead of killing a fellow inmate, or worse – one of the visitors that day. Inmates like Patterson dread the outside world, it's why they are relocated here, it's a kind of half-way step. Acclimatization. You know he's a former gang member? Well, his parole will be conditional upon many factors, one of them being that he is forbidden to have any contact with his former acquaintances and motorcycle club. For him, and others like him, that's tantamount to no life at all. It's not unusual therefore for an inmate like Patterson to prefer the option of remaining incarcerated on a permanent basis, to grow old and die in prison."

Warden Maedel rubbed the top of his head and seemed unaware of, or unconcerned by, the resulting statically charged spikes of enduring hair. He glanced beyond the small, rectangular window at the top of the wall to the left of his desk. A single, white vapour line began its languid dissipation in the otherwise unscarred blue sky.

"Did you know Patterson well?" Cuzzocrea asked.

"Of course." Maedel was still watching the contrail as it fluffed and skewed. "Nice enough guy. Quiet. Had a part-time placement at a local car detailing facility in Collwood. Model inmate by all standards, head of his pod. He'd just completed all of his quals ready for parole."

"Any recent changes in his behaviour? New visitors? Anything at all," asked Munro.

Maedel twitched his strikingly priapic nose and Cuzzocrea noticed a golden nasal pube had descended and curled around the rim of his right nostril.

"Nothing recent." Maedel's brow furrowed. "Patterson had completely turned himself around prior to being relocated here. Only ten years ago he slit an inmate's throat at Kent for stealing his milk but now he is, or was, a dream prisoner. No trouble. Ever."

"So, he'd turned himself around, you said. In what way?" Cuzzocrea wondered.

"Gentlemen, James Henry Patterson found God. A born again Christian. A bit of a zealot, actually, preaching left, right and centre. He led prayers and a bible study every Sunday without fail. He called himself an 'ascetic follower of Christ the saviour' and he believed that severe self-discipline and the denial of any and all forms of indulgence, brought him closer to God – or Jesus, or whatever. He would fast, but he'd always inform us of his intentions and the duration of the fast so we didn't misconstrue it as a hunger strike. He was passionate about his religious beliefs and rituals."

Cuzzocrea's interest was piqued, "Did he practice any mumpsimus customs?"

Maedel communicated his confusion by scrunching his dick-like nose.

Cuzzocrea elaborated: "Any flagellation? Penitent acts? Ritualistic in nature and unreasonable when taken out of a religious context."

Maedel thought for a moment and then replied, a glimmer of understanding dancing in his skull, "Yes, actually. The strangest things. He refused to sleep on his bed, he said he wished to rise above the need for comfort. He would take ice baths too, freezing cold, iced water. Also, he believed that God provided all the nutrients we need in nature so he would eat all sorts of bugs and plants, even slugs. You know, we have to be very careful when it comes to religion. We can't infringe upon an inmate's religious freedoms."

Cuzzocrea smiled and shook his head. Munro recognized in his partner, an 'aha' moment.

"How did Patterson escape?" Munro asked the warden.

Maedel huffed and rubbed his head again. "Surely you've read the report."

Munro took a step towards Maedel's desk. "Warden Maedel, I wish that our job was as easy as reading a couple of statements or a report. If you don't mind, we would really like to hear your version of events, directly from you."

"My statement has already been documented." Warden Maedel pinched a sliver of dry lip skin between his teeth.

Munro shrugged. "We can go over your head on this. Hell, we can even caution you and pick up where we leave off in an interview room at the station?"

"Come on, let's not get like that. God knows I have enough problems." Maedel puffed his cheeks, his puckered lips farted the air out as he relented to Munro's pressure. "Fact is, I don't know how he escaped. Still don't."

"There was an event here on Sunday?" asked Cuzzocrea.

"Yes, jeez, that makes the whole thing worse. We'll never get permission for performances again. Patterson ruined that privilege for everyone."

"Performances?"

"We have our own theatre troupe – actually that's the wrong word entirely. I told Sandra that from the off, a theatre troupe is a group of peripatetic, travelling performers so describing a cast made up of convicts as a 'troupe' is oxymoronic."

"Who is Sandra?"

"Sandra Moore. She's a local acting coach, she works with the inmates. It's proven to be highly beneficial. They have weekly rehearsals and they put on shows once a year, open to the general public. It boosts morale, highly motivational and quite therapeutic. Also, the shows are great P.R. for us."

"Was Patterson involved in last Sunday's show?" asked Cuzzocrea.

"The Might Company – M.I.G.H.T. stands for The Mochetsin Institute Giving Hope Theatre."

Not caring what the name of the company stood for, Cuzzocrea reiterated his question, "And Patterson?"

"Yes, he was involved. Everyone was. This year's show had a carnival theme and we set up the gym and the basketball court like an old-fashioned fete, games, stalls, a coconut shy and pin the tail on the donkey, that sort of thing. The inmates were all dressed like carnies and each was in charge of his own event or stall and then there were the actual actors, the cast in the play itself. Patterson was in charge of the petting zoo, a little pen on the basketball court with goats and pigs, rabbits and so on. Everyone was monitored the whole time."

"Clearly not, Mr Maedel," Cuzzocrea corrected the warden. "When was Patterson's disappearance noted?"

"Once the play started and the audience was seated, all of the inmates who had been in charge of stalls were then tasked with setting up the ocean view marquee on the lawn with refreshments."

"Was Patterson present at that time?"

Maedel hesitated and peeled the dry skin off his bottom lip leaving a fuchsia lesion.

"Warden?" Munro prodded.

"He prays at three o'clock sharp, every Sunday. Always has, the whole time he's been here. I told you, he's a zealot."

"What time did the performance start?" Munro already knew the answer.

"Three," replied Maedel. "I'd given permission previously for Patterson to be allowed to return to his pod house for afternoon prayer. He had gotten agitated, you see, when Sunday's itinerary was distributed. He had a panic attack just at the thought of missing his prayers. I spoke at length with him and he made a fair point that if he were Muslim we would have to respect salat. So, it was agreed that he could return to his house at three, pray and then join us in the gym for the remainder of the play."

"So he left for prayer at three. Unaccompanied?" Cuzzocrea asked.

"At about ten minutes before three and yes, unattended. This *is* a minimum-security facility." Maedel was defensive. "Once the refreshment tent was set up, the inmates were allowed to watch the remainder of the show at the back of the audience. That was at about three thirty, three thirty-five maybe."

"By which time he had been absent for almost an hour?" Munro shook his head.

Maedel looked guiltily at the policemen and nodded. "I'm

afraid so. Although, if you factor in that he usually prays for twenty minutes…"

Cuzzocrea and Munro shared a look, Munro barely stifled a laugh.

"Mr Maedel," said Cuzzocrea, "Patterson wasn't praying. Not last Sunday and probably not ever in his life."

Maedel's cheeks reddened and quivered with embarrassment.

"We'll need to take a look around," said Munro.

Locked in a disturbing reverie, Maedel absently pointed to his door. "Officer Hammond should be outside. He's giving you the tour."

"Just before we go, Warden," Cuzzocrea began, "I take it you've already had the subaquatic perimeter searched?"

Munro looked a question, Cuzzocrea explained.

"The two thousand twelve escape I began telling you about it earlier? Kessler wasn't an escapee, he was a drug dealer. His supplier would throw drugs in hermetically sealed jars through the barrier of razor wire that lies in coiled runs under the water along the shoreline of this facility. It's too high to swim over and too low to swim under but evidently, as Kessler's booming trade proved, if you're careful enough and can hold your breath like an olympian, you're able to receive regular shipments of heroin via the 'impenetrable' barbed bulwark. Unfortunately for Kessler something must have gone wrong that day because he became entangled and drowned. His body was only discovered three weeks later when a stench began emanating from his bloated carcass at low tide and, of course, the fresh abundance of scavengers attracted to the site. There wasn't a whole lot left of Kessler by the time he was found. But his drugs were bone dry."

Munro raised an eyebrow and turned to the warden for a response. Maedel acquiesced that Cuzzocrea's telling of the story was accurate and assured the police officers that a thorough investigation of the submarinal perimeter had come up empty.

"Let me just address the elephant in the room," said

Munro. "Why the hell did anyone build a prison here? It's a security nightmare."

Maedel shook his head, defeated. "It was originally a quarantine centre for immigrants. It wasn't designed to keep criminals in, just sick people. Feel free to take a look around, gentlemen, and if you need anything else, I'm, well, you know where I am."

As they left the office, Cuzzocrea paused, he looked at Maedel and wondered if the man had yet considered tying a noose around his neck and saving himself the humiliation and denigration that awaited him. *Probably,* thought Cuzzocrea, *and if he hasn't yet, he will.*

Leaving the frazzled warden alone, searching for a contrail now long gone, Cuzzocrea joined Munro in the corridor where they were met by an inappropriately joyful Officer Hammond for a tour of the Mochetsin Institute and a further waste of crucial investigative hours.

CHAPTER 16 - THE MARIONETTE

Ali's cell phone vibrated in a circle on the table. The ear-piercing text tone reveille alerted her to the fact that David was on his way home.

"Fuck," said Ali as she read the message.

"What?" asked Marlene.

"David's done for the day. I have to get some food organized."

"What time is it?" Marlene checked her watch. "Four thirty? My, time flies when you're talking murder. I have to go anyway."

"Okay. Thanks Marlene. You want to do the same tomorrow?"

"Sure do. I have a little gathering I'm going to tonight so I'll do some undercover investigation – get my Sherlock on."

"Sounds good."

Marlene opened the front door, stepped out onto the front porch and turned to Ali.

"Actually, my Watson, you're the Sherlock here. For what it's worth, hon, you might want to free yourself from that kitchen sink. It's the one good thing that came from our couples counselling in the nineties – being the self-proclaimed do-it-all-er of the house, the cook, the cleaner, the shopper, the grass cutter, not good for you or your marriage."

"I know." Ali exhaled.

"No, you don't because you got that text and instead of

feeling happy that David was on his way home, you panicked. You were cool as ice at that crime scene the other day yet the idea of not having your husband's supper ready for him, filled you with terror. Do you think that's healthy?"

"I know, it's just…"

"That's what you did in the first year of being a stay-at-home mum and new wife, right?"

"Yes."

"It's a mistake a lot of us make. I did it too. You have to imagine that if you and David were divorced, he would work, come home, cook, clean, do laundry and you'd split parenting right down the middle, right?"

Ali nodded.

"You have to keep that in mind. Your role as his wife is defined by your relationship with him, not by how much you do for him. That's slavery and really only a few steps removed from being the kind of victim we've been thinking about all day. That isn't you. You're clearly a highly-intelligent woman, Ali, think about the dynamics of your relationship – I'm sure neither you nor David wants you to commit to a life of servitude just because you fell in love."

"You're right, Marlene. I know you are."

Marlene smiled kindly. "Rome wasn't built in a day. Saved my marriage though, sex is way better when you shed the resentment that goes with being everyone's doormat."

"You know, I'll need to know more about that couples counselling stuff."

"I'm an open book." Marlene headed down the steps. "Same time tomorrow?"

"Good with me," replied Ali. "Bring more of those strawberry sweets."

"Sure will. Bye."

Marlene marched up the hill of the drive and Ali remembered their first encounter, each of them in the spaces they inhabited now, and regretted her castigation of the woman.

"Hey, Marlene." Ali took a stance reminiscent of her

pugnaciousness of that day. "You can use the fucking drive any time you fucking like."

Marlene stopped and laughed, holding her crotch to avoid leakage. "Well, thanks a effing lot, bitch."

Ali laughed and added, "Hey, Marlene? Why don't you have a cell phone?"

"Brain cancer." Marlene waved the hefty subject away as she continued up the steep slope and added, "It's all part of the couples counselling story. Another time."

...

Back in her kitchen, Ali was attempting the world record for vegetable chopping. At least she could make it appear that the stir-fry was planned rather than thrown together as an afterthought. She imagined Marlene would be tutting at her right now but her conflict remained. David had cooked for the past two nights and no, that shouldn't be a problem but Ali just wasn't ready to overhaul their relationship. Besides, she wanted to enjoy her husband, not greet him at the door with another conflict or worse, a worry. Ali knew that when the simple routines, the basic functions of the household begin to fall apart – or become obsessively intense – she slips. Her mental hold loosens. Her quotidian achievements, or the lack thereof, are reliable indicators of her mental health and the man she loves, her protector, watches for them all the time. Better for all for Ali to be the marionette with the sardonic smile tethered to the puppet master of wifedom than to pile the threat of her mental fragility atop the shoulders of her husband.

CHAPTER 17 - THE BROWN-NOSER

Neophobia is a fear of the new. Cuzzocrea had long since deduced that Patterson had patiently dissembled his true intent by the meticulous building of an audacious façade of religion and neophobia. The façade had fooled most of the idiots charged with his confinement, but not the idiot that is Corrections Officer Jacob Hammond.

"I told them all. I warned them," said Hammond, resting an elbow on a shelf next to the pigeon hole lockers, his thumbs hooked in the belt loops of his trousers as he watched Cuzzocrea and Munro retrieve their belongings and their guns.

"Tell me more." Cuzzocrea rolled his shirt sleeves up to his elbows.

Hammond, who had the blond-haired, rosy-cheeked, puppy-fat look of an overgrown five-year-old boy, was happy to continue. "Patterson wasn't institutionalized, he was just playing the system so he could transfer here. The religious stuff? Bullshit."

Cuzzocrea nodded, Hammond continued: "He played them all, but not me. The fucker enjoyed too many sixty-nines for someone who believes in the bible. This place is a modern Sodom and Gomorrah."

Munro interjected, "Patterson's gay?"

Jacob Hammond laughed. "They're not gay. They might give it, take it, suck each other's dicks but if you called them gay? No, sir. It's just what they do. They might be locked up but their urges aren't. Bet you don't know this, it's usually a shocker for people…we have to supply them with lube and condoms and dental dams. For health and safety reasons."

Hammond opened the security door and held it open for the police officers to egress to the entrance foyer.

"Everyone?" Munro asked.

"As far as I can tell, everyone who's done more than a couple of years, yeah." Hammond continued as he led them out, "So, here? With long-term prisoners? Yeah, at least the odd blow job."

"The sixty-nine thing, is that what Patterson's into, then?" Munro stepped past Hammond, who was holding open the outermost door of the main building, the heat of the dwindling afternoon didn't hesitate to infiltrate his pores.

"Nah, not just that. Cigarettes, pop, chips, candy are all currency for sex but if you just agree on a mutual need, you better sixty-nine so there's no backing out when one blows his load."

Munro blinked away the image and wiped a trickle of perspiration from his temple as another one took the baton in the sweat relay race being run on his forehead.

"Patterson was an escape waiting to happen. He was never a good prisoner, known for throwing piss and shit on officers, he slit someone's throat once, he made bitches of all his cell mates and then suddenly he's perfect? He finds Jesus? Yeah, like that washes. I could see it in his eyes, always planning. Just waiting."

"I don't disagree with you, Officer Hammond," said Cuzzocrea checking his watch. "Thanks for the tour. It was very helpful."

"No problem guys. This way, I have to let you out of the last gate too." Hammond led the way, turned and continued ahead, walking backwards so he could face the officers. "Say, if you're all done for the day, I'm just about to clock off and I'm on my way to the Mochetsin Café. I'm meeting a couple of buddies there. You're welcome to join us."

Hammond flashed two rows of straight, too-white teeth.

"Thanks but the day isn't over for us," said Cuzzocrea.

"Gotta eat, don't you?" Hammond persisted.

"A Big Mac and fries on the way back to the station," said Munro.

Hammond turned and dropped back to Cuzzocrea and Munro's pace.

"Well, that sucks. So, you think Patterson killed that girl?" Hammond asked.

Munro met Cuzzocrea's eyes. "What girl?" Munro asked Hammond.

Jacob Hammond smiled his cloying smile again and wagged a finger at Munro. "Aw, don't do that. Like you guys aren't looking into that. The dead girl found on Alder Beach Trail this week. You think it was him?"

"Do you?" Cuzzocrea watched Hammond process the question.

Finally, he replied, "Was she raped?"

"Can't answer that." said Munro.

"Right, yeah, classified shit, eh? Well, if she was raped then, hell yeah," Hammond answered.

"He doesn't have previous for rape," said Cuzzocrea.

"Na, but these bikers, they're all like that, you know, their women are just gashes, good for one thing. And there's a few split asses in here can attest to his healthy sex drive."

"I'm sure," said Cuzzocrea. "Tell me, Hammond, you think he went to all the effort of that elaborate escape just to rape and murder some girl? A sexual relationship wouldn't be a parole violation upon his November release."

Hammond nodded his acceptance of Cuzzocrea's point. "Jeez, these guys are all sick fucks, I got no time for any one of them."

As the men approached the outer gate of the complex, Hammond pulled out a white plastic card, pulling its attached, retractable string to its fullest extent from the black casing attached to his belt. He pressed the card against a similar sized box located adjacent to the lock on the gate. A red light on the box turned green and the gate buzzed open.

Hammond held it open with his foot, allowing Munro and Cuzzocrea passage.

Cuzzocrea pointed to the card. "Patterson would have needed one of those to get out of here. Any idea how he may have gotten his hands on one?"

Hammond smiled, checked over his shoulder conspiratorially. "Like I said, sexual favours are for sale in here. Whoever it was wouldn't be the first or the last guard in history to have a thing for an inmate."

Hammond responded to Cuzzocrea's questioning gaze. He held his hands up defensively.

"Hey, don't go there. It wasn't me. I got plenty of gash of my own around, I don't need no skanky inmate sucking my dick."

Hammond laughed the gate shut behind the officers. He called after them, "If you guys change your mind, you know where I'll be, enjoying the Workman Burger at the café."

Munro stared incredulously as Cuzzocrea returned to Hammond, his cell phone out. "What's your number, Jacob? I'll call if we free up."

"Awesome! Seven, seven, eight, two, five, zero, seven, seven, seven, seven. All the sevens!"

Munro raised a goodbye hand to Hammond as his partner joined him and they headed to the car park.

"He's a fucking creep. You can't be serious, Rey," said Munro.

"Na, I just want his number for future reference, that's all." Cuzzocrea completed the contact information page and put his cell phone back in his pocket.

"So what d'you think? What's the deal with Patterson?" Munro asked.

"He's hiding out on the Tsawataineuk land."

"The? Huh?" Munro was confused.

"The forest here and over there, all round this place is First Nation Tribal land. The Tsawataineuk Band. He's there. Living off the land, filling himself with bug protein and sleeping rough. That's what he's been preparing for all along, the fasting, the refusing to sleep on a bed, eating bugs. It was all to lay low here until the search for him dies a death."

"And then?" Munro asked.

"And then he'll be on his toes, he'll head for Nanaimo to his old hunting ground where he'll be welcomed with open arms by his former M.C."

"So we going to make the Tweta...whatever land, the focus of the search."

Cuzzocrea shook his head. "No-one's getting a warrant for that. The most you could hope for is a meeting with the tribal council. Maybe they'd allow a search if it was for a missing kid but I doubt it. We'd probably be given a not-so-friendly *go fuck yourselves*."

"So what are you going to do? You're sure he's not our perp. We can't just sit and wait for him to surface in Nanaimo. Our case'd be dead by then."

"I'll think of something." Cuzzocrea reassured his clammy partner. "That creep Jacob Hammond might just come in handy though." Cuzzocrea smiled at Munro.

"In that case, whatever you've got up your sleeve, I'm in," said Munro.

"Good, let's get that Big Mac and come back later."

CHAPTER 18 - YOUTUBE AND THE FOREST

"Muuum!"

Sandy's tone reminded her of the days when Kenny was little and he would take great delight in shitting in their shared bath, leaving his sister clinging onto the edge of the tub terrorized by the bobbing poo's proximity to her.

Ali paused her episode of *The Real Housewives of New York City* (a guilty pleasure) to respond to the holler of the Dalglish Family Crier.

"Yeah?" Ali resented the disturbance. She and David were cosy together on the couch, Ali marathoning the new season (which was so far proving to be Ramona's most melt-downy, attention-seeky ever) while David snored rhythmically beside her.

"You might want to take a look at this, Mum."

Ali rolled her eyes, her mind had just begun to still and she was feeling functional and sane – a guaranteed side effect of watching the undignified, warts-and-all unravelling of another person's life, the addictive psychological reaction that has resulted in the western world's obsession with reality T.V., not to mention the fattened bank balance of people like Andy Cohen and Ryan Seacrest.

Ali propped herself up on an elbow; David moaned. Sandy was staring open-mouthed at the screen of the Mac. Ali debated whether to go to her daughter or to ignore her and press play, then she thought about the future ramifications of the 'human zoo' phenomenon of the reality

T.V. genre and decided she was entirely too educated to buy into it.

"What is it?" Ali peeled herself out of her husband's embrace.

"Mum! Come see!" Sandy urged.

Ali huffed and thought: *If it's a cat playing a piano, I'll shove that mouse up your arse.*

David moaned again and spread himself out across the newly-vacated space.

"Okay, I'm up. What is it, Sandy?" Ali stood behind her daughter as she moved the cursor to play a YouTube video that would last three minutes and forty-nine seconds. Ali thought, *If this is a video of a cat playing a piano for three minutes and forty-nine seconds, I'll shove the entire bloody computer up your arse.*

After a moment of buffering, shaky footage appeared on screen. It was a cell phone video. Ali's mind registered familiarity but she couldn't quite place the scene until she read the title printed below the video: LITTLE BRITAIN VS R.C.M.P.

"I was searching episodes of *Little Britain* and this was in the suggestions. It's you, Mum."

Ali's gut clenched. She grunted in anticipation of her own embarrassment. Her vanity felt the bruise of the *Little Britain* reference (she hoped it was an insult regarding her height and nationality, not any sort of likeness she might bear to either David Walliams or, worse, Matt Lucas).

"Fuck," said Ali, shepherding Sandy out of the swivel chair and taking her place.

"Kenny!" Sandy yelled excitedly through the kitchen hatch to her brother who was putting the top layer on one of his famous five-decker ham-and-mayo sandwiches, "It's mum, on YouTube, you gotta see, it's sooo bad!"

Ali shushed her daughter and raised the volume to its fullest.

Ali, flanked by Sandy and Kenny, who was happily crunching his toasted piece of art near her right ear, began to recall what lay ahead in the footage recorded during Monday night's meeting. The new tension in the atmosphere had managed to rouse David from his peaceful slumber. He now sat upright and was looking puffy-faced over the back of the couch at them. Ali tried to avoid his eye.

The shaky video hastily zoomed in on YouTube-Ali – her forehead vein was on form – the frame wobbled as the aspect zoomed out again, she was standing at the rear of the Pioneer House and all eyes in the room appeared to be on her.

"*Mrs Dalglish. And you, Sergeant frigging Hewer, can suck my tone's dick.*"

Ali cringed as Kenny and Sandy laughed and high-fived behind her. On the screen David appeared, crabbing along Ali's row of chairs. He began talking to Ali and he grasped her elbow.

"What did you say, Dad?" Kenny asked.

"What is it?" David said from the couch.

"Footage from the meeting the other night," said Ali quietly.

"What?" David heaved himself off the couch, all four dogs were rats to his pied piper. David joined his family at the computer.

Ali watched as YouTube-Ali snatched her arm free of David's grasp and responded to him.

"What did you say, Mum?" asked Sandy.

"I can't remember," Ali lied. She'd actually told David to 'lay off the fucking Kool-Aid, I'm getting some answers from this twat if it kills me.'

Ali's hands went to her cheeks as she psychically begged her YouTube avatar of the past, 'please don't, please don't, please don't'.

But of course, YouTube-Ali was already stomping her way down the centre aisle to the stage and to Sergeant Hewer. Ali watched, horrified at the sight of herself in full temper and also by the fact that she'd clearly gained a good ten pounds since last time she'd seen herself on film. Maybe there was a Matt Lucas reference in the title, after all.

And then it began: *"I'd like to speak to you, Sergeant Hewer. I'm more than happy to do it in private if that would make you more comfortable."*

Hewer licked his lips, straightened up and said, *"Here is fine, Mrs Dalglish, it's a public meeting."*

Did Ali just see her YouTube-self smile? Yes. She watched herself enjoying the prospect of going into battle with the poor man. Intent on diminishing his superiority.

"You were saying?"

"Look, Hewer, no offence intended, but I don't think you know what the hell you're doing."

Kenny giggled through a mouth full of toast and ham.

"Mrs Dalglish, I'm going to ask you to calm down and to check your attitude, please."

"Ooh. Did he just tell Mum to calm down?" Kenny was delighted.

"Oh kiss mine, Hewer, you jumped-up piece of shit. And, before you even start – contempt of cop is not a thing. I can be as rude as I like to you, it's not against the law."

"What's not a thing, Mum?" asked Kenny. David shushed him.

"I'm a concerned member of this community calling you out on your bullshit. Now, please tell me that this investigation is not in your hands. Please! Because if it is, I will have something to say about it. This is a major crime and, trust me when I say this, it is time sensitive, yet here you are ponsing around with your little man here, having a chit-chat in this quaint municipality with all your frigging mates? Look at you, giving it the large like a total muppet. This is a VIIMIS case, and you know it!"

Ali quite honestly could not recall saying any of those words. Her shoulders were on a tense, speedy migration towards her ears.

"And what do you know about VIIMIS, Mrs Dalglish?"

"Duh! I have Google, you pleb."

"For your information, VIIMIS are on their way. I'm simply overseeing the case in the meantime."

There was an audible gasp in the room and murmuring that the cell phone microphone couldn't decipher.

"If everyone would like to take their seats, we can get going with these statements."

"Excuse me?" A new voice echoed in the Pioneer House. It was Marlene who now appeared in the bottom left of the screen. The photographer – Ali remembered the fat little bitch who had been flirting with the doctor and hated her even more now that she'd labelled Ali as *Little Britain* – moved towards the front of the room to include Marlene in a loose three-shot, Ali remembered that it was at this moment in the Pioneer House that she had noticed the cell phone was capturing the exchange and now watched her old self peering scornfully at the camera as YouTube-Marlene continued:

"I think Ali has a very good point. Even if she has put it across in...her own...way. This meantime? How long is that? Because there is a girl – a poor girl who has been killed. If, God forbid, it was my daughter, I'd want to know that the police were looking for the person who did it. Not chatting with all of us. And, also, shouldn't statements already have been taken? It really doesn't seem to be happening in the way I imagined it would."

YouTube-Ali seemed to be oblivious to Marlene's support but Ali knew that was just a front, she remembered being surprised but very grateful at the time.

Ali watched as her avatar made her exit. *"Here's my signed statement, Hewer. Pass it on to someone who knows what the fuck they're doing."*

Ali watched with interest as her YouTube-self exited and she was able to witness a few seconds of the room's reaction: Hewer picking up her statement, the gossipy women in the front row, Dr Labreque laughing with the mayor and, sadly, David joining the two men and shaking his head along with them.

The video ended.

"Oh em gee, Mum! That was awesome," said Sandy.

"Send this to me, can you, Sandy?"

"Sure." Sandy eagerly took her mother's vacated chair.

"Like I needed to relive that," David said as Ali passed him on her way to the kitchen.

"Oh, David, it's had twelve views and two of those were us. It's not going viral any time soon." Ali clicked the kettle on.

"Why are you getting her to send it to you?" David said as Ali bypassed him and saw the mess left by the making of Kenny's five-tiered sandwich.

"I've been hoping it would be uploaded," Ali said. "Kenny! Can you clean up in here, please?"

"On it!" Kenny called back.

"Why would you want that on YouTube?" David asked.

"David, please. I don't need you getting in my face right now. I saw the girl filming it, okay? I was dreading it ever being uploaded until I realized that it could help Marlene and I with the investigation. It's a great way for us to see who was in the room."

Ali felt the weight of David's silence and knew he was watching her as she prepared two mugs for tea. She hated moments like this, she always felt so self-conscious and that feeling was intensified by the unflattering image she had of herself now she'd watched herself at her ugliest.

"What are you doing, Ali?" David's voice faked empathy.

"David. Don't. Don't lecture me. Just…stop telling me what I can or can't do. Stop it." Ali held herself against the worktop.

"Ali, you're embarrassing yourself."

"What?" Ali was astonished by the statement.

"You're making a fool of yourself."

Ali was dumbstruck, not by a lack of words but by a torrent of them. A farrago of vicious retorts flooded forth, boiling up like lava and Ali knew she did not possess restraint enough to pluck anything relevant from the confused mass. She left David alone in the kitchen.

…

"I fucking hate you." Ali told the ugly light fixture above her bed. Her constant companion during all her miserable moments. Ali's heart pumped with suppressed...*suppressedness*. God, she wished she'd stormed off to the balcony instead, at least then she could have had a fag. Her bedroom was an utterly joyless space bereft of even a T.V. – although having witnessed her own amateur version of the *Real Housewives of Mochetsin*, she guessed her viewing pleasure would be greatly diminished as a result. Talk about karma.

Ali was faced with several options: she could stay ensconced in the airless bedroom, gasping for a smoke and arguing in her own head all night; she could return to the kitchen and continue the argument with David; she could nip for a fag *then* continue the argument and really give it to the fucker, thus purging herself of all that remained unsaid. The choice was easily made and driven by the severe lack of nicotine in her system.

...

As David was joining his wife on their deck, Cuzzocrea and Munro were heading deeper into the Tsawataineuk Forest. Although the capture of the fugitive, James Henry Patterson, was the primary motivation behind their evening hike, the last thing either of them wanted was direct contact with the escaped prisoner.

Cuzzocrea was no stranger to the use of unconventional methods based on a hunch but even as they crunched deeper into the woods he knew that an unwarranted search of private property was pushing it too far. It was, however, a risk worth taking because if his hunch was right, he could tie up the Patterson distraction thus allowing the VIIMIS team to focus on the actual case they had been assembled to investigate.

Just ahead of Cuzzocrea, Munro heaved his less-than-athletic frame up an embankment. Although the canopy of the dense forest provided a blessed shelter from the heat of the day, Cuzzocrea noticed that Munro's sweat-saturated shirt was stuck to his back.

"Can't see much this way," Munro said from his new vantage point.

"I'd get off that if I were you," warned Cuzzocrea.

Munro looked at the hillock on which he stood. "Why?"

"It's a tumulus."

"Huh?" said Munro, turning to face Cuzzocrea.

"A burial mound. And if the aboriginal beliefs about them are right, then you're inviting some serious negativity into your body by standing on it."

Munro failed to disguise his urgency as he alighted from the barrow. "I don't believe in all that crap, anyway," Munro said bravely, once he was on solid ground again.

"You know, I wouldn't put it past Patterson to use it to his advantage though. Sacred ground? It's a guaranteed place of peace, undisturbed."

"Let's go round it and see what's down that way then," suggested Munro.

Cuzzocrea nodded his agreement. They headed deeper into the forest.

...

"I'm worried about you, Ali." David leaned against the chimney as Ali smoked in her usual spot by the door on the balcony.

"No you're not, David. You're worried about you."

"What the hell are you talking about?"

"Truth is, it's you who's embarrassed, you think I'm making a fool of *you*."

"That's not true, Ali."

"Yes it is and do you know what? Maybe I am an embarrassment to you. Maybe I do show you up but you can't keep me locked away like something you're ashamed of."

"I'm not ashamed of you."

"Yes, you are. I saw you at the end of that video."

"That's not fair."

"And you're pissed off that I'm investigating this murder."

"Ali! Listen to yourself – you're not investigating anything, you're just a…"

"Just a what? Just a what, David? What am I?"

"This isn't your job anymore."

"I know that, believe me. I'm *just* what? What am I *just*? Just a wife? Just a mother? Just a woman? What?"

"Ali, for God's sake. It is not your job. Please, just let it go."

"No! I fucking won't. I won't let it go because it is what I'm good at. I should never have stopped doing it in the first place, but I did. For you. What the fuck was I thinking? I must have been out of my fucking mind."

"Hey. That's not nice."

"No, it's not. It's horrible. It's vile, but it's fucking true. I worked so hard, David and I got somewhere, you know? I was at the top of my game and I thought I could do it all. You think you're going to be young forever but then one day you wake up and you're past it. Nobody sees you anymore. You're done. Is that okay? Do you think that's a fair price for me to pay? Because I had children, what I was great at had to disappear? And what? It's unfair of me to be angry about that?"

"You didn't have to leave. Nobody made you, it was your choice."

"Really? Were you going to give up your job and stay at home with the kids?"

David didn't answer.

"No. Because at the end of the day, it's the ones with the fucking vaginas who have to make the sacrifices. It's us who come last."

"Oh, please. I do not need one of your feminist rants

right now."

"You're getting one, David. I regret giving up my job, I am so pissed off that I had to and I've been going slowly out of my mind ever since because every day that passes the world carries on without me and I haven't mattered a jot. Done nothing. Been nothing. Now, I love my kids so much, and I am glad that I've given them my full attention and love but now that they're older, don't you fucking dare tell me that I'm not allowed to do something. Don't you fucking dare!"

"Why is it, no matter what we argue about, you always turn it around to be about your career?"

"Because that's the only argument there is? Don't you see that? That's the only problem."

"So go back to fucking work, Ali. If that's what you want. Bring in some fucking money. Please."

"First of all, fuck you! It's that easy, is it? I'd have to retrain here, just like you had to. Qualifications don't carry over, David, you know that. How would Canada make all its fucking money from us if we could just move and work? Huh? No, you have to spend thousands to requalify."

"So do it then."

"I can't. We don't have the money and who the fuck is going to run this house and home school Kenny if I go back to full-time education for five fucking years? You?"

"Yes."

"That's a laugh. First of all, you nearly shit a brick this week 'cause you had to cook twice so don't stand there and pretend it's not an issue. Second, for me to requalify it would take at least five years and about sixty or seventy fucking grand. Third, home schooling Kenny? You probably think that's a piece of piss too, maybe you could do in your half hour lunch, eh?"

"I don't know what you want."

"I'm doing it! That's what I'm saying. I want to investigate this murder. I want to see where it goes. It's the closest I've come to feeling like I can contribute for a long time. I want to do that."

"But what's the point? It's weird. It's degrading. You and Marlene sticking up pictures and case notes all over the dining room? What's next, taking statements? It's not *real*, Ali."

"You are a prick, David. You're a fucking prick!"

"Don't shout at me like that."

"Well listen to me then! I'm telling you – I'm always telling you. You just don't hear me."

They both fell silent. A fresh breeze buffeted Ali's hair as she crossed to the rail and looked out over the ocean. The fat moon hung pink and low in the lilac sky.

David approached Ali from behind and wrapped his arms around her waist. "I feel like you're not okay."

Ali stiffened and pulled away from his embrace. She turned to him.

"I feel irrelevant. I feel like nothing. I'm empty and the old Ali, she's dead, David, she's gone." Ali swallowed back her tears, determined that her words shouldn't be diluted by pointless emotion. "I want to feel alive again. I need a purpose. That's what this is all about."

Ali's chin quivered as she fought against her own self-pity.

"Maybe you should go and see someone again." David shrugged.

Ali stepped back from her husband and it struck her that David was incapable of understanding. He couldn't see her. When did he stop seeing her?

"You're not happy," David added.

Suddenly exhausted by her plight and the futility of trying to express it, Ali left him on the balcony to ensconce herself once more within her joyless bedroom to lick her mental wounds.

...

Cuzzocrea and Munro crouched at the edge of a clearing. An

outcropping of boulders shone pink in the light of the ascending moon. Beyond the rocks was a decrepit fifth wheel trailer, the type you can attach to the back of pickup trucks. While the once-white vehicle bore the char of fire, Cuzzocrea imagined it could make a perfectly suitable abode for a wanted fugitive on the lam.

Munro looked a question. Cuzzocrea shook his head and indicated that they should quietly retreat.

Once they were back at the perimeter of the Tsawataineuk Forest, where it jutted up against the prison boundary, Munro asked his question aloud.

"Shouldn't we have looked inside? Made sure he was there?"

"Too much of a risk with no warrant. It's a hunch but it's a strong one. We have little to lose."

"So what now?"

"Now I'm going to put a call into our friend, whatshisname?"

"Hammond, Jacob. But, Rey, if he tells anyone that we put him onto it, that we told him where to look, we're in deep shit all the same."

"I'm not going to tell him, I'm just going to suggest where *I* would look if I could, if my hands weren't tied, you know? If I'm right about this guy's psychology then he won't be able to resist. He will genuinely believe that it was his idea. He'll want to take credit for cracking the case himself because he's not bright enough to know he's been played. Ideally he'll tip off the authorities in charge but let's hope he's not egomaniacal enough to actually want to apprehend Patterson himself. That's the only risk factor."

"And if he does?"

"Then I'll have underestimated his potential for doing truly dumb shit."

...

In the Mochetsin Café, Jacob Hammond looked at the screen of his phone as the call disconnected even before his thumb had time to tap the red 'end call' disk.

He swirled the remaining third of a sleeve of Granville Island beer as a brilliant idea formed in his mind.

"Who was that, Buddy?" Matt, one of Hammond's friends, asked him.

"Oh, a cop buddy of mine. We're working on a case together," Hammond replied.

Matt was impressed, "Oh yeah?"

Hammond shrugged. "I can't say much about it but…he was picking my brains on something."

"Yeah?"

"Uhuh." Hammond downed the remainder of his beer, patted Matt and his other friends goodbye. "Catch you guys later."

Behind the wheel of his Ford F150, Hammond imagined how it would feel if he single-handedly brought the man hunt for Patterson to an end. He'd bet good money that that shit would even impress Cuzzocrea and his partner. They might even put in a good word for him. Maybe they'd see that he could be an asset to their team. Maybe he could do some undercover stuff for them.

Hammond, lost in his thought, turned the key in the ignition. The engine remained silent, he'd gotten carried away imagining celebratory drinks with his buddies and the cops and maybe even a front-page piece in the *Mochetsin News* – hell, even the *Times Colonist* – although he should be wary of publicity if he was going to need a low profile for undercover work. He shook his head at his folly, he'd forgotten to blow into the breathalyzer. It had been retrofitted (at his expense) six months ago once his driving ban for the D.U.I. was lifted. Now he was free to drive but to start his truck he had to blow into a tube to prove he was under the legal limit in order for the engine to start.

Hammond pulled the coin drawer under his dash open and grabbed a couple of pennies to suck, knowing that the copper reacted with alcohol giving a negative reading, although he knew from experience that the trick didn't work when he'd had more than a couple of sleeves. Last weekend at his sister's fire-pit party, having imbibed too many shots of tequila, his levels were way over and so he'd had to get his six-year-old niece out of bed to blow in the tube for him. He'd managed to drive almost all the way home before the system had required another sample and then, since he was over the limit, the engine had cut out, the lights began flashing, the horn wailing until he removed his key and locked the vehicle, abandoning it at the side of a road and walking the remainder of the journey home.

Hammond spat the coins into his palm, blew into the tube and his truck rumbled to life. Bruce Springsteen was singing about his glory days. Hammond turned the C.D. changer dial all the way to the left to play track number one, his favourite. As Hammond headed home, thumping his steering wheel to the beat and singing about being born in a dead man's town and ending up like a dog that's been beat too much, he wondered if that old taser in the shed still had juice and which drawer held the box of shells for dad's old twelve-gauge shotgun.

CHAPTER 19 - SUSURRANT

The secret was in the salt. The simple solution was sitting around the bend. After weeks of trial and error and many initial mishaps, a pile of dented lengths of copper tubing lay discarded in a corner of his workshop. The notion came to him as he watched a child tipping multicoloured sherbet from a long, plastic tube into her mouth as she waited in line to meet Santa in his mall grotto.

The simple act of filling each tube with salt before attempting to force them into the desired ring shape ensured that the all-important cylindrical circumference remained. First, each ten-metre length must be sawed into six smaller parts; the shortest being eleven and three eighths; the next four increasing incrementally in length; and the longest measuring thirteen and four eighths of an inch. One end should be plugged and soldered then the salt must be funnelled up to the brim. The open end should be sealed only enough to contain the substance within but should also allow for inevitable, but minimal, displacement of the salt during the coiling process. Then, with the aid of a vice and by carefully and gently hammering (with a cotton-covered mallet to prevent pitting or denting) and twisting and pulling (with pliers also covered in cotton so as not to leave pinch marks) a perfect circle can be achieved. Once all the rings are complete, one has the beginnings of perfection.

Only the beginnings.

The real perfection is achieved by the patient

commandeering of measurement and time.

The first six rings cover a length of three inches and seven eighths – only three eighths over the average natural length of their necks – and so, apart from the fitting process itself, it's not uncomfortable to wear, not even once the weights are applied to the bottom ring, both forward and aft.

On day one they are adorned with their first six rings, as a welcome gift. After one month, coil number seven is fitted. That remains, to do its work, for seven months. Coils numbers eight, nine and ten are all added at six-month intervals. Once all ten are in place, the magnificence is beyond imaginings. Pride dwells in the resourcefulness it takes to find a way. To take a common specimen, of which there is an abundance, and transform it into something more deserving of its fate, rather than hoping to stumble upon one who is naturally blessed with such a rare and exquisite length of neck.

After a full seven hundred and thirty days is spent, a measurement of six inches and three eighths is achieved and the result is astonishing.

The process can be beleaguered. His first seven-hundred-and-thirty-day cycle culminated in a heavy disappointment. But his patient assiduousness paid off through a series of ingenious solutions, an intricate contrivance thwarting defeat. No more would he be feckless enough to rely upon a single piece of work at a time. After all, the same amount of effort, care and inculcation can be spent on many as on one. It would be, therefore, imprudent to deny oneself a bountiful harvest of fruit for one's labour.

In comparison to that initial failure over two years ago, last week's failure seemed marginally less devastating thanks to the understudy. With necessity being the mother of invention and ennui being the child of boredom, the introduction of an understudy became imperative and now it paid off in troves. And so the project metamorphosed into a feat of derring-do that vaulted beyond its meagre beginnings.

The road to success should be travelled first in the mind,

only then can one see a failure lurking around the bend and have the means of rectifying it sitting patiently around the next. And now, as he unshackles his first understudy, releasing her from her stocks for the last time, he is joyous and proud of his adroitness.

Her cognitive senses sufficiently numbed, he carries her through to the last of her dwelling places, where she will be laid out and will await him.

Within the walls of his lair he is exalted. Omnipotent. And on this, the seven hundred and thirtieth day of this cycle, in his sacristy, he prepares. Except, unlike a priest, his vestments are removed. The stole, un-kissed.

The arcane pleasures are nascent now and lie only a few steps and mere moments away.

Once prepared he is still. He learned long ago how to savour the potential of the act. The eve of the moment is profuse with hedonistic delectation and should be supped and sipped at. This stillness prior to his reward is the gourmand's appetizer, the soup first tasted with a sniff.

Stepping through the inner door of his sacristy, he stoops his way through the sombre waiting room. His glorious menagerie.

The climax of two bygone years is inexorable now and the weight of its proximity sits deeply within him. The anticipation of his savage release stirs inside him, writhing in his gut, as he passes his still-ripening ladies in waiting, immured in their coppery keeps.

And beyond, he enters the final chamber. The snug in the depths of the earth. The amber glow of the cast iron stove is just enough to darkle her eyes, their aperture pinned by opiates.

Upon the stove a copper tea kettle babbles softly, percussion to her vaguely audible susurrant whisperings. It is lyrical and poetic. A childish rhyme? Or is it futile supplication? How interesting it is that with each assignation thus far, they have all sensed the finality of the chamber. The nearing of their end as if the crags of the walls whisper it to them as they are laid upon the swathe that will soon be their papoose, the fabric sarcophagus of their ascent to the ultimate resting place.

On bended knee he searches those eyes for a glister of hope and the twinkling therein triggers the first of the synaesthesia he craves and his dick hardens against her breast in response to the strange resilience of this creature's spirit.

He issues a susurration of his own against her damp cheek,

"Anon."

Brute force, it turns out, is the most efficient means of removing the ferrules of copper. The first time he had employed a ring cutter, the type used to remove never-taken-off rings from the aged and fattened fingers of the recently divorced, but the noise and vibration of the device imposed upon the solemnity of the chamber and disturbed the peace of the moment. The gouting of the encased salt sullied the manumission and instilled the wrong type of fear – fear of the tool rather than fear focused entirely upon him.

Palms outward, he persuades his fingers between flesh and metal, crowding the tight space and constricting her ability to breathe and temporarily occluding the passage of arterial fluid. The opiates are no match against the brain's fervent need for oxygenated blood, and so her eyes are increasingly protuberant in their bony sockets, her temples throb and her once-dispirited gaze is alive with terror.

Saliva fills the basin of his mouth as he waits for a motor response, a twitch of fingers and only then he pulls outward and apart. The circle becomes an open ellipsis and a ring is removed. Breath returns, eyes die again. He places his palm upon her heart, it thrums a relieved tattoo.

Sucking back his spit, he moves a hand to each floppy tit. He gently kneads them, the pretence of a kind lover. She watches the walls and he wonders if this is how she lay and allowed herself to be degraded in her previous life by accepting alms from stinking strangers, her licentiousness a dissolute raft to the next fix. He pressed his fingertips into the flesh of her breasts, pressing his entire weight upon her, her skin blanching white under the pressure, each blotch a halo to his digits.

Dirty fucking whore.

A stifled mewl? He clawed his fingers into fists, gripping hard the tissue of each tit, squeezing and twisting. Her eyebrows rising slowly and finally a tear spills, pooling in the socket then fleeing over the bridge of her nose.

And so back he goes to the delicious removal of the coils, their old coppery brilliance hinted at by the lambent flicker of the flame as each is slowly removed. Slowly. So slowly that the process is an almost intolerable tease, faking perpetuity but merely a prefatory, ephemeral cruelty. A trickle of the future pelting he will mete out.

Her heart canters. The aperture of her eyes begins to blacken wider. Soon the pain and the horror will be unbearable for her. She will no longer be cushioned against it. Her unmedicated self will emerge to finally meet him in all his glory.

There it is. Her neck, unsheathed. The weakest part of us all. Home to the precious conduits of life and yet it is bare. There is no bony cage protecting it, no sheet of muscle. Whatever or whoever created man was punctilious in the intricate creation of our meat-suits but was disastrously short-sighted with the neck. Or perhaps the flaw was entirely deliberate.

He, however, was not so short-sighted. Each and every detail had been carefully anticipated and all the items needed were carefully laid out like a surgeon's tools – the paraphernalia of torture.

Unseating himself from her belly, rising from his place straddling her torso, he poured the simmering water from the kettle into the bowl, dipping a cloth into it. He watches as she moans unease and tries to move her head, her wasted muscles barely respond and her eyes drift back to the crags of the wall.

As he dips the cloth into the bowl, the steaming water

bites at his fingertips. While the skin of her neck must not be scorched, the thin skin on her inner thighs is delightfully responsive as he carefully pours droplets from the roiling kettle onto them. The skin reacts immediately, first reddening then blistering as it cools – a double delight ready for popping and peeling later. Her lips part, her eyes seek, the searing drops make her toes curl. The opiates are prescribed to ease chronic pain yet pain is the antidote to them. Her mouth curves in a grimaced response to the strafing burns.

Holding the saturated flannel aloft to cool further, he allows it to piss away its heat onto her bare stomach then he slaps the rest of its power pendulously against her fetid cunt. It is finally cool enough to be patted safely around her glorious neck, cleansing the grime and smeg previously unreachable beneath the coils. Readying the site for the first bite.

Straddling her once more, thumbs driving upward, close to piercing through the hairy skin of her armpits, he lowers himself onto her. His stiff dick onto her belly. His ribcage denting hers. then lips against skin, the lick of tongue, saltiness of aged sweat and the tang of cuddling copper. Finally, the first graze of incisors, his jaws open, just a little for just a little nip. And a nip, and a nip and now a sharp, clenching nip and the first of her blood is punctured forth. He retreats a few inches and watches it bead like a single sphere of an unripe blackberry.

Barely noticeable is its tiny but frenetic quiver as it expands minutely. He licks it into a strip and watches as a new ball forms. He stills. Mesmerized. He holds himself back, denies the temptation within to bite deep, to gouge and to rip and devour.

For he learnt long ago how to savour the potential of the act.

PART FOUR

THURSDAY 12TH APRIL

CHAPTER 20 - WHY I DON'T HAVE FRIENDS

Ali watched life fade from the kitten's wide, blue eyes as her fingers squeezed shut its throat so tightly that its trachea skewed and bent itself out of shape in her grip and forced the creature's tongue to loll comically from its mouth. The claws that had so viciously scratched her fell limp and suddenly the cat looked like an under-stuffed toy version of its former, hissing self. She threw the tabby-grey body to the ground only for her heart to leap in fright again as she noticed the arrival of a platoon of pirate ships at the end of the wharf upon which she stood.

"It's okay, there are some nice pirates too, you know."

Ali looked at the face from which the voice had come: her long dead Uncle Spence. Ali stared incredulously at him, wanting all at once to hug him and to flee from him. Uncle Spence stepped up to the dead cat and looked down upon it. The corpse reanimated, shivered and shook itself to its feet, arching its back as if merely waking from a peaceful sleep, and padded happily beside Spence along the quay toward the majestic, black-sailed vessels. The cat turned and meowed at Ali but the sound wasn't a meow, it was a word: Mum. Mum. Mum.

Waking with a start, Ali saw that the word had come not from feline lips but from those of her daughter, Sandy, who was standing above her, gently pushing at Ali's shoulder, trying to wake her mother from a hydromorphone-induced coma-deep sleep.

Ali forced her focus onto Sandy as what had once seemed real retreated to its rightful place in the file-cabinet of her mind marked 'What-The-Fuck Dreams' and reality heaved its way upon her consciousness.

"Marlene's here." Sandy's whisper was as loud as anyone's normal speaking voice, indicating that Marlene's presence had pissed the girl off.

"What time is it?" Ali's tongue felt fat and furred and she imagined her breath must be equally thick and heavy. She hoped that the mug her daughter was cupping in her hands was full of hot, sweet tea.

Sandy, perhaps reading Ali's mind or maybe the desperate pleading of her eyes, placed the mug on Ali's bedside table and said, "It's only half past bloody seven."

"What?" Ali rolled onto her side and ached as she propped herself up on her elbow. The tea was a soul-nourishing remedy and the first sip was enough to spark life back into her brain. "Ooh, that's good. Thanks, baby. Why's she here so frigging early?"

"Dunno. She woke the dogs." Sandy readjusted the towel turban on her head. "I was just out of the shower."

"Okay. Sorry. Tell her I'll be out in five, will you?"

"'kay." Sandy left in a drop-shouldered huff. Ali rolled her eyes, as she often did in response to the teenager's strops. Taking another sip of her tea, she headed into the en-suite bathroom.

"This is why I don't have friends."

CHAPTER 21 - C.O.D.

"So, we have an I.D.?" Superintendent Doug Shaw snatched at his earbuds, pulling them free as he entered the VIIMIS task force office.

Corporal Paul Abbott jumped to his feet. "I think so, sir."

"Think? Elaborate, Abbott." Shaw's voice carried a warning.

"The description of our vic matched that of a missing girl from Abbotsford, sir. Last seen in July of two thousand twelve."

"And?" Shaw took his place at the front of the room, hands on hips, quickly regaining his resting heart rate following his daily run.

"I'm confident. The description matches, so do the photographs. I've asked the parents to come in. They're on their way from Abbotsford right now. I'm picking them up at the ferry terminal at two. We should have confirmation later this afternoon. Sir, I thought it was better to have them come in rather than sending them our photograph via e-mail, it would have been disturbing for them and I wouldn't have asked them to come unless I was pretty sure."

"Good call, although if it is their daughter, it's not going to be any less harrowing to see her in the flesh, so to speak. But at least you'll be there with them. Liaise with a bereavement counsellor here prior to their arrival and see if you can have them present at the M.E.'s office. Good work, Abbott."

"Thank you, sir." Abbott took his seat. His brief smile of relief quickly dissipated under the promise of a grim afternoon.

"Trina?" Shaw nodded to his head of forensics in a way that had Munro nudging Cuzzocrea.

Munro leaned into his partner's ear. "Definitely fucking. You know, I heard they're sharing a room at Bear Mountain Lodge."

Cuzzocrea ignored Munro as Trina Walsh stood and began her brief. "Well, Cuzzocrea's theory turned out to be sound, the M.E.'s C.O.D. was inconclusive until I put it to him. We worked through the night and we now have a conclusive cause of death."

Cuzzocrea sat forward, resting his elbows on his knees. Shaw gave him a slight nod of approval. Cuzzocrea was relieved that his eleven p.m. e-mail (detailing his analysis based on the Dalglish woman's theory) to Shaw had been taken seriously enough to be forwarded to the Medical Examiner – via Trina, of course, making Cuzzocrea wonder if indeed Munro was right about Shaw and Walsh sharing a room after all.

Trina continued, "The analysis of the necrosis in the tissue surrounding the victim's wounds – specifically those of the neck area – along with lividity present on the right-back areas except on her shoulders, outside right tricep, outer right thigh, hip and backs of her heels – supported the tetanus theory. Further investigation of the victim's heart with induced isometric contraction resulting in a tetanic response correlating with and highly indicative of tetanus, allowed him to conclude that she died as a result of generalized tetanus, the specific C.O.D. being a cardiac arrest as a result of heart seizure."

"Okay, we have a cause of death. What else did he come back with?" Shaw said.

"The hair strand test isn't back yet but the toxicology screen showed high levels of an opioid – Dihydromorphine – a derivative of morphine, a commonly prescribed narcotic for the treatment of moderate to severe pain both in tablet and liquid form.

"Evidence of sexual assault: tearing and scarring on the vagina walls. No presence of semen. The M.E. indicated that vaginal penetration was made by a rigid, foreign object inserted violently and at regular intervals over a long period of time.

"There was evidence of physical torture, bruising and swelling of the breast tissue, the nipples bore evidence of severe injury consistent with the application of pliers or clamps. The skin on the inner and outer upper thighs, stomach, back and buttocks had been burned repeatedly with the application of boiling liquid, probably water, resulting in second- and third-degree burns. Her thighs had also been bitten – human bites – but only partials could be taken, it would seem our perp used only his canines and one upper and one lower incisor, so sidelong bites probably in a deliberate attempt to avoid the possibility of a dental record match being made.

"This factor led us to conclude that the removal of the rectangular section of the skin on the victim's neck was a further attempt at destroying evidence made by his teeth. There was only minor injury to the internal tissue of the neck and no punctures of the arterial or veinous systems of the throat. The removal of the rectangular section of the upper and lower epidermis resulted in a complete and skilled excoriation of that section of skin with no damage to the flesh below and was probably done with the use of a skinning knife, normally used for skinning the hide from deer. Our sample knife and the one that gave us the most similar cut was the Havalon Piranha Bolt. The M.E. provided me with an example.

"The removal of the neck skin was the only injury inflicted post mortem.

"Moving on to the defining and unique feature of the victim: an attempt had been made to lengthen the victim's neck unnaturally over time with the application of some sort of neckwear. The act of neck lengthening is most notably practiced by the Padaung women of the Kayan people of Burma. The women are known as the Kayan Lahni, meaning long-necked Kayan, but are referred to as The Giraffe Women by tourists to the Ban Mai Nai Soi refugee camps of Burma.

"Brass neck coils are applied to the 'Giraffe Women' around the age of two and the neck stretching is almost entirely illusory. Although the vertebrae are forced apart and the intervertebral discs absorb liquid to fill the resulting space, the effect is actually caused by the forced deformation of the upper ribs and collarbone which twist at a forty-five-degree angle, causing the look of a longer neck. Our victim's neck measured just over six inches and while that is longer than average it isn't as long and wasn't as narrow as seen in the Padaung women. However, examinations of markings on the neck, bruising and indentations on the clavicle, distortion of the angle of the rib cage, fluid in the intervertebral discs, calluses on the underside of the jaw and on the clavicle, the presence of fungal dermatitis, the presence of treated pressure sores on her buttocks and distortion of the cervical vertebrae indicate that not only was a neck lengthening device worn for over a year, but the victim slept in an upright, seated position, with the weight of her body hanging down – the weight of such sped up the process.

"She was moved from the scene of her death post mortem and once rigor mortis had ended but prior to significant putrefaction – so she was moved between twenty and twenty-six hours after death, the variance dependent upon the ambient temperature of her environment at the site of her death. Time of death: approximately between the hours of oh five forty-five and eleven forty-five on Sunday, eighth of April. She was carried and placed on the trail. She was not dragged.

"The cadaver had been washed down with a solution of a nitrogenous cationic surface-acting agent called benzalkonium chloride and triclosan – two common ingredients found in many anti-bacterial hand sanitizers and so we have no conclusive D.N.A. from the bites, no skin was present under her fingernails and, as I said before, no semen was present. We did collect fibres – harsh, nylon, dark grey, the type used in car mats and, interestingly enough, on the walls of cinemas but I'm guessing on the former. The other fibres collected were of a soft cotton variety, light blue and turquoise. Soil was taken from underneath her toenails and we are yet to get word back from the lab as to its features and components. We removed several small splinters of wood from the scalp just beneath her hair above the nape of her neck.

"Her stomach was empty and she was undernourished and vitamin deficient, primarily lacking vitamin D. Muscle wastage was consistent with a long-term, chronic non-ambulatory state. Her liver was slightly distended and her kidneys showed signs of dehydration. We suspect that the opioids – perhaps other narcotics too – were used on a regular basis but we'll know more on that when we get the hair analysis back." Trina sat.

Shaw took a breath and exhaled slowly. "Well, he may have taken his time but he's certainly given us a lot to go on. Rey? I want a full analysis based on the M.E.'s report. How soon can you put a profile together for us?"

Cuzzocrea had already begun to formulate one in his mind. "A few hours, as long as I can focus on that and that alone."

"Meaning?" Shaw enquired.

"Patterson, sir."

Shaw nodded, thought for a moment and shifted his gaze to Munro, "Munro, you're on Patterson. I want you to work alongside Sergeant, whatshisname...Hewer. He's heading the local P.D. search."

Munro nodded his acceptance of the order and mumbled through the corner of his mouth to Cuzzocrea, "You sneaky fuck, Rey."

"What was that, Munro?" snapped Shaw.

"Nothing, sir. Yes, sir." Munro's chubby cheeks reddened.

"Good." Shaw peeled his glare from Munro and placed it back on Cuzzocrea. "Rey, I need to speak with you." Shaw turned to Eden Harrington, his special victims officer. "Eden?"

"Sir?" Eden had pen and pad ready for instructions.

"While we await Rey's analysis, I want you to comb the database for sex offences in the Greater Victoria region – specifically assaults involving sadistic torture, rape with foreign objects…Trina? Any indication as to the type of implement used in the rape itself?"

"Only that it was rigid. There was no debris found in the vagina so we can rule out anything of a softer variety like wood or anything covered in paint and the injuries were certainly not caused by anything pliable like a rubber or latex dildo or vibrator. Large, long and cylindrical, longer and thicker than the average penis." Trina shrugged, sorry she couldn't be more specific.

"Got that, Eden? Also, biting – and the use of clamps or pliers."

"Yes, sir." Eden scribbled busily in her pad as she crossed to a computer workstation at the rear of the room.

Cuzzocrea crossed to the front of the room toward Shaw who was ripping his velcro iPhone sling from around his bicep as he spoke to Corporal Abbott.

"Abbott? Locate the on-duty grief counsellor or whatever they have here, might be a family liaison officer, ready for this afternoon's I.D."

"Sir." Abbott hurried from the room, overtaking a sulky Munro at the door.

Cuzzocrea stood before his superior, "Sir?"

"Rey. This tetanus theory? It worked out for you."

"Sir."

"Tell me about your source, this Dalglish woman."

CHAPTER 22 - WE'RE HAVING A MEMORIAL

When Ali joined her in the dining room – their makeshift incident room – Marlene was lecturing a trying-to-appear-interested Kenny on the merits and techniques of skim boarding at low tide.

"Hey," said Ali, rescuing Kenny from the uncomfortable interaction. She then rescued him further by asking him to take the dogs out for a walk. Kenny's eagerness to escape Marlene's company was betrayed by the speed at which he left the room.

Ali addressed Marlene, "Marlene. A little early, don't you think?"

"A smidge, but we have a memorial service to arrange by seven this evening."

"Huh?"

Marlene held up the top sheet of a pile of yellow, home-printed flyers.

Ali took the flyer. In large, bold lettering at the top of the page it said, 'IN MEMORIAM' and below it informed the reader that a memorial service, followed by the release of lanterns, would take place tonight, at seven, in The Pioneer House. A book of condolence would also be available to pay tribute to 'THE ALDER BEACH GIRL'. The nondenominational service would be facilitated by Reverend Arthur Underwood of St. Margaret's Church, Mochetsin.

Ali looked at Marlene. "Okay?"

"You said he would attend memorials or funerals – in

fact, I think you said he would *definitely* attend memo —"

"Yes." Ali acknowledged the fact. "But how do we get this out in time? How can we be sure he knows about it? Shouldn't we delay it and advertise it – that feels wrong – spread the word during the interim?"

"This is Mochetsin, Ali. Every pod leader has been informed personally, by me, and they will spread the word. Also, Peter's doing his part through the municipal hall, leaving you and I to go door to door with these." Marlene, laid her hand on the pile of flyers.

"What? Every door?"

"Wow, you need coffee. Not every door, just the doors of properties that fit with your profile."

Ali ticked the idea over in her mind. She walked over to the investigation wall and looked at the generic silhouette on the right side, the representation of their unknown subject. Finally, she turned to an expectant Marlene.

"Fuck it. Yep."

Marlene clapped her hands together, "Yes! Now, let's plan our route."

CHAPTER 23 - HUNTING THE PREY

Calling in sick was easy. Jacob Hammond had never taken a day off yet and so doing so wouldn't raise suspicions of malingering.

He'd parked his truck on Cedar Avenue, a safe distance from both the prison and the native land through which he was currently trespassing.

With his backpack on he would pass for a hiker and even if a native were to catch him on the reserve, he could plead ignorance and claim to be a tourist who had wandered off the beaten path. But the contents of Jacob's backpack weren't the regular accoutrements of hiking or tourism, a bundle of nylon cable ties to be used as handcuffs later and his shotgun shells.

He hadn't managed to find the old taser but, wrapped in the rolled sleeping bag he'd found stuffed in a cobwebbed corner of the shed and suspended horizontally from the velcro loops at the bottom of the rucksack, was his dad's old twelve-gauge shotgun – the double barrels freshly sawn off in his shed last night so it could be concealed within the mildew-spattered sleeping bag. And because it was just more badass that way.

Jacob took each step tentatively. Conscious of the crackling of every dried twig and of the rustling branches as he zig-zagged between and ducked under them. He was even aware of a tiny yet irritating whistle emanating from his right nostril when he exhaled through it. He pinched his left nostril shut and snorted out hard, clearing the offending blockage from his nasal passage. The whistling ceased.

Jacob couldn't remember feeling so alive, here he was hunting down a fugitive – a known killer – each careful step bringing him closer to a better life, one in which he would be appreciated and celebrated, a hero. Patting his trouser pocket, Jacob checked that his cell phone was still there, he intended to capture the selfie of all selfies once he'd subdued Patterson. He would kneel on one knee, above the cuffed prisoner, hold his gun across his chest like the special forces guys do in their photographs, he'd set it as his banner *and* his profile photo on Facebook. Hell, it would be a great addition to all the similar framed photos in his house of him and his dad after hunts except this time he wouldn't have any antlers alongside the shot.

Past a little hill, crouching low behind a cluster of big rocks, Jacob caught sight of what looked like a burnt out fifth-wheel trailer. He carefully slipped the padded straps from his shoulders and lay the rucksack down at his feet. He slipped the twelve-gauge from its musty tunnel and set about loading it.

...

Jacob Hammond wasn't the only one being quiet in the woods that morning. Patterson had prepared himself well for wilderness living and evading capture. It was imperative that he left no trace of himself lest those traces become a trail of breadcrumbs that could lead to his capture. As such, Patterson knew the importance of burying one's shit.

As he pinched off the last of his morning constitutional, a familiar face wandered into view. Patterson froze and watched as Hammond crouched behind the rocks. The fuck-wit corrections officer, a snivelling little creep, stretched up and was looking over the rocks at the trailer, ignorant that his prey was finishing a shit just ten feet away, in a bush southeast to Hammond's north.

Patterson pulled his undershorts and pants up slowly. In one smooth movement, he dropped silently to his knees, buttoned up and kicked the mound of soil back into the toilet hole. As he watched Hammond pull a sawed-off shotgun (the type Patterson and his crew had used a bunch of times) from the bottom of his backpack, Patterson felt a tingle of excitement – the presence of such an illegal gun meant that Hammond wasn't part of the official hunt for him. He'd come alone.

Silently picking up his metal cudgel (a short length of piping he'd wriggled free of the trailer's defunct plumbing system) Patterson got to his feet, crouching low, shoulders hunched. The hunter became the prey.

CHAPTER 24 - WHO IS ALI DALGLISH?

Superintendent Shaw was of the belief that a brief should be precisely that and so Cuzzocrea mentally scrambled to condense Ali Dalglish's biography down to a skeletal, bullet-pointed concentration. Only the most pertinent and pivotal events in the woman's impressive history made the cut.

"Ali Dalglish, née McFee born nineteen seventy-four in Edinburgh, Scotland. Matriculated at Cambridge in nineteen eighty-eight – matching a two-hundred-plus-year-old record held by William Pitt the Younger set in seventeen seventy-three, a record still held to this day, as the youngest person to be enrolled in the university – touted as a child prodigy, she caused a ripple of media attention at the time and she was even featured on a popular T.V. programme called *Blue Peter.*"

Shaw, characteristically unimpressed by the savant aspect of Dalglish's story, snapped his fingers in quick succession and so Cuzzocrea moved on to his next mental bullet point.

"By the time she was twenty she was a fully qualified criminal psychologist and a forensic pathologist. Dalglish worked exhaustively and garnered a reputation as a bit of a secret weapon in the police's back pocket. She was instrumental on a series of major, high profile crimes in the U.K."

"All of this in her early twenties?" Shaw folded his arms, looking only marginally intrigued.

"She opted out in two thousand and one following the

birth of her youngest child but she did come out of retirement briefly to work the famous Edgbaston Murders in two thousand and two."

"And now she's here."

"Yes, she and her husband, along with their two children, have permanent resident status and became landed immigrants in two thousand and eight."

"What about the husband?"

"David Dalglish. A career firefighter from Manchester, England. Currently employed by the district of Mochetsin at the fire hall."

Once dismissed by a more than usually impatient Shaw, Cuzzocrea followed orders to head to Mochetsin in the hope that he could speak further with Dalglish, in a strictly unofficial capacity. Her involvement would have to remain off the record due to the fact that she wasn't an accredited or licensed medical professional in Canada but also because of a disturbing fact that Cuzzocrea had omitted from his briefest of briefs: Ali Dalglish's history of mental illness.

CHAPTER 25 - THE ADDRESSES

Ali helped to strip the lady bare as she peeled the curling bark of the Arbutus from its ochre, red trunk, frozen in a perpetually twisted squirm in the field alongside the Mochetsin municipal hall. The many-ramped building looked more like an expensive nursing home and had the melancholy air of a hospice rather than a council hub.

Marlene was inside, making good on the promise of her connections within the community and had assured Ali that she had a friend who worked in the property tax department who would provide her with addresses for the men who had made it onto their suspect list.

The two women had cross-referenced the list of men present at the site of the body in Pioneer House later that day and had gone as far as to study the footage – much to Marlene's entertainment – of Ali's cringe-inducing YouTube appearance.

As Ali had imagined it would be, the footage was a boon and had brought to their attention the presence of men at the meeting that they would otherwise have been unaware of, one of whom Marlene knew only vaguely by sight but who she was confident volunteered as a firefighter. It made sense, therefore, to consult David about the man's identity. Because Ali hadn't spoken to David since their argument – and had no intention of doing so thank-you-very-much – the pursuit of David's input was delegated to Marlene.

Ali was growing more comfortable by the second with

the notion of not having to answer to David, of not seeking his approval any more and she was beginning to wonder if this is how couples first begin to separate from each other spiritually. Free of the house, under the shade of the Arbutus tree with bees drunkenly humming to and fro between flowers, in quiet, all-consuming contemplation of evil, Ali felt happy. She felt like the old Ali, the authentic Ali was waking up from a one-and-a-half-decade sleep.

Marlene had tracked down David under engine nine. David had identified the freeze-frame image of the man in question as Jacob Hammond who used to volunteer at the fire hall but who had been forced to hand in his pager following a driving ban some months ago.

Ali's phone trumpeted the arrival of a text message from Sandy who, at Marlene's request, was reluctantly on the hunt for sky lanterns in a Glandford party supply shop. The text read: *found them. colours or white?* Ali replied *white*, because a memorial shouldn't be colourful.

Marlene hurried out of the municipal hall doors and trotted down the long wheelchair ramp, waving her incident pad above her head. "Got them."

The two women headed for Marlene's car. Ali lit a cigarette. "So, Marlene, run me through this list while I have a smoke."

Marlene licked her index finger and flicked back through pages in her notebook. "We have: Robert Labreque – our swinging doctor, easy, he lives on our street; our very own mayor, Ed Dunlop; Charlie Chaud…"

"…the red-neck I was arguing with that day on the trail?"

"Yes."

"That reminds me, that day, you were calming him down and I heard you mention a name, a woman's name. I meant to ask you about that."

"Annie. Annie Chaud. You'd have seen her that night at the meeting, she always wears a shawl, she's on the council? Anyway, I've found that no matter how big and ugly they get, men are always terrified of their mother, it was a sure-fire way to get rid of Charlie that day, it's also the way to calm him down whenever he's drunk and causing trouble at the café too. He's been banned from there a half-dozen times."

"Okay, who's next?" asked Ali.

"Mr Winston."

Ali shook her head. "No, too old remember? Too frail."

"Ah, that's right. My mistake." Marlene scribbled over Mr Winston's name with her biro, "Carter Burrows."

"Okay, he was the guy at the back of the hall in the video, right? The postal worker? Who else? What about this ex-firefighter?"

"Jacob Hammond. I think he's worth looking at because he works at the prison which strikes me as the kind of job someone who couldn't get into the R.C.M.P. would do, eh?"

"The prison? What prison?" said Ali.

"The Mochetsin Institute," Marlene replied.

"There's a fucking prison here?"

"Yes, there's a prison here. How do you not know that?"

"Because no bastard thought to tell me, Marlene."

"I suppose it's not the sort of thing stated in a rental agreement. It's okay, it's minimum security."

"That's not okay, Marlene. What kind of inmates? Young offenders? What?"

"No, lifers who are due for release. The Mochetsin Institute gets them ready for release here. They work for local companies, finish school and get their diplomas, that sort of thing."

Ali was shocked by the information and was briefly stumped for words. "We're on a man hunt for a violent murderer, possibly rapist and it never occurred to you that the presence of a minimum-security facility in Mochetsin, housing life-sentence prisoners, would be at all relevant?"

Marlene considered Ali's point. "Well, when you put it like that...I'll take you up there if you like."

"Do you know anyone there?"

"What do you think?"

Ali smiled and shook her head. "Okay, so that's how many?"

Marlene counted down her list. "Five. Not counting David and Peter, or Greg Hewer and his constable."

"Let's keep our husbands and the two coppers on the back burner for now, shall we? Our list is way too long already."

"Okey dokey but you said that if you were married to a psycho, you wouldn't know it so back burner it is, but not scratched off entirely, like Mr Winston."

Ali opened the passenger door. "Whatever you say, Marlene but I'm confident that if David had an outhouse full of girls on our property I'd know about it."

Inside the car, Marlene pulled her seat as close to the steering wheel as she could get, clicked her seatbelt in place and checked her mirrors before turning the key in the ignition. "Five addresses then."

"You want me to put them in Google Maps?"

Marlene huffed her disapproval, tapping her skull, she said, "Google Maps! I'm the only Google Map you need, Ali Dalglish."

Ali smiled as Marlene showed promise by revving her engine, lurching speedily from the parking stall only to swiftly drop down to a glacial thirty – a speed she had maintained from Alder Beach Road all the way to the municipal hall. Marlene sat upright, peering over the steering wheel at the section of road directly in front of the car.

"I would warn you about the dangers of sitting too close to airbags, Marlene, but since I could run faster than you drive, I'll not bother."

Marlene's focus on the road didn't waiver. "Lots of police around at the moment, not to mention deer, tractors, cyclists. Can't be too careful, Ali."

Ali was glad that there were only five addresses on the list.

CHAPTER 26 - HAMMOND'S END

It was the unmistakable smell of old carpet that he first became aware of. The heavy mustiness of festering damp sweating its way upwards in the humid air and at the tail end of it, the ammonia sting of cat piss. The odour had the effect of smelling salts to a punch-drunk boxer mid-fight and Jacob felt like just such a boxer with the jabs of wooly nylon from the squashed shag pile against his cheek, the trail of saliva he didn't dare suck back was slick at the corner of his mouth and the pulsing throb that was a haymaker inside his skull.

Not wanting to open his eyes just yet, it felt important that he should try to remember what had happened to him first. His mind was scattered, jumping from last Saturday's hangover to last night in the shed, sawing off the end of a shotgun. For a long moment Jacob failed to remember why he had taken a hacksaw to his dad's old gun in the first place.

Then, in a sudden lurch of vertigo that forced his eyes to roll open in search of equilibrium, he remembered it all. The gun, the cable ties, the forest, the fifth wheel and loading two cartridges into the barrels of the gun then the skin-splitting blow to the back of his head, the force of which had slammed his forehead onto the rocks he'd been hiding behind with a deep crunch.

The carpet had once been pink but was filthy with grey and black patches of grime, his face was inches from the formica wood-panelled base of a seating banquette against which was stuck a variety of hairs including one long, wiry pube. Suddenly the carpet was more redolent of unwashed hairy balls than of piss. Jacob spat the trail of saliva from his mouth lest it become a bridge for a serried army of germs and bacteria.

The action of spitting gave him a double helping of pain and a cripplingly disheartening realization. The pain at the back of his head was at once hot and cold; Jacob guessed that his scalp was gaping open. His forehead smarted with a sharp sting, the grazes he must have suffered as a result of head-butting a rock. But what caused him to dismiss either injury as being of any importance was the fact that not only were his wrists and ankles cuffed – probably with the cable ties he'd brought with him – his trousers and boxers were scrunched down below his knees.

Jacob tentatively rolled onto his back, crushing his blood-fattened hands underneath him. He was inside the burnt-out fifth-wheel trailer he'd been ready to invade. The memory of fire had left a smoky black residue on the walls and the ceiling, a square sky light had melted, dripped then cooled again leaving curled, twisted icicles of brown plastic suspended from the opening. What had once been a window above the banquet was now just a rectangular hole, an old sheet patterned with orange and brown florals was nailed across it, one loose corner waved cheerfully to him in the breeze. As far as he could tell, he seemed to be alone.

Jacob tried to sit up but his stomach muscles wouldn't allow it, they scrunched and quivered an attempt at strength only to shudder into relaxation. Air grunted from his lungs, through his vocal chords and sounded out his body's gruff rebellion against action. Jacob lay back down, the gash at the back of his head sucking all the pubes and germs and old piss from the rug into his flesh.

Jacob was a crier. Always had been. His babyish tears, his

habit of 'turning on the waterworks', as his dad had called it, often resulted in physical punishment because Jacob's dad 'didn't want no pussy for a son'. Jacob shuddered back his emotions now and blinked away his tears. He listened for sounds; he could barely hear past the pounding of blood in his own ears but there was the gentle flapping of the window sheet and...something else...what was it? Whistling. Someone outside was whistling. As he listened, the whistling started to get louder. No, not louder – *closer*. Jacob's heart thudded fast, pounding against his ribcage.

The whistled tune wasn't the cheerful type made through licked, pursed lips but the bitter snake-like sound pushed through gritted teeth. Ignoring the pain of the wound as it rolled wider because of his movement, Jacob nonetheless looked all the way above and behind himself to an open door. The only entrance and the only exit. As a shadow glanced up the jamb of the open doorway, Jacob rolled onto his left side, and bringing his knees up towards his stomach, he pushed with his feet against the opposite wall, managing to shove himself almost to a seated position with his shoulders half way up the cladded banquette's base. His eyes were drawn to the blot of claret on the carpet where his head had been.

The shadow slipped through the doorway and slid down the kitchenette cabinet's, positioned just beyond the threshold, becoming one with the shadow-black filth of the floor. The light of the day was stolen as the doorway filled. Jacob blinked sweat, maybe blood, from his eyes. The trailer rocked in response to the visitor's weight as he entered. Patterson loomed large, the twelve-gauge hanging in his left hand, and through whistling teeth he welcomed his prey,

"Officer Hammond! You really are a stupid, fat fuck."

Jacob panted. He dared to hope he could negotiate with the man – he was, after all, trained to deal with potentially dangerous prisoners.

"Patterson," Jacob warned, "you're already in a lot of trouble."

Patterson smiled. "Trouble ain't a stranger to me, fatty Hammond. You know that."

Jacob tried to wriggle himself higher up the banquette, the rigid edge of the framed seat stabbed into his wound, making him wince, a whimper left his lips.

Patterson whistled a laugh between his teeth.

"I'm not alone, Patterson."

"Yes, you are."

Jacob's chin dimpled, he licked at his bottom lip to mask the precursor to tears. "You really think I'd be stupid enough to come here without back-up?"

Now Patterson really laughed, throwing his head back in rapture. Jacob pulled his hands apart as far as he could, desperately hoping he could apply enough pressure on the vinyl restraints to make them snap open or even stretch but managed only to make them cut deeper into the flesh of his wrists.

"Where'd you park?"

After a moment, Jacob replied, "Where the police are waiting."

"Fuck you!" Patterson stepped up to Jacob and stared down at him. "Drop it will you, fatso? You did come alone because you're exactly that dumb. Now, you tell me where your truck is and I'll think about letting you go." Patterson squatted, peering into his prisoner's eyes. "You scared, Hammond?"

Jacob reluctantly nodded and the admission caused his chin to crumple, quivering beyond his control, hot tears shimmered in his eyes. "Please let me go, Patterson. I'll help you. I'll help you get away and, and, I won't tell anyone. I swear. Please. Let me go."

Patterson was almost nose to nose with Jacob, his breath rancid, "You scared 'cause your pants are down?"

Jacob nodded a fat sob.

"You know, fatty, I ain't no stranger to trouble and I ain't no stranger to a lot of shit you don't even wanna know about."

"Patterson, I've always been good to you, haven't I?"

"Good to me? You've always been good to me? Fuck. Is that what you think?"

Patterson snarled as he pushed the sharp metal of the gun's barrels against Jacob's raw forehead. Jacob tried to pull away but managed only to bump the open flesh at the back of his skull onto the surface behind him. The hopelessness of his predicament burst forth from him as he yawned a pathetic wail, a bubble of snot filled and burst at the end of his nose.

"Please. Please don't hurt me," Jacob begged. "I'll take you to the truck. I mean it."

"You really are a fucking specimen, Hammond. Tell me where you parked it."

"I'll take you to it, that's the deal. Okay?"

In a blink, Patterson reached behind Jacob, grabbed the middle finger of his right hand and snapped it all the way back. The broken digit lolled diagonally against Jacob's other fingers as his eyes widened, his scream silenced by the intensity of his fresh agony.

Still holding the gun against Jacob's head, Patterson spoke calmly, "Nine more where that came from. Where's the fucking truck?"

Gasping like a dying fish out of water, Jacob tried to speak but his diaphragm was cramped tight, his lungs powerless captives.

"What? I can't hear you, you stupid dollop of shit. What you saying?"

Jacob, cheeks burning, heart galloping, slobbered out the words, "Cedar…Cedar Avenue…it's down the hill, to the…"

"I know where it is. You think I didn't study the roads round here? You fucking cunt."

Jacob hiccupped a semblance of control, his face sticky with tears and snot and spit. He watched as Patterson placed the gun on the kitchenette countertop and, to his horror, as he unbuttoned and unzipped his trousers.

Jacob kicked out wildly with his bound feet as Patterson approached him, lazily stroking his fattened penis. Jacob shouted at him, "No! Please! Patterson! You can't do this!"

"I'm going to split you in two, you snivelling, fat fucker."

Jacob screamed. He screamed as loud as he could and he kept screaming, the pitch rising higher and more desperate until Patterson stuffed a stinking rag in his mouth, forcing it down his gullet. Fumes evaporated across his face, up into his eyes. Gasoline, the rag was soaked in gasoline. Jacob's eyes scrunched tight as he gagged on the rag, his stomach lurched and fizzing bile baulked up, meeting the soaked cloth on its way and burning his throat. With nowhere else to go on a determined upward journey, the stomach acid spewed out of Jacob's nostrils.

Patterson hooked his hand under Jacob's left armpit and in one unbelievably powerful heave, pulled Jacob up and over, ramming his chest onto the cushioned seat of the banquette, his neck twisting uncomfortably as his head was rammed against the ninety-degree angle where seat met backrest.

Patterson positioned himself above Jacob, whistling through his teeth again but pausing to delight in Jacob's muffled squeal of pain as he snapped another finger back so far that the nail touched the scrunched, purple skin of his wrist.

Jacob bucked furiously as Patterson pulled his cheeks apart, gargled up and spat out a slimy glob of phlegm and as it landed on Jacob's defiantly puckered anus Patterson exclaimed, "Bullseye!" and then commenced his jaunty whistle as he forced himself inside.

CHAPTER 27 - ED DUNLOP

Marlene's car scrunched over Mayor Ed Dunlop's pebbled, almost majestic drive with its herbaceous borders and amateur topiary. One bush, Ali noticed, was trying to resemble a giraffe. The house was as ostentatious as any Ali had ever seen with its pretentious black and white mock-Tudor frontage.

"Please, are we really expected to believe that a Tudor-era family built this two hundred years before the first British settlers arrived on the fucking continent?" said Ali.

"What d'you mean, hon?" asked Marlene as she somehow managed to pull to an abrupt, whiplash-inducing stop even though she couldn't have been doing more than five kilometres an hour.

"Never mind. Just the house. It's beyond tacky – denotes a lack of historical knowledge *and* style."

"Well, you can't blame Ed and Theresa for that, they bought it from the Mormons, the Jorgensens, after their son offed himself in there."

"I can blame them for not tearing it down or burning it to the bloody ground."

"You stay here, I'll knock on and see if anyone's home." Marlene headed towards the house then stopped and returned to the car, grabbing the flyers from Ali. "Hey, you snap a picture for the wall, your phone has a camera, right?"

Ali watched Marlene, armed with her bundle of yellow flyers, approach the huge out-of-keeping-with-the-fake-era-of-the-house double doors and rap loudly with yet another architectural faux pas, a Tutankhamen brass knocker.

As per Marlene's request, Ali took a picture of the house and hoped to God that they could scratch the mayor's name from their suspect list so the image of Ed Dunlop's vomitus house wouldn't have to pollute her dining room wall.

A woman opened the door and Marlene chatted to her. The two of them sported the same hairstyle – dyed white blonde and helmeted with a pint of Elnette lacquer – one of two styles favoured by women of a certain age in Mochetsin, the other being a close-cut grey crop. The women with the helmet hair all wore comfortable slacks and fuck ugly shoes with a cotton blouse or a twin set while the cropped set favoured hiking gear. Was it something in the water? Or maybe Dr Labreque prescribed the same menopausal medications that were actually a secret weapon of a population hungry government who preferred women past the age of reproduction to become as sexless and as invisible to the opposite sex as possible so as not pose a challenge to young women with non-withered ovaries? Ali felt even happier that she had been excluded from the local G.P.'s patient roster and made a mental note to change the filter in her water jug later.

Marlene jogged excitedly to Ali's side of the car and opened the passenger door. "Ed's off today, chest infection, he's round back. Come on."

Ali got out of the car and followed Marlene around the side of the house and couldn't decide whether she was happy or sad that the mock Tudor theme didn't extend to the gable ends of the building until she spied that the rear exposure picked up the scheme again and felt nauseous.

The rear garden was an English pastoral scene – Ali could almost hear Henry VIII's 'Greensleeves' – with beautifully manicured lawns and geometric flower beds framed with carefully trimmed box hedging, a smattering of varied and well-established trees and a garishly colourful, gigantic fountain featuring three killer whales spitting up into the air, all of them held aloft by demonic-looking cherubs who were themselves, gayly pissing.

Marlene called out, "Ed? You back here?"

Ed Dunlop stepped out from under a wooden lean-to structure, almost completely obscured from view by an impressive mass of climbing hydrangeas and wisteria. At the sight of him, Marlene gasped: wearing a black leather apron and long plastic gloves (the type you would see on vets, shoulder-deep in a cow) both the apron and the gloves were smeared with blood that scintillated in the sunlight and in his hand was a long, curved knife.

"Back here. Oh, Marlene! Hey, hey."

Marlene waved and whispered to Ali as they approached the bloodied mayor, "This is either a bad joke or we've got him. Hmm, on the hunt for a killer…out pops nice Ed Dunlop, mid-slash."

Marlene seemed to search Ali for an expert opinion. Ali didn't have one, she shrugged. "I'm lost for words."

Under the slanted roof of the lean-to structure hung the fresh carcass of a newly eviscerated stag. Ed, standing in a puddle of spilled, black guts was skinning the animal starting at the ankle and flaying the skin expertly down the legs.

"Marlene. Peter send you for some venison?"

"No, but we will take some when it's a little more like steak. Ed, this is Ali, my neighbour."

Ed turned to look at Ali and scanned her from foot to head making Ali feel like he was working out how best to flay her. With a smile as pretentious as his house, he offered his hand out to shake. Ali refused the insane offer of a bloody handshake and wondered if he'd forgotten that his gloves were smeared with deer innards or if that was precisely the sentiment with which he intended to greet her.

"Ah, yes, David's wife. Hello. So, what can I do for you pretty little ladies today?"

"Just letting you know…"

"If it's about this memorial, I know all about it. Very nice thought. I'll be there, of course."

Through the hanging clusters of immature wisteria buds, Ali scanned the grounds. No outhouses except for one shed, cloaked in creeping Virginia and barely big enough to house the ride-on mower Ed must own to maintain his golf course standard expanse of lawn.

"I'll be getting sausages made this time, if you want to put an order in," said the mayor.

"Not for me, Ed. They gave Peter a bad case of the gas last time," replied Marlene.

"And you?" Ed pointed his knife at Ali.

Marlene nudged Ali. "You want sausages, Ali? They're good but very rich."

"Um," Ali gave the mayor her own pretentious smile, "no thanks. You know, I just love your house."

Ed Dunlop stood proud at the compliment and stepped out from his puddle of bowels to look up at his house. He shielded his eyes from the sun with a drippy glove as he gazed up lovingly.

"Yep. She's a keeper, that's for sure. Lot of maintenance though."

Ali mirrored his stance, "I can imagine. How many bedrooms?"

"Oh just six but she's got seven and a half baths."

"Wow, six bedrooms?" Ali enthused, "On how many floors?"

"Funny you should ask that, but then you are a Brit, after all. Three."

"Three floors, Ed?" said Marlene. "I thought it was just the ground and an upstairs."

"Aha!" Ed pointed up a finger to ready the women for their lesson. "That's what you might think but you see, in England, she'll know this," he nodded rudely towards Ali, "space is hard to come by, everyone's just crammed into every inch of land and well, this is a typical English home, you see."

Ali's grin was beginning to weaken despite her effort to maintain it. She cleared her throat to suppress the rillet of corrections she wished to make.

The mayor continued, "So, there, you see? In England, if they need more room, they go *up*, not *out* like us. There's a couple of sneaky little attic rooms up top, in the eaves. Hot as hell but the grandkids love it up there. Very C.S. Lewis."

"Well, you learn something every day," said Marlene.

"No cellar?" asked Ali.

"Cellar?" the mayor laughed at her. "Oh, you mean basement?"

Ali only thought her authentic answer: *No, I mean cellar, you jumped-up, brainless twat.* She giggled a dumb shrug in lieu of honesty.

"Alas, no basement. So much as I would love my own man cave, the only way I get peace and quiet is by getting out there and putting a bit of lead in these suckers." He hitched a thumb back in reference to the once-majestic stag.

"Aren't you a lovely man," Ali sniped.

Marlene, sensing a change in the atmosphere, grabbed Ali by the elbow and ushered her back down the way they had come, calling to Ed as she went, "So, anyhoo, got to go. I left a flyer with Theresa. Hope that chest infection clears up. Look forward to the venison. Love to the family."

Back at the car Marlene put the air conditioning on full blast and wafted the underarms of her blouse in front of the vents. "You really do have a way about you, Ali. What charm school did you graduate from?"

"Fucking Cambridge. By the way, I was perfectly polite. It's not my fault he knows fuck all about British property."

"What can I say? Ed Dunlop knows everything – or thinks he does." Marlene slowly reversed along the driveway, towards the Mochetsin Road. "So? What do you think?"

"Skilled with a knife. Probably...*definitely* a misogynist. Appearances are of high importance to him. I didn't get the feeling there was anywhere on that property suitable for the job but he does, by his own admission, spend time away hunting. He could have somewhere else."

"He's still a suspect then?" said Marlene as she pulled out

onto the main road.

"Yes, but he lacks the genius I expected. God, he's a twat."

"Oh, Ali. I hate that word."

"Twat?"

"Yes."

"You prefer cunt?"

"Lord have mercy." Marlene waved to a car that had slowed down behind her as she struggled to find the D for drive. "Where next?"

"McIvor Road. Charlie Chaud – our favourite redneck."

Marlene assumed her driving position, nipples bouncing against the Subaru ellipsis on the steering wheel.

Ali asked, "Can I drive please, Marlene? I want to get round these next four houses by Tuesday."

Marlene snorted. "I've seen you drive." Her snarky comment was accompanied by a snarkier glance but Marlene's cockiness was short lived as she swerved onto the gritty hard shoulder. She corrected her position and refocused on the stretch of road directly ahead of her. "Better to arrive ten minutes late in this life than fifty years early in the next."

Ali smiled and wondered at exactly what age Marlene was expecting to die.

CHAPTER 28 - PIN THE TAIL

Patterson leaned back against the little kitchen area to regain his breath. Today was another hot one but that was okay because kismet was working in his favour – he'd be free of this stinking sweat box in no time.

He looked around for something to wipe his cock with and finally ripped the ugly sheet from the window; he wouldn't be needing it anymore anyway. He gave his arse a wipe while he was at it too because that fucking Hammond had disturbed him half way through a shit so he'd had to snip and move.

He looked at Hammond, the dumb fuck. He'd passed out maybe, or maybe he was just in shock – first time he'd been banged probably. Looking at Hammond, ass splayed, bent over that seat then at the grotty (now grottier) sheet in his hand, Patterson had a great idea. He was always going to fire the shit hole but now he could fire two shit holes at once.

The old gas can he'd found was as pointless as a priest in a brothel for someone evading detection so he'd been keeping what gas there was in it for his final departure when he'd always planned on setting the trailer ablaze but now he soaked his dick rag curtain with its contents.

He sloshed the rest of the gas all about the interior of the shitty trailer he'd been more eager to escape after just four nights than he had his whole time in prison. He splashed some on Officer Hammond's sweaty face too, it was stinging the fat shit's eyes. Oh fuck, that fucking crying. This guy needed putting out of his misery.

Taking the soaked sheet, he opened Hammond's ass with one hand, a turbid stream of jizz, blood and shit seeping out of it down to his ball sack. Patterson shoved the cloth into Hammond's arse and trailed it out towards the door with him as he backed out of the trailer, taking with him his new gun, the backpack full of goodies, Hammond's boots and a set of keys to a Ford.

Hammond was crying again, probably thinking that getting rammed up the arse was the worst thing that could happen to him but that sorry sucker was about to wish for that ten times over in place of what was coming.

Patterson stepped clear of the trailer door, took his lighter from his pocket and leaned in. He lit the end of the orange and brown floral fuse.

He watched the fire consume Hammond's new tail then he watched it consume Hammond.

CHAPTER 29 - CHARLIE CHAUD

The number 3662 was painted in white on a tree trunk at the bottom of the pot-holed, dirt drive shaded by low-hanging boughs of ancient firs all nodding their tips to the west having grown to their fullest in a region battered by regular south-easterly winds.

If Ed Dunlop's house was the tackiest in Mochetsin, Charlie Chaud's would be voted the scruffiest. On the way up the drive, Ali noticed the scattered remnants of a spilled garbage can along a rut in the verge.

It would be inaccurate to describe the steep, two-tracked gradient as a drive since driving up it proved to be a physical exertion for Marlene who had to pull herself even closer than usual to the steering wheel to see over the dash. Perhaps someone who had driven the slope a thousand times, memorizing every curve and the altering proximity of the flanking ditches on both sides, would feel confident enough to relax back into their seat for the trip.

The top of the drive opened up to a clearing that fancied itself as a parking area come turning circle. As if it had been set-dressed for the shooting of an episode of *The Beverly Hillbillies*, the area was home to a handful of broken-down trucks and cars in various states of disrepair as well as a variety of discarded beer bottles and cans that littered the knee-high brush and broom bordering the clearing.

Marlene turned the engine off. The two women sat, wordlessly observing their surroundings. The house was positioned high atop a hill and although the sky was as bright as anywhere else in Mochetsin the area seemed glum, the wind whistling ominously through trees that rustled secret whisperings to one another.

Ali and Marlene got out of the car. Ahead of them a rocky humpback jutted from the hill upon which stood Charlie Chaud's house with its warped cedar clad roof. Many of the shingles were split, their weather-silvered edges curling in on themselves. Much of the roof was carpeted with furry moss; a raven busily pecked lumps of it free and tossed them down the pitch of the roof where they rolled into a length of guttering that had worked free of its downspout and stuck out at an angle from the house.

An effort had once been made to pretty up the neglected place; a gnome with a menacing grin, the point of his green hat cracked and gone, was cheerfully pushing a wooden wheelbarrow of long dead plants.

"Does Chaud live here alone?" asked Ali.

"Yes. Annie, his mother, used to live here but moved into the assisted living place on Rocky Point Road a couple of years ago after her hip replacement. Charlie made her, she didn't want to go."

"Why not? I'd have thrown myself down some steps or smashed my own hip with a frigging hammer to get away from this place."

"I've never been up here before but I'm sure Annie would have had it nicer than this. Charlie lacks finesse, shall we say? Seems he's not one for visitors. Actually, I'm hoping he's not here and I can just slip a flyer through his door."

A family of deer, munching on forbs nestled within the long grasses, stopped to look at the women as they crested the hump and headed to the house. With a twitch of an ear and a bored chew the antlered leader of the pack led the herd away at a languid pace over another buttress of rock (upon which stood a redneck art installation – a pyramid of Molsen cans) and disappeared behind the house.

The exterior of the house was shambolic, an old velour

couch furnished what should have been a front lawn and on a makeshift deck comprised of six fork-lift pallets stood a pink acrylic bath, not a hot tub or a paddling pool but an actual, normally-found-in-a-regular-bathroom-bath, two-thirds filled with green water. The scummy meniscus was an oily grave to a range of bugs including one daddy longlegs who was endeavouring to resist death by turning in endless circles upon the surface. A red hose running from behind the house and over a tarpaulin-covered stack of firewood, hung from a nail in a two-by-four post, rammed but not concreted into the ground which served as the tub's shower head.

Marlene, referring to the bath, said, "Maybe it's nice on a starry night?"

"What's next? A toilet round the back so he can shit under the full moon?"

"I'll try the door." Marlene pinched her nose as she passed the couch, "Oh, that thing stinks like a bag of dead weasels."

As Marlene approached the door, the moss-tossing crow shrieked a warning and took flight. Its shadow slipped over the wood pile and a white blob of poop splattered the Subaru's windshield. After her second series of raps on the faded burgundy front door, Marlene turned with a shrug.

"He's not in, thank God. Let's take a little look round back, shall we?" said Marlene.

"You sure he's not home?"

"His truck's not here."

"Maybe it's one of them?" Ali nodded towards the elephant's graveyard of vehicles.

"No. He delivers chips. He drives a cube van with the 'Old Dutch' logo plastered all over it."

"Worth the risk then, I reckon."

The back of the Chaud house was only accessible over the rocky mound the deer had disappeared behind. Ali and Marlene traversed it and a breathtaking view, sweeping over the treed valley below and out to the Olympic mountain range of America beyond, opened up before them. The wind buffeted them and Ali felt cold for the first time in days. Marlene held her arms out at shoulder height like a rapturous scarecrow.

"Oh, that's heaven," said Marlene and peeked at Ali sidelong. "I get the sweats. They're torture, you'll see."

Ali looked up at the house. Green paint peeled from its siding revealing the canary yellow that the house must once have been. An empty, cobwebbed humming bird feeder, the plastic of the vessel-singed sepia over many hot summers, was at the mercy of the wind and tapped a staccato upon the window frame from which it hung.

From their new elevation, Marlene and Ali had a clear view of the expanse of acreage that made up Charlie Chaud's land. A tall, skinny shed, reminiscent of yesteryear's outside privies, stood fifty metres or so to the right of them.

"What is that, Marlene? A toilet?" asked Ali.

"I think it might be over the well, actually. See how it's wrapped in black plastic? To keep wildlife out and to protect it from contamination." Marlene pointed to a flattened area where the grass looked unusually healthy, "That'll be the septic field. I can smell it when the wind blows."

Marlene turned and looked at the house, "Hey, there's a basement window," Marlene descended the outcropping, "Curtains are open, lets have a nosey."

Ali and Marlene carefully picked their way through the thorny bushes that lay between them and the small window which was positioned higher than it had looked from their raised position. Even on tip toes, Ali couldn't see over the ledge. Marlene was slightly taller than Ali but could still only see the ceiling and the top of the walls as she looked in, tutting her disapproval.

"Typical."

"What?" asked Ali.

"Smutty posters. Must be his bedroom. Find something for me to stand on, will you?"

Ali looked around and noticed a square entrance in the

house's exterior wall, low down and almost obscured from view by another spiked bush.

"I'll have a look in there," said Ali, drawing Marlene's attention to the hole.

"Good idea, must be a crawl space, maybe access to plumbing and electric."

Ali squeezed herself along the wall, her denim shirt snagging repeatedly on the grasping thorns. Finally she dropped down to her knees to see if there was anything inside the crawlspace that could be used as a boost. The opening was curtained by a white blanket of spiderweb and Ali, familiar with the artist's work having encountered the same webs whilst pruning an overgrown flower bed last autumn, recognized the wolf spider's nursery web. Wolf spiders are huge, fanged fiends that hunt down their prey rather than snaring them in webs – its web served only one purpose, to house the young over which the mother watches carefully. Beyond the web, nestled in the gloom of the crawlspace, lay a bucket – perfect for the task of raising Marlene high enough to peek through the window – teasingly within reach but unplunderable for one as scared of arachnids as Ali.

"Fuck."

"You find anything?" called Marlene.

"A bucket. Wait, I'll get it."

Summoning her reserves of bravery, defiant of weakness and pathetic fear, Ali pushed her hand into the web and brushed it aside. The web was a sticky glove that no amount of shaking of her hand could dislodge so instead she wiped the length of her forearm on her jeans and gritted her wilting bravery between her teeth. Ali reached her hand inside the dark void and wiggled her outstretched fingers, her cheek flat against the outside wall, trying to grasp the rim of the bucket but managing only to make it skid farther from her.

"Shitting fuck nuts."

There was nothing else to do; she would have to crawl in there, shoulder deep at least, to get the bucket.

"Fuck fuck cunting toss-face." Ali cursed her predicament, her lack of courage and the anabolic steroid-injecting meaty spiders of Canada.

"Oh my God! What is all the drama about?" asked Marlene from the relative safety of the window sill.

"Fucking spiders. Just a minute," Ali snapped. She took and held a deep breath as if she were about to dive into a treacherous body of water, dropped to her hands, briefly scanned the opening of the hatch and went for it. During the brief seconds she was inside the dank crawlspace she took note of an old charcoal barbecue and a pile of fur that made her think a fluffy animal had been ripped apart under there but that turned out to be the ripped out stuffing of a cushion that matched the velour sofa out front. Ali grabbed the bucket and was shuffling her retreat when she felt a distinct weight drop onto the centre of her back and knew it had to be the solid carapace of the mama wolf spider. Her fear was confirmed as she sped up her exit and the weight sped up its ascent of her body, scuttling from the centre of her back, upwards, between her shoulder blades, towards her neck.

Outside the crawlspace Ali screamed, threw the bucket down and ripped her denim shirt off, thankful that the buttons were press studs. Ali peeled the cuffs from her wrists, trotting maniacally on the spot as her panic reached an eye-jiggling crescendo. Ali threw her shirt down on the ground and ruffled her hair, her scalp felt like it was crawling with baby spiders. She caught her breath – topless but for her bra – and looked at Marlene who stared back at her, mouth agape. As Ali's fluttering heart began to calm she felt a burst of laughter rise but before it came to fruition, it was stymied by a voice from above.

"What you doing back here?"

Marlene's startled look hadn't been because of Ali's inelegant strip show but because Charlie Chaud had appeared on the rock behind his house. Ali crossed her arms across her chest and looked up at him, her eyes adjusting to the bright sky beyond him. Charlie Chaud was wearing a dirty green coverall and holding what seemed to be two small, steel cages, one in each hand.

"Charlie!" exclaimed Marlene. "You nearly gave me a heart attack."

Charlie eyed Ali in such a way that she immediately swept up her shirt and pulled it back on, caring not if it was home to a thousand wolf spiders.

"I…we were just looking for you." Marlene headed to him, forcing his glare from Ali.

"Oh yeah?"

As she climbed up onto the rock, Marlene poured unctuous charm to deflect Chaud's suspicions. "Yes! You are just the guy I need."

"What fur?"

"You don't have any sky lanterns do you?" said Marlene as she signalled for a now buttoned-up Ali to follow her as she side-stepped the rubescent nastiness of the man. As they passed him, Ali noticed that the cages were humane rat traps, a rodent in each, one was attempting to escape and another, larger and black, was happily finishing the smear of peanut butter that had obviously lured him into the trap in the first place. Marlene shepherded Ali behind her and headed toward the front of the house, all the while exuding charming innocence.

"Sky what?"

"Lanterns, hon. You know the ones. You light them and they go up, up, up, into the sky?"

"No," said Charlie following the women with a heavy-foreheaded scowl on his face.

"Oh, darn it. Well, I'll just have to try someone else then. We need them for the memorial tonight, you see, for that girl we found the other day. Well, I thought to myself, I should let Charlie Chaud know because he was there too and then I thought, ooh, I'll see if he has any of those pretty sky lanterns while I'm at it."

Evidently Marlene's verbal diarrhoea was a fine pest repellent as Charlie Chaud followed them only as far as his outdoor tub, over which he remained sentry.

"I've left a note all about it under your door, Charlie."

Charlie Chaud stood above his bath, seeming to enjoy their fumbled retreat with a sneer that implied he could smell the bullshit spouted by Marlene. Charlie's gaze shifted to Ali as he lasciviously licked his lips and grinned just before dropping the two rat traps in the water, the steel cages submerging fully and quickly, fat oily bubbles popped on the surface of the scuzzy water. Charlie winked at Ali.

"In the car, Marlene," Ali muttered.

"Oh yes," agreed Marlene.

The women made hasty their escape. Inside the car, blindly stabbing her key around the ignition, Marlene asked, "Is he still there?" The key found its slot and slid home, the engine started the first time, as it always did, but Marlene had a look of relief upon her face when it did. "Is he coming?"

Ali looked out of the window as Marlene completed a three-point turn with all of the finesse of a learner. "No. He's just standing there, fucking nutter. Just go."

Marlene drove faster down the roller coaster hill than Ali had previously thought her capable of. The car bumped over tree roots and slammed into potholes, Marlene's face was full of determination and Ali had to hold onto the dash to keep herself from bouncing out of her seat. The excitement, however, was short-lived as Marlene deliberately slowed to her signature fuck-all-mph, squinting at her speedometer, once the tyres met with the safety of McIvor Road.

After a brief silence both the women began to laugh, their tension dissipating. Marlene held her hand out to see if it was shaking; it was.

"Means nothing, could be early Parkinson's." Marlene smiled, dismissing the significance of her trembling hand. "I nearly pee'd myself, just so you know, when I saw him standing up there, but, again, that means nothing, I only have to sneeze and I've got Niagara falling."

"We should be careful about snooping like that, Marlene, we are looking for a killer."

"I hear you. I do not want to be the next one found butchered."

"Agreed?" Ali asked.

"Agreed." Marlene confirmed. "I take it Charlie Chaud is still on the list?"

Ali nodded. "Oh yes. I'd say he's up there."

"In your expert opinion, how would you describe him?"

"Well," said Ali, "he's disorganized, he's not charismatic in the least and clearly doesn't give a shit about appearing normal. I'd guess that he has an average, if not below average I.Q. That all goes against our profile, *but* Charlie Chaud is a hulking sleazy fuck with a penchant for torturing things smaller than him. He gave me the creeps. I saw him looking at my tits, and that wink? Just before he drowned the rats? Also, that property is massive and his truck, the crisp truck you said he drives?"

"Chips."

"Yeah, crisps. That must have been parked somewhere hidden, somewhere in the trees otherwise we'd have seen it. He's dominant and controlling, he made his own mother move into a nursing home. He's basically one horrible fucking bastard so yes, he stays on the list."

CHAPTER 30 - CUZZOCREA SCREWED UP

<FYI.HMMND PHND SCK. V UNUSL. SHLD B WRRYD?>

Cuzzocrea frowned as he deciphered Munro's embarrassing attempt at text savviness. Once he worked out that HMMND stood for Hammond, it was simple, and yes, he did begin to worry.

In his job, Rey Cuzzocrea was expected to make accurate readings about a person's psychology, not by relying on gut instinct but through the implementation of proven scientific profiling techniques as well as his wealth of knowledge and understanding, training and experience. Perhaps he had impetuously analysed Hammond. He wasn't, after all, a suspect, he was just a means to an end, a puppet on a string that Cuzzocrea had enchanted into life so that a few corners could be cut.

Cuzzocrea had taken the corrections officer to be a garrulous, dim-witted approval seeker. An obeyer of rules, a sheep, a follower, and so hinting to Hammond as to the possible whereabouts of Patterson *should* have inspired him, in an anonymous, muse-like fashion, to simply tip-off the relevant authorities, take the glory and feel like a hero for fifteen minutes. Of course the worst-case scenario had glanced Cuzzocrea's mind at the time but he had batted the possibility away due to the time-sensitive nature of the VIIMIS murder case. After all, Hammond actually going after the escaped convict himself would require a bullheaded audacity he hadn't picked up on in the man. There had been an element of latent machoism but only the type that draws a man like Jacob to a job in corrections anyway – a negligible gauze of courage barely concealing his true cowardice and vulnerability. Surely Cuzzocrea hadn't missed something vital and misread the man entirely.

Just to salve his conscience and so that he could reassure his partner, Cuzzocrea ran Jacob Hammond's name expecting to see that he was indeed a rule obeyer, a sheep, a follower and would therefore have a clean police record. No such luck. Cuzzocrea, alone in his car, blushed with shame as he scrolled down the laptop screen.

"Oh shit." Cuzzocrea called Munro on his cell.

Munro answered immediately, "Rey? You get my text?"

"Yep, that's why I'm calling. Listen, don't text anything else about it, okay?"

"Shit. What are you saying, buddy?"

"Nothing. Just…let's tread carefully on this one," Cuzzocrea rubbed his closed eyes. "I may have misread the guy."

"What? Misread him? Rey, we talked about this, remember? You knew this was a risk, you said it yourself."

"I know. What's done is done – we don't know anything yet, for all we know Hammond could be sick, he might have food poisoning from his what was it? The *workman burger* he said he was having."

"What makes you say you misread him then?"

Cuzzocrea delayed his response, by relaying the information he was highlighting his own ineptitude. "He has a record. D.U.I.s, one resisting arrest and a domestic assault. All within the past year. It's like he used to be a goody-goody and now, all of a sudden he's… I didn't see it, I didn't pick up on it."

"Well you dropped the ball on this one, buddy. If he's not sick – and I really hope he is – if he did go after Patterson and it all went south, if they find out that we sent him there...what if he fucking tells them, Rey? It's our jobs we're talking about."

"I know. That's why you've gotta shut your mouth and quit texting me. I'm in Mochetsin now, he lives down the road. I'll head to his house. Hopefully he's there and I can do some damage limitation."

"I'll tell you what damage limitation we should be doing, we should be telling Shaw about this. Come clean early then it's just a fuck up, nothing that can get us fired...or worse."

"Let me check out Hammond's place first, okay? Just keep your pants on till then."

Cuzzocrea ended the call and wished he had some science to lean on right now because his gut instincts were painting a very grim picture for him.

CHAPTER 31 - THE ITALIAN STALLION

"Well. This isn't much, the whole place is as big as my kitchen." Marlene screwed up her nose as she looked at Jacob Hammond's modest, beige stuccoed rancher. "It's a subdivided parcel. His neighbours are close, no privacy."

"Good. We need to narrow our suspects down." said Ali, getting out of the car.

The women entered a small covered porch at the front door of the house. Marlene pressed the doorbell, waited and pressed it again.

"Nobody home." shrugged Marlene, "Probably at work. Come on."

Marlene headed out of the porch and disappeared around the side of the house. Ali rushed to catch up.

"Marlene!" Ali found Marlene with her nose pressed up against the back-door window, her hands cupped against her face and the glass to shield the sun and enable her to see clearly inside. "Marlene, I thought we agreed that we weren't going to snoop. We made this mistake already once today, remember?"

Marlene replied with her nose still pressed to the glass, "If we managed to talk our way off Charlie Chaud's property without being shot or gnawed by rats, I'm sure we can talk our way round one of your husband's firefighters."

"What do you see?" asked Ali as she quickly assessed the back yard; there was a large shed, not much smaller than the main house itself, a workshop.

"Nothing, he's straight and he lives alone."

Ali was surprised. "Oh? How'd you work that out then,

Columbo?"

Marlene moved along the rear of the house to peer in another window. "Because it's a pig sty. Also, Marge in the tax office told me she knows his ex-girlfriend."

"I'm going to look in this shed but if there're spider webs I'm out of here," said Ali to an unresponsive Marlene who was busy tutting at the sight of what Ali assumed to be another room fit for pigs.

The workshop door was ajar so Ali pulled it open; the hinges were reluctant with rust. The shed seemed to be piled high with a ravel of garden tools, old hoses and electrical cords. A work bench was littered with empty plant pots and hanging baskets as well as a box of tangled Christmas lights. Not the shed-come-workshop of an organized psychopath.

Ali, nerves still chattering from her encounter with wolf spiders and weirdo rednecks, jumped when Marlene pulled the door from her hand and joined her in the entrance to the shed.

"I don't know, Ali. Seems like a regular guy. A slob, but a regular guy. You know, he's too young for the profile too – his house is overlooked. What's your feeling?"

"I'm inclined to agree. Bottom of the list. If he turns up tonight we can assess him further."

"Good. I'll pop a flyer through his letterbox."

"Come on then," said Ali, pushing the shed door closed again.

As they rounded the front corner of Hammond's house, another car, a blue Prius, was parked beside the Subaru. The women stood still.

"Not again. Seriously?" said Ali. "I told you we shouldn't have gone spying."

"Mrs Dalglish?"

The voice came from the front door of the house. Ali and Marlene looked towards the covered porch where a tall figure was stepping out.

"Inspector Cuzzocrea," said Ali.

Cuzzocrea approached the women, holding out his hand

to first shake Ali's and then Marlene's.

"Marlene, this is Inspector Cuzzocrea, he's with the VIIMIS team. This is Marlene McKean, my neighbour."

Marlene clucked as she eyed the handsome police officer, shaking his hand for too long and eyeing him head to toe. "I remember you mentioning him. Strange name, Cuzzocrea. Any relation of Doug in Coombs? Where they have the goats on the roof?"

"No. No relation." Cuzzocrea politely peeled his hand free of Marlene's vice-like grip.

"Italian, isn't it? Cuzzocrea?" persisted Marlene.

"Yes. On my father's side, obviously. So, ladies, what brings you here?" Cuzzocrea asked.

Ali studied Cuzzocrea's countenance and detected deceit therein. "I really want to ask you the same question, Inspector."

Cuzzocrea met Ali's eyes and realized, for the first time, how it felt to be the subject of a profiler at work.

Marlene cut the tension. "We're delivering flyers."

Marlene handed a yellow sheet to Cuzzocrea whose brow furrowed as he read. He lifted his eyes to Ali. "How very community-spirited of you."

The remark was loaded and Ali felt suddenly transparent. "Marlene's idea."

"I guessed." said Cuzzocrea, his glassy eyes penetrating Ali's soul, making her flush and forcing her to break eye contact but, feeling his relentless stare upon her nonetheless, she denied the intimidation and looked back into him.

"How's the investigation going, Inspector Cuzzocrea?" asked Marlene.

"It's going." He smiled kindly.

"Any suspects?" asked Ali.

"I'm afraid that's classified," replied Cuzzocrea.

"Classified?" Ali snorted. "You're not the CIA. What about Hammond? Is he a suspect? Is that why you're here?"

"No."

"He is, isn't he?" Ali prodded.

"Mrs Dalglish…" Cuzzocrea began.

"Well Marlene, looks like Hammond makes it back onto our suspect list after all," said Ali.

"Looks like it," agreed Marlene.

"Suspect list?" said Cuzzocrea. "You're conducting an investigation?"

"Oh yes we are," said Marlene.

"And we're making some headway too, aren't we, Marlene?" Ali said to Marlene who nodded. Ali continued, "Obviously I'd love to share our findings but, well, they're classified."

Ali smiled at Cuzzocrea who narrowed his eyes, a hint of crow's feet wrinkles framed them adding to his appeal. Ali felt the bitter punch of yet another male-biased advantage in life: men age and become sexier; women age and disappear.

Cuzzocrea put his hands in his pockets. "I'm here on a separate matter."

"Oh, what's that then? You here to tidy up?" suggested Marlene.

Cuzzocrea paused. "Hammond works at the Mochetsin Institute. He's helping out on the Patterson escape. Nothing to do with the girl on the beach." As soon as the words left Cuzzocrea's lips the two women shared a shocked look. Cuzzocrea scolded this latest dilution of what was normally his sagacious mind. What the hell had gotten into him? Two major slip-ups in less than twenty-four hours.

"When was the escape?" enquired Ali, piqued.

Cuzzocrea, harm already done, relented. "Sunday afternoon. And before you jump to wild conclusions, no, the escapee is not a suspect."

"Why not?" asked Marlene. "What was he in for?"

"That's irrelevant," said Cuzzocrea.

"Well, not really, young man. I think I have the right to know – as both a concerned citizen and as a resident of Mochetsin," said Marlene.

"I'm really not at liberty to say, I'm not even officially involved in that case."

Ali had been reading Cuzzocrea's face and his responses, "It's okay, Marlene. I get the feeling that Inspector Cuzzocrea is very careful about who he chooses to eliminate from an enquiry. Also, it's likely he escaped hours after our victim was already dead." Still watching the man, Ali added, "You're a profiler?"

"A criminal analyst, yes."

Ali saw in his eyes an active, perceptive intelligence she was intimately familiar with and felt his recognition of the same quality in her.

"Mrs Dalglish, I'd like to sit down with you at some point. I passed on the thoughts you shared with me the other day and, in fact, your theory turned out to be correct."

"Tetanus?" asked Ali.

"Yes."

Proud of the vindication on behalf of her friend, Marlene nudged Ali with a sharp elbow to the ribs. The strange intensity between Cuzzocrea and Ali was momentarily broken. Ali's mouth was suddenly dry and her head swirled with the ramifications of her theory having been correct.

Ali's voice was quiet. "You can catch me tonight, at the memorial, I suppose."

"I will," said Cuzzocrea, concern darkening his eyes as he observed Ali's reactions.

Ali felt clumsy as she crossed the patchy front lawn and felt clumsier still when she slammed the crown of her head against the car roof as she was getting in, a reverberant throb instantly took up residence across the top of her skull. She slid into the car seat muttering quiet *fuck-fucks* as she slammed the door. Avoiding eye contact with Cuzzocrea by busying herself with the seatbelt latch, she was sure he was scanning her again with those obtrusive eyes of his. Marlene joined her in the car and waved to the inspector from behind the windshield as she began her too slow reverse manoeuvre from the drive onto Daisy Farm Road.

"I'll take him and a five-pound-bag of potatoes any day of the week and twice on Sundays, thank you very much."

said Marlene, through her teeth like a ventriloquist, perhaps in the hope of preventing Cuzzocrea from reading her lips.

"What does that even mean?" asked Ali.

"Ooh, those eyes. He almost did with one look what takes half a tube of KY to do for me twice a year."

Ali laughed. "Marlene!"

"What? I am a woman, you know. I still get the odd twitch when I'm faced with a delectation like that particular Italian stallion back there or, of course, Charles Bronson."

"Charles Bronson? The prisoner?"

"What? No. Charles Bronson."

"The actor?"

"Yes," said Marlene, "James Bond."

"What? Charles Bronson wasn't a Bond."

"Oh, come on, he was one of the best…wait, not Charles…Pierce! Pierce Bronson."

"Pierce Brosnan?"

"Exactly."

"Twice a year?" asked Ali.

Marlene nodded. "New Year and Peter's birthday."

"Not your birthday?"

"Ali, hon, I want presents on my birthday, not a chaffed chuff." Marlene saw Ali's expression. "Don't tell me I've shocked the unshockable Ali Dalglish?"

"A bit," admitted Ali.

"Take it from me, when the change comes you should get on hormone replacement; it might increase the risk of breast cancer but at least you'll have enjoyed sex till your premature end. Speaking of sex…there was a bit of chemistry going on back there, would you agree?"

"Oh, you think you're in there with the Italian stallion do you?" said Ali.

"Me? Now, I know I'm a total milf but I meant you, hon. That man couldn't take his eyes off you."

Ali couldn't agree more and, with a growing sense of foreboding, she began to wonder why.

CHAPTER 32 - THE TRUCK

Emerging gingerly from a bosk of woods and skid-stepping down a slope, Patterson slipped through the bark palisade that separated the rustic, bucolic native reserve from the too neat and too contrived squares of suburban lawns that made up Cedar Avenue.

The F150 was easy to spot; it was the only vehicle not parked on a driveway or tucked safely away in a double garage. The street was deserted and the only movement was a paper bag eager to escape the snare of the empty blue recycling bin it was trapped under. The blue bins lay carelessly discarded at the end of every drive on the road and Patterson could still hear the gassy wheeze of the recycling truck as it stopped and started on its rounds in a nearby street.

His toe knuckle skin was beginning to chafe. Patterson had washed his socks earlier that morning and had hung them on a branch to drip dry just before Hammond had happened upon his hideout. The socks were still sopping wet by the time the flames had begun to lick out of the old fifth wheel and so Patterson's bare toes were now curled and pinched inside the boots he had taken from Jacob Hammond before he'd watched the sucker's skin crisp and bubble like a pig's on a spit. The guy had small feet but the discomfort would be worth it to put the canines off his spoor should they decide to get dogs out tracking him.

Once he was in the truck, however, the issue of a scent

trail would be irrelevant – all that would lie between him and his ultimate freedom was the Malahat Pass, a treacherous stretch of road cut through the mountains between Victoria and the rest of Vancouver Island. The only route in or out and Patterson's final hurdle.

Patterson smiled as the truck peeped a response to its key fob and clunked open. Taking his place at the steering wheel, dropping the backpack onto the passenger seat, he felt a tingle of excitement at his good fortune. His bid for freedom was supposed to have taken much longer. He'd prepared himself for several weeks of survivalist living in the forest, always on his toes, never able to truly relax, outsmarting the authorities by remaining close to the prison, hiding in plain sight, instead of fleeing as fast as possible like other escapees.

It had taken years to turn his behaviour around, to paint a believable picture of himself as a religious nut, a reformed con seeking the ultimate forgiveness, penitent and worthy of parole. The key had been to ensure his placement in the Mochetsin Institute, a laughable excuse for a prison. He'd even been able to prepare himself there for his escape by watching programmes like Survivor Man, Bear Grylls and Man Tracker – none of which raised a flag of suspicion because the focus was preparing inmates for release, allowing them semi-freedom to acclimatize to the burgeoning world of conformity. But that world, a world where you work for 'the man', where people treat you like something tracked in on their shoes, where your ability to dominate is eradicated by the control imposed upon ex-cons by a pompous, superior society, didn't hold any appeal for Patterson.

Patterson found the ignition and turned the key. Nothing. He tried it again and again but was rewarded only with silence. The silence was frustrating in that the engine wasn't even attempting to tick over, no coughing of audible clues as to a mechanical malfunction. Patterson's work placement as an inmate at Mochetsin had been in a car detailing shop, a quality valeting service, and had nothing to do with the mechanical workings of vehicles but he felt confident that taking a look under the hood wouldn't be a complete waste of time.

The street was still quiet, quiet enough for a fugitive to pop the hood and take a look at the engine under it. Patterson could see nothing out of place so, leaving the hood up, he returned to the driver's seat and turned the key once more. Nothing. The dash was illuminated though and when he pushed the button on the stereo the unmistakeable mumbled monotone of 'The Boss' issued forth making Patterson all the more frustrated – the trip over the Malahat and along the desolate New Island Highway with Springsteen blasting in his ears was so appealing and yet lay irritatingly out of reach. Patterson punched the steering wheel. The battery wasn't dead. There were no warning lights on on the dash, why wouldn't the piece of shit truck start?

Patterson took another look at the engine, fiddling with it as best he could by unplugging things, blowing on the connectors and replacing them. The dipstick showed a healthy level, there was sufficient water and coolant, even screen wash. Reaching his extent of mechanical knowledge, Patterson dropped the hood. He checked the sky above the trees, so far there was no sign of smoke from his fifth-wheel pig roast, but he knew it wouldn't take long for the fire to consume the ancient, pre-retardant innards of the trailer and send up thick plumes of toxic black.

He looked at the idle truck, his comfortable escape wagon; the grill grinned at him gleefully enjoying this bitter plot twist.

"Fuck!"

It was time for him to act. He'd irreparably damaged his hideout, raped and murdered a corrections officer and now he was exposed with no means of escape but two screwed up feet festering in size ten boots. Reaching over the centre console, grabbing the backpack from the passenger seat, Patterson twisted the key again, a trickle of hope teased him with a fantasy of the truck rumbling into life for him. The truck was dead. Patterson slammed the door shut and kicked it hard, dinting the panel and further chafing his ready to blister toes.

"Having trouble?"

Patterson turned to see an elderly man at the end of a drive in the act of retrieving his empty recycling tub. Patterson's heart pounded, he held up a hand hoping the gesture would nip the unwanted interaction in the bud but it seemed that kismet was enjoying its reversal and had made an illegal u-turn, determined to conspire against Patterson as the cardiganed codger started across the street to him.

"You need a jump?"

Patterson glanced about him, checking for other witnesses, twitching curtains or more Stepfordesque suburbanites eager to help.

"Na, I'm good."

Patterson dipped his head and headed to the rear of the pickup. It was time for him to vamoose.

"Say, I got leads," the approaching man called to Patterson as he retreated.

Patterson took off, too aware of the bundled twelve-gauge hanging from the bottom of the rucksack. He would be loath to kill the man, not out of a sense of empathy but more because it would draw attention to his whereabouts and would probably lead to an intensified search resulting in his demise. Picking up his pace, Patterson was ready to dart through the palisade again but hoped to steer clear of the native land now he'd torched a section of it. He looked back at the wannabe hero and saw that he was looking into the cab.

"Hey Buddy? You left your keys!" the man called.

Patterson walked on faster still as the man called out to him, something about an ignition device? It didn't matter, he had to get away fast if he had any chance of finding somewhere new to lie low for a few days. He had to disappear and so into the woods he dipped, through the trees, across creeks and up into the hills in search of a new hide.

CHAPTER 33 - THE MAIL MAN

Lunch was eaten at a patriotically umbrellaed picnic table outside the Mochetsin Café and as Ali watched the comings and goings of a surfeit of happy patrons she mused upon the fact that the establishment, free of any local competition, could only expect a better income if it was printing its own money.

It seemed that Marlene knew every one of the customers by name. Ali remained happily and anonymously excluded under the red and white hued light of the umbrella. The superficial niceties bandied across the lawn between their table and the pathway leading from the carpark to the café entrance epitomized the kind of light chit-chat Ali had always fallen short of perfecting.

Although her appetite had been satiated twenty minutes since, Ali speared the meaty shrimp, profuse and abundant within the varied leaves of a salad big enough to split four ways and still satisfy all four members of her family with scraps left over for the dogs. Canadian dining etiquette left much to be desired. Empty or no longer required plates were removed by eager bussers regardless of whether the entire table had finished eating whereas in Britain it was bad form for anything to be removed from a dining table until the last fork was laid to rest alongside the last knife, placed diagonally across the empty plate in the 'twenty past four' position.

Marlene had everyone in her crosshairs and it didn't take

Ali long to realize that her superficial jollity was a charade to disguise the cunning detective she fancied herself to be. In the same breath as she issued a fond farewell to a passersby, Marlene would turn to Ali and confer on the possibility that they harboured murderous intent regardless of any and all defining characteristics. Twice Ali had to reel Marlene in and remind her that they were on the hunt for a man capable of carrying a dead body some distance either up or down a sloped trail – the general demography of the café's customers being couples old enough to have conceived Ali whilst in their thirties, ruled all of Marlene's recent suspects out.

"Do you know, I can't remember a single suspicious death in Mochetsin, never mind an actual murder before." Marlene said before crushing the last of her red snapper wrap into her mouth.

"That's not to say there hasn't been a murder or a suspicious death," said Ali. "Sometimes people do get away with murder, you know. Especially in an ageing community like this, when someone who was already ill dies, or when someone seventy or eighty years old dies, flags of suspicion aren't necessarily raised."

Marlene swallowed and licked at her teeth as she looked at Ali, "I suppose you do get cynical in a job like yours."

"It's not cynicism, it's realism. Probability. Statistics. Human nature, I'm afraid. Crime rates rise with the population, the more people, the more deviance and the higher likelihood there is of major crime being committed."

"So, where you come from there must be a lot of crime, huh?"

Ali nodded. "It played a significant role in our decision to leave the U.K."

"Because of all the cases you'd worked on?"

"No, actually the deciding factor was the growing youth culture problem. Gangs of kids kicking a father to death in front of his children just because he dared to tell them to stop jumping on his car or setting fire to his bins or shoving fireworks up cats' arses, whatever the reason, doesn't matter, the papers were littered with stories like it every day. It's a very scary situation and our kids were just young enough not to have gotten themselves involved with the wrong kind at school…"

"The wrong kind?"

"It does sound snobby, I know, but believe me when I say there *is* a wrong kind and there's a lot of that kind in every bloody school and outside every local shop – those rare shops that managed to survive the recession, that is. David and I faced different worries to those of our parents when we were teenagers. They were only worried about smoking, drink, drugs and pregnancy. We had to worry about anti-social behaviour orders, men in transit vans kidnapping, raping and torturing our kids, sick fucks walking into nursery schools and shooting our babies as they practiced their ABCs never mind the very real possibility that they would end up part of a gang of thugs with no compunction whatsoever about stamping on the skull of a man trying his best to protect his family."

"Why here?" asked Marlene.

"Canada? Its beauty. It's not overpopulated, crime statistics are good. It's peaceful, the air is fresh and unpolluted. It has a national health service and everything is covered if you can wait the agonizing first few years of poverty and luck that it takes to find a job offering benefits. But mainly, it was the nature that called to us, the eagles, the whales, the bears – so long as I don't encounter one eating from my trash."

"So, here you are, in paradise and then this happens."

Ali nodded and remembered a fitting quote by John Bunyan: "Then I saw that there was a way to Hell, even from the gate of Heaven."

"Big human trafficking area though, you know, the Pacific Northwest? I watched a Nightline programme all about it just last Christmas." Marlene picked snapper from between her two front teeth with her pinkie nail.

"There's no escaping the human propensity for evil, Marlene. No matter where you hide, sooner or later it's going to stare you right in the face."

"You have to admit *that* is cynical."

Before Ali could respond, Marlene's attention was diverted across the street to the corner store,

"Ooh, ooh, ooh, look, there's Carter."

A skinny, shaven-headed man wearing a postal worker's uniform was exiting the store carrying three boxes in his arms.

"Carter? Carter Burrows?" asked Ali, the name ringing a bell of recognition. "He's on our list, isn't he?" Ali watched the man struggle to open the back of his small cargo van, a magnetic Canada Post car topper on the roof, and place the parcels inside.

"Carter!" called Marlene, holding her hand up high. "Bless him, he might not hear me, he has hearing trouble. Head injury. Yoohoo! Carter!"

Marlene's shrill call carried across the road, Carter turned. He looked at Marlene for a moment before he recognized her. Carter closed the rear of his van and dropped his keys, allowing them to dangle from a chain attached to his belt. Eyes on the pavement, Carter stepped up to the curb and stood, feet together like a child who had recently been taught the green-cross-code. He checked for traffic carefully, twice in each direction, before appearing to stall. He concentrated hard on taking his first step. Once in the street, however, he picked up his pace and walked in a comically fast manner reminiscent of a 1920s over-cranked film.

"He just does the Mochetsin route on Tuesdays and Thursdays. It's part of a community outreach programme. Linda McNicholl, our actual postie, is getting on a bit and so she arranged, along with Canada Post and whatever authority it is that oversee Carter's welfare, for him to take her route twice a week and deliver any parcels dropped at the store. It's very good for him. Keeps him motivated."

If Marlene hadn't already informed Ali of Carter's head

injury she could have easily deduced that he suffered from neuromotor problems. She noticed an almost imperceptible reluctance in his right leg – not a limp but a slight delay in response – his left brain had been injured, the synapses were firing but communication between the brain and the effector neurons in the spinal cord were diminished, explaining his concentrated delay when stepping into the street. He also held his head at a peculiar angle, cocked slightly to the left, sometimes indicative of damage to the sound receptors in the effected portion of the brain as a result of severe traumatic injury or even concussion.

Carter reached their table, dipped his head under the skirt of the umbrella and smiled down at Marlene with yellowed teeth, gapped and short, a common tell of those who'd suffered childhood neglect and malnutrition. He reached out a sinewy arm and shook Marlene's hand.

"Hi Mrs McKean."

Marlene took his hand in both of hers and patted the back of it, pulling him down to sit on the bench next to her. "Come sit, Carter. I want you to meet a friend of mine. This is Ali. Ali Dalglish."

Carter's eye contact with Ali was fleeting and timid. He spoke to Marlene, "555 Alder beach Road, V9C 4AB."

Marlene laughed and patted Carter's shoulder, "That's right." She smiled at Ali. "No-one's safe with this one around, eh Carter?" She placed her finger gently on his forehead, "He's like our very own rain man, never forgets a name or an address, do you, Carter?"

Carter shrugged bashfully. "Nope."

"Hi Carter," said Ali.

Carter looked at Ali once and then away. He looked at her hands and away again before daring to finally meet her eyes. Ali smiled her kindest smile and held her hand out to him. So boyish was his manner that the manly hair on his knuckles and forearms were a contradiction, his handshake was flaccid but his fingernails were neatly trimmed and very clean, Ali could smell the faint miasma of hand sanitizer on them. Maybe he was beleaguered by more than faulty neurons, maybe his dysfunctional childhood had resulted in the manifestation of many dysfunctions in him, obsessive compulsive hand washing? Misfiring synapses? Carter was a mass of nervous ticks and flinches and seemed relieved to pull his limp fingers from Ali's palm. Ali felt embarrassed on behalf of Marlene for her perception of Carter as a funny jester, an entertaining *Rain Man* parlour act.

"Now Carter, we've been looking for you all day." Marlene's condescension was relentless. "Ali and I are doing a very important job and we might just need a little bit of help from you."

"Me? Why?" Carter patted his buzz-cut hair above his left ear and Ali noticed the pinched, white skin of an old scar which stretched from above his ear all the way back and behind it.

"Well, now…"

Marlene was interrupted by a loud, ululant wail like a World War II air raid siren. Carter stood up looking towards the source of the alarm, his head skimming under the umbrella skirt and, with excitement sparkling in his eyes, he turned back to Ali and declared, "David got a fire call!"

CHAPTER 34 - IT'S NOT CARTER

David was driving the lead in Battalion 1, the white-helmeted chief was in the passenger seat, on his radio. Engine 6 and Tender 5 were in pursuit. David pulled up at the junction of the Mochetsin Road and spotted Ali at the picnic table with Marlene and Carter, nodded to her and turned right out of the junction speeding out of view, lights blaring and sirens parping.

Carter was evidently enthralled and waved to each fire truck as it passed.

"I wonder where they're off to?" said Marlene.

Carter turned and began to walk away.

"Wait. Carter?" said Ali. Carter turned to look at her. "You said 'David got a call.' You know my husband, David?"

"I know everyone." He turned to Marlene. "You wanna see where they're going, right? I'll find out for you."

"You do that, hon." Marlene smiled as she watched Carter head over the grassy meadow which lay between the café and the fire hall.

Ali was confused. "Where's he going?"

"Oh, Carter is obsessed with fire trucks, fire halls, all things fire. Loves the sirens," explained Marlene. "He's a staple part of all the departments around here from Bear Mountain to Glandford, Sooke and his favourite, of course, ours."

"And he's going to find out what the call was? How is he

going to do that exactly?"

"In the radio room of course, see the printout."

"Doesn't that strike you as weird?"

"Weird? No." Marlene seemed baffled for a moment. "Wait. You can't really think that Carter could have done it. Oh my, Ali. I only let his name stay on the suspect list as a joke, hon, until you met him. It's Carter. He's a sweetheart."

Ali didn't respond but watched Carter all the way to the fire hall as he disappeared inside it.

"Ali! Carter Burrows wears velcro runners because he can't tie his own shoes! There is no way he can be a serious suspect. You just finished lecturing me on being suspicious of anyone unable to carry a body on that trail – even if he was capable of murder, he would never be capable of that, he can barely cross the street." Marlene's jowls trembled as she squeezed out her impassioned defence.

"He gives me the creeps." Ali stated the fact unapologetically with a nonchalant shrug.

Marlene stared walleyed at Ali as she wiped her hands on her red paper napkin. "That's not very nice. In fact, I think you're being a bit mean."

"I'm not being mean. I'm telling the truth. He's creepy, and it has nothing to do with his disabilities."

"You sure about that?" Marlene stood and pulled her handbag onto her shoulder, taking a wad of flyers out of it. She handed half to Ali. "Here, you put some under wipers in the carpark, I'll see if they'll put some up inside."

"Have I upset you?" Ali asked.

"No," Marlene lied.

Ali stood. "I have, haven't I?"

Marlene looked at Ali. "I thought we were on the hunt for a vicious killer, a murderer, not a witch hunt. Carter's an innocent. He's been bullied and victimized all of his life."

Ali bit the end of her tongue, now was not the appropriate time for one of her acerbic truths. She fought the temptation to tell Marlene that her own treatment of Carter was bullying with a friendly face.

"Marlene, if we do manage to work out who was responsible, the likelihood of that person being someone you already know, maybe even someone you like, is very real. Our suspects are all Mochetsinites."

"Charlie Chaud is one thing, even Labreque or Ed or that prison worker but not Carter. I shouldn't have let him be on the list, it wasn't even funny in the end anyway."

"Okay, look, forget it. Carter's off the list. Done. Okay?"

Marlene managed a hint of a smile. "Come on, we still have to get these out there and then get to Christine and Robert's place."

Although they shared a smile, Ali could tell she'd crossed a line with Marlene as she watched her enter the café. She felt a wave of depression, noticeable because of its unusual infrequency since she and Marlene had teamed up on their quest, crest upon her heart. Ali deeply regretted her unerring ability to say and do things that repel people. Of course it made sense that friction would happen, their bond wasn't a naturally built one; it was fused in crisis under extraordinary circumstances and while their time together had almost been fun thus far, underneath the veil of companionship was, had to be, a base of determined motivation on Ali's part – the very real and very urgent hunt for a monster. Ali wondered if their friendship – one she had grown to truly enjoy – would survive the task ahead. She likened their dynamic to that of a bridezilla and the bridesmaid who would never speak to her again once the reception was over such was the bride's display of egomania and self-absorption on the run up to the wedding.

What was worse, Ali was already diluting her style of working in consideration of carrying Marlene along on the ride. Although, doing so had actually proven to be beneficial during the process of oiling the hinges and scraping off the rust from her neglected skill-set. By having to explain her thinking, her theories and deductions as she went Ali had been able to gently wade into what so often became a turbulent, tempestuous sea, to wade and paddle and now tread water, toning her muscles and strengthening her lungs in readiness for long unchartered depths. Once Ali did have a lead, and she would find that lead, she would become lost in it, focused and determined. Ali was a tenacious seeker of evil and she sought that evil no matter what the cost. It was the reason she had had to step away from her job so many years ago because it was an all-or-nothing scenario. How could she possibly have the needs and wants of her family in mind when that mind was so singularly intent upon the grimmest of quests?

As Ali placed the last of her flyers on a windshield, Marlene was trotting along the café's pathway to her. Happily, Ali noticed that Marlene's previously serious demeanour had made way for her signature exuberance.

Suddenly Carter appeared, his white ankle socks took turns emphasizing the quickness of his short stride. As he neared, Marlene sent Ali a brief look and Ali took it for what it was: a silent warning. The atmosphere altered somewhat as if Marlene had conjured a protective bubble of maternal defence around herself and Carter, a bubble that Ali felt excluded from.

"Mrs McKean? Structure fire. On the reserve." Carter nodded, taking a big gulp of air to regain his spent breath, clearly proud of himself as he relayed the information.

"Oh thank you, hon. Here," she handed him a flyer, "you be sure to be there now, we need your help, don't forget." Marlene patted Carter's shoulder and led the way to the car, leaving Carter frowning at the yellow sheet.

Marlene reversed out of the parking spot. "There won't be much left of it."

"Huh?" asked Ali.

"The structure. They have to get permission you see, from the native band, to go onto the land and put the fire out."

"That's crazy."

"Tell me about it."

Marlene tooted her horn to an only mildly distracted

Carter, still engrossed in the words upon the flyer, as they passed him by.

"Can he read?" asked Ali.

Marlene tutted and glared at her. Ali held her hands up, pleading innocence.

"I'm serious. He looks like he's struggling, that's all."

"Of course he can read. He's a bit slow not stupid. He's a mailman for God's sake. How'd you think he memorizes all that stuff? And he drives. You can't get your 'L' if you can't read the test, can you?" Marlene yielded for a car and followed it out onto the Mochetsin Road.

In the interest of self-preservation, Ali decided to divert the topic of conversation away from Carter Burrows. "So, Dr Labreque's house then?"

"Yup," said Marlene who was doing at least thirty-five kilometres an hour.

Ali must have *really* pissed her off.

CHAPTER 35 - CUZZOCREA NEEDS ALI

The deeply-shadowed trail provided Cuzzocrea with welcomed cool tranquillity, shelter from the sun and from the vicious whip of admonishment he'd been lashing himself with ever since Munro's text concerning Jacob frigging Hammond – a pain in the butt distraction he did not need.

The tail end of a strip of police tape, still tethered to the bark of a nearby tree, clapped in the wind, a quaver to the sea's adagio, and served as a prod which pulled his mind back to the pertinent matter each time it drifted to dwell upon his own doubt and his strange yet undeniable preoccupation with the Dalglish woman.

Three days ago this patch of the Alder Beach Trail had been abuzz with police activity. Floodlights had been stationed at three points to illuminate the ground upon which the dead body of a young woman, exposed in every way, had lain lifeless. Cuzzocrea recalled wishing a similar fate upon Trina Walsh, the VIIMIS's head of forensics, at the time as she'd adamantly claimed the site as her territory well into the early hours of Tuesday morning, vehemently barking at any of the team who dared to step near the ground surrounding the corpse, subject of her keen, squirrelly style of evidence gathering.

Cuzzocrea's analysis was almost complete but a lone visit, free of anyone wearing a white forensic coverall and bootees, to the site where victim and perpetrator had shared their last moments together was a crucial part of his process and always managed to imbue him with a more focused sense of the subject, as if in the ether of the site there remained an essence of the killer, of his innermost drives and wants.

Cuzzocrea knew him. He had known him for a while. Not just since his very first visit to this, the shallowest of graves, but earlier, an older knowledge. The defining difference between a conventional detective and a criminal analyst had less to do with evidence and more to do with an intrinsic understanding of the darkest possibilities, the odious depths of the most sinister minds.

The killer had left the victim here to be found, not because he is careless; he isn't careless. Not because he is a rookie; he's killed many, many times before. And not because he cared that she should be laid to rest somewhere beautiful; for he is incapable of kindness. He left her here, displayed her here. He was testing the police. Taunting VIIMIS and so Cuzzocrea began to understand his drives, his wants. VIIMIS must have missed him before, must have been on his tail. He would have enjoyed watching them puzzling over his work, basked in the glory of outwitting them. That attention, his glory, must have been taken away at some point in the past. Was it a case that had been overlooked in some way? Handed over to regular police? A cold case, perhaps?

Here, with the effluvium of the killer's evil being absorbed transdermally into him, Cuzzocrea became sure of three things: the decapitated body of a woman, washed up on the Sooke shores two years ago, had been a victim of the same killer; to avoid the disappointment of his work being overlooked once more, he will kill again; and Ali Dalglish would be the one to find him. Hopefully before that happened.

CHAPTER 36 - THE HAYLOFT

Sirens blared to the west. Patterson scrambled into a shallow, leaf-filled ditch like a fox avoiding the screaming herd of beagles.

He panted, no longer aware of the skinned toes that had so recently stung with his own sweat as he'd humped at a pace through the woods and up the valley, avoiding yards and steering clear of dwellings as best he could.

The sirens were distant but close enough for him to conclude that they were heading in the direction from whence he came.

He pushed himself up the embankment. To remain still, unsheltered at any point would not serve him well. He scrambled, pulling at brambles and thistles and nettles, oblivious for now to their venomous pricks. He climbed higher, his lungs clenching, burning.

Finally there was a barn, neglected and partially collapsed in on one side of the roof. He nestled himself against an abutment on the barn wall to rest and to quell the throb of his hot blood.

Eyes wide, Patterson listened as the siren became less of a keening wail and slipped away through a sorrowful, anticlimactic lament into silence.

He stood out from his hiding place and looked over the valley he had scaled. In the distance he saw a black cloud rising through the distant trees of the native reserve. The fire. The sirens must have been the fire trucks in response to it.

Patterson laughed as quietly as he could and blew out the contents of his sticky nostrils. Of course police on the hunt for him, had they been notified of his presence by the woollen vested do-gooder on Cedar Avenue, would hardly signal their advance by blaring their sirens for him.

Still, once that blaze was tackled, the fire-dicks'd call the cops and then the hunt would be on. They'd probably canvas the area, they speak to the old guy, they'd put two and two together fast enough and then they'd get the dogs out.

Patterson had to find somewhere to hide. Somewhere nobody would stumble across him — God knows he didn't need another Hammond walking up on him. He stepped out from behind the barn. It was one of two buildings on an overgrown property. He looked up at the barn to a pair of doors, doors leading to nothing but a break-neck fall — a hayloft. If he could get up there he'd have a hideout and a birds-eye view of the valley. Peace and quiet enough to safely lay low, overnight at least.

CHAPTER 37 - CHRISTINE'S APOCALYPSE

The tension between Ali and Marlene had finally dissipated once Christine started leading them onto her rear deck – the site of the infamous hot tub swinger gatherings.

Christine had ushered them onto floral-cushioned patio chairs before returning indoors to prepare coffees. Marlene was full of mischief and pulled Ali by the arm to the hot tub, lifting the blue vinyl cover.

"Go on, touch it. I dare you."

"No fucking way. Not after what you told me goes on in there." Ali took a step back.

"I know. You could probably get pregnant just by smelling it." Marlene giggled. Not satisfied with mere threats, she reached into the tub and splashed a handful of water at Ali who jumped back to avoid it, knocking over a planter full of lavender.

"Fuck!" said Ali. "You're like a bloody kid, Marlene."

Ali and Marlene scrambled to clean up the mess they'd made; Ali scooping up handfuls of soil and Marlene pressing the plant back into its pot. Christine arrived with a tray of coffee and after-dinner mints.

"I'm afraid we knocked your planter over, Christine." Marlene's apology struck Ali as insincere.

"Oh, don't mind that. Robert's jet-washing on Saturday morning anyway. Here, come sit." Christine placed the tray on the glass-topped coffee table as Marlene took the chair next to Christine and Ali the one opposite.

"We were just admiring the hot tub," said Marlene. "Lovely model, where'd you get it?"

"Barton's on the Sooke Road." Christine poured coffee into all three mugs. "It's the deluxe model, of course. Cup holders, lights, music and custom cedar steps. Cream?" Christine asked Marlene.

"Hmm, and one sugar thanks," she replied.

Christine looked at Ali, eyebrows raised in question.

"Same. Please," said Ali.

"It's a big one. Lights? Under the water?" asked Marlene.

"Oh yes. The colours change in time with the music. Top of the range." Christine stirred the coffees.

"I bet you can get a few people in there, eh?"

"We do have some fun hot-tub parties, that's for sure."

Ali rubbed her lips together to suppress her amusement. Coffee served, Christine sat back into her chair and crossed her legs.

"The more the merrier, that's our philosophy. Actually this weather is supposed to hold through the weekend so Robert and I are having a little get together tomorrow night." Christine sipped her coffee. "You're welcome to come along if you're free and if you promise to actually stay past eight thirty this time."

Marlene choked mid-swallow. Coughing, red-faced, to clear her lungs of liquid, it was several seconds before she was able to respond.

"I can't, sorry. I have a drum session on Friday."

Ali sensed, due to Christine's deliberate avoidance of eye contact with her, that the invitation didn't extend to her.

"You play the drums?" Christine's question was more of an accusation of deceit.

"Not drums as in a rock band," Marlene explained, patting her recovering chest. "Shamanic drums, a drumming circle. Our shaman, Colin, has a moose hide powwow and the rest of the group have mostly deer skin ones, mine is horse and cedar."

"How interesting." Christine was insincere. "I can't say I

condone the practice. Robert and I are supporters of PETA."

"Well don't go round to Ed Dunlop's today then," said Marlene. "He's butchering a deer as we speak."

"Slightly different," scoffed Christine. "Killing a deer for food is entirely incomparable to killing one so you can stretch the poor thing's pelt over a drum."

"What rubbish Christine. First of all, all of the animal is used and then it is meditated upon, thanked and worshiped. It's an ancient and noble process and I can assure you that none of the dead beast's bits end up with ice burn at the back of a chest freezer in someone's garage. Oh, by the way, nice leather shoes. I suppose it's okay to skin an animal for footwear is it?"

Christine smiled, knowing she had managed to rile Marlene. "Clothing, food, shelter – all necessary parts of human existence, so yes. Drumming? Not so much."

An uncomfortable silence followed. Ali sipped her coffee as Christine and Marlene made a point of looking in different directions, making a childish show of ignoring each other.

"This coffee's nice." Ali broke the silence in an attempt to inspire a ceasefire. Christine turned her eyes to Ali and stared at her as if she were an insolent child who had chirped in on a private adult conversation.

With a sour expression, Christine spoke to Ali, "Kicking Horse. Cafetière blend."

Another silence ensued until Marlene, clearly swallowing her pride for the sake of the purpose of their visit, relented. "Robert at the surgery?"

"Mmm." Christine confirmed smugly. Ali wondered if her arrogance was because her husband was at his surgery or as an acknowledgement of one-upping Marlene by having her back down first. Ali concluded that Christine probably carried with her an air of smugness regardless and wondered why the two women ever chose to spend time in each other's company at all.

Christine turned her gorgonesque gaze to Ali once more. "So, Ali? I've yet to see you at a pod meeting."

Ali, beginning to feel like an insolent child, fumbled an excuse. "No. I...ah...I prefer to keep myself to myself."

Christine's head nodded on the end of her neck like a mean bobble-head. "All well and good until you need a water rescue and shelter following a catastrophic event."

Marlene groaned, "Oh Christine."

And the air between the women transformed from mere awkwardness into the charged tension usually a prequel to physical violence. Ali jumped in her seat as Christine slammed her cup onto the coffee table with such venom it was a wonder the glass hadn't shattered.

"It's coming Marlene, mark my words. And it's about time you and Peter stopped burying your heads in the sand about it. Preparedness, Marlene. Preparedness will be the key to survival."

Marlene turned to Ali, "Christine is of the belief that *the big one* is coming." Marlene punctuated the big one with rabbit-ear fingers on her free hand.

"The big one?" Ali just had to ask, the tête-à-tête was proving to be better entertainment value than half-price-cinema-Tuesdays (in her opinion, Canada's very best invention).

Marlene explained: "An earthquake big enough to split Vancouver Island in two and send it the same way as Atlantis."

Christine huffed. "A slight exaggeration."

"I'm the exaggerator here? That's a good one." Marlene laughed.

"It wouldn't *sink* us, that's just silly. It would break us up into a cluster of smaller islands." Christine turned to Ali and continued, "Studies have proven that it isn't just a possibility, it's a guarantee. Just a matter of time. And if you happen, geographically speaking, to be situated on one of the gigantic fissures that open up...well...it's goodnight. *But* if you do survive the initial quake and the tremendous aftershocks, then you'd need to be prepared for absolute chaos – tsunamis, injuries, disease, a complete breakdown of infrastructure, the displacement of thousands of people. The northern half of the island would be completely cut off from civilization…"

"Except by boat from the mainland which would take like twenty frigging minutes – grizzly bears swim it for God's sake. Christine, you're more dramatic than that science guy in the film with The Rock, what was it? *San Andreas*." Marlene interjected.

"Oh, the movie about the very fault line upon which we are bold enough to perch? Marlene, I have done extensive research on this matter, as you know. This isn't fiction, I'm not just making it up. I'm prepared, not just to survive but to help others in the aftermath. You should be too."

"Oh twaddle! Ali, pay no mind to her hyperbole, we'll all be dead and long gone *if* it ever happens but we are far more likely to have destroyed the Arctic tundra and melted the polar icecaps with our belching pollutants first, rendering earthquakes a thing of legend since we'll all be living on rafts like Kevin Bacon in another silly movie."

Ali suspected Marlene had meant to say Kevin Costner in reference to his post-apocalyptic ocean-based flop but refrained from participating in the debate as the two women stared daggers at each other.

Christine straightened her blouse and added a further snide remark, "I didn't realize you were an expert seismologist, Marlene."

"That's funny 'cause I realized that you *aren't* one a long time ago."

"So you guys must be really prepared then," Ali said to Christine, "for when the big one hits."

Christine's eyes narrowed defensively as she considered Ali, "Yes. Yes we are."

"So food, water?"

"Medical supplies, fuel, generators, pumps, tools, clothing and blankets. Our boat, of course. And a lot more besides.

We collect all sorts of things, donated primarily by pod members — the ones who actually take an interest in the welfare of their community, that is, but then you prefer to keep yourself to yourself."

Christine's manner was flat-out contentious and Ali was slapped in the face by the blowhard's gall; she felt her inner troll stir and would've liked nothing more than to humble the arrogant bitch. However, Ali employed an otherwise uncharacteristic level of restraint, mindful of her cause. Marlene raised her eyebrows to Ali, perhaps impressed but more likely disappointed by Ali's self-control.

"Where do you store it all?" Ali asked as pleasantly as she could.

"Pardon me?" Christine asked.

Marlene seamlessly picked up on Ali's line of inquiry, "Yes, where d'you guys keep all that stuff?"

"In the coach house, you passed it on the way in," Christine responded.

"Coach house? You mean that shed by the gate?" Marlene snorted.

Christine gave a false laugh, her eyes were not amused. "Hardly a shed, Marlene, it's a double garage with a fully-equipped rental suite upstairs."

Marlene turned to Ali and gave her a sly wink. "There's no way you have a full suite in that little thing Christine."

"I assure you there is a suite and it's actually very nice. We remodelled it in ninety-seven, thank you very much." Christine stuck her sizeable chest out.

"Oh I think this is another one of your exaggerations. Ali you have to watch this one for that."

Christine stood. "Clearly, Marlene, the purpose of your visit was to decry my views, upbraid me with your vitriolic criticisms and generally vex me so if you don't believe me, not that I have anything to prove, then why don't you take a look at the coach house for yourself…on your way out?"

Christine took Marlene's mug from her hands and placed it on the tray. She cleared her own mug and Ali was quick enough to take the hint by putting hers alongside it before it could be snatched from her by the hag – an action that would have surely forced Ali to obey the snarling troll within.

"I must get on. Lots to do and less time to do it now I'll be attending an impromptu memorial for a girl I've never met as well as having to sweep up the dirt on my deck. I must say, Marlene, I am thrilled that you popped by."

On her way to her door, Christine threw a last, pitiable, Parthian shot over her shoulder, "Jealousy is a terrible thing you know. Most unbecoming," then swept into her house leaving Ali and Marlene to make their exit via the deck stairs leading to the lawn.

"What a horrible bitch," said Ali once they were in the car.

"Toxic. That's the word I always use when I think about Christine Labreque." Marlene three-point-turned the car to face their exit. "It's little wonder Robert has a wandering eye.'

"You really think she meant it, us taking a look in that coach house?"

"Oh yes, she's all about the look-what-I-have. Can you imagine being married to her?"

"I imagined ramming my fist back her throat when she was talking to me like that."

"I was shocked that you didn't, in all honesty."

"I only held back so that we could get information.'

"I know that. I, however, didn't hold back for the same reason." Marlene boasted.

"Genius move, by the way, using her own pride against her so we could look in her suite slash double garage."

On cue, Marlene pulled to a stop outside the wooden structure. "Here we are at Chateau Labreque's infamous *coach house*."

"Pompous git."

"Tell me about it, sister." Marlene said, much to Ali's amusement as they entered the building.

The downstairs area was home to a single-prop, silver fishing boat.

"Hardly a Bayliner. This isn't a double garage, at all. You can barely fit a pushbike in here with that thing." Marlene looked inside a selection of plastic-lidded crates. "She's praying for a disaster so she can lord it about – a self-appointed commander in chief – rescuing people who, once they found themselves safely in her vessel, would be looking for the nearest *fissure* to throw themselves overboard into. Honestly, I'd rather die than be indebted to her."

"There's no love lost between the two of you I see. Makes me wonder why she invited you to her party."

"Because she has a serious case of social-climberitis. She hates me because I'm more important and far more influential than her. It's not friendship – it's her keeping her enemies closer."

"But she has a lot to lose, with them being swingers. I'm sure that's something she'd rather keep from her pod members."

"You're kidding, they're not ashamed of it. They call it *a lifestyle*, like it's perfectly frigging normal. And she has the cheek to look down her nose at me for my drumming."

Ali picked up a screwdriver from a nearby workbench and held it up to Marlene. "Hey, Marlene? It would be a terrible shame if H.M.S. Labreque were to sink."

"Don't tempt me. Let's have a look at this amazing suite, shall we?"

Ali led the way up the stairs to an open-plan bedsit with a small kitchen area in the corner. The roof was open to the rafters and featured two skylights and, although the central passageway had plenty of headroom to the apex, the majority of floorspace was rendered unusable under the eaves.

"Very nice – for a family of munchkins," said Marlene. "You'd be okay," she added with a smile at Ali.

"So is this the only other building on their property, apart from the house?"

"They have a wood burning stove so there must be a

woodshed of some sort – maybe they call it the log retreat – apart from that, nothing."

"And Labreque's car is that red sporty thing."

"Yes, and don't we all know it when he races it up and down the street."

"But that boat's on a trailer. Does he have another car to tow it? A pickup maybe?"

"I think Christine has a hitch on her Escape. I know for sure they only have the two cars."

"Okay, so," Ali thought aloud as she descended the stairs followed by Marlene, "this place is clean, not soundproofed and close to the road. His car is entirely unsuitable. What about the house? Are you familiar with it?"

"Yes. It's level entry basement style. You enter at the front, there's the kitchen to the right, the lounge which leads to the deck then the ground drops away at the back. It's sloped so you go downstairs to the bedrooms which are on the basement level. If my memory serves me correctly there are three bedrooms down there. The master with an en suite and the other two rooms are Jack-and-Jill with one central bathroom between them. There's a laundry room down there which leads through to a storage area. I was in there once, last Mochetsin Day to borrow fairy lights for the bandstand."

"So this storage room?" asked Ali.

"The usual, there's a heat pump, boxes, Christmas decorations. It's not big. I can't clearly remember, though there could have been more to it. It would make sense if it ran the length of the house, so it is feasible that there was another part to it that I didn't see."

Ali was lost in thought, staring at the boat.

"What do you think then?" Marlene asked her.

"Can't say either way. We need to investigate further, that's for sure. We need to speak to Dr Labreque this evening, get a feel for him."

"You'll get a feel for him alright if you're not careful." Marlene headed out of the garage and pinched Ali's bum as she passed.

"Ow!" exclaimed Ali.

"Not just his eye that wanders you know."

"Oh my God, Marlene!" Ali said as an idea sprouted in her mind. "Your second moment of genius today."

Marlene spoke to Ali from across the car roof, "Really? Why? What did I say?"

"You're going to chat up the good doctor and get me invited to that party tomorrow night."

Marlene shook her head. "No. You don't want to go to one of their parties."

"Yes I do. It'll get me inside to explore that storage room."

"You remember what I told you about their parties, right? I don't know David well but I'm guessing he might be a little uncomfortable with a hot tub full of baggy pee-pees and old Dick – *literally old Dick*, Dick from the Esso station on The Parkway, he's a regular at their get togethers."

Ali laughed. "That's why I'm not taking David."

"You can't go alone; it'd be like a lamb to the slaughter."

"Precisely why you're going to come with me."

Marlene opened her mouth to respond but Ali held a finger up to stop her. "No arguments. You said you could get me in anywhere, remember? Before we started this whole thing? It's all in the line of duty, Marlene. All in the line of duty."

Giggling with glee, Ali got into the car leaving a drop-jawed, ashen-faced Marlene mulling over the prospect of her second 'slinger' party.

CHAPTER 38 - MUNRO'S DONE

Cuzzocrea paid no mind to the speed limit on the country road as he approached Cedar Avenue. Waiting for him when he arrived was his partner, Munro, looking even more clammy than usual, pacing the length of a Ford pickup. Cuzzocrea pulled up alongside his partner.

"Got your text. What's up?"

"Good news and bad – and before you ask, I'm giving you the good news first because that shit's only lasting a minute. Pull up over there."

Munro pointed to his Corolla, parked on the opposite side of the street, outside a house where an elderly gentleman was pretending to prune an azalea – pretending because his shears were merely snipping the thin air over the bush as the man rubber-necked his interest in the police presence on his street.

Cuzzocrea arrived at the pickup just in time to gulp a lung full of Munro's freshly sparked up smoke, reminding him of his nicotine- and alcohol-fuelled college years.

"So? What's the good news?"

"Mochetsin fire just managed to extinguish one hell of a conflagration – that's a big-ass fire according to their chief."

"And?"

"And…it was a trailer, Rey. The fifth wheel we found? Well once the fire was out, the remains of a man were discovered inside."

"Okay." Cuzzocrea was hopeful.

"Here's the good news, buddy." Munro pulled on his cigarette and gulped back the smoke, speaking on his exhalation, "The hunt for Patterson's over."

Cuzzocrea blinked, relief was his initial reaction but he noticed that Munro's clammy tension persisted. "And the bad news?"

"His boots – Patterson's boots? Prison issue with his number inside, that's what it's based on. They were outside the trailer, on the ground about six feet away. But you see this truck?"

"Yeah."

"This truck belongs to…"

Cuzzocrea knew the answer instantaneously "…Jacob Hammond."

"You got it."

"Fuck." Cuzzocrea ran his fingers through his hair and paced towards Munro's car and back again. "Tell me everything."

"So, when the call came in about Mochetsin responding to a fire on the Tsawataineuk land, it triggered alarm bells and I was just down the road at the prison so I headed up there. I got there as they'd discovered the boots and the R.C.M.P. were called. Not long after that, I got a call from a uni', he'd been called to an address on Cedar Avenue regarding a suspicious male."

Cuzzocrea glanced over his shoulder at the man who was now making no effort whatsoever to feign an interest in azaleas. "This guy?"

"Yep. Mr Luckinuk over there had an interesting interaction with a man who had no idea his truck was fitted with an ignition interlock device. When the guy ran away, Mr Luckinuk assumed that he'd been attempting to steal the vehicle and called nine-one-one. The description of the guy?"

"Patterson."

"You got it again, buddy, you are on fire!" Munro clenched his teeth in a grimace of nothing less than detest as he pointed his cigarette at Cuzzocrea's face then pulled it back and lit a new smoke with the ember of the old one before continuing, "You always know best Rey, don't you. You just fucking do this shit, do whatever you fucking want and the rest of us just drag our retarded-fucking-selves along. I told you that we should have come clean, we should have told Shaw, been upfront. Rey, we could have gotten a team here this morning and we could have prevented this. We could have gotten a team here, even without warrants, on the perimeter, and we could have stopped this from happening to Hammond."

"We don't know it's him. It could be Patterson."

Munro stared at Cuzzocrea incredulously. "Look, I'm not some hot-shot analyser with degrees from wherever, but I can tell you exactly what happened here and for once you're gonna listen. You thought it was a waste of your talent – and that's an actual fucking quote – to investigate Patterson's escape…"

"…because I wanted to focus on the girl."

Munro stepped up to Cuzzocrea, his fists clenched, his jaw tightened but he restrained himself as he caught a peripheral view of Mr Luckinuk and stepped back. "I told you to listen the fuck up, so listen the fuck up or I swear I will fuck you over. You drag me on an unwarranted search – not your first, by the way, because you just fucking know…you just *know*, Rey, don't you? You know Patterson's there, and guess what? You were right, we find a trailer, it fits with your estimation of his movements and with your voodoo fucking knowledge and so what do we do? Do we go through the appropriate channels? Do we redirect the search? Do we follow procedure, Rey? No! No because Rey fucking Cuzzocrea doesn't do appropriate, he doesn't wait for procedure, he's above that shit. So Rey fucking Cuzzocrea, in his infinite fucking wisdom calls a redneck with a record to do our dirty work for us."

"I did not send Hammond in, that isn't what I was doing."

"No? But you played one of your mind games with him, didn't you? One of those mind games you play with us *mere mortals*. Except this time it got someone killed because I'm willing to bet my pension — not that I'll be getting one if I'm dishonourably discharged — that the black, dripping corpse back there with a set of once pearly whites grinning out at me was not James Henry Patterson but Jacob fucking Hammond and you know what? His death is on you, Buddy, pure and simple."

Cuzzocrea felt his blood pool around his ankles and his knees sag. His head swam as he leaned against the truck, mindful still of evidence corruption yet unable to support his weight. His partner's empathy was not forthcoming. Munro chose instead to twist the knife he'd plunged.

"You know it's only a matter of time before they I.D. that body and I'd be neglectful of my duties if I didn't follow up on this line of enquiry." Munro motioned to the truck.

"I know."

"So here's what I'm going to do. I'm going to follow up, I'm going to do my job and I'm going to keep you out of this for as long as I can because — even though you're a selfish sonofabitch — I don't want this to be the end for you. But you need to come up with a plausible story once your number shows up on Hammond's call list. Fuck, Rey, you were probably the last person to speak to him."

"Not necessarily."

"Shut the fuck up and get out of here. I'll cover for you because that's what good guys do, they cover their partner's back. But if it turns, if it comes to it and there's a choice between my career and protecting you?"

Cuzzocrea looked at Munro as he stepped past. Munro spat on the ground near Cuzzocrea's feet, flicked his cigarette butt ahead of him and squashed it with his next step, heading for an excited Mr Luckinuk.

Cuzzocrea was suddenly envious of a simpler life, of a man like Luckinuk for whom such events brightened an otherwise monotonous day, events that had clawed a new darkness into Cuzzocrea's already bleak soul.

CHAPTER 39 - SHOW ME YOURS

After a few hours at home to shower, dress and saran-wrap meals for her family, Ali entered The Pioneer House just in time to witness Marlene in full-blown brown-nosing mode with Christine and Dr Labreque at the far end of the hall. She recognized the same unctuous charm Marlene had employed earlier in the day when they'd encountered the rat-drowning Charlie Chaud at his squalid abode.

Ali read the body language of the triumvirate from across the room and deduced that the doctor was the driving force behind the couple's swinger lifestyle – he as good as poked his bulging groin against Marlene when they shared a brief hug. Christine's rictus of false acceptance betrayed her underlying insecurity and jealousy – *a terrible thing, most unbecoming.*

Spotting Ali in the entranceway, Marlene laid a hand on Robert Labreque's elbow and began, quite obviously, to talk about her with him. The interlocutors all turned in unison to look at Ali. Marlene was clearly negotiating Ali's invitation as her 'plus one' tomorrow night. While Christine's visage portrayed her vaguely concealed distaste, Dr Labreque shot a slimy grin in Ali's direction. Ali's stomach tightened as unwelcome and grotesquely eidetic images of the man naked, pouring himself over her body, wormed their way into the forefront of her mind.

Ali snatched her head around to avoid the possibility of interaction and in the vain attempt to shake the images free.

She noticed Sandy, at a nearby table, setting up Marlene's sky lanterns.

"Hi sweet," Ali hugged her daughter from behind. Sandy squirmed from the embrace. "What's up?"

"Mum, I spent all day running round Glandford for your new BFF and now she's treating me like hired help. I have to build these stupid things."

"Hardly *build*, you only have to take them out of their packets."

Sandy was sullen. "If it's so easy, why don't you do it? I see that you've had time to get home and doll yourself up."

Ali looked down at her black Armani trouser suit – a relic of her former high-earning life which she'd found hidden amongst cardigans and body warmers in the back of her closet. She hated to admit it but for the first time in months she'd actually tried to look as good as possible. The worst part of it was that her motivation had been to impress someone other than her husband.

"Oh, Sandy, stop moaning. You are such a drama queen. It's for a good cause."

"If it wasn't for Carter I'd have been here all night with these stupid things."

Ali's heart stepped up a beat. "Carter?"

"Yeah, he's been putting the candles in."

Ali scanned the room. "Where is Carter?"

"He's gone to get us a coffee from Tim's."

"What?" Ali snapped.

Sandy turned to her mother, hands on hips. "Oh my God, Mum! Calm down – he's just a guy who offered to help me, it's not like I'm gonna date him."

The desire to throttle her daughter was rare but not entirely unusual when the teenager dared to square up to Ali. Ali resisted the desire to slap the stupid out of Sandy and opted instead to admonish her privately in a whispered tone, "Listen to me, Sandy. I'm going to tell you this only once – you stay away from that guy, you understand me?"

"Why? He's totally harmless. God, Mum, why don't you

just lock me up in a tower. Weirdo."

"How the hell would you know if someone is harmless or not?"

"Oh, I'm sorry I'm not some frigging professor of psychology. What? Just 'cause he's slow, he's dangerous? That's pathetic Mum."

"Sandy Dalglish, I am warning you, drop the attitude and straighten up your face. You're acting like a brat."

"No I'm not. *You're* acting like some crazy lunatic running round with little old ladies, like you and Marlene are Cagney and Lacey. Dad's right, you know, you are losing it again. You need help."

"What did you just say to me?"

Sandy blushed, realizing that she'd crossed a line. "Sorry."

"You bloody better be, lady. We are going to have words when we get home tonight."

"I didn't mean it, it just came out." Sandy's eyes watered.

"Get on with what you're doing. Where is your bloody father?" Ali couldn't see David in the room. Her temper was rising and her wrath was so intense that she couldn't care less if her signature head vein was throbbing.

"He's still at the hall. Mum, I'm so sorry, I didn't mean it, it's just that I'm so tired."

"Oh suck it up," Ali snapped before her maternal love swamped her frustration and forced her to suddenly forgive her daughter. "It's okay. Forget it. Look, you get home if you like, as soon as you're finished here. And I meant what I said about that Carter guy, you don't need to be rude but I do want you to keep your distance; you don't know him and you certainly don't know he's harmless. I met him earlier and I just felt that there was something…off…about him. Okay?"

Sandy nodded. Ali stepped away from the table. She could feel herself cracking. David's arrow of betrayal had struck true into her Achilles heel, empowering her already omnipotent enemy, an enemy she battled fiercely every day – her own mind.

Ali's hurt was thick, lumping in her throat. Ali tried to choke it back, her hands trembled as she reached for her phone. She knew she was coming apart, here, now. In a public place surrounded by people close to, but far worse than, strangers – people she lived near, people who would be only too quick to gossip and point and vilify if they were to witness her breaking down.

Fury was second only to humour as the most dependable weapon in Ali's arsenal but she felt bereft of both. Ali tried for anger but in place of its usual abundance was only a well, deep with anguish, where her heart should be.

The nastiest of her demons was replaying Sandy's words and had conjured for her the conversation David must have had with their daughter for her to have said such a thing; a cruel ridicule of Ali's diseased predicament from the very man who should be her champion, her protector. As the demon looped possible scenarios and hurtful images – David laughing with Sandy as they bitched about her, David gossiping with co-workers – Ali's bitterness multiplied and the bitterness brought with it a long-buried resentment harboured toward a husband who had once witnessed the signing of commitment papers with her name on them.

Ali's knees buckled under the pressure of the internal onslaught and a horribly familiar panic overwhelmed her as her lungs contracted and barred admittance to air.

Silver rain sluiced her vision as she donned a pretence of calm and walked out of Pioneer House, gasping as quietly as possible, desperately trying to force oxygen into her lungs. Her temples throbbed and felt like they were bulging as if trying to puke her thoughts from her brain. Fat, hot tears blurred her vision as she made it around to the back of the building just in time for her anxiety to clench a grip upon her already enervated spirit.

Vaguely aware of a presence – a man, tall, forceful, his hand slipping around her waist, pulling her to him – Ali's world spun from her as the perfect blue sky above her turned black.

...

Over a decade since his last smoke, Cuzzocrea had shamefully purchased a pack of Peter Jacksons and a disposable lighter from The Mochetsin Country Store on his way to the Pioneer House having left Munro to deal with Jacob Hammond's F150.

His pink lungs were repulsed by the intake of smoke and ferociously spewed its invasion causing a series of sharp, rasping coughs that prickled Cuzzocrea's airways and watered his eyes.

The cigarette was a metaphor for all his misjudgements over the past few days, his latest in a long line of bad ideas. Cuzzocrea was crushing the almost full-sized cigarette into the grass when Ali Dalglish had appeared from around the corner. He was about to say hello when he noticed that something was wrong with the woman. She wasn't so much walking as stumbling, her hands feeling their way along the wall like someone struck suddenly blind.

Cuzzocrea had wasted no time in getting to her, seeing that her face had the ashen pallor of someone about to pass out. He'd managed to scoop her to him just as she'd lost consciousness. It was merely a matter of seconds before her cheeks had pinked up again but with her face upturned to him, her head resting against his bicep, he was able to indulge himself in a private study of her archaically precise features – an indulgence he had desired and had denied himself since first meeting her, a preoccupation he could perhaps blame for his recent absence of mind.

The intimate, voyeuristic nature of the moment made him feel like a naughty child peeking through a keyhole. Holding her petite body against him was achingly exciting and yet he willed her eyes to open as much because he felt afraid – albeit irrationally – of being caught with her in his arms but more so because he didn't want the moment to be tainted as it would surely be if it were to be witnessed by a passing stranger, someone only marginally less understanding than he of the woman's strange magnetism.

With disappointment and relief in equal measure, Cuzzocrea watched her blink back to consciousness. An ambiguous expression veiled her face as she looked into his eyes and he was unable to determine whether her furrowed brow was an indication of confusion or anger.

"What the fuck?" said Ali Dalglish as she pushed herself from Cuzzocrea's chest to stand on her own two feet, allowing the man to determine that she was indeed angry.

...

Loss of control being her ultimate nemesis, Ali was able to tap into her arsenal after all and once she regained consciousness, once oxygenated blood pumped through her brain once more, she found herself in the arms of Inspector Cuzzocrea. She disguised her embarrassment with an act of defensive independence. Although she was compos mentis enough to appreciate that he had not only prevented a possible traumatic injury and that there were far worse places she could think of to find herself, her overwhelming reaction was one of shameful resentment.

"What happened?" she asked.

Cuzzocrea held a hand out to her, aware that she wasn't yet entirely steady on her feet. "You passed out."

"Shit."

"You need to sit down."

Ali acquiesced and lowered herself to the ground, leaning her back against the wall of Pioneer House. "What I need is a fag."

Cuzzocrea raised his eyebrows in amusement.

"A cigarette," explained Ali. "Not a fag – another cultural difference and one that could make me unpopular if I said it in a gay bar."

Cuzzocrea dropped his new pack of Peter Jacksons into

her lap as he joined her on the ground. "I knew what you meant," he said.

"You smoke?" asked Ali.

"Used to, in college."

"And now you just carry a pack around with you in case you happen upon damsels in distress with a nicotine addiction?"

"No, and I get the impression you don't often need rescuing." Cuzzocrea pulled his lighter from his pocket and lit Ali's cigarette.

"Bad day?" asked Ali.

"How'd you guess?"

"Usually what causes my nicotine relapses."

"And you? Bad day?" Cuzzocrea asked.

"How'd you guess?" Ali smiled and shook her head. "I am extremely embarrassed right now."

"Don't be. What happened?"

Ali was quiet as she as she ran through all of the truths she had no intention of sharing with him. "No idea. Skipped lunch, must be that."

"Okay."

His eyes met hers and the knowledge therein reminded Ali that Cuzzocrea was trained, as was she, to detect evasions of truth. She shrugged, the closest she was able to come to an admission of guilt. "Whatever. So, how long was I out?"

"A few seconds, five maybe."

"That's not so bad. I fell asleep on the tube once, in London, and I woke up with everyone around me laughing."

"Why? What did you do?"

"God knows. I got off at Tottenham Court Road and caught the next train."

"Maybe you were talking in your sleep."

"Or maybe I farted. That was my real fear."

Cuzzocrea laughed. "I don't think so."

"Oh please, why not? Because I'm a *lady*?" Ali used her poshest of voices, "And *ladies* do not pass wind."

"Really? You know for a genius, that's kinda dumb," said

Cuzzocrea.

Ali looked a question.

"Passing wind – as you put it – does come with a particular after effect that you would have been aware of," Cuzzocrea explained.

Suddenly Ali understood. "Damn! That is stupid of me. Do you know that I've wondered about that bloody tube ride for years and that never occurred to me? Inspector, you just solved the mystery of the sleeping woman on the train."

"Not really, you still don't know why the other passengers were laughing at you but I am glad that we can get off the subject of you farting."

Ali smiled. "Why? Would that freak you out?"

"It doesn't fit with the image I have of you in my mind."

Ali looked at him. "Well, if that image is of a genius who doesn't digest food then you have me on a pedestal from which I can only fall."

"I don't think so." Cuzzocrea looked away as the admission left his mouth.

After a moment, Ali saved him from his apparent embarrassment, "So what made your day bad enough to pick up where you left off on the cancer front?"

Cuzzocrea blew his cheeks out and rested his head against the wall. "I screwed up. Bad. Maybe."

"On the job?"

Cuzzocrea nodded.

"Official warning screwed up? Because you're talking to an expert in that particular field. I never met a boss I didn't piss off."

"I wish it were only that." Cuzzocrea looked at Ali, his eyes narrowed in a mock warning, "I don't want to talk about it."

"Bollocks." Ali narrowed her eyes right back at him. "I'm trained to read deceit too, you know. *All* you want to do is talk about it, to tell someone and purge your soul. I can see it in your eyes."

Cuzzocrea stood up and offered Ali his hand, "I'll make

you a deal, Mrs Dalglish, you tell me the truth about your anxiety attack and I'll tell you the truth about my screw up."

Ali allowed herself to be pulled from her place on the ground. "No deal. There is something I want you to tell me though."

"What's that?"

"The victim's time of death. I can't narrow down suspects without it."

"I'm surprised you haven't already deduced it to the nearest second."

"Inspector, I'm good but I'm not that good."

"What's your guess?" Cuzzocrea's eyes glittered with expectation.

"Sunday the eighth."

"Time?"

"Early morning, anywhere between eight and eleven, maybe?"

"Not bad. Our M.E. determined between five forty-five and eleven forty-five."

Ali thought for a moment. "You know, that might not even help, in terms of alibis."

Cuzzocrea nodded. "I thought the same thing. Because of the tetanus, I know. She could have, most probably did, die alone."

"Precisely. What you could do with is an approximate time on the cuts being made; they were inflicted post mortem. It'd be tricky though but not impossible."

"Well I showed you mine, now you show me yours."

"Inspector Cuzzocrea! That is a highly inappropriate suggestion."

"Your suspects. Your profile."

"Damn it." Ali joked, "Why would VIIMIS need a housewife's opinion on this investigation?"

"Not VIIMIS, me. And you're hardly a housewife – that's not pedestal talk, it's fact."

"So you did look me up then." Ali wondered about Cuzzocrea, wondered why he was humble enough to seek her help, to admit that he'd gone to the trouble of researching her and how he'd watched her have a panic attack yet acted like it was no big deal, taking it in his stride rather than holding it over her as proof of her weakness. "One condition. You don't call me Mrs Dalglish ever again."

"Sorry. Why?"

"Two reasons: it makes me feel old, and if I get my hands on my piece of shit husband any time soon I'll either be widowed or reverting back to my maiden name faster than goose shit slides through a tin horn."

"Wow, that's pretty fast. Okay, deal."

Cuzzocrea offered his hand and Ali shook it.

"Step into my office – otherwise known as Pioneer House – and we can start by having a few one-on-ones with some suspects," Ali said and remembered that she was still holding Cuzzocrea's cigarettes. She offered them back to him. Cuzzocrea refused them.

"Keep them. I'm rethinking the whole cancer thing," he said.

"Cool because I'm not. I've been rattling around this world causing trouble for entirely too long already," said Ali as she led the way back to the front of the building. Cuzzocrea followed.

CHAPTER 40 - SPIRITUAL CONTRACTS

Although Ali despised organized religion – the product of a less than happy union of a Protestant father and a Catholic mother – she did have a natural inclination towards a set of spiritual beliefs that resonated in the core of her being regardless of and contradictory to her naturally scientific brain and her educational background.

Rationally speaking, her spiritual vibration made no sense and veered towards mania, however, it was deeply and intrinsically hers – one of her many secrets. As such, Ali believed in the notion of spiritual contracts and the idea had allowed her a greater understanding and empathetic capacity for the otherwise random if not heinous acts of others.

Embracing the assumption that such contracts are entered into by the (yet-to-be-assigned a foetus meat-suit) soul, under the guidance of a source energy, a creator?, *perhaps* God, then it would be one's spiritual duty to honour the contract on the earthy plane for one's soul to advance and evolve. Within this theory one would interact with a small group of souls – all of the people one meets during their lifetime – as either a major or minor player in one another's individual spiritual contract.

Although a residual consciousness of the fact would be detrimental to the process and to the destined outcome of any previously agreed upon journey of learning, Ali believed that a fail-safe, atavistic knowledge is triggered at the moment one encounters someone imperatively central to one's contract – whether they, or you, are to play a positive or negative role in the experience, the intensity of feeling is determined and proportionately equal to the significance of the relationship – how pivotal the communion is with regards to the ultimate goal.

Just as one can feel love instantly, so can one feel hatred. It stands to reason that if it is possible to fall in love at first sight – to know without doubt that someone is to be your lover – it is therefore possible to feel the antithesis, an instinctive dread, and to know without doubt that someone is a mortal threat.

As Ali sat on a windowsill at the rear of The Pioneer House with Cuzzocrea next to her, she felt two undeniable truths itching in her soul. First, there was someone in the room who was so diabolical, with such evil that she knew undoubtedly that not only was he the killer of the girl on the trail but that his dark energy was so intrinsically linked to her that it was as if one could not possibly exist without the other, that the contract drawn up for each of them ended with the other's name. Second, and more chillingly, Ali had an instinct, a knowledge, a twinning with the man beside her. The effervescent bubbling of something terrifying existed between Cuzzocrea and herself – it was not malevolent, it had no dangerous undertone, it was exquisitely enticing and yet it repelled her more than the other evil because, spiritual contract or not, it was just as likely to reduce her life as she knew it to the pile of rubble it had been endeavouring to become for some time. The prospect left her spiritually adrift.

"Is that your daughter?" Cuzzocrea was looking at Sandy who was unhappily breaking down the empty packaging of the sky lanterns before squishing them into a black refuse sack.

"I know, unbelievable isn't it? I don't look old enough," Ali joked.

"You don't."

"Shut up. I was only kidding. How arrogant do you think

I am?"

"How old were you when you had her?"

"Young. I did everything young. Do you guys have any suspects?"

"You do realize I'm not allowed to discuss anything with you, I'm not allowed to divulge anything I know with you or anyone else. I could get in a lot of trouble."

"Inspector Cuzzocrea, I promise with every atom of my being that I would never betray your confidence and I would never be anything less than discreet."

"Rey."

"Pardon?"

"My name. If I'm going to break my oath of secrecy with you, perhaps it's better if you know my name."

"Okay." Ali smiled at him.

Lost for a moment as he returned Ali's smile, Cuzzocrea visibly switched back on. "Suspects. If only we'd gotten to that stage. The Patterson escape eclipsed the investigation – it was by trying to hurdle that problem that I might have landed myself in trouble. I'm looking into prior convictions right now but so far I've only come across petty crimes, a couple of domestic assault charges, a plethora of D.U.I.s and possession charges and an unlawful weapons charge but that guy's eighty-three now. There was a malpractice suit against the local G.P. but it was dropped following a significant settlement."

"Dr Labreque. He's over there, the sleazoid in the pink shirt."

"Is he on your list?" Cuzzocrea asked.

"One hundred per cent. He gives me the willies. I've tasked Marlene with getting her and me invited to his wife-swapping party, actually some sort of swinging orgy type thing, tomorrow night so I can take a closer look at his place and getter a better –"

"– woah. You can't do that." Cuzzocrea looked shocked.

"I can do whatever I want. Unlike you I'm not bound by the constraints of the law."

238

"Wait a minute, first of all – a wife-swapping, swinging orgy?"

"I'm not going to get involved."

"It's a dangerous position to put yourself in, you're out of your mind."

Ali shrugged. "Some would argue. I'll be safe. Anyhow, I'll have Marlene with me – she'd probably kick seven shades of shit out of anyone who tried it on."

"Wife swapping aside, hypothetically speaking, if Labreque is the killer and you go snooping, he catches you or even thinks you're on his tail, you put yourself in his sights."

"Not the first time I've been bait."

"I can't let you do this, Ali."

"Luckily it's not your place to *let* me do anything. Listen, there's the possibility that he has a secret room in his basement, as soon as Marlene and I confirm that fact or find it to be untrue, we're out of there – no hot tubs, no potluck, no old Dick."

Cuzzocrea huffed his disapproval.

"God, if you're that bothered then sit outside in your car, watch us go in and come out. If there's any sign of trouble we can alert you and you can swoop in on your steed."

"How? Wear a wire?"

"That's a bit dramatic, isn't it? Do you always have a propensity for being O.T.T.? I'll take my phone, how's that for genius?"

Cuzzocrea still wasn't sure.

"Seriously, how long would it take for you guys to get a warrant to search a local doctor's house? Without any evidence or cause, with no real link to the case? There's no way. Do it my way and your investigation leaps forward."

Ali watched as Cuzzocrea mulled the idea over, gently biting on his bottom lip, an action that felt intimate enough for her to find an excuse to look elsewhere.

"Okay," he said reluctantly.

"Just so you know, Inspector, you better drop this whole

over-protective thing right now. I may have fainted earlier but don't mistake that for weakness. I am not a damsel and I am not in distress. I can look after myself. Understand?"

"Sure."

"It's actually fucking offensive."

"Okay." Cuzzocrea held his hands up in surrender. "Fair enough, I apologize."

Ali, satisfied with his acknowledgement, continued, "Suspect number two: Ed Dunlop – His Worship – or whatever bollocks it is that's expected here. I encountered him this morning wielding a bloodied knife."

"Wow, you really get right in there, don't you."

"Indeed I do. He was skinning a deer at the time but, as you and I both know, skill with a skinning knife would be a biggie on our tick list. Also, he's a prick, self-centred, quasi-charismatic, all about superficial appearances, married, hunter, power hungry – what politician isn't? I don't suppose you have anything on him?"

"Squat. He's clean," replied Cuzzocrea.

"Doesn't surprise me although our killer wouldn't be reckless enough to have besmirched his reputation with convictions. Too clever. Too meticulous."

"I concur. Any plans to check for secret rooms in his house? Maybe attend an S&M event there?"

"Ha ha. No. If he does have a murder room it's somewhere separate from his home. Definitely off site."

"I'll look into it, see if he has any other properties. I'm also gathering C.C.T.V. footage from any cameras – few and far between around here – to see vehicles moving in and around the area on the evening of the eighth into the morning of the ninth, see what turns up. I'll do a check on the vehicles of all of your suspects."

"Now this guy is vile. The one eating the burrito over there. Charlie Chaud."

"He flagged on our system."

"Doesn't surprise me. What for?"

"One of the domestic assaults."

"Let me guess, the victim was his mother?"

"Officially I can't say but...how did you know that?"

"Just putting stuff together – two and two making six. I'm not even going to tell you about my encounter with him lest you revert to protective father mode."

"You know I did swear an oath to diligently perform the duties required of me. It would be remiss of me to be anything other than protective when you tell me that you intend to put yourself in danger."

"Actually I looked up the oath that you took and it doesn't mention the public at all, no protect, no serve just vowing to serve Queen Elizabeth II and to keep each other's secrets – very cabal-like. I don't know what he looks like so I couldn't even point him out to you if I tried but we were looking into Jacob Hammond, the prison guard? As you probably know since you caught us snooping at his house."

"He's not here.'

"And you're confident he isn't a suspect?" Ali asked.

"Yep. So they're all of your suspects? Based on what?"

"There's one more. All of our suspects were either present on the trail the day that the body was discovered, attended the town meeting later that day or were present at both events. It sounds thin, I know, but the best place to start given our lack of resources and in consideration of the profile. Our perpetrator would feel compelled to watch the fallout, the effects of his work upon police officers and members of the public alike. The entire process would be pointless if he were unable to bask in the reflected glory."

"Hence the memorial."

Ali nodded. "Marlene's idea but a fantastic lure. It reminds me of some tactics we used to employ back home. Putting parents of a missing child in front of a room full of T.V. cameras for an appeal is how you get to watch them either genuinely react or do a bad job of acting."

"I have a feeling that your profile will be similar to my analysis. I also stated that he would be local and would involve himself in the investigation and attend all public events in connection with the murder."

"I don't like this guy here," Ali whispered to Cuzzocrea as Carter Burrows passed them and approached Sandy, taking the black bag from her and offering to take it out to the trash. Carter noticed Sandy's Tim Hortons cup on the table and shook it to check that it was empty before throwing it into the trash bag too then leaving through the front door, presumably to find The Pioneer House trash receptacle.

"Carter Burrows," Cuzzocrea replied.

"You know him?"

"I do. He's a regular at Glandford."

"Meaning?"

"He knows a lot of the older guys, one of those groupie types. He had a dysfunctional childhood – junkie mum, dad locked up more than he was out, a series of stepdads, some of whom abused him. My theory with guys like that, cop groupies, is that they had so much interaction with cops during their formative years and following highly traumatic events that their brains twist the association with police officers into a positive, like the kids of cancer sufferers who become depressed once the parent recovers because all of the kindness and attention that outsiders lavished upon the family, suddenly ceases."

"Well, he's still on my list of suspects, despite the fact that Marlene almost hung me out to dry today when I suggested it – I swear, if you join the choir and tell me the guy's harmless too, I'll rip your nuts off."

"I quite like my nuts so I won't. I wouldn't go as far as to say he's harmless – I know for a fact that he isn't – but given his mental incapacities, I doubt he has the intellect to have carried out the crime."

"So he isn't harmless? Elaborate."

"Now, that *would* be crossing the line but suffice to say there was a youth record that has since been sealed; it may even have been expunged."

"Hmm. I'm keeping him in view, not front and centre

maybe but at least in my peripheral."

Ali saw David enter through the front doors. Still his tall, broad, undeniably handsome self, yet her usual feeling of excitement at the sight of him had not only diminished, it had vanished and in its place was a desire to cause him pain. Whether physical or emotional seemed to matter not, her appetite for vengeance at the sight of him outweighed rationale.

"Here." Ali handed her phone to Cuzzocrea. "Put your number in here for me will you? I hate talking on the phone so I won't answer unless I know who's calling."

Ali gently pressed her breast against his arm.

"Okay." Cuzzocrea angled the screen to her. "It's locked."

"Five-five-three-seven," she brazenly whispered into his ear. Even as she did it, Ali understood how basic her actions were, game-playing fit for a schoolgirl but she wanted David to feel jealousy. She wanted to inspire in him an insecurity forgotten during the course of their long marriage, to remind him that he wasn't entitled to her, that her loyalty to him wasn't guaranteed but her side of an agreement to cherish each other.

But games are only played well by the players of them. Ali was built for honesty, brutal, in-your-face honesty and so her attempt was clumsy and embarrassingly amateurish. She was Icarus to the sun. In such close proximity to Cuzzocrea she detected his masculine scent, a brute musk that gently permeated an overtone of soap and deodorant. It produced in her a physiological reaction that was simultaneously arousing as she tightened and humbling as she looked at the man who she was bold enough to imagine could be attracted to her.

Ali pulled back, feeling doubly stung by her inadequacy, Cuzzocrea was intent in his pursuit as he created a new contact in her phone but spoke quietly to her without averting his eyes from the screen.

"You might want to stay there a little longer if you really

want to make him mad."

Ali felt herself blush. "Am I that transparent?"

"Or am I just good at my job?" Cuzzocrea smiled as he returned her phone to her.

"I'm sorry."

"Don't be. Although it could technically be deemed sexual harassment, it's not every day I have beautiful women pressing themselves up against me so I'll let you off with a severe reprimand."

"Hello." David approached them, Cuzzocrea stood up off the ledge to greet him.

"David, this is Inspector Cuzzocrea. Inspector, this is my husband, David."

The men shook hands in the unmistakable way two men do when they're sizing up the competition. Ali felt marginally satisfied.

"I hope my wife isn't making a nuisance of herself. She's got it into her head that it's up to her to solve this case. I told her to back off, but you know women."

Cuzzocrea didn't share in the amusement as David laughed but instead opted to politely excuse himself.

"He's got a stick up his arse." David took Cuzzocrea's place next to Ali. "So what's going on then? The word is out that you and your dumpy friend have been harassing Mayor Dunlop on his day off."

Ali was lost for words. Where would she begin? The effort of even remembering a starting point, the moment David's insensitivity had become intolerable, was exhausting in itself. David had surpassed even *his* well-honed ability to piss her off, now he was publicly belittling her. It was his game, an intricate ploy to make her independence of him so uncomfortable that she would scurry back for comfort within their home where she could be a good little wife again and shelter from a cruel world, exposure to which seems to cause myriad marital problems.

Now Ali reversed her regret of pushing her tits against Cuzzocrea. Now she wished she'd have thrown caution to the wind and found her way through his zipper and grabbed his dick too.

"I see, we're still not speaking then?" David shrugged and stood.

"What do you expect?" Ali asked.

"I expect not to walk in on my wife cozied up to some random guy for a start."

"David…"

"…go on. I'm sure it'd be bloody murder if the tables were turned."

"I can't. I just cannot talk to you right now because if I start, it might just get to bloody murder."

"If that's how you want it, fine by me. I'm only here to rescue Sandy. She texted me and told me that you two have roped her into your scheme. If you want to play cops and robbers – or inspectors and bored housewives – then go ahead but leave the kids out of it, okay?"

"That's rich."

"Meaning?"

Ali, all too aware of her surroundings and the show she'd made of herself during the last public gathering in the space, tried to swallow the wrath that had her eyes burning in their sockets. "Sandy let me in on your discussion with her, regarding my mental status. Apparently I need help?"

David nodded without compunction. "Nothing I haven't already said to your face, Ali. I'll see you at home. Don't be late, I'm up early."

David gestured to Sandy. Glancing back at her mother, Sandy left with David. Ali found herself alone, both literally and figuratively, and as the lump of emotion returned to choke shut her throat, she defied its power.

Cuzzocrea was watching her from across the room where he was speaking to the mayor.

In that very instant Ali built for herself a fortress within, a metaphorical rampart – each stone hewn with a chisel of hate and if ever asked she would pinpoint that exact moment as the one when David had lost her; the very second she separated herself from her domineering, manipulative husband. David would sleep tonight on his side of a barrier of pillows separating him from a wife already divorced from him and unaware that he would never again enjoy her trust, her companionship or the life of quiet servitude he had worked so hard to impose upon her.

Ali was alone.

Unburdened.

Lighter.

As her spirit untethered itself from a domestic situation that had suffocated and repressed her for almost two decades, she felt the resurgence of a state of being she had forgotten was even possible:

Ali was happy.

CHAPTER 41 - A DANGEROUS CLAUSE

Let my soul be lifted up,
Let my spirit take flight
And join the heavenly beings,
The Saints and the Apostles.
Let me sleep in the arms of Angels.

Let my passing not go unnoticed
Yet dwell upon it, not.
Do not feel sorrow or pain for me
For I am free; I am saved; I am light.
Let me sing with the Heavenly Angels.

Death is our earthly end but our soul's rebirth,
Where we soar in tranquil rapture.
I have not gone, I am forever with thee
And I shall watch over you with love.
Let me dance and twirl with Angels.

I am no longer bound by time,
I cannot suffer indignity or strife.
I am in the lightness; I am in the joy;
I am the laughter; I am the embrace.
Let me fly upon the wings of an Angel.

Ali wondered what was nondenominational about referencing angels and heaven as reverend Arthur

Underwood concluded his service. Like a bad actor playing the role of village vicar in an am-dram play, the Reverend slowly closed his book of weird prayers for the dead. Air displaced by the closing pages wafted his feathery white nasal hair and he nodded solemnly from his place on the stage.

Marlene dabbed at her eyes with a cotton handkerchief. A few days ago Ali would have sneered at the show of emotion, assuming it to be fake; a bid for attention. However, having gotten to know the woman very quickly, understanding her essence – a common phenomenon amongst people whose bonds are necessitated by crisis – she could see that Marlene was genuinely touched. It was suggestive of her not being a mere spectator of tragedy but possessed by a cognizant understanding of it. Ali wondered if Marlene's ebullience in her quest to find the Alder Beach girl's killer may be driven by her own story, a deep sadness layered beneath her otherwise jubilant alacrity.

Reverend Underwood announced that a book of condolence was available for all who should wish to pass on their prayers and messages of sympathy and that anyone who wishes to take part in the release of the sky lanterns should collect one from the table and congregate on the lawn outside.

"Are you okay?" Ali asked Marlene.

Marlene pulled herself together, sniffed and slapped her thighs before grasping one of Ali's hands. "My heart breaks. Parents shouldn't bury their children. It's not the natural order."

"What's worse? Burying your child or not even knowing that they died?"

"I suppose the latter," Marlene said, eyelids hooded with a depth of compassion unique to those who have suffered similar tragedies. Ali decided not to pry.

"I'm going to thank Reverend Underwood," said Marlene before heading over to the stage.

Ali stood and turned to face the rest of the room. People were congregating in small groups, everyone far more subdued than they had been prior to the service. She wondered how many in the room were damned with Marlene's ability to relate to a parent's loss. She absently prayed to any denomination of god for dispensation from such a curse.

Dr Labreque was at the other end of the front row in which Ali stood. She was aware of his baritone voice as he chatted with a couple who flanked their obviously bored tween daughter. Ali always tried to keep an objective point of view when it came to suspects; maybe it was because she was out of practice or just that she was functioning purely in an amateur capacity but she couldn't shake off Labreque's sleazy stench. Even if he wasn't guilty of murder he had an air of depravity pungent enough to warrant suspicion and she instinctively wanted to keep him a distance from easily enamoured, impressionable young women.

Charlie Chaud was smoking just outside the front doors, a wannabe dust devil gyrated past his feet as the early evening breeze mustered itself for twilight. Chaud didn't strike Ali as the sensitive type and so it beggared belief that he would be at a memorial service simply to pay his respects. Of course, his mother was present – she was fussing over sky lanterns in yet another crocheted shawl, this time composed of chenille blues and turquoises – and so that could be his one and only reason to be there. However, the guise of giving his mother a ride to Mochetsin could have facilitated a grim need, a need to watch and enjoy the aftermath of a tragedy of his own making.

Cuzzocrea was the epitome of a detective at work. Managing to blend in, to become part of the furniture and go wholly unnoticed, despite his height and good looks. Sitting on the windowsill they had previously shared, Cuzzocrea was subtly scanning the room, monitoring interactions, reading facial expressions and body language. Like a magnetite lodestone he drew her to him; she scrambled for a believable excuse as the distance between them shrunk.

"I'm going out for a smoke. Charlie Chaud's out there

too. Maybe worth having an informal chat with him?"

"Samantha Giesbrecht," Cuzzocrea said as he stood and reminded Ali of her diminutive stature.

"Who?"

"The Alder Beach girl. She's been I.D.ed by her parents. Samantha Giesbrecht. Nineteen. Runaway from Abbotsford, reported missing by her parents in two thousand twelve. History of addiction and mental illness. The parents identified her body a little over an hour ago."

Ali looked over at Marlene, who was shaking the reverend's hand, and caught her attention with a wave. Marlene was smiling as she approached them, her grin favouring Cuzzocrea. But Marlene's smile faded quickly when Ali supplied her with the victim's name and age.

"She would have been seventeen when he took her then. Just a baby." Marlene commented, "I'm going to tell Underwood, he can offer up a prayer."

Ali nodded sympathetically as she watched Marlene return to the stage. "Do you feel it?" she said to Cuzzocrea. "The sadness?"

"Never. The day I do, I'll find myself another line of work."

"What do you feel?"

"Guilt."

Ali nodded. "Fag?"

Cuzzocrea nodded and they headed out of Pioneer House together. "Seventeen?"

"Seventeen what?"

"Marlene said he'd have taken her when she was seventeen."

"A theory of mine. He keeps them for at least two years before he kills them."

"Neck lengthening?"

Ali stopped and looked at him. "Your people came up with the same thing?"

"Yes. It seems so random, how the hell did you deduce that without a lab or X-ray equipment?"

"The bruises, the indentations in the underside of the jaw and along the clavicle. And her neck was unnaturally long and thin. Obvious really."

"I don't think so."

"Take another look at her or pictures of her and you'll see. Once you know it, you'll see it."

They continued to and out of the front doors, "I think he uses…" Ali silenced herself as Carter Burrows brushed past her, heading out to the lawn with his lantern as fast as the hitch in his step would allow. "Copper tubing which he coils somehow around the victim's neck, adding more and more coils as time passes and the neck narrows and lengthens – although it doesn't…"

"I know, it doesn't actually lengthen, just an illusion."

"Do you know there are people actually choosing to do it? Like getting big holes in your earlobes or tattoos, what's next? Ceramic plates in your bottom lip? I'll tell you this, they'll all be sorry when they age and just look like sad old gits or develop Alzheimer's and they're in a nursing home dribbling oatmeal and needing their arses wiped for them by a bunch of carers to whom they are a novelty freak show."

"Wow. The future's bright in your mind, huh?"

"I despise the ageing process. The worst part is, it's so fucking inevitable." Ali slapped her neck and wondered how many years it would take before mosquitos granted her their version of permanent residency and left her blood alone as they seemed to with actual Canadians.

Ali lit her cigarette and relished the intake of smoke as Cuzzocrea stepped over to Charlie Chaud. She watched as he introduced himself and offered his credentials for Chaud's perusal. The snob in Ali wondered if Chaud was even literate enough to read an I.D. Charlie Chaud's body language informed her that he was a natural born miscreant with a recalcitrant attitude. Another tick in the suspicion box.

Suddenly there was a mass exodus of lantern carriers to the patch of lawn. In the distance Ali could just hear the snore of the sleeping beast that was the ocean. The eastern sky was a deep periwinkle blue blushed with rose cirrus and peppered with the first winking diamonds of the darkling sky.

Ali stepped to the lawn as the lanterns were lit, their paper bellies buttered with flickering light, held aloft and ready to take flight. From inside the building behind her came the dulcet tinkling prelude to Rachmaninov's opus twenty-three. The lead lantern raised itself up, gently buoyed by a set of arthritic fingertips belonging to old Annie Chaud who then watched, her hands clasped to her chest, as it lethargically spiralled upwards lazily trailed by the others. One by one the lanterns cuddled up to the breeze and drifted skyward.

Ali wondered if Samantha Giesbrecht's soul was watching and if so, was she touched by the sight of a group of strangers in this anonymous Canadian municipality honouring her passing?

Samantha Giesbrecht's spiritual contract had been fulfilled. Ali's was yet to be.

As she watched the paper balls of diffused light head southward, Ali felt more than ever that she was about to honour a dangerous clause.

CHAPTER 42 - PATTERSON PLUNDERS

Every bone in him ached but Patterson could be grateful for small mercies – he had shelter, comfortable enough now he'd set out a makeshift bed on a pile of old straw, and food in his belly.

He had waited, secreted at the uppermost level of the hayloft in the old barn for a couple of hours at least. Until the last of the smoke from his previous hideout had finally dissipated and the sirens had fallen silent. Only then had he dared venture out, firstly around the perimeter of the barn where he'd happened upon a rusty old bale hook, the wooden handle rounded and smoothed by years of relentless toil, discarded amongst the knee-high, beige grass.

The property must have been a working farm at some point. Broken down fences and skewed posts of fences long-gone marked the plot edges of fields whose only remaining crop was the ever pervasive Scotch broom, the scourge of Vancouver Island. The persistent yellow bushes served as a treat to Patterson's eyes since he and his fellow inmates were sent, summer after summer, to farms and roadsides to hand-pull the shit out. He was no longer anyone's free labour.

The broom served him as much as a symbol of his newfound freedom as camouflage. Crouching low amongst the weeds he was obscured from view as he cut through the fields to what appeared to be the only residential building on the site.

A small, brown house with vinyl siding and an asphalt-shingled roof, Patterson assessed the house for a while from his vantage point amongst the rogue plants. There was no sign of life, no movement within that he could see through the three windows visible on the rear elevation. There was a skinny, steel chimney and although no smoke emanated from it, it was a warm enough day to warrant no supplementary heating, so he proceeded with caution.

Staying low, his senses on high alert, his new bale hook at the ready. He was more than willing to stick it through the throat of anyone who risked compromising his freedom but was already playing a dangerous game, leaving a rookie trail – first fat Hammond then the codger on Cedar Avenue.

Patterson slid his back up the ridged siding on the back wall of the house, next to a window he assumed to be that of the kitchen since there was a bottle of dishwashing liquid on the sill inside. He gingerly spied within. It was the kitchen, small and grotty with many of the cabinet doors missing and a pot-strewn stove on the opposite wall to a steel sink that was under the window through which he now confidently peered.

Patterson moved along the wall to the next window. Inside was a couch and two high back chairs either side of a brick fireplace, home to a black wood-burning stove. Nobody in the living room either, Patterson felt hopeful that the house was empty. The next window along was of opaque glass patterned with frosted leaves – the bathroom. The smallest section of the two-part window was open a chink and he decided that if further investigation found that the inhabitants were indeed out, he could, at a push, gain entry through it.

Rounding the side of the house he poked his head out to check the front. No vehicles. All still. He clambered over the rocky ground, slipping once, his foot snared in a hole while his forward motion continued, twisting his ankle badly. He cursed Hammond's stupid fucking boots, not only had they scraped the skin from all his toes but had also, as he noted in the hayloft earlier, begun to shed a cheese-smelling residue from the navy-blue inner lining that clumped between his sweaty toes and was fusing to the, as yet, limpid puss that the raw flesh on his toe knuckles had started to excrete.

Through the house's front windows (of which there were three) Patterson saw through to the same living area, this time alongside the stove; a double bedroom with an old, oak chifforobe in the corner, identical to the one his granny used to keep her 'Sunday best' dresses in; and one smaller bedroom, Spartan and tidy enough to pass muster in a military academy.

By now sure that the place was free of people, Patterson moved swiftly to the only door of the house, time now being of the essence. Finding his way through what must have amounted to decades worth of unwanted newspapers, magazines and a variety of empty jars and tubs in the open vestibule area, he tried his luck with the knob to no avail. The door was locked and so he made his way back around to the open bathroom window. With a severe limp to his gait now that his ankle had swelled, throbbing thickly with every pound of his weight upon it, Patterson was careful not to find the same foothold as before.

Accessing the open window proved harder than he'd expected, his paunch scraping on the fixed half of the latch. He eventually birthed his way through and spilled headfirst over the sink, his shoulder slamming on the avocado ceramic as he fell to the linoleum floor. The bathmat was still wet. He pulled himself up, grasping onto the pedestal sink for support and doing his best to ignore his new injury. Someone had recently taken a shower, probably that morning, and would likely return at any moment. Speed was imperative, he needed to gather the things he would need and get back to the safety of his barn where he could wait out any revived search for him in peace.

The matter of utmost urgency was fuel and so he headed directly to the kitchen. Opening drawers and cupboards as he went, stuffing a half-eaten Slim-Jim from the counter into his mouth, he searched the room. Patterson gathered everything that he might need but that wouldn't be necessarily missed upon the return of the homeowner: a tin of beans, a spoon, a can opener, a pack of hickory stick chips that may well be missed but he couldn't resist the lure of the tasty treat; a tin of dollar store stew, two cartons of apple juice, a couple of bottles of water, a black liver-spotted banana and a take-out carton of something Asian from the fridge. He found a white bin liner under the sink in which to carry his groceries.

He'd need to keep warm, although the past few nights had been comfortable, this was Van Isle and the weather is notoriously changeable. Spring could easily shrink back to its late-winter former self in a snap and if that happened, Hammond's crappy sleeping bag wouldn't be enough. In the double bedroom he found a pile of blankets where shoes would usually be at the bottom of the hanger section of the old wardrobe. He took an orange one with a silky tangerine-coloured trim at the top as well as a pink cardigan – this wasn't the time for vanity, however, he couldn't help but be mindful of his M.C. comrades and how they'd never let him live it down if they saw him wearing it. The drawers were filled with gash stuff: old lady belly-warmer panties and bras big enough to support watermelon tits. No socks. He needed socks.

Unlike the rest of the house, the second bedroom was neat and sparse. The bedding was pulled tight and tucked neatly between the wooden frame and the mattress, a cream-coloured sheet was folded over the top end of the itchy-looking, grey blanket. A set of drawers stood to the left of the single bed. Inside, Patterson found a multitude of socks to choose from, arranged in precise rows and bundled in such a way that no toe was in sight. He desperately needed socks if he had any hope of protecting his damaged feet and of staving off infection but by disrupting such order he would leave evidence of his plundering. Deciding it was worth the risk, he dropped a pair of Clorox-white sport socks into the bag, his feet already soothed at the sight of their potential comfort.

In the bathroom, Patterson turned the hot faucet on full and allowed the water to run. He carefully peeled the boots from his feet, one of the toes on his left foot was reluctant to detach itself from the stinking lining until he pushed harder against the heel of the boot with his other foot, wincing at the sting as nature's band aid remained inside the boot and the sore wept.

Pooling his trousers and boxers around his ankles and removing his shirt, Patterson grabbed a tatty floral hand towel from a plastic ring on the wall and soaked it with the now searingly hot water. He squeezed the cloth almost dry then scrubbed at his armpits, groin and between the cheeks of his ass. While he filled the sink with water as hot as he could take, Patterson pulled up his trousers and rolled them to his knees. He turned the faucet off and placed one foot at a time in the steaming basin, letting out a gasp of painful relief at this first step toward healing.

Patterson treated himself to a comfortable shit – frankly, it was such a delight that it would have been worth killing the homeowner over it had he, she or they returned before he'd finished, in fact it would have been his second kill as a result of a disturbed shit that day.

By the time he flushed, his feet were dry enough for the socks which he carefully pulled on and wriggled his toes within.

Next he checked out the small, glass-fronted medicine cabinet above the toilet and took from it a bottle of medicine – heavy-ass shit, anything with 'morphone' at the end of the word was good enough for him and all the better in liquid form. The name on the bottle implied that the prescription had been filled by the male of the house – the one with the Spartan room and the neat socks. Nothing else in the cabinet was of much use to him but he did take one of several bottles of hand sanitizer, it would work as an adequate antiseptic wound wash for his toes later.

Happy with his stash, Patterson left by the front door –

his energy way too depleted to attempt a safe landing via the bathroom window through which he had entered. He figured that the homeowners would assume they had simply forgotten to lock the front door behind them; this *was* Mochetsin, the place was stuck in a time warp and the locals probably thought the world was 1940s safe enough to leave doors open all the time anyway.

Now, back in his hayloft, his blanket over his new hay bed and his toes on the mend, Patterson was comfortable in the pink cardigan that even smelled a little like Granny. He gazed out through the massive hole in the broken roof at the evening sky beyond. It was a purply-blue with wisps the colour of his cardigan and he could even see the twinkling of the first stars of the night as he chowed down on delicious cold beef stew.

CHAPTER 43 - BLOOD ON HIS HANDS

On any other night in April Cedar Avenue would be dark but for the glow of porch lights and from windows. The penny pinching District of Mochetsin has never installed street lights throughout the borough. This fact, it could be argued, contributes to the high rate of motor vehicle incidents in the region – the number one culprit being the inflated number of impaired drivers on its roads since the municipality has no police presence.

Local governments are only obliged to establish a rural police force in areas where the population exceeds 5,000. The truth is, Mochetsin's population leaped 5,000 half a decade since but the local council fudges official figures for three reasons: to avoid the expense of building and staffing a dedicated police station; to avoid the expense and upheaval caused by having to convert their volunteer fire hall into a fully staffed, well-equipped one; and, most pertinent of all, to keep things just the way they are, thank you very much!

Mochetsinites are renowned for their stalwart refusal to change. Suggestions of an amalgamation with neighbouring boroughs caused fierce protests in 2003 and no council leader since has dared to propose such outrageous forward thinking. Such reluctance isn't merely in resistance to change but also to protect their multi-million-dollar profit margin, profits they would be obliged to share in the event of an amalgamation with other rural communities, all of whom function in a perpetual dance between the red and the black, credit and debt. Things like street lights, road repairs, salaried first responders – the general facilities and basic infrastructure required for the efficient operation of a community – cost money and if all of the money was to be used on such frivolous superfluity, how would the local council then be able to fund the lamb spit roast on Mochetsin Day?

Cuzzocrea hated incestuous little places like this as much as those places and their denizens hated him, hated *all* outsiders. The rape of Cedar Avenue had commenced. Invaded by a litany of outsiders and strange illumination alike. All the houses on the street were awash with the red and blue beacons of the numerous emergency vehicles present as well as the cold white light of the two portable floodlights (the hum of their diesel-fuelled generators as much of a disturbance to the quiet neighbourhood as the lights themselves), both focused upon Jacob Hammond's F150, allowing scene of crime officers to search for and gather evidence.

The rain had brought with it a sudden and significant drop in temperature over the past hour. The wind had picked up too. Continuous swirls and whistles were punctuated by brutal gusts that threatened a blackout as, with each squalling rush, branches seduced the power lines they intended to sever.

Munro and Cuzzocrea, having donned their VIIMIS wind cheaters, sat wordlessly together in the shelter of Munro's Corolla. The driver's side window was open a crack to prevent the windows from clouding with their exhaled breath; the wind moved through it with a petulant lament like the finished chanter on the last squeeze of the bagpipe.

"They need to sandbag that sucker." Munro was captivated by the buffeting of one of the portable floodlights.

"What time is it?" asked Cuzzocrea, lulled by the sound of the wind and too dozy to look at his own watch.

"Ten after nine. He's been up there for an hour now,"

replied Munro.

"What kind of a mood is he in?"

"His usual cheery self. You know Shaw. Probably extra pissed off because he's been called out to the field when he could be boning Trina."

"You honestly think they're having an affair?"

"You don't?" Munro asked.

Cuzzocrea had to admit that since the seed of an affair between his boss and the head of forensics for the team had been planted in his mind by Munro, the idea had begun to take root. "Maybe."

"Shit," said Munro looking in his wing mirror and already opening his door. "He's coming."

Cuzzocrea and Munro met Superintendent Doug Shaw at the rear of Munro's car. For the first time, Cuzzocrea noticed how thin and feathery his boss's hair was as it was sucked upwards in the wind's vortex.

"We have an interesting development, gentlemen," said Shaw, putting his hands on his hips.

"Is it Patterson?" asked Munro.

"Dr Colling just finished up there, he's the on-call dentist for The Mochetsin Institute. He's not the most cheerful of souls but he was able to confirm that it's not Patterson."

"Fuck." Luckily for Cuzzocrea, his expletive was issued quietly enough to be lost to the wind and went unnoticed by Shaw.

"That's not all. Coincidentally enough, the inmates aren't the only people he performed dentistry upon at the institute."

"He I.D.ed the remains?" Munro asked. Cuzzocrea held his breath.

"Colling recognized his work during the examination – bridge work performed only a week ago on three molars. He I.D.ed the body as that of one Jacob Hammond, a prison guard at Mochetsin."

After a brief pause, Munro faked enlightenment, "Wait a minute. We met him, this Hammond guy, he gave us a tour of the place."

"Rey?" Shaw turned to his inspector.

"Yeah…I remember him."

"And?" asked Shaw.

Cuzzocrea hoped he wasn't looking as guilty on the outside as he was feeling on the inside. His next words could condemn him. It was likely that Shaw was asking his opinion genuinely however it was also a possibility that Shaw had already been made aware of the truth. Cuzzocrea briefly pondered the likelihood of his partner's betrayal. Could Munro have ratted on him to save his own skin? Cuzzocrea was about to evade the truth. In a matter of moments his reputation could be irreparably tarnished, his career over. However, it would be premature to hang the noose around his neck just yet – after all it was better to be hung for a sheep as for a lamb.

"Jacob Hammond. Confident, average intelligence, seemed straight-forward enough. Had a good understanding of the ins and outs of the prison and of the inmates. He was certainly helpful." Cuzzocrea nodded and shrugged, indicating that he'd reached the limit of his understanding with regards to Hammond.

Munro cleared his throat nervously. "Didn't you take his number, Rey? Remember? You said you might need to ask him a couple of things."

No sooner than Cuzzocrea felt well and truly stabbed in the back by his partner did he then realize Munro's angle. During an ensuing investigation of the dead guard, Hammond's phone records would show evidence that Cuzzocrea had called him.

"Oh yeah, I forgot."

"Did you call him?" asked Shaw.

"Yep. Just a little later that evening."

"Why?" Shaw frowned.

Cuzzocrea's mind scrambled upon a justifiable reason for the call. "I asked him about the swipe cards the guards carry them on retractable lanyards. They're the only way of accessing the gates and doors in and around the complex. I, *we*, theorized that Patterson must have had one in his possession to make the clean escape that he did. I asked Hammond how Patterson might have gotten his hands on one."

"What did he say?"

"Actually, sir, he implied that some guards might trade stuff like that for sexual favours."

Shaw looked at both of his officers. "Either of you get the feeling he was playing you?"

Cuzzocrea and Munro shared a look and replied 'no' in unison.

Shaw nodded thoughtfully. "I've been speaking with Sergeant Hewer, it seems Hammond's conduct might have left something to be desired over the past year or so. He was arrested on a D.U.I., his truck there was fitted with an ignition interlock device following a six-month driving ban after which he appealed to the court and requested a restricted driving licence. The court awarded it on the condition that his truck be fitted with the device for a full two years and that he only uses the vehicle to get him to and from his place of work. Unfortunately for Hammond that didn't include his journeys to and from the local fire hall where he had volunteered up until that time. He was also involved in a domestic assault, the charges were later dropped. He certainly went off the rails."

"You think Hammond was Patterson's accomplice?" asked Cuzzocrea.

"That's the assumption Hewer is now working upon. It explains how Patterson managed to escape so easily, why Jacob Hammond came to be in that trailer and the breathalyzer explains why Patterson was forced to abandon his getaway truck."

"So Hammond helps Patterson escape, Patterson sits tight here for a few, Hammond shows up once he feels it's safe to do so to get Patterson out of Mochetsin?" Munro suggested.

"Patterson decides he's better off alone, was probably just using Hammond from the off and always planned to take him out of the picture. There's clear evidence that a sexual assault took place in that trailer before it was set alight. The fire chief says an accelerant was used, probably petrol, and the source of the fire emanated from Hammond's body. Basically Patterson tied Hammond up, bent him over, likely had his way with him then set him alight and left him to burn. He took Hammond's keys, took Hammond's boots for whatever reason, gets to the truck, can't start it. He encounters Mr Luckinuk then takes off in that direction. Soon thereafter smoke sightings alert Mochetsin Fire Rescue, Mr Luckinuk calls us and the rest is history." Shaw concluded.

Cuzzocrea felt himself relax. It couldn't be more plausible and believable if he'd have planned it himself.

"So what now, sir?" asked Munro.

Shaw pulled his collar up around his ears and zipped the front of his wind cheater. "Patterson's on foot and we know the general direction he was headed in. Hewer's called in the K9 unit for a search. Munro, you're no longer on this, you're back on the Giesbrecht case. Patterson escaped hours after our official time of death so I'm declaring officially that James Henry Patterson is no longer a suspect in our case. The time for caring about public perception is over – let Hewer deal with the locals on that one. Briefing in the a.m. as per usual. Have a good night officers."

"Sir," Munro and Cuzzocrea spoke once more in unison.

Once Shaw had pulled away in his black SUV, Munro turned to Cuzzocrea.

"By the skin of your teeth, buddy."

Cuzzocrea shook his partner's hand. "Thanks for getting in the thing about the call, I overlooked that. Shit though, I still feel bad. Hammond didn't help Patterson but now that's all he'll be remembered for."

Munro headed to his car door, raising his voice above the wind. "Fuck him, for all you know he *was* helping Patterson and when you told him about your suspicions as to his whereabouts, maybe it spooked him and that's why he came out here. I wouldn't lose any sleep over it now, you're free and clear."

The portable floodlight finally succumbed to the wind's power of persuasion and clattered loudly to the ground. The tempered glass cover remained intact but the sound of tinkling glass shards behind it implied that the delicate bulbs had smashed and was confirmed by the fifty per cent dip in white light on Cedar Avenue.

"I told you that needed sandbagging. See you in the morning." Munro brushed excess rain from the top of his hair before getting into his old car and driving away.

As Cuzzocrea made his way to his car, he tried to convince himself that Munro was right. The assumption could be justifiably made that Hammond had been working in cahoots with Patterson and that his untimely death was a result of his own criminal behaviour and not Cuzzocrea's bad choices. But no matter what, he knew deep down, in the place where everyone sequesters their truth, that Jacob Hammond's blood was on his hands.

CHAPTER 44 - CLEAN-UP CREW

Ali had never been the type to 'join in'. Never one for clubs or group activities and she hated corporate bonding days with a vengeance. It wasn't that she was anti-social, necessarily, just that she didn't tend to like people all that much – especially during organized group activities or sports where the average human can't help but succumb to the mind-bending power of their own ego.

Ali despised inane small talk and found it impossible to don a smile for the sake of social charm, however, on the wings of Marlene – a social butterfly if ever she'd seen one – Ali found that she was actually beginning to feel like part of the community. It was a feeling that had thus far eluded her throughout the unusual course of her life, a life starved of a normal childhood and the important friendships made during those all-important, formative years in order to feed a hunger for academic brilliance.

A week ago Ali had looked upon Mochetsinites as a weird bunch, a clique she had no intention of infiltrating. Now, folding chairs along with a small crew of willing volunteers, she could almost imagine herself joining the quaint little hamlet's incestuous throng of apologists.

The group who had remained after the memorial service to clean up Pioneer House (a task that simply required the folding of rows of chairs and stacking them neatly in an annexe room behind the stage in readiness for 'Jean's Jazzercise', scheduled for the following morning) consisted of Ali, Marlene, Christine Labreque, Annie Chaud, Theresa Dunlop and Carter Burrows.

Marlene had briefly popped home to feed and walk her beloved Webster. However, as it turned out, the trip had been subterfuge so she could smuggle back a bottle of her home-brewed blackberry wine and a pack of red, disposable cups.

With the chairs away, the room echoed Christine's footsteps as she crossed it and handed a black trash bag to Carter.

"Here you go, Carter, just do a round and pick up any bits we missed, will you?"

"Sure thing Mrs Labreque."

Christine joined the other ladies who were sitting in a row on the edge of the stage as Marlene made her way down the line, handing each lady a cup and filling it half way with blackberry wine starting with Theresa Dunlop who refused the beverage.

"Not for me, I'm the designated driver tonight for Annie and Christine."

Marlene shrugged. "Really?" She moved on to fill a cup for Christine. "Where'd Robert go?"

"Your guess is as good as mine. He's off playing poker probably – he knows I hate gambling. Took my car so he'll be as drunk as a skunk when he gets back and will have left it somewhere random for me to pick up tomorrow."

Ali was next in line, Marlene filled a cup for her before moving along the row.

"Annie?"

"Yes please," said Annie Chaud, her cup shaking in her Parkinson's trembling hands. "I'll have Theresa's share. I like to have a nip before bed, helps me sleep."

"Careful now, you know this stuff can blow your head off," warned Marlene.

Annie laughed. "I remember. Bingo night last year – I wasn't myself for a few days after that. Played havoc with my bowels."

"Oh, that was a bad batch; I think the bottles weren't cleaned properly. This one's better," said Marlene as she poured her own and took a gulp. "Nectar."

"I thought your boy was driving you home, Annie," said Marlene.

"You know Charlie, he'd had enough of the sentimentality. Said we were acting like Americans."

The women laughed and nodded to each other in agreement. Ali sensed that there was no love lost between Canadians and their American neighbours.

"I don't mind taking her home. Ed's off on a night stalk anyway," said Theresa Dunlop.

"A night stalk?" asked Marlene.

"Deer. Ed says the best hunting is a night. I just think he likes playing with those night vision goggles of his."

"What does he need another deer for? He just skinned one today," Christine chirped.

Theresa looked at Christine. "How the hell do you know that?"

Christine jammed a thumb in Ali's direction. "She told me."

"No I didn't. It was Marlene who told you that, actually." Ali corrected her in as polite a manner as she could manage.

Christine pulled a well-that-told-me face and didn't seem to mind that Ali could see her. "Sorry, Mary Poppins. My mistake."

"Never mind her, Ali," said Theresa Dunlop. "Christine's bark is worse than her bite. I must say, I am intrigued by your and Marlene's investigation, it must be lots of fun."

"Ooh, that reminds me. Carter, come here will you?" said Marlene.

In response to Marlene's request, Carter immediately dropped his trash bag to the floor, made a tentative first step, his head tilted to one side, before speedily crossing the room to stand before her. Ali was keenly observant.

Marlene filled a cup halfway for Carter and pressured him to take hold of it.

"No, go on. It's bad luck to toast without a drink. Theresa, here's a little for you too."

"I can't. I told you, I'm driving. How would it look for the wife of the mayor to drive under the influence? Not to mention the fact that these premises aren't licensed." Theresa was adamant even as Marlene pressed the cup into her hand.

Annie Chaud tutted, "Spit it back out after the toast, if you must."

Marlene raised her glass. "To Samantha Giesbrecht – that's the name of the dead girl incidentally. The inspector informed us of her identity earlier this evening. May she rest in peace."

They all raised their cups and took a drink of the blackberry wine which Ali found to be less of a nectar and more of an uvula acid wash.

Theresa Dunlop made a show of spitting her mouthful back into her cup. "You all saw that, didn't you? Just for the record."

Annie Chaud groaned in response. Carter was in full support. "I did Mrs Dunlop. If you need a witness, I saw you spit that out."

"Thank you, Carter." Theresa smiled kindly at him.

Christine knocked back the rest of her drink and stood, pulling her handbag strap over her head so it hung diagonally across her torso. "Hate to be a pain ladies but I have a big day tomorrow so, Theresa, do you mind if we make tracks?"

Theresa stood. "I'm bushed myself. Annie?"

Annie appeared to be less than thrilled that her nightly 'nip' was to be cut short. She downed the rest of her wine, a trickle of the purple fluid puddled in a crease at the corner of her lips. Carter helped her to her feet and readjusted her shawl as it had slipped from one of her shoulders.

Annie pressed her hand to his cheek, her thin skin was papery dry and almost translucent where it stretched tightly over her arthritic knuckles. "Sweet boy."

"Nighty night, ladies. Thanks for helping to clear away,"

said Marlene.

Theresa addressed Ali and Marlene, "Now, you two must fill us in next time. I want to hear all about your detective adventures and I for one want to know more about that mysterious inspector of yours." Theresa waved behind her as she and Annie left together, arms linked.

Carter had already gathered and disposed of both Annie's and Theresa's cups as they'd passed him and now took receipt of Christine's as she paused to say goodbye to Marlene and Ali. "So, I'll be seeing you both tomorrow evening then?" Christine's smile was sour enough to spoil milk. "I'm sure Marlene's probably already told you, Ali, Robert is just thrilled that you'll be joining us."

Ali matched Christine's sour grin. "I'm looking forward to it, Christine. Thank you so much for the invitation."

Christine stared at Ali for an uncomfortable few seconds of silence, her smile remained but her eyes were wider as if she were trapped in a horrifically jolly reverie. Finally snapping back to consciousness she spoke, "Okey-dokey-daddy-dog. See you then."

As Christine spun to face the door then flounced out, Ali half expected to see her disappear in a plume of green smoke, wringing her hands and crying about how Ali had ruined her beautiful wickedness.

As Christine left the room, the atmosphere becoming lighter as a direct result, Carter returned to his work picking up debris from the parquet floor. Marlene kicked off her flats and sat next to Ali on the stage, stretching her legs out in front of her and fanning her toes. "Christine is known for being a bit of a bitch and, boy, has she got her daggers out for you, Ali honey."

"Great! That's all I need."

"Pay no mind. Like Theresa said, her bark's worse than her bite. I wouldn't be too shocked, though, if the rumour mill starts turning about you. That's her M.O. as we detectives would say. She already made a point of mentioning to Theresa that she'd noticed you and David having a spat earlier."

"What? Nosy twat."

Carter turned to look at Ali, clearly shocked. "That's a bad word, Mrs Dalglish."

"There's worse where that came from, Carter. This one has a mouth like a sewer. It's funnier in her accent though, don't you think?"

"I don't know, Mrs McKean."

"Shit bum bugger fart piss willie bastard balls fuck fuck fuck twat cunting spunk." Ali rhymed off a quick demonstration of her swearing skills. If Marlene wanted sewer mouth, she'd get sewer mouth.

Carter stared at her, open-mouthed. Marlene laughed. "Look at his face! Oh, Carter, it's okay, sweet." Marlene laughed harder. "Ooh!," She crossed her legs tight. "Am I glad I wore my Depends! So, Carter? You remember I told you that Ali and I are doing a very important job? That we might need your help?"

"Yes?" Carter approached Marlene, dragging his trash bag behind him.

"I don't know if we should involve Carter, Marlene," Ali said.

"Nonsense. Carter's a letter carrier – no better way to get around unnoticed than in a Canada Post van."

"That's true, Mrs Dalglish. I can go everywhere."

Marlene leaned forward, her face serious. "We are investigating the murder of that poor girl who was killed."

"Are you?" Carter dropped the bag and knelt on the floor like a child ready for story time.

"Yes we are and we are doing a very good job of it because Ali, well, she's good at things like this, aren't you?" Marlene turned to Ali for confirmation.

"I don't think this is approp –"

Marlene interrupted Ali's protest. "She used to catch bad people all the time in England. That was her job, you see?"

Carter's eyes were full of amazement as he looked at Ali, "Was it?"

Ali smiled reluctantly in response as Marlene continued, "Soo, Carter, we are on the lookout for a very bad man who we think might live here, in Mochetsin."

"No." Carter frowned at Marlene.

"Yes." Marlene nodded.

"Who do you think did it?" asked Carter.

"Well, that takes time. First you have to have suspects, people who *could* have done it then you rule them out for various reasons and hopefully, at the end, you're left with one. That one would theoretically be the one who killed her." Marlene explained.

"Okay." Carter's head tilted more as a look of concentration took over his face.

"So far we are looking at Ed Dunlop, Robert Labreque and Charlie Chaud." Marlene's words alarmed Carter who shook his head in disbelief, "Oh, no, it's okay. Nothing to worry about yet, like I said, they are just suspects. There is a prison guard too but so far we haven't tracked him down and the police say that it wasn't him."

"The police? Are you a police lady?" Carter asked Ali.

"No."

"Oh." Carter looked back at Marlene. "What can I do?"

"Well, to start with, you just need to keep your eyes open for anything suspicious, any comings and goings as far as those three are concerned. But even if there's something else suspicious, maybe someone we haven't thought of that you think is acting a bit odd maybe? You let us know." Marlene consulted with Ali. "Maybe Carter could find out where they all were on the night the body was left, Sunday? Early Monday morning?"

"Oh, I think that'd be wrong," Ali replied. "Carter shouldn't be going around asking stuff like that."

"No, no. You're right." Marlene spoke to Carter again, "Between us, and don't go telling anyone, Ali and I have been snooping today – in all of their houses. We nearly got caught once by Charlie Chaud so you have to be careful. Just keep your eyes peeled for now."

Carter straightened. "Eyes peeled?"

Marlene laughed, understanding Carter's confusion. "Oh, hon. It's just a saying. It means to keep a lookout. You shouldn't ever try to peel your eyes."

"Okay, Mrs McKean." Carter stood, picked up his garbage bag and gave Marlene a small salute. "Carter Burrows at your service." Carter hiccupped a laugh, his lips revealing his diminutive, dirty teeth. "I'm going now."

"Okay. Drive carefully now, you had some of that blackberry wine, remember?" Marlene reminded him.

Carter nodded, took Ali's red cup from her, then Marlene's and deposited them in his trash bag and made for the door.

Marlene called after him, "Hey, Carter? You want to know something funny?" Carter turned to listen. "Now, this is before she knew you but Ali here originally thought you should be a suspect too. Isn't that just too funny?"

Marlene laughed. Carter didn't.

"It's okay now she knows you. You're not a suspect anymore."

"Mrs Dalglish?" Carter spoke to Ali. "Is Sandy going to be helping us too?"

Ali's stomach lurched as her daughter's name left his lips, "Pardon me?"

"Is Sandy helping too? Because she's real book-smart. She said so."

"No. No she isn't. Helping, I mean." Ali felt her skin prickle with goose bumps as Carter nodded, accepting her answer but with a look in his eye that belied his apparent retardation.

He left.

Marlene leaned conspiratorially against Ali's arm. "I think someone might have a crush on Sandy. I caught him watching her earlier, bless him, and he told me that he thought she was the most beautiful thing he'd ever seen." Marlene stood. "Right then, I'll be getting back. I don't know who's missed me more the past few days, Peter or Webster.

Come on, I'll need to lock up after you."

Ali slowly stood and absently brushed the back of her trousers.

"Are you okay?" Marlene asked Ali. "You look like you've seen a ghost."

"I'm okay. Look, I'm sorry if this offends you, Marlene, but I'm really uncomfortable with you involving Carter in this."

"Oh tish! He loves helping, he'll get so much out of this. Look, I promise I won't tell him anything else. Is that fair?"

"Okay."

"You ready for this party tomorrow night?"

"God, I nearly forgot about that."

"You should wear something slutty."

"What? Are you wearing something slutty?"

Marlene winked. "Oh yes, I'll be wearing the sluttiest thing I own." Marlene shepherded Ali out of Pioneer House and fussed with locking the door.

"I'm thinking we should go to Victoria tomorrow, check out shelters and food banks, soup kitchens? I'll get a picture of the girl from Cuzzocrea and we can ask around about her."

"Real detective stuff. I'll look out my trench coat."

"I wouldn't go that far."

Marlene held her hand out in the rain. "How else am I going to keep dry?"

"Oh. Okay, I see. Shit, I'm tired. See you tomorrow, Marlene."

"Night night."

...

Inside her Porsche, Ali demisted her windscreen with the heater on full blast. She watched as Marlene drove off at a snail's pace. The rain pattered sharp ticks on Ali's windscreen and looked like a thousand silver pins darting through the beams cast by her headlights.

Ali watched Carter as he headed to his van, returning from the outdoor trash can. He stopped in the penumbra of her lights, a daring doe, looking at her. Could he see her? She waved at him to continue safely across her path. He seemed fused to the spot, dazzled by the lights. A mean streak in Ali wanted to rev the engine and run the creep over. After a moment, Carter scuttled off to his van. As she selected first gear and released the handbrake, Ali decided that tomorrow she'd ask Cuzzocrea for more than just a picture of Samantha Giesbrecht. She wanted to see Carter's sealed youth record too.

CHAPTER 45 - THE HOMECOMING

Patterson was grateful for the blanket and the cardigan now the night had taken a chilly turn and the rain was coming down. He was glad too that the section of roof above him was intact and of the many leaks that had appeared over the past hour or so, none of them happened to be above his bed.

He'd pushed wide the hayloft doors and the opening allowed for the passage of a refreshing breeze, the tail end of the more powerful gusts beyond that forced soaring pines to bend to the west like a line of withered old men silhouetted against the night sky, fat with grey clouds and full of ominous portent.

The rain would pass soon enough. He'd already tempted the gods by questioning the staying power of the nicer weather of the past few days and so he'd vowed to only think positive thoughts regarding the climate until he was finally back in Nanaimo.

He rubbed his knuckles up and down the centre of his chest, the banana he'd eaten had turned, the blackened patches had fermented enough to be considered alcoholic and had left him with the metallic burn of acid reflux in his tubes. He stilled and sat upright. Was that the sound of a car? Crunching over gravel? He listened closely, with shallow breaths.

His suspicions were confirmed as the withered old man trees were brushed by a sweep of yellow light, first up and then across. The trajectory of the movement of the light allowed him a dependable guess that a car had pulled up to the house, first facing the trees lining the farthest perimeter of the property before turning away again and coming to a stop in front of the little brown house itself.

Patterson felt it was safe to assume that whoever the inhabitants of the house were, they rarely, if ever, crossed the overgrown fields to enter their condemnable barn and yet his heart thumped in his chest as if he were in imminent danger, his senses focused.

A rustling to his left startled him disproportionately since it was only the scurry of a mouse – one of many he seemed to be sharing the loft with. Breath bated, Patterson listened carefully, the wind was louder all of a sudden and was pissing him off until he heard the distinct slamming of a car door, confirming that someone was indeed home.

Whether as a result of boredom or simple curiosity, Patterson itched to know more about his unsuspecting landlords. He debated the possible risks versus rewards of crawling through the Scotch broom once more and finding out who was in the house. From his earlier rummage through it, he guessed: one little old lady and her grown son, nephew or maybe a grandson. Ex-military, considering the presentation of his immaculate room.

Knowing that within that house, right now as he sat burping banana in a windy hayloft, lay a set of car keys and therefore his means of a full and proper escape was almost too much for him to bear. He had a bad track record for self-discipline, he'd always been an instant gratification kind of guy – whatever he wanted, he took, regardless of rules, laws or consequences. It was the outlaw way.

But was it too great a risk to satisfy this particular itch? If the male of the house was indeed ex-military, he could be dangerous. What if he was a yank? A former Marine like Patterson's buddy, Tyler Baylock – one dangerous motherfucker who lived by the motto, 'No better friend, no worse enemy' and Patterson knew from years spent alongside Tyler how that motto translated into practice.

Of course, the neatness of that bed could just as well have been a habit picked up inside. The guy in the house could just as likely be an ex-con as an ex-Marine. Patterson was yet to let a fellow inmate get the best of him. Sure, a few had tried, it was the nature of the beast, but none who had tried had come off the better for it. One guy had ended up worm food, his hot blood sprayed up the walls of the chow hall.

Patterson lay back on one elbow and reached for the backpack, sliding it over the straw to him, and reached into the sleeping bag (a treat he was saving till the moments immediately before he wanted to sleep to truly appreciate its downy comfort) and retrieved the twelve-gauge hidden within.

Former Marine Corps or not, two shells to the chest would be the ultimate equalizer. But shotgun blasts are loud, the noise would travel. Patterson would at least have to off the old lady too – something that would be a stoop too low, even for him.

The debate ping-ponged in Patterson's head until he felt like his brain might spew out of his ears like raw clay.

"Fuck!" he exclaimed through gritted teeth. On one hand he could go for it, creep up to the house, scope it out. He could even wait until they were asleep then gain entry somehow, put a couple of rounds in the guy, one in the granny, get the car and be through the Malahat an hour later. Or he could hang tight in the loft, get a good night's sleep, assess the situation better and eradicate the risk of further complicating his egress from Mochetsin and further fanning the fire of law enforcement on his tail.

From the corner of his eye, Patterson caught movement outside. Light upon the trees again. Not as bright as the headlights had been, not by half and the movement of the light was frenetic, not the smooth sweep of a vehicle as it turned. It was the bobbing light, he was sure, of someone walking with a flashlight.

Surely to fuck it was not someone making their way to

the barn. If that was the case then he should just put the shotgun barrel in his mouth and fire a slug into his brain because that would mean that luck was working one hundred per cent against him. Maybe the old woman was a witch or a psychic or a fucking tea-leaf reader because that would be the only way, short of hidden cameras for anyone in that house to know that he was hiding up here in the middle of a rainstorm.

The light bobbed faster, covering only the lowest portion of the trees and some of the grass as the wind blew it back and forth in clumps. Whoever was out there was heading towards the tree line itself. Patterson frowned; he hadn't explored the entire property but he was sure that nothing of note lay in that direction. Why the hell would anyone be going out on a pointless stroll into the forest on a stormy night?

A skinny figure, flashlight in hand, appeared. Framed perfectly between the hayloft door jambs across from Patterson, he was fast and nimble, half-running, half-striding. The sureness of his steps indicated a knowledge of the path beneath the man's feet.

Patterson ducked down, feeling conspicuous and able to imagine his illuminated visage from the point of view of the torch bearer should he sweep its light in the direction of the barn. The figure stopped, dropped his flashlight to the ground and stooped. Seeming to peel the grass from its rightful place upon the earth, he then rolled it back on itself like it was a hearth rug.

Patterson watched, bemused as the figure then heaved up and over to the right what appeared to be a door in the earth. Patterson wondered if it was a storm shelter but dismissed the notion. Mochetsin was often battered by winds and rains but never anything truly destructive enough to warrant the installation of an underground storm shelter. Patterson scuttled forward on his stomach, closer to the opening for a better look, the wind kicking up tiny particles of dry hay into his face. Patterson pinched his nostrils shut –

the last thing he needed was to be rumbled by an involuntary sneeze.

The figure picked up the flashlight and shone it into whatever void had now been opened, knelt down and reached a hand deep within the earth. Patterson couldn't discern whether he had perceived or imagined the clicking of a light switch but that was what he heard as a sudden wash of light from what must have been more than a solitary lightbulb illuminated the man from within the hole. The man stood, hooded in a slick, black raincoat, a pointed, pink nose was all that protruded forth to indicate his humanity before he clicked off the flashlight and descended quickly into the ground whilst pulling the door above him closed as he went, snuffing out the light and returning the property to its former dark and barren, storm-battered self.

A new debate raged in Patterson's mind as he remained belly down on the hay. He could barely see the exact spot where the mac-clothed demon had opened his gate to hell.

"What the fuck?"

The allure of the car keys – no doubt left unguarded on a kitchen counter or hanging from a hook on a wall – seemed to pale in comparison to the new allure of a secret tunnel to God-knows-where and God-knows-what.

Little hidey holes like Mochetsin were renowned for pot grow-ups and major trafficking operations of both the human and narcotic variety. Patterson had a knack of spotting a criminal enterprise from a thousand paces – it was a case of 'takes one to know one' – and what he knew right now was that he'd just witnessed the door to a secret scam, quite literally, open before him.

Maybe luck was once more working one hundred per cent in his favour after all. What better way to go home to his crew than with a stash of gear? Maybe even a car full?

Now that would be worth killing a granny for.

CHAPTER 46 - ALI'S HOME

Apart from the usual barking welcome home by her four dogs, Ali found the house to be peacefully quiet and still. Oscar, her black and white Newfie (her secret favourite), was particularly happy to see her and Ali had to allow him to complete his ritual of rubbing and pushing and of wiping his slobber on her suit trousers before he would allow her passage through the rest of the house. Any owner of a Newfoundland knows that every now and then, particularly following a prolonged absence from their company, you must indulge the protective and loving dogs in their moments of intense, almost bullying displays of affection – affection that borders on admonishment – then thank them with an ear rub and a series of echoing thank-you pats against their barrelled ribcages. They are bred protectors of people and become frustrated by their powerlessness to protect an owner who is out of the home. Newfoundlands have even been known to systematically clear entire lakes of otherwise happy swimmers to minimize the risk of a drowning.

Sandy was in her dimly lit room, on the edge of sleep, her iPad propped against a pillow on her tummy, scrolling through Tumblr. Ali waved a goodnight to her daughter. She could hear tinny music from Sandy's earbuds and wanted to tell her daughter to turn the music down a notch but Sandy was clearly still displeased with her mother, returning Ali's wave with as much enthusiasm as a dead fish. Ali closed

Sandy's door and blew out a deep breath, ridding herself of the negativity. Now that a flush of happiness had begun to dawn in her soul again, Ali was determined not to allow herself to be brought back down by anyone. Sometimes those who love us the most are the ones who, perhaps inadvertently, drain us of our joy.

Kenny was already fast asleep. One of his size twelve feet poked free of the bedclothes and reminded Ali that her baby was becoming a man. He'd fallen asleep watching a D.V.D. The menu screen of Sons of Anarchy was on a loop, Curtis Stigers was moaning about riding through the world all alone while various black and white visuals of cast members looking solemn, mean and somehow becoming un-tattooed, repeated every ten seconds or so. Ali found the remote nestled within the crumpled Liverpool F.C. comforter and clicked the television system off, plunging the room into sleepy darkness but for the gentle light that emanated from the snake tank in the corner.

In the main room of the house, Ali perused the wall that had become the hub of her investigation. She removed any notes regarding the prison guard and wanted to add a new series of notes regarding Carter Burrows but resisted. She knew that Marlene held the man in her affections as did, it seemed, all the women in Mochetsin. Ali hated to be swayed by gut feelings – it was dangerous to fixate upon any one suspect if nothing more than instinct pulled you in that direction – but fixated she was, regardless that Carter Burrows – as far as anyone knew him – didn't actually fit the profile. Her *own* profile.

The key was that Ali needed more information on him so that she could, at the very least, discount him as a suspect. Perhaps by knowing more about him she could pinpoint the characteristics in him that produced her atavistic disdain for him. She sent a text to Cuzzocrea and after a brief conversation back and forth, agreed to meet with him in the morning. After pouring a double gin and tonic, Ali sent the inspector an e-mail. She wondered what Cuzzocrea was doing at that moment, was he in bed? What was he thinking about? Then she remembered pressing herself against him earlier and his cool reaction to that. Butterflies fluttered in her tummy but their wings were laced with guilt.

Ali tiptoed through the master bedroom. David's sleeping form was barely visible past his barricade of pillows – God forbid he should actually touch his wife during the night. Ali stepped around his side of the bed. As she stood watching him Ali felt sure her husband was faking sleep. His eyelids were shut determinedly tight, the eyes beneath them reacting to the intermittent pulse of red light given off by his fire service pager on the bedside table. Ali's suspicions were confirmed as his deception was betrayed by the cell phone on the floor next to the bed when the screen illuminated as it received a muted text. Ali stepped over the phone and read the screen. The sender was simply 'WORK' and the message content consisted of a single letter: 'k'. Obviously David was mid text conversation with a mysterious entity known only as 'WORK' but wished to conceal the fact from his wife by faking – badly – sleep. Ali went to the en-suite bathroom and reached around the door for her bathrobe, wondering when childish games had become an acceptable part of her relationship with David. As she left the bedroom, a bitter sense of loss for something once beautiful swelled in her heart.

CHAPTER 47 - DID THEY FLEE?

Routine disrupted. No time for ceremony, no disrobing can be done, his feet thump down each step, a bulb brushes the wet hood from his head. His fists clench in fury.

It isn't possible. There's no way one of them could have found their way out but someone had been in his house, someone had stolen food and water and socks. Someone had washed in the bathroom and someone had carelessly left the front door unlocked.

Careful measures are in place to avoid such a calamity. A biological phenomenon must first have taken place, a supernatural speeding of a carefully measured metabolism. The navigation of a labyrinth of his making, locked from above in his absence.

For one of them to escape his lair would require assistance from an outside party and the only living beings aware of this place are the ones he hoped to find exactly where he'd left them. Two in stocks. One in the chamber.

Reassuring himself as he goes that they must, *can only be,* secure in their places, he continues through the tunnel. He feels his anger stabbing, fury mounting, promising himself not to unleash his wrath upon them – an act that would only bring about another disappointing end to a long-awaited harvest. They cannot be gone, they are bereft of help, they are forsaken by all but him.

Never before has he felt the danger of discovery, the proximity of a threat to his work. It is the woman that has unnerved him. The policeman, the crime unit, he fears not for he has watched them – *him* – fail before. They were no match for him two years ago and they are no match for him now. They are outwitted indeed. Inept. Incompetent. Irrelevant.

The woman though, she sees him. She knows. Her drooping, old, dumb, bitch friend would have to sport a neck of copper herself before understanding dawned in that minute brain of hers, a brain only capable of supporting basic motor function. But the Dalglish woman – how he'd like to humble her, how he'd revel in her discomfort, her pleas. How he'd make her see the real him, the true power of him, his awesome superiority over all the scuttling cretins of this world. How she'd marvel at his deviousness, his devotion to his quest and his unmasking.

He is forced to dishonour the sanctity of his sacristy – a price must be paid for that alone – and hunch down, hurrying through his secret warren to their door.

CHAPTER 48 - CUZZOCREA JUDGED

Rey Cuzzocrea wasn't much of a sleeper at the best of times and in the best of circumstances but particularly not during the course of an investigation and whilst confined to a single bedroom in a tacky bed and breakfast decorated by a woman with a disturbing owl fetish. A heinous watercolour print of one of the birds loomed above the twin bed and judged him with golden eyes and feathery horns.

He pushed his open laptop down towards his knees and lounged back as best he could in the slipcovered tub chair with his feet propped on the end of the bed. Although her profile was fastidious and insightful, indicative of her expertise in criminal psychology – not to mention the fact that the woman had somehow managed to hit two major bullseyes regarding cause of death and a defining aspect of the killer's M.O. just by looking at the body – Ali Dalglish's suspect list was weak.

Still, a weak suspect list beats an empty one and so, since he'd managed to come up with diddly-squat, Ali had one up on him already. He'd managed to keep the details of his investigation under wraps with vague and ambiguous answers to her questions – less to do with confidentiality and more as an attempt to prevent Ali Dalglish from discovering that thus far he had conducted himself in an amateurish manner worthy of a lowly gumshoe. He'd even managed to get a man killed, regardless of what Shaw, Munro or anyone else may say. Cuzzocrea felt the weight of Hammond's demise upon him and the owl, for one, was in full agreement.

He'd received a text message from Ali Dalglish a little over an hour ago. In it she'd requested he provide her with the most recent photograph of Samantha Giesbrecht that the R.C.M.P. has on file. Once she'd explained her intentions, Cuzzocrea had agreed to deliver the print to her in the morning.

Following a confirmed identification, the obvious next step in an investigation is to focus on victimology and so Ali Dalglish and her sidekick, Marlene McKean, intended to interview the homeless population of downtown Victoria, hoping to find someone who knew the girl and may therefore have information regarding anyone she was in contact with or had befriended. Although he was frustrated that Ali was a step ahead of him, he hoped he could suppress his ego enough to allow her to take the lead in his stalled investigation. For the greater good.

Two further requests were made of him over the course of their brief conversation via text: his e-mail address and Carter Burrows's youth record.

The e-mail address was easier to supply her with than the criminal record would be and she'd sent him an e-mail (the subject box contained the words: 'Now show me yours!') empty but for an attached file simply labelled: PROFILE.

He'd read it through twice and noted the similarities between his own analysis and her profile, relieved not only because they were clearly on the same trail but because when the time did come to 'show her his' he wasn't likely to embarrass himself. What Cuzzocrea now struggled with, however, was why she seemed so focused on Burrows as a suspect. He didn't fit her profile which called for an unknown subject of high intellect – an I.Q. of over one sixty; an ability to manipulate and control people; to manufacture a life that gives the illusion of normalcy; and that he would most probably be married. Carter Burrows seemed to be the antithesis of every one of these vital points.

What perturbed Cuzzocrea more than so many aspects of the profile working *against* Carter Burrows as a viable suspect were the numerous aspects of the profile that seemed to work *for* Ali Dalglish being a suspect. Granted, he knew nothing of her childhood except for the fact that she was a child prodigy and held a joint historic record for academic achievements in Britain but, working under the assumption that she'd suffered abuse as a child in a dysfunctional household then under the greater assumption that she was capable of murder, Ali Dalglish had profiled herself and sent that profile to an investigator on the case. That action in itself was a major bullet point of the Dalglish profile – *the killer would become involved with the investigation, the killer was taunting the police and a community he felt excluded from.* The sexual assaults were inflicted with the use of an object. Ali had stated that the killer may be impotent but what if the killer used an object not because he couldn't achieve an erection but because the killer doesn't have a penis?

Cuzzocrea threw his laptop onto the bed and rubbed at his forehead. Was this an actual lead or just the musings of a man who found himself in the shadows of incompetence cast by the brilliance of her competence. Was this misogyny? His own insecurities twisting a talented, intelligent and undeniably attractive woman into a fiend? He sat back again and looked at the painting of the owl and the owl told him he was indeed a gigantic loser.

CHAPTER 49 - WASHING IT ALL AWAY

Ali went to the only other bathroom in the house and drew a steaming hot, many bubbled bath. She slipped into it, careful not to spill her G&T. For Ali, crying was a display of weakness, it was a pathetic, purposeless show of emotion but she also knew from past experience that every now and again, regardless of how tough one wishes to appear one must let it all out. It was a matter of self-preservation because Ali had learnt that to hold it all in for too long was very, very bad for the soul. She'd been there before and eventually that shit'll make you snap.

The tub in the kids' bathroom was small even for Ali and so she was forced to rest her feet on the lip at the tap end. This position turned out to be of benefit every time the cooling water needed a top-up of heat as she found her feet to be extraordinarily dextrous in their ability to turn the hot tap on and off, allowing the rest of her body to remain submerged in the therapeutic, lavender scented water.

Against her own better judgement she managed to stave off an outpouring of raw emotion and had instead swallowed it all back and cloaked it in bitterness and resentment, as is her wont. Tears were the least of Ali's battles. She fought a daily battle against depression – the rarest and most vicious form of it, medically untreatable due to unusual brain chemistry rendering the taking of antidepressants, particularly twinned with anti-anxiety meds akin to playing Russian roulette with every chamber full.

Ali was blessed to be part of the two per cent of the world's population with genius level intelligence but cursed to be within another two per cent of people referred to at the end of every pharmaceutical company advert for mood altering medications: *May, in rare cases, result in new or worsening suicidal thoughts or actions.*

Ali had received the diagnosis upon being discharged from St. Fillan's Hospital for Forensic Mental Health Care three years ago with a warning that she mustn't take antidepressants particularly SSRI's, anti-anxiety medication, or to use smoking cessation aids (most of which are laced with antidepressants).

Ali shrugged away her blight, it was an evil, old friend that had lurked within her for as long as she could remember and she knew the early warning signs of an up-coming crisis – dreams about gleefully throwing oneself from towering viaducts or chopping your own head off. The brain dysfunction that makes you think you wrote a shopping list about bread and milk but which actually looks to anyone else like a heart monitor's print-out, or forgetting your own name and even the fact that you have children.

Ali ignored an escaping tear and used her foot to add a torrent of steaming water to her bath. She took a swallow of her liquor as an army of tiny bubbles tickled her back on their way to the surface.

CHAPTER 50 - THE NEED FOR REVENGE

This is their waiting room, he likes to call it 'the stockroom' – an amusing double entendre. There they are. Subdued and compliant as ever. Absent yes, but only mentally, in a chemical fugue. Powerless and immobile.

No escape was made. No escape was ever intended. Within the final chamber (he is loath to enter in his otherworldly guise and in such a fluster for it is unbecoming of his standing within these hewn walls) she lies there still, awaiting his presence. Doe-eyed and eager for his attention she turns her head to see him, a dark crust has furred the edges of his work. The pustules have hardened and the flaps of skin recoil from him. He wants her now but the ritual must be observed. He will return to her soon.

He adds a special fuel to the fading fire and watches as the brown plastic of the cup's lid curls at the kiss of the flame. It makes him wonder if, not too far from here, the pouting, virginal lips that had earlier tasted its creamy contents were now feeling a sudden, inexplicable heat. Was she now touching those lips in response to the strange sensation? She had been ignorant of his gift, stirred into the hot coffee she'd been so grateful to receive. He'd watched her eyes flutter closed, her head tilt back to reveal a naturally elegant neck and the tight descent of her oesophagus as she'd taken the seed he'd deposited within the drink and drank deeply of his cream. To the very last drop.

Someone had been in his house. Someone had evidently

rummaged and stolen. Someone had snooped. Who had spent the day snooping? That stinking bitch, the Dalglish whore. She would have to pay and by making her pay he would force her to focus on matters other than him. With her attention diverted to matters of grief and desperation she would be unable to meddle further in matters with which she has no business.

He pressed his hand to the glass of the stove door and thrilled at the scurry of heat beneath his fingers as the words on the Tim Horton's cup first bubbled and then blackened: *Always fresh*.

He smiled as he decided upon his next step. He'd need to make a call to 911 from a pay phone. He needed Mochetsin Fire to be otherwise engaged for a while.

CHAPTER 51 - PATTERSON WATCHES

Patterson waited patiently, his eyes trained upon one patch of grass in the field before him, for the secret door in the earth to open once more. His mind was a swirl of curiosity in desperate need of satiation. He scraped the black, gritty dirt from under his fingernails with a canine tooth. He was eager to get down into that hole and see what his mysterious, no doubt profitable, prize might be.

It was fate or kismet or luck. Had to be. Unexpected twists and turns had led him to this barn in the middle of nowhere. Twists and turns that would have stymied a lesser man and thwarted escape. Such hurdles could have, *should* have, landed him right back in maximum security on the mainland, no chance of parole, no privileges. Then he'd have to kiss the opportunity of a future escape, or a legitimate release, a big sloppy one right on the rear end.

Fat Hammond. Hammond's piece of shit truck not starting. 'Charitable Charlie' with the Trump comb-over on Cedar Avenue. All those weird events that should have culminated in his recapture had instead forced him back into the woods and upwards to this place because fate or kismet or luck was giving him another chance.

Just being free and back in Nanaimo seemed like a second-place ribbon to the idea that he could bankroll his future too and maybe even that of his niece who had been raped and battered at the age of fifteen by the president of a rival organization – The Devil's Fang whose various body parts (most of which Patterson had taken great delight in removing *before* he let the fucker die) were found in separate shallow graves in the front lawns of other Devil's Fang members' homes. Now, he wouldn't even have to rely on the handouts and generosity of his brothers-in-arms. Patterson was convinced that the hole in the ground was a tunnel to a secret fucking treasure. A fortune. This shit was Patterson's lotto 6/49 moment and he was about to hit the motherfucking jackpot.

The long grass surrounding the hole illuminated, first in a strip of light at ground level then sweeping out and up as the door to it was raised, this time from the inside. A hooded head followed the arm that was pushing the hatch cover up and over; it landed with a dull thud. The man climbed out of the hole, turned and knelt before it. Patterson saw the same pointy nose poking out of the hood like a flesh gnomon on a sundial as he reached back into the hole and snuffed the light from within it. Patterson made a mental note of the light switch's approximate location within the mouth of the aperture for later reference.

Now using a flashlight to see, the hooded figure hauled the door back into place, closing the hole. There followed a metallic chinking but Patterson had never let a padlock stop him before and remained unfazed. Stepping over the sealed entry, the man unrolled his rug of grass, rendering the secret underground store non-existent to the untrained eye. Patterson liked the guy, not enough to prevent him from filling him with lead, but enough to give him a tip of his equally nefarious cap.

Patterson's toes wriggled with excitement as the man made his way through the field. Patterson was unwilling to wait longer. He was ready to follow the guy to the house and take out both him and the owner of the big panties and pink cardigan.

Patterson rolled onto his side, keeping only half a lookout for the man as he did so. He reached for the twelve-gauge and pulled it up to his side but accidentally knocked the bale hook with his foot as he did so. It slid across the wooden mezzanine of the hayloft and teetered agonizingly at the edge. Patterson didn't have time to pray before the thing tipped and spilled over the edge. As it fell it clattered noisily against a rung of the ladder before landing softly in a pile of straw below.

Patterson immediately returned to his stomach, head low, daring himself to peek out at the field. "Fuck," he whispered to himself. Why hadn't he just stayed still for a couple more minutes? He gingerly spied out across the field, hoping to find it empty, maybe the noise of the wind had deafened the man to the sound of the falling hook. No such luck. The dark figure was standing in the middle of the field and looking up at the barn. Patterson ducked his head as far as he could whilst still keeping the figure in view as the man took two steps towards the barn and trained his flashlight beam across it.

The gaps between the planks of the wall allowed the light to permeate the barn in bright strips that travelled across it towards Patterson's hiding place in the loft. He flattened himself against the floor, his cheek firmly planted in the mouse-piss-soaked hay. He held his breath and dared not look until the light finally retreated along the wall and slithered through the gaps again. With the barn returned to darkness Patterson still did not dare to look out of the hayloft doorway until a sudden, vicious gust of wind squalled through it, kicking up a pelting of straw and mouse droppings and slamming one of the loft doors shut before clattering it back open again to slam against the outside of the wall as it screamed its retreat. The door banged so forcefully that a fresh dusting of ancient crap drizzled down from the roof. As the door bounced to a rest, its handle jangled metallically, producing a sound not entirely dissimilar to that caused by the metal bale-hook hitting the wooden rung. Patterson felt hope once more and peeked out at the field just in time to see that the man was satisfied that he had deciphered the source of the noise and was clearly on his way back to his house.

Patterson rolled onto his back and allowed himself to breathe again.

Kismet? Fate? Luck? Whatever it was, it was wearing thin and running out of patience.

Patterson's eyes widened as he heard a car door slam, an engine cough to life and watched the retreating glare of headlights before waiting for the sound of the vehicle to fade into the distance. He took it as a sign. This was his chance and all he needed was for whatever force it was that had taken him under its wing to trust in him a little longer. Long enough to gain entry to the shaft and evaluate its contents then get to the house and do what needed to be done before taking a seat on that neatly made bed to await the return of the mystery man and his getaway vehicle.

CHAPTER 52 - THE PAGER

Ali drank the last of her gin and tonic – she wasn't supposed to drink either but, fuck that for a game of soldiers. Sometimes looking forward to a drink was the only thing that got her to seven p.m. She huffed as she heard David's pager pealing from their bedroom followed by the frantic madness as he rushed from the house leaving their pack of dogs barking at the front door. That was her cue to forsake her relaxing bath and settle the house down again.

Once in bed, sleep came easily to Ali but even as she drifted off, she prayed to a god she was almost sure was real that her dreams be free of viaducts and hacksaws because severe depression was always listening and fed upon the sufferer's own thoughts of it – like the saying someone had used the other day at the meeting, what was it? 'Speak of the devil, and he's presently at your elbow', a Christine Labreque special if ever there was one. *Damn*, thought Ali, as she remembered she was due to attend the Labreque swingers' party tomorrow night.

During the night Ali was only vaguely aware of David's return, his entrance accompanied by the expected barking of four attention-hungry dogs. Although she'd sensed his presence in the master suite and his weight on his side of the bed, Ali had forced her eyes to remain shut – *two can play at that game, David* – and he'd left the room soon thereafter. Maybe he preferred the couch to his side of the barricade? Later, some time in the early hours of Friday morning, she was aware of his departure from the house once again but this time the pager had remained silent.

CHAPTER 53 - THE HERO

Some crazy-ass, tin-foil hat-wearing conspiracy theorist had evidently worked his paranoid butt off creating what Patterson had decided to name 'The Rat Run'.

He'd opened the door in the field easily, despite the fact that its deadbolt was padlocked, by smashing the bolt from the door with the butt of the gun. The light switch was a thin string of metal balls dangling from a steel disk screwed onto the wooden framework of the platform within which the hatch door nestled when closed. He had descended a set of steep stairs, the central structure of which was originally a simple wooden ladder. Planks of wood, two-by-fours and impacted dirt had been added to form a crude stairway leading down to a tunnel.

The tunnel was a massive, corrugated metal pipe, tall enough to stand in and trussed with crossed beams at its entrance, once in the middle and again at the far end. A trail of bulbs, the cable connecting them was hooked to the ceiling at intervals, provided more than adequate lighting and by the end of the passageway, heat too.

The Rat Run was an appropriate name for two reasons: three of the suckers had scurried past him already and the place stunk of rat piss and shit. At the end of the tunnel was a round door, except it wasn't really round, it had just looked that way to Patterson as he neared the end of the circular pipe. Sliding another deadbolt open, this one was padlock free, Patterson pushed the wooden door open and stepped into a small, circular room lit by a single bulb on the same length of cable as the others.

The walls looked like they had been carved with spoons, there wasn't a straight edge or a corner in sight. Directly in front of him was another wooden door with a deadbolt like the last. To his left was a wooden chair, next to that was a brown velvet curtain hanging from a rail. To his right was a mirror surrounded by polaroid photographs.

No drugs. No stash of cash. Behind the curtain was some serious gimp gear, leather suspenders and steel studs and a set of chaps that'd get you killed in any self-respecting motorcycle club. Patterson stepped over to the mirror and studied the photographs surrounding it, some of them yellowed and faded but all of them with a grim theme. Young girls, naked, tied up. Some serious S&M shit. But as he looked at the pictures Patterson noticed that all the girls were expressionless regardless of what twisted stuff was happening to them. One girl was in a yoke, the kind you see over the shoulders of yaks and oxen carrying heavy loads up mountains. Another girl's tits were pulled out to each side, so much so it looked painful, her nipples in clamps at the end of wires but again her face was emotionless, she wasn't reacting to pain, in fact she looked half asleep. One girl's face was obscured from view but whatever was stuffed in her pussy was like no dildo Patterson had ever seen – it looked rigid and solid and certainly wasn't designed to bring pleasure.

As he scanned the multitude of pictures and blank faces Patterson began to wonder what the fuck he'd stumbled across here. What was this place? Some sicko's pleasure dungeon? Patterson was the first to admit he'd done some mean shit in his time but these pictures crossed a line, they depicted something darker than mere perversion and he had to turn away when the images began to stir something darkly arousing within him. He was determined to keep the threat of a stiffy at bay.

Patterson was beginning to feel cheated and found

himself about as pissed off as he could be. Finding a great pile of cocaine or heroin or even fucking hash seemed about as likely as finding rocking horse shit. The dilemma that he was now faced with was whether to proceed through the next door or just count his blessings and get the fuck out.

Okay, so this is the creep's jerk-off room. So what? It didn't mean there wasn't a huge narco operation through the next door. Except there was a stronger smell of piss and shit now, but it had the tang of human faeces, meatier and less earthy than before. Well, if it turned out to just be a toilet back there, he would turn back, see the night through in the hayloft then head out at first light.

Patterson checked the two cartridges in his shotgun and snapped the barrel shut again. With the ultimate equalizer in hand, he proceeded through the next door.

A rush of warm air clouded his face and with it came a strong stench of festering human, everything that stinks on an unclean body. Not just piss and shit, but sour sweat, hair grease and the stuff that comes out from between your teeth when you floss and the white smeg that gathers and goes fungal in moist folds of skin. Within that myriad of fetidness was a fresher, more subtle smell but one that pricks at the survival instincts; it was the almost indiscernible hint of fresh wounds, the smell that causes a dog to seek out and lick at a pin prick, the smell of early onset infection.

Patterson's stomach turned, a reaction most unusual for him. He paused in the doorway to regain his composure and to allow his eyes to adjust to the gloominess of the room, larger than the previous one but also lit only by a single bulb.

The ceiling of this room was much lower than the last and so he had to stoop slightly as he stepped in. Against the mud wall directly in front of him Patterson saw that, running the entire length of the room, a wooden bench had been installed and was bolted to the ground. Sitting upright on the bench, four feet or so apart, were two naked girls. His initial reaction was to raise his gun at them until he noticed that they weren't aware of his presence and posed no threat to him. The wooden bench upon which they were seated had large holes bored through it at intervals along its length, each of the girls was seated over their own hole, their arms lay lifeless at their sides, their hands resting on the bench like the hands of boxed puppets.

Toilet holes. Patterson glanced below the bench and saw that there was a steel bucket under each girl, ready to catch their waste. But these girls weren't just enjoying the pleasure of a communal bathroom experience and they weren't sitting upright because they were alert; they were out of it. Another plank of wood ran the length of the room, this time a little higher than their shoulders, their heads above the plank – through it – their bodies below.

Patterson stepped closer to the girls, his knees felt fat and weak like his legs might buckle under him and give way at any moment. He swallowed to suppress a puke promising throb in his tongue.

The shoulder-height plank had been sawn in two along its length with cutouts big enough for only a neck in intervals that exactly corresponded with the toilet holes below. Each of the girls was trapped by the neck. This was the yoke type contraption he'd seen in one of those pictures.

Despite the ambient warmth, Patterson felt cold beads of sweat prickle his brow and a slap of dismay hit him. He looked at each end of the neck plank. On the right side it was attached to the wall with steel anchors and bolts. On the left it was housed in a boxed socket and secured with a pair of rings and a padlock, presumably so that the planks could be separated at that junction to place the girls in the stocks and take them out again as needed.

There was another door to the left of the room. Patterson stared at it, dumbfounded, dreading what may lie beyond its threshold. Turning back to the girls, their skin waxy with perspiration. He whispered to them, "Hey. Hey, wake up."

They didn't stir. They certainly weren't dead, he could see their ribs moving with each breath. He touched one of the girls, on her cheek. She was the one nearest to him with long, dark hair hanging nearly to her skinny waist. She looked young. Eighteen, maybe nineteen but no older than that. He prodded her cheek again but she didn't respond. It was then that he noticed that the girls weren't only locked into the plank, they were locked *onto* it too.

Around each girl's neck was some sort of a collar, orange metal, separate rings. One of them had more rings than the other but the highest ring on both had been fastened to the plank above it with a combination padlock and rings.

Patterson pulled at the plank, wondering how much give it had, how easy it would be to free the girls from the contraption. He hadn't realized it until that moment but freeing these girls and getting them the fuck out of there had become his only motivation. Fuck the jackpot, fuck the Malahat and fuck if he had to spend the rest of his life inside, there was just no way he could live with himself if he were to turn his back and leave them now.

The plank was heavy and secure but it wasn't the padlocks that daunted him.

"Hey, lady. Wake up," he whispered to the girl with the long hair again but again there was no response. He pulled up her eyelid, her eye swam up as if she were trying to see him but then drifted to her left. Her pupils were so pinned, they were barely visible.

Heroin?

He'd seen the effects of it before but the girls didn't appear to have any track lines. One of the girls had some old scars on her forearms from shooting up but nothing recent. Not on their legs either.

Patterson turned to the closed door, the mystery door and took a readying breath. He had to see what lay beyond it. There could be another room with more girls because neither of the girls in this room were any of the ones pictured in the polaroids he'd seen in the jerk-off room.

He slid the bolt open and pushed the door away from him. He was greeted at once by a more intense blast of heat and all the smells of the previous room but accompanied by the coppery scent of blood.

Girl number three took no finding because no attempt had been made to hide the sorry wretch. She was illuminated only by the light of a corner wood stove, its chimney disappeared through the ceiling and Patterson imagined it must pop out of the ground within the line of the perimeter trees above ground. She was lying on a blue blanket, her arms and legs stretched wide. She was cuffed at her ankles and her wrists. A thick chain ran from the cuffs to rings embedded into the walls on either side of her.

Patterson's usually strong constitution crumbled and the old banana he'd eaten resurfaced on his tongue. He held back the vomit as best he could with his free hand but the contents of his stomach, the cold stew, the Slim Jim and one of the bottles of water spewed out from behind his palm, splattering his cheeks, his boots and the dirty floor.

She was in a hellish state, her pussy was swollen, blistered red and raw and from inside it protruded the black object he'd seen in the photos. The skin on her stomach and on the top of her thighs was splattered with strips of blistered flesh, some of the blisters had burst and were crusting up, some were like cloudy snow globes and bulged with fluid still. Her neck and her shoulders and the top of her chest were all bloody, skin was missing and torn, the same damage was evident along the length of her inner thighs. Patterson puked again as he watched a black fly enjoying a strip of the raw flesh there.

She was barely alive. So skinny that Patterson thought he could make out the grey of her rib bones beneath her skin. Her stomach was concave and bobbed along with her fast, shallow breaths. Her eyes were half open and he could see them gently drifting from side to side as if she was watching an imaginary T.V. above her. Her teeth were prominent and looked like they belonged to a far larger skull than hers, her lips peeled back from them so she looked like she was enjoying the imaginary broadcast.

Patterson's stomach knotted. He butted his ass back

against the door and put his hands on his knees, resting his weight against them. Shaken to the core of him. Many times in his life, Patterson had been described as 'evil'. By the judge that sentenced him, both of his ex-wives and almost everyone who managed to find his wrong side. Over the years he'd embraced the adjective, it was a badge of honour hard earned on the outlaw battlefield. But now, having witnessed the detritus of *true* evil, the human debris of a dark soul, Patterson was purified in comparison, baptized with a new sense of humanity and he willingly shed himself of any similarity between him and the monster responsible for this sorry sight.

He'd watched the man come and go. He'd entered the guy's house, eaten his food, he was wearing his socks.

In the doorway between both rooms, Patterson looked at the imprisoned girls and felt helpless. There were no other doors, that was something at least, so he was only faced with freeing the three of them. If he were to free them from their chains and padlocks he'd still have to get them out. They were all smacked out of their heads, they'd never be able to climb or run or even walk. He wondered if he'd even be able to carry them all up that ladder to ground level and then what? How would he get them to safety? What if the monster were to come back in the middle of their manumission?

There was no other option. He'd have to leave them and get help. He swiped the back of his arm across his vinegar-tasting mouth and spat again. Pulling himself up to standing on legs like those of a newborn foal, he backed out of the rooms, internally apologizing and reassuring the helpless waifs who, he knew, were blissfully unaware that he'd even been in the room with them.

James Henry Patterson felt something new and entirely overwhelming within him and he began to cry. As honest despair hiccuped out of him, it brought with it all of his anger and the cold viciousness with which he'd thus far navigated life. Tears blurred his vision and his nose dripped and tingled with a sour buzz. Patterson realized then, for the first time in his life, what heartbreak is. His actual heart – nothing imaginary, nothing arty-farty, the organ itself – ached and sagged in his chest and he sobbed for the innocence, spoiled and battered and trapped in the monster's hell hole.

In the jerk-off room again, Patterson felt hatred. Hatred for the beast he'd watch come and go from this place. He lashed out at the walls, screaming his fury. As he did, he tore down the curtain, pulled the seedy gimp gear from the hangers and scratched the polaroids off the wall before slamming his boot into the mirror and shattering it.

Once he'd sniffled himself to a semblance of calm he once again looked at the pictures, this time scrunched and half-buried in the loose dirt of the floor. None of the girls in the two rooms behind him were photographed and Patterson realized that many more must have suffered the same fate as them but had been finished with and disposed of somehow. The floor might contain the only proof of what had become of them. Patterson bent to gather the images up, he'd need them, he'd show them to the police and then they'd believe him, they'd have to look for this place and make the bastard pay.

Patterson only managed to shove three of the pictures into his pocket before he heard the outer door, the hatch to the outside world, open. A stiff breeze of fresh air ruffled his hair and goose-pimpled his flesh with the chilly arrival of evil in the pipe. He looked along the tunnel ahead of him as two booted feet started to descend the ladder stairway.

The sick fuck was back. Patterson looked around. There was nowhere to hide now that the curtain was crumpled on the floor. He grasped his gun to his chest and held himself flush against the wall only partially obscured by the open door. His heart pounded. He had the upper hand thanks to the two shells loaded in the shotgun but still he felt...what was it he felt? Shit fucking scared, that's what.

Patterson's upper hand was ripped from him when the

lights were snuffed. What's the use of a gun in utter darkness? Subterranean darkness is a darkness like no other. It is not merely the absence of light; it has weight and it touches you, bears down upon you. It sucks the oxygen from the air and places such pressure around you that your eardrums swell and whistle-pop like when you're speeding too fast downhill.

As the darkness wrapped itself upon his eyeballs, Patterson had no choice but to head for the deepest depths of the lair, past the sitting girls and into the final room where the ruined girl lay and where there was a light that couldn't be switched off – the light from the corner stove then he could take aim and send this sucker to a hell of his own.

Patterson understood that this guy probably knew every inch of these rooms and that tunnel yet he himself was utterly disorientated. He dropped to his hands and knees as quietly as he could and began to proceed in the direction in which he imagined the door to the second room lay. It was impossible to be silent, the gun chinked every time he progressed. He prayed that whoever this fiend was, he might be hard of hearing or deaf. Deaf would be a massive bonus right now because Patterson was pretty sure that his own heartbeat would give away his location, never mind the clinking firearm.

He felt out ahead of himself, sure that he must have reached the threshold between the room he was in and the one housing the two sitting girls but was dismayed to feel the velvet of the heavy brown curtain beneath his fingertips. Patterson adjusted his angle, hoping that he'd pointed himself in the right direction this time and crawled forward three chinking hand-steps.

Feeling again with his hand outstretched he was heartened to discover that he had reached the doorway. Fuelled by refreshed hope Patterson shuffled eagerly forward but his eagerness was his downfall. From behind him came the thudding, echoing steps of the crazy bastard – he was running full pelt through the pitch-black tunnel, gaining on him fast and leaving Patterson with no option but to throw himself over onto his back, raise the double barrel and shoot it blind into the darkness.

Searing light flashed and the decibels of the shot clattered his eardrums so they hummed and muted themselves. His brain pushed against the back of his eyes as the red ghost of the gunshot's flash branded itself on his retinas.

Then a weight was on him, it slammed upon his chest, the gun was yanked out of his hands. Patterson grappled madly hoping to grab hair, grip a face or tear skin but he was overpowered.

The monster must be a nocturnal beast, able to see in the dark and wavered not in bringing about Patterson's demise. Patterson's fingers on his right hand were crushed in the man's fist then yanked back as a simultaneous blast hit his face. It was a cracking blow, bones audibly fractured as something huge and solid and inhuman smashed into his face. Patterson was unable to react to the blow, not simply because it had dazed him but because it had baffled him. What the fuck was the guy hitting him with? It was hard and soft, it was cold and warm, both sticky and slick. The massive, furred club struck his face again, his nose snapped sharply out of place and the darkness prickled with silver spots.

Patterson's face was coated with a creamy coldness, salty and vaguely recognizable. In the brief second that it took for the next, more brutal blow to fall he realized that he was slick with blood but that the blood was not his own – it was cold blood and besides, even a busted nose doesn't bleed that much.

He was struck again and he felt his lips split in the middle against his teeth, his mouth instantly filling with burning, thick blood of his own. The mystery weapon felt like a cinder block wrapped in a fur coat, the tail end of which painted wetness over his forehead as his attacker's weight lifted from his chest. Patterson gargled. His left eye socket was smashed and the shards of bone surrounding his eyeball poked at its juice once the lights were switched back on and he tried to look to the side to make sense of the befuddling object being wielded by the nutter.

Blinking away the crimson paste from his good eye, Patterson spluttered his own blood from his gullet and rolled onto his side, his skewed jaw screamed in protest. He looked at the madman.

Standing in the doorway to the 'sitting room' loomed the hooded man he'd watched crossing the field earlier that night. In his left hand was the shotgun, from his right dangled a black ball of fur, way larger than a soccer ball and not perfectly round, it hung from a smaller patch of the fur and twirled slowly, painting a circle of Christmassy red dots in the dirt. As the thing turned, Patterson caught sight of what looked like a big, black nose. An animal's nose. The madman had beaten him with the head of a huge animal, its barely visible black eyes stared lifelessly out of its dead skull, mocking Patterson as it spun lazily above him.

The hooded man let go of the animal's ear and the ball of fur dropped to the ground with a thud. Patterson managed to raise his hands in a last but futile attempt to survive. The twelve-gauge flashed.

PART FIVE

FRIDAY 13TH APRIL

CHAPTER 54 - BAD DISGUISED AS GOOD

Hindsight is twenty-twenty. If you're lucky there have been only a handful of truly bad days in your life but, whether those days are many or few, in *hindsight* you knew the bad was coming.

Human beings perceive many things with senses numbering many more than five. We are instinctive creatures. We possess atavistic knowledge – passed onto us through our D.N.A. by ancestors who walked the earth decades, centuries and millennia ago and who, having befallen a fate at the hands of a foe, whispered to themselves, 'I knew it' and the power of this acknowledgement lives on in them, becomes a part of them beyond the demise of their flesh and bones and whispers to their descendants, informing them of danger.

The whisper lets us know a stranger entirely, yet we talk ourselves out of trusting that knowledge because it isn't based on a tangible experience. For instance, your energy sinks the day you meet 'Jenny', a co-worker, perhaps, at your new place of work. Although she is smiling and she is chatting you somehow know that you can't trust her. You tell yourself to ignore the sinking feeling because 'Jenny' seems harmless and she hasn't done anything to you, she hasn't because you've just met her. So, you suppress your instinctive mistrust of her, you deny your nonsensical revulsion towards her. But sometime later, in the future, be it in days or weeks or months or years, you find yourself saying

'I knew it!' because 'Jenny' turned out to be a treacherous, duplicitous, back-stabbing bitch. You *knew* it. You knew it because 'Jenny' possessed a quality that was present in the persecutor of a distant, long forgotten ancestor whose genetic code informed your own.

For Ali, Friday the thirteenth would be one of those days and would live up to the negative associations attached to the date by the superstitious. A day that she would look back upon in hindsight and ponder upon the fact that she had started it off somehow *knowing* that it was going to be bad.

But the bad was cloaked in good.

Although her dreams had been weird – in that twisted, dream-like way where the newly sprouted fish gills on your inner thighs are being studied by a team of goggled scientists and you're embarrassed by the worm of poo that spews from the new anus in your armpit as they prod it – twisted indeed but mercifully free of viaducts and self-slaughter.

However, as a mere newborn in terms of happiness (maybe happiness is an exaggeration, more like peeking out from under her worn blanket of depression) Ali had awoken with a defensive, mistrusting tinge to anything resembling joy within her.

She looked at David's side of the bed. She had slept alone last night; he'd left the bed and then the house.

Ali pressed her face against his pillow, breathing in the scent of her husband and wrapped her arms and legs around the barricade of pillows between her side and his. She closed her eyes and indulged in a pretence, a pretence that they were happy and in love again and she was cuddled up to him. She remembered the comfort that holding him close brought to her, the familiarity of their intimacy and wondered when, *how*, they had drifted apart. Was it just since she and Marlene had found Samantha Giesbrecht? Surely not. The rot must have set in long before that.

Ali released pillow-David from her embrace and rolled onto her back. The ugly light fixture glared down at her, studying her, analysing her just like the fish-gills the scientists in her dream had.

Under its accusatory gaze, Ali acquiesced that if her relationship with David was indeed over then it was probably because of her – not her fault, because that was a different matter altogether – but, *because of her.*

It was an admission she accepted only briefly before her natural inclination towards vicious defensiveness seeped into her soul like acid on litmus and threatened her refreshing serenity with visions of ripping her husband's balls off and serving them to him, smothered in tomato sauce on a bed of spaghetti. She didn't want her happiness to scuttle away again, at least not before it had a chance to bloom properly. She asked herself again if she was feeling true happiness or was she pink-clouding on the back of the elevated drama of the week. The pink cloud was a dangerous thing to ride. The pink cloud was the paradigm of bad disguised as good.

Showered and dressed but unable to remember the last time she'd eaten, Ali's body demanded calories and so she spread not only a layer of salted butter on her toast but also a layer of Marmite followed by a thick smear of palette gluing peanut butter and washed it all down with a massive mug of heavily sugared tea.

The fatty breakfast was as uncharacteristic as the fact that she'd consumed it all before her first cigarette but she remedied her misdemeanour by smoking two in a row, the second lit from the ember of the first.

The morning seemed to have inspired uncharacteristic actions in everyone as Kenny was particularly quiet and unusually disciplined on the personal hygiene front – he had showered and was wearing clean clothes by eight thirty. But before Ali took pride in her parenting skills, she realized that she'd been so distracted by the week's events that she'd forgotten about Kenny's mock exam, scheduled for later that day.

She decided to allow her son the pleasure of thinking he had one-upped his mother – not entirely for selfless reasons but more because she hadn't even written the damn thing yet and Marlene would be arriving any minute for their trip to Victoria.

As if Marlene had been cued from the wings, the doorbell chimed and the madness of the morning began. Ali opened the door to a rosy-cheeked Marlene, unable to fend off the canine welcome because her arms were full.

Ali pulled her dogs back, counting only three and vaguely bemused by that fact but overwhelmingly curious as to the contents of Marlene's numerous bundles.

"Morning, Marlene. Come in. What's all that?"

Marlene negotiated her way past the dogs and dumped her load down on the dining table.

"I made some sandwiches," she said as she pointed to a large, black, Save-On-Foods bag-for-life. "And some blankets, sweaters and a couple of Peter's old winter coats. I'm sure he won't miss them, probably doesn't even know he still has them, honestly."

Ali looked in the bag-for-life, at the pile of individually wrapped sub sandwiches featuring a variety of over the top luxury fillings including prawns in thousand island dressing and brie with what looked like a caramelized onion relish, the type Ali used to splurge on at Christmas from Marks & Spencer.

"That's one shit load of sandwiches. You must have been at it all night."

"Well, I figured, if we're going to talk to homeless people then we should give them something in return, so, food and warmth."

"Nice."

"Peter says, better that than money to buy crack or crank or whatever it is they put in their veins or pipes."

"Or even just cigs and booze, huh? I've asked Cuzzocrea for a picture of the Giesbrecht girl. Maybe it will jog a few memories."

"Super. So, are we stopping at R.C.M.P. on the way? We're taking your car, right? I'm excited to get in a Porsche.

We can burn it on the highway."

Ali laughed. "Yeah. But no, Cuzzocrea said he'd drop it off here this morning."

"Ooh, the personal touch." Marlene checked the time, a white, cotton handkerchief was folded neatly into the space between the watch's gold bracelet and her freckled wrist. "The Salvation Army at the bottom of Johnson Street serves a breakfast of sorts until nine thirty so we should aim to get going as soon as possible."

"Okay, I'll text him, see where he is."

No sooner had Ali's phone whooshed with the sound of her sent text than the doorbell chimed again. Ali headed for it but was beaten to it by Sandy who was dressed for work and already opening it, holding the barking dogs back expertly with a leg and the snarking chihuahua under her right arm.

Ali heard Cuzzocrea's voice, "It's okay, Sandy. Let him in."

Sandy stepped back from the door, Ali could see that she was blushing and as Cuzzocrea stepped into the house, she understood how the sight of the man could have such an effect of a young girl – who was she kidding? He had the same effect on her too *and* Marlene who, Ali could hear, was quietly cooing as the tall cop smiled and joined them in the dining area.

"Morning ladies."

"Good morning, Inspector." Marlene rolled the final 'r' in inspector like a pantomime baddie. "How did you sleep?"

"I didn't," he replied.

"I'm not surprised with her thread count." Marlene snorted.

"Pardon me?"

"Elouise Dompierre. Cheap sheets and plastic flowers." Marlene explained, "You're staying at the Owl's Roost B&B, right?"

Cuzzocrea looked stunned. "How do you…"

Ali shrugged. "It's Mochetsin. If you shit, someone brings

you toilet paper."

"Mum!" Sandy chided from behind Cuzzocrea.

"What?"

"Gross. I'm going to work." Sandy pulled on her hoodie and tied her scarf around her neck. She flicked her hair out of it like she was auditioning for a Garnier Nutrisse ad.

"Okay sweet, can you take the dogs out for their morning shit first?" Ali smiled at her daughter.

Sandy huffed with a mixture of disgust and desired rebellion but restrained herself from vocalizing either, probably, Ali suspected, to appear as mature as she possibly could in the presence of the inspector.

Ali quashed a smirk. "Where is Oscar, by the way? I haven't seen him yet today."

"Oh, yes. The Newfie. I thought my trousers were clean," said Marlene. "Where is that magnificent beast of yours?"

"Maybe he's on the beach?" suggested Sandy. "And, by the way, can you please remind dad that I'm not five any more? He doesn't need to tuck me in."

"Okay, but I don't know what you're talking about," said Ali.

"He must have come into my room last night because I woke up and I couldn't move, my comforter was tucked in under my mattress all the way up to my shoulders *and* he'd switched my lamp off. I hate that."

"Sandy, honey, what can I say? He's a firefighter, they have a habit of ensuring that all electrical stuff is off at night – something to do with dragging charred children out of buildings in the middle of the night and crushing the bones of their tiny chests doing C.P.R., I suppose." Ali's eyes warned her daughter that a cocky response would land her in very embarrassing waters.

"Whatever." Sandy called the dogs to her and headed for the back door.

"She's not very happy with us," said Ali to Marlene.

"Ali, she's a teenager, they're never happy with anyone," said Marlene.

Cuzzocrea held up a manila envelope. "I have the photograph for you. It's the most recent one the parents had of her."

"May I?" Marlene asked Cuzzocrea.

Marlene took the manila envelope and stepped away to look at the photograph within.

Cuzzocrea held up another envelope, this one much fatter than the first. "The file you requested."

Ali took it. "Thank you."

Cuzzocrea crossed to her and spoke quietly, "Do I need to remind you what would happen to me if anyone…"

"Say no more. I promise, for my eyes only. Besides," Ali whispered quietly to him, "I think Marlene'd have me publicly flogged if she knew I had it."

Cuzzocrea nodded and took his vibrating phone from his pocket. He answered the call and stepped away to speak privately.

Ali placed the secret file on the table. Marlene's shoulders betrayed the sad weight upon them as she looked at the photograph and pinned it to the victim section of the wall, just above Ali's sketch of the body as they'd found it, discarded in the bushes on Alder Beach Trail.

Ali didn't have the heart to mention that pinning it up right now was pointless as they'd need to take it with them to Victoria and instead stood shoulder to shoulder next to Marlene as she studied the face in the picture.

Samantha Giesbrecht looked like any happy, pretty teenage girl. Squinting a cheerful grin to the camera, shielding her eyes from the glare of the sun on what must have been a family trip to the beach – the photo had been cropped so that its only focus was the girl but Ali could see the edge of a woman's arm around Samantha's shoulder, maybe her mother's, and the pointy tip of a dog's ears peeking into the bottom of the shot.

Ali felt a stab of compassion. She had a hundred pictures just like it of her own kids. God forbid their images ever found themselves posthumously placed on an incident board.

Startling Ali out of her grim funk, Cuzzocrea spoke, "I have to go, there's been a development." He noticed the wall. "Wow. You two aren't kidding around."

"A development?" asked Ali. "Something you want to share?"

"Not yet. I'll let you know if it's pertinent. What time are you ladies leaving for your…"

"Orgy?" Marlene smiled cheekily at him. "Seven?" Marlene suggested.

"Works for me," agreed Ali.

"Remember our agreement?" Cuzzocrea said as he headed for the door. "You show me yours…if you happen upon anything significant downtown…"

"You'll be the third to know." Ali nodded.

Ali heard Cuzzocrea's confident steps descend her stairs accompanied by the cacophony of barking emanating from the fenced dog run which lay at the other side of the driveway. As his car ascended the drive the dogs barked louder than before but quieter than usual since they lacked the shuddering bass of Oscar's voice.

"Kenny, honey?" Ali called out.

Kenny was in the kitchen – undoubtedly preparing one of his many-layered creations capable of putting even Marlene's bag of luxury sandwiches to shame – he popped his head through the housewife's hatch. "Yeah?"

"Do me a favour and go find Oscar after you've eaten, will you?"

"On it." Kenny disappeared again, still doing a masterful job of flying under mum-radar.

"Okay then, we're off. Call me if you need anything. Or dad, if you can't get a hold of me."

"I don't know if he'll have a signal on the ferry, but okay," said Kenny, dipping into view through the hatch and licking some mayo from the butter knife.

"Don't lick the knife," said Ali. "What do you mean? Ferry?"

"The Salt-Spring thing. He texted Sandy early to leave a note for you," said Kenny. "Here. Kinda dumb though, why not just text you?"

"Hmmm." Ali pulled the lilac sheet of grocery list paper to her and read David's note, written by proxy in her daughter's neat hand:

Hey,
Dad says he got a call and stayed after it to get a head start on loading up the trucks for the Salt Spring Island course. He said he wanted to go for a run anyway and didn't want to disturb us so showered at the hall. He said he loves us and he'll see us on Sunday night.
xxx

"Fuck," said Ali.

"Problem?" asked Marlene.

"No. Yes. Shit. I forgot David was on some course this weekend."

Ali's heart ached, she'd been so wrapped up in herself, she'd also forgotten about David's trip and she felt lousy because of it. Now the distance between them was literal too. "Oh well, not much I can do about that now," Ali said, scrunching up the note and allowing her spiritual litmus to blanch. If she focused on David's pettiness, his refusal to communicate directly with her, she could almost hate him more than herself and that felt marginally better.

"Shall we?" said Marlene, her arms full again.

Ali took the sandwich bag from her. "Let me carry that." Ali followed Marlene to the front door, grabbing her car keys from the hook next to it as she passed. "Bye, Kenny. Love you."

"Bye," he spoke with a mouth full of triple-decker.

Ali crashed into the back of Marlene who had stopped short of the threshold. "What?"

"Just thinking, we'll need that picture with us downtown – that's why you got it, right?" said Marlene.

"Fuck a duck!" Ali exclaimed as she returned to the photograph and pulled it down from the wall. "What the hell is wrong with me?"

"Early menopause? Maybe dementia?" replied Marlene in a matter-of-fact manner. "You should watch 'Still Alice', to prepare yourself."

"Thanks, Marlene. You're like…spittoon soup for the soul."

CHAPTER 55 - THE DEATH PIT

Having pulled on his Tyvek coverall and boot covers (he decided there was no need for the purple medical gloves since Trina Walsh wasn't likely to let anyone touch anything within a wide radius of the site anyhow) Cuzzocrea slammed his trunk shut and headed over the field towards his approaching partner.

Munro's face was comically squishing out from within the tight elastic of his white coverall hood. He belched as he met Cuzzocrea, burping out a hot, oniony waft and thumped his sternum.

"I went grazing round Costco last night instead of paying for food and that frigging samosa is repeating on me something wicked."

"What do we have?" asked Cuzzocrea.

"We have ourselves a bona-fide death-pit, my friend," answered Munro.

"Another girl?"

"Nope. An actual death pit, used by the Mochetsin Public Works crew. Come over and look, then I'll explain."

So excited was Munro to show off the death pit that he practically skipped towards the cordoned section of the field. As he watched Munro gallop ahead of him, Cuzzocrea was reminded of the tubby kitchen paper men in the Sponge Towel advertisement on T.V.

The death pit was appropriately named. Ignoring the reason for the VIIMIS presence on site, Cuzzocrea counted more than fourteen visible roadkill carcasses each in various stages of decomposition, consisting largely of deer but also racoons, one owl that would have his landlady in need of a paper bag and several squished squirrels.

"What the hell?"

"I always wondered what they did with roadkill. They dump it in pits like this. Makes sense, I suppose, it's not like you see stag graveyards all over the place."

"Man, it stinks."

"Yep. You get used to it after half an hour or so."

Cuzzocrea crouched down at the edge of the pit.

"Stay back, four hundred metres, Cuzzocrea." Trina Walsh shouted from the other side of the pit where she and her forensic team were labelling evidence bags and laying them out on a white table, the sort of table usually used for condiments and hotdog rolls at a tailgate party.

Cuzzocrea waved in an effort to appease her – what did she think? That he wanted to dive into the carrion festooned hole?

"So, looks like we found our escaped convict then." Cuzzocrea studied the spread-eagled body lying across the top of the heap of death, face up and, strangely enough, wearing a pink cardigan.

James Henry Patterson's face was battered and bloody and he had a black, gaping hole in the centre of his chest.

"What do we know so far? asked Cuzzocrea.

"According to Walsh, prior to death he suffered significant blunt-force trauma to the face. As you can see, he died of a single shot to the chest. The wound is consistent with a shotgun round fired at close range," Munro said.

"What about the injuries to the face?"

"That's where it gets really freaky. At the site of all of the facial injuries, Trina found animal fur, hair actually. It's dog hair."

"He was mauled?"

"Nope. The black and white thing you can see under him?"

"What the fuck is that?" asked Cuzzocrea. He moved forty-five degrees, anti-clockwise around the mouth of the pit and crouched again at his new vantage point. Although covered in blood, it was clear that the black and white creature was heavily furred; its wide paws and a fluffy white tail was all that could be observed of the animal under Patterson's splayed body but the length of the beast's spine, judging by the distance between its front paws and back paws, had to be two-thirds as long as the man on top of it.

"Not a bear, with those markings," Cuzzocrea thought aloud.

"Buddy, it's a dog. Decapitated too."

"Roadkill? Is that what caused the decapitation?" asked Cuzzocrea.

"Nope, the head was severed."

Cuzzocrea stood, slowly. His mind ticked over and he was already dreading the rest of Munro's report.

"Initially, Trina thought that the dog hair in Patterson's wounds was a result of his proximity to the animal in the pit – cross contamination. But then she found that the dog hair and other debris consistent with the canine's pelt was imbedded in the wounds, so much so that her theory is that he was…wait for it…probably beaten with the decapitated head of the dog. What the fuck, buddy."

Cuzzocrea took a steadying breath. "Where is the head?"

"It's not visible in the pit but she's yet to move Patterson or the dog so it could be underneath them."

Cuzzocrea headed around the pit to Trina Walsh.

"How long before you move him?" he asked her.

"Couple of hours, we're still gathering evidence and documenting the site."

"You think this is connected to our investigation?"

Trina Walsh snapped a surgical mask in place across the lower two thirds of her face and pinched the embedded metal strip across the bridge of her nose. "That's your job, Inspector. I'll gather the evidence, you do with it what you will." Trina stepped past Cuzzocrea and headed towards the death pit, passing Superintendent Doug Shaw, followed by Munro, as they joined Cuzzocrea.

"Sir," said Cuzzocrea, standing straighter than before.

"Rey." Shaw nodded curtly.

"So. We have Patterson," said Cuzzocrea.

"That we do." Shaw watched Trina Walsh stepping into a rope harness and fastening it around her pelvis.

"Are we treating this as a separate case?" asked Cuzzocrea.

"Officially, yes, for now," said Shaw, turning back to Cuzzocrea. "But let me ask you, what does your gut tell you, Rey?"

As he considered his answer, Cuzzocrea watched Trina carefully descending the steep sides of the pit, supported by one of her team at the other end of the rope and knew that the safety harness was not because she would find it grotesque to fall into a pit of dead things but more because she was preserving evidence and therefore had to be careful of each and every step she took within it.

"Unless there's something scary in the water, it's unlikely we suddenly have more than one murderer operating in a little town like Mochetsin." Cuzzocrea replied.

"I concur. I'm inclined to think we have one perp, responsible for both the girl and Patterson."

"Could have been a citizen acting in self-defence who killed him, panicked and dumped the body," Munro chimed in.

"Too brutal a kill," replied Shaw. "Too cold. And dumped here? According Mayor Dunlop, this place is a bit of a dirty little secret and not exactly common knowledge. It's not flagged on tourist maps, that's for sure. Has to have been a local, a long-term local, someone in the know, even at the centre of the community. Not only that, someone capable of murder and of decapitating a dog and using its head to beat Patterson before shooting him at point-blank range."

"Could be revenge for Hammond?" Cuzzocrea offered.

"Perhaps. Only problem with that theory is that Hammond's death isn't in the public realm yet. We haven't tracked down his next of kin."

"It's a different M.O. to our killer's," said Munro.

"Yes, but if it was a spontaneous attack, not planned by our psycho, then anything goes, right? Freaky neck lengthening is the modus operandi we're using as a distinguishing feature in our investigation, yes, but that doesn't rule out our un-sub's capacity for violence and brutality in general," said Shaw.

Cuzzocrea nodded.

Shaw continued, "I think there has to be a link. Too much of a coincidence to have two separate maniacs at work, like you say. It defies statistical probability."

"Yes." Cuzzocrea thought for a moment and then asked, "The dog, sir?"

"What about it?"

"You don't happen to know what breed it is, do you?"

Shaw frowned. "No." He called out to Trina who was carefully stepping between stag ribs, "Walsh?"

"Sir?" replied Trina.

"What breed is that dog?"

"It's a Newfie. A Newfoundland? Landseer, specifically. I need three evidence bags, now. Doug? I have something."

Superintendent Shaw and Cuzzocrea, followed by Munro, crossed over to the pit as Trina was handed the clear evidence bags by a member of her team. They watched as she placed the items in the bags. Trina made her way back to the edge of the pit and reached up to Doug Shaw, handing him the three new pieces of evidence.

"These were in his trouser pocket," said Trina.

Inside the bags were dirty, crumpled polaroid photographs. Shaw studied them then handed them along to Cuzzocrea and Munro.

"Look at the second girl's neck," said Trina Walsh.

Three different girls were featured in the photographs, one seemed to be asleep yet her nipples were in clamps, the clamps attached to what looked like wires, each breast was being pulled away to each side of her body at what looked to be a painful extreme. The second girl was locked into wooden stocks around her neck but below the wood and wrapped tightly around her neck was a coil of copper tubing, the kind that both Trina Walsh and Ali Dalglish had theorized to be the implement used to lengthen the neck of Samantha Giesbrecht. The third girl was splayed at the legs and a large, cylindrical object protruded from her vagina.

"This confirms our suspicions, the two cases are linked." Doug Shaw turned to Cuzzocrea but he was already crossing the field, on his way back to his car.

"Rey?" Shaw called.

"I may have something, sir. I'll look into it and report back," said Cuzzocrea. He pulled back the hood of his Tyvek and unzipped it to find his phone.

He decided that it was best to remain firm but vague for now, no need to cause unnecessary alarm but as soon as he sent his text he would be heading for one place and one place only:

555 Alder Beach Road.

CHAPTER 56 - ALI PUTS HER FOOT DOWN

Ali was just pulling the white parking stub out of the Fisgard Parkade meter when she received Cuzzocrea's text message:

<important development. meet at your place asap. no panic - obey speed limits! :)>

Ali snatched the card from the slot and ran up the slope, back to her car. Marlene was retrieving her alms from under the hood of the Porsche – a trunk space which had initially dumbfounded Marlene until Ali had explained where the engine was positioned in a Porsche and why.

"Put it back, Marlene. We have to go."

"Huh?" Marlene asked.

"We have to get back to Mochetsin."

Marlene was about to protest but, having taken note of Ali's facial expression, decided instead to drop the goods back into the trunk, at which point she flapped her hands in mild panic. "You shut this, I don't know how."

Ali made sure Marlene's fingers were free of the hood before lowering it down and then clicking it firmly shut by pressing the heel of her hand down on the Stuttgart badge.

As Marlene placed herself in the passenger seat, she asked, "What's going on, hon?"

Ali fastened her seatbelt and fired up the engine. "I got a text from Cuzzocrea. There's been a development."

Ali and Marlene sat in silence as Ali utilized her powerful

engine and sped out of Victoria, taking the View Royal route to the Island Highway, blatantly ignoring the speed limit unless she spotted a police car or passed a school zone where she was forced to drop to an infuriating thirty kilometres per hour.

Ali was no stranger to police jargon. Their code, the way they addressed 'Joe Public', a code employed in certain situations as a pre-emptive means of controlling a potentially volatile or highly emotional situation. Whenever cops say words like, "no panic" or "take a seat" or "remain calm" you can guarantee a shocker is coming. Combine any of those with the acronym A.S.A.P. and you know a shit storm is heading your way.

Ali knew that Cuzzocrea's text was deliberately vague but that the subtext was a message to her – not just a mere development regarding the case but some event that involved her specifically. But the most unnerving part of the message was easily the smiley face emoji at the end of it. Cuzzocrea didn't strike her as the type to use that sort of crap in his communication with her or with anyone else. It was camouflage.

Then a horrible feeling of dread descended upon Ali. What if something terrible had happened? To David? To Sandy, maybe? Or little Kenny? What had she been thinking leaving Kenny home alone with a fucking murderer out there somewhere? Fuck! She'd been drinking the small-town Kool-Aid and taken her cynical eye off the ball, shit, shit, shit. Kenny wasn't just home alone, she'd sent him out to look for the fucking dog!

Ali put her foot all the way down on Veteran's Memorial Parkway. At her side, Marlene gripped the leather sides of her seat and pressed her sensibly shod feet into the footwell.

CHAPTER 57 - THE SHOCKED PATHOLOGIST

He heard the determination, the anger in her engine as she turned onto Alder Beach Road. It was no surprise that the woman had defied his request for her to remain under the legal speed limit. It had been only seventeen minutes since he'd text her – it would take a law-abiding citizen double that time to get back from downtown Victoria. It was no surprise to him because Ali Dalglish didn't strike him as the type of woman who would happily do what someone else told her to do, actually she seemed more likely to do the very opposite just to prove a point.

If his suspicions were correct it was that particular aspect of her personality that may prove problematic for him today because it was likely he would have to order her to behave in a manner counterintuitive to her to preserve her and her family's safety.

Ali killed the engine after freewheeling her nippy Porsche down the steeply sloped driveway and got out, slamming her door behind her.

"What happened? Where's my son?" she hardly waited for an answer as she took the stairs to her front door two at a time.

"I checked on him when I arrived. He's fine," said Cuzzocrea, following her up the stairs and into the main living area of the home, followed by Marlene.

Ali kissed Kenny on the head, he barely noticed her as he was wearing headphones and appeared to be watching a

YouTube video of other people reacting to YouTube videos. Ali sent two text messages before turning to Cuzzocrea and Marlene.

"I'm checking on Sandy and David." She gestured impatiently for Cuzzocrea to speak. "So?"

Cuzzocrea looked toward Kenny. "We might want to speak in private."

"Is it Sandy or David?"

"No," he replied.

Ali exhaled. "Thank God. Okay, balcony then I can have a fag and normalize my blood pressure."

On the balcony, Ali lit her cigarette and held the smoke in her lungs before blowing it slowly out again. She'd insisted that Marlene remained present. Not only were they partners but Ali had a feeling that she'd be needing Marlene's support.

"Come on then, hit me with it," Ali said.

"Your dog. The one that was missing this morning," said Cuzzocrea.

"Oscar?"

"Yes. Can you describe him for me?"

Ali frowned. "He's a Newfie. Big. Like a hundred and eighty, two hundred pounds, big. A Landseer, black and white. Why? Don't tell me you scared the shit out of me just because someone found my fucking dog."

Cuzzocrea began, "The body of James Patterson, the escaped Mochetsin Institute prisoner, was discovered this morning."

"Oh my," said Marlene.

"Go on?" said Ali.

"He had been severely beaten about the face and he was shot through the chest at close range."

"Okay, Cuzzocrea. How does this involve me and my frigging Newfie? I know we have an agreement to share information but I'm not an idiot, there's no way you'd have rushed over here and called me back from Victoria just to tell me that a guy had been found dead, especially a guy you'd already ruled out of the investigation in the first place."

"His body was dumped alongside that of a dog. A Newfoundland. A Landseer Newfoundland, specifically."

Ali absorbed the information as best she could, of all the possible scenarios she had flirted with in her mind during the drive back, not one of them had involved her dogs.

"Before we rush to any conclusions, is there any way that we can confirm that the dog is your Newfoundland?"

"He wears a red collar, there's a disc attached that's engraved with my phone number."

Cuzzocrea shook his head. "Any other means of identification?"

"Not too many Landseers around, Inspector," said Marlene. "I'm pretty sure he's the only one in Mochetsin."

"I need to be able to confirm it." said Cuzzocrea.

Ali raised her cigarette to her lips, her hand was shaking. "Yes. The…the PIT."

Cuzzocrea stepped closer to Ali, "Excuse me?"

Ali's eyes glazed as she smoked, she wasn't listening to him anymore.

"What do you know about the pit, Ali?" Cuzzocrea pressed.

Ali was as stunned as she could ever remember herself being, she tried to shake herself free of the day-dream-like state she had become trapped in bit couldn't, she heard Cuzzocrea asking her a question, he was being overly persistent, aggressive even.

"Ali, what do you know about the pit?"

His tone had a harshness about it that pissed Ali off enough to bring her back to her present reality again. "What the fuck? Who do you think you're talking to?"

"The pit. Anything you'd like to tell me, Mrs Dalglish?"

Ali stepped closer to Cuzzocrea and glared into his eyes, meeting his challenge. "*Mrs Dalglish?* I see you have quite a way with the victims of crime, Inspector. Oscar, he has a PIT tag – a Passive Integrated Transponder? Arse hole."

Cuzzocrea sighed, relieved. "I apologize."

"You can get a vet to check it, he'll be in the database under my name and contact info. It's between his shoulder blades. What did you think I meant? What's the deal with the PIT?"

"I'm going to make a phone call, okay? It's important that we I.D. the dog first."

Ali huffed impatiently, pissed off that Cuzzocrea was failing to get to the fucking point but grateful for the helpful distraction that her impatience with him was giving her. As Cuzzocrea stepped away to make a phone call, Marlene hugged Ali.

"Oh, hon. I'm so sorry. Poor thing."

Ali took the hug. Resting her chin on Marlene's shoulder, she asked, "Hey, Marlene? You get the feeling that isn't the worst news we're going to hear?"

Marlene held Ali at arm's length and looked at her. "Oh gosh, don't say that. You heard back from Sandy and David yet?"

"Not yet." said Ali.

Cuzzocrea ended his phone call and returned to the women.

Ali didn't hesitate to address him, "The PIT thing. Explain that reaction of yours, please."

"Okay. The body of Patterson and that of what we will assume, for the purposes of this conversation, is the body of your Newfoundland were found in a pit. A pit used by the local public works crew."

"Oh God, the stag pit?" said Marlene, she turned to Ali to explain. "It's where they dump the animals they collect from the side of the roads, the ones that have been hit by cars. It's in a field owned by the council, over by the golf course."

Ali stubbed out her cigarette. "So what? When I said PIT, you immediately thought what? That I dumped my dog there?"

"Look, it was just an unfortunate coincidence, that's all. I mean, who uses the actual scientific acronym for their dog's microchip?" said Cuzzocrea, holding his hands up.

"A scientist, maybe?" Ali replied, "Look, Cuzzocrea, can you please get to the motherfucking point here? What the fuck does my dead dog – if it is him – have to do with this Patterson guy?"

"The dog was decapitated," said Cuzzocrea.

Ali swallowed and camouflaged her shock with a level of outward professionalism she'd had to don in many stomach churning situations during the course of her career. "That can happen as a result of blunt force trauma, the kind sustained during a high-speed motor vehicle versus soft tissue impact."

"Our head of forensics – and this is yet to be confirmed by her..."

"Get to the point, Cuzzocrea, I'm a big girl."

"She thinks that the dog's head was severed by someone who then used the skull to beat Patterson prior to shooting him dead."

Ali was still, her brain whirred as it painted graphic and disturbing images across her mind. Marlene covered her mouth with her hand; she too must have been visualizing similar images, her eyes flicked from Ali to Cuzzocrea and then back again.

"So whoever killed Patterson, killed my dog first? Is...is...that where you are?" Ali asked the inspector.

Cuzzocrea nodded.

"There's no chance Oscar was roadkill? Just a hit and run thing?"

"Maybe," Cuzzocrea lied.

Ali saw through the lie. "It's personal, then."

"We need to look into that possibility. I'm going to report back to my Superintendent. You'll be staying here?"

Ali nodded.

"I'll stay with her," said Marlene.

"No, there's no need for that, Marlene. Really, I'm fine."

"Tish and pish. I'll get the kettle on." Marlene went inside the house, rolling up her sleeves as she went.

Ali looked at Cuzzocrea. "You know this has to be linked to Samantha Giesbrecht, right? That's a conclusion worth jumping to…statistically speaking, the likelihood…"

"I know. My super and I already discussed it. Stay here. Please?"

Ali sensed his genuine concern and smiled at him, "I will." she watched him leave.

On her way back into the house Ali received a text message from Sandy; she was okay and half way through her shift at the diner. As relieved as Ali was, she had to deny any sentimentality or even grief for Oscar – she had to remain focused now. There would be time for emotion later. Privately.

As she passed him, Kenny pulled back his headphones. "Hey Mum, you want me to go look for Oscar now?"

"No, it's okay baby. Why don't you go to your room and play a game or watch a D.V.D. or something? Marlene and I need to work up here. Okay?"

"What about school?" Kenny asked, the picture of innocence.

"Because you're already hard at it I see." Ali pointed at the paused YouTube video on the screen of the Mac.

"I was just about to start." He smiled.

"Yeah, right. Let's have today off, bud." Ali ruffled his hair as his eyes widened with happiness.

"Cool. Can I have a can of Coke?"

"Don't push it," Ali warned.

Kenny could barely hide his glee at having the day off but also, as far as he was aware, managing to wriggle his way out of a mock exam too. He unplugged his headphones, logged out of his user account and dashed out of the room.

In the kitchen, Marlene was squeezing a tea bag against the rim of one of the two steaming mugs she had prepared.

"Find everything okay?" said Ali.

"Funny how everyone puts stuff in the same place in kitchens. You have your tea making supplies in the very same cupboard as Jean Torrell used to."

"Makes sense if Jean also had her kettle plugged into that wall socket, it being the only one in the kitchen." Ali smiled

"Aha, suppose so. You take sugar don't you?"

"Give me three please, Marlene."

"Three!" exclaimed Marlene. "You won't keep that waist for long on three sugars in every cup. Moment on the lips, lifetime on the hips," she warned.

"Just for the shock. I'm shaking a bit and I don't want anyone to see." Ali held her trembling hands out in front of her to demonstrate.

"Well, well, well, Ali Dalglish is human after all. Let's get this cup of tea in you and sit you down for a minute."

Marlene carried the cups of tea to the dining table. Ali sat down in a chair facing the wall of investigation, Marlene took a seat at the head of the table.

Ali sipped her tea and felt comforted by it. "Quite a shocker, have to say."

Marlene, blew the surface of her tea in short, successive bursts before finally slurping it loudly. "You know, I have some really good pot at home. Romulan Mist. You want me to roll you a joint, hon?"

Ali laughed, almost choking on her tea, "You smoke wacky baccy? Marlene! I am shocked."

"Everyone knows it should be legal already. It is in the freaking States, should be here too. Besides, this is B.C., hon, we all puff a little. You get your hands on any of our medical records and you'll see that we all suffer from chronic pain so we can get a card for the medical dispensary downtown."

"Under normal circumstances – not that there could be a normal circumstance following the news that some maniac cut off your dog's head and used it to batter a fugitive – I'd say 'hell yes', but since I have a feeling Cuzzocrea's coming back with his law enforcement buddies, probably best if I'm not stoned when they question me."

"They're going to question you?"

"Of course. I would."

"They can't think you had anything to do with it? Surely."

"I think I might have, yes. Indirectly," said Ali, supping her tea again.

CHAPTER 58 - THE UNRAVELLING

Since David had yet to reply to a single one of her text messages – the most recent one being: *Call me, you fucking idiot!* – she'd resorted to phoning him using the redial button, over and over again. At first her calls had been redirected to voicemail after the usual five rings but now they were going straight to his pre-recorded outgoing message. Ali slammed her phone down, the fucker had switched his phone off.

"No signal, my arse."

"What's that?" asked Marlene. She was busy making a pyramid of her sandwiches that she'd retrieved from Ali's car, displaying them in the opening of the kitchen hatch.

"David. He's playing silly buggers. Just switched his phone off. Why would he do that?"

"Did you tell him about Oscar?"

"No. I just said that I needed to speak to him, that it was important."

"Why didn't you tell him? He needs to know."

"Because I'm not in the mood for one of his lectures. He'd blame me. He always does. What are you doing with those sandwiches?"

"They need to be eaten and, like you said, Cuzzocrea will be back with his colleagues to question you."

"Did you check on Webster?" Ali asked.

"Peter's got him. You know, I don't think I'd be able to hold myself together like you are if it had been Webster instead of Oscar."

"Maybe I'm just a cold-hearted bitch."

Happy with her pyramid of snacks, Marlene turned to Ali. "You might be able to fool some people with that tough act you've got going on, Ali, but not me. I can see right through it."

Ali smiled. "I suppose it's a coping mechanism. Detachment."

"I wish I had that skill. I'm afraid everything seems to get me right here." Marlene pointed to her heart, or at least, Ali noticed, where most people *think* their heart is located.

Marlene pulled out a chair and sat down with Ali at the table. "Remember when you asked me why I don't have a cell phone?"

Ali nodded. "Brain cancer, you said."

"We lost our daughter. Eleven years ago this November."

"God, Marlene, I'm sorry."

Marlene nodded and smiled sadly. She pulled the photograph of Samantha Giesbrecht to her from where Ali had placed it in the centre of the table. "Nobody should have to bury their own child. It's upside down."

Marlene arose and crossed to the wall, pinning the photograph back in its place. She adjusted it so that it was perfectly straight. "Charlotte's cancer was a living hell for us all and then to lose her after watching her fight for so long…but to know that your child was murdered? That some psycho had taken her and done…things…to her and then killed her? And dumped her body? I cannot imagine what kind of hell that must be."

"We'll get the bastard, Marlene, you watch. And it won't change what happened to that girl but it will help her parents. The torture is in the not knowing. Thinking that someone got away with it. The least we can do now is catch the fucker and see that justice is served. Maybe then those parents will, at the very least, have some sort of closure. Without that, the grieving process is a never-ending loop. A cycle of despair, like all the confusion and the guilt, the anger and the helplessness is on eternal freeze frame."

"Do you believe in heaven, Ali?"

Marlene wasn't the first parent of a dead child to ask her that and Ali knew that now wasn't the time for negativity or even ambiguity.

"Absolutely," said Ali.

Marlene inhaled deeply and touched the photograph of Samantha Giesbrecht. "So do I." Marlene turned to Ali, eyes wide. "I hear cars."

Ali remained seated as Marlene rushed to the door and opened it, she called back to Ali, "Yes, it's them, hon, the Italian stallion and his cronies."

Marlene flitted between looking out of the door and turning back to Ali as she gave a running commentary of the events on the drive. "Three cars. Cuzzocrea is leading the pack, followed by a big, black car and a light brown one – maybe gold – bit of a rust bucket, actually. Well, that's rude! The rust bucket just took a chunk out of your grass border – you should get them to compensate you for that. Ooh, the inspector is out, so is the little man from the black SUV. Bless, he's got a bald spot at the back of his head, that's how Peter started. Rust bucket is out too, he's like the human version of his own car, badly maintained and beige. Okay, Cuzzocrea's talking to the little one now – that must be the boss, I think. They're going through some paperwork. Ooh, rust bucket just looked at me."

Ali watched as Marlene smiled and waved.

"I don't like him at all." Marlene said through her grinning teeth. "I think they're looking at our profile, you know. They must be talking about us. Very suspicious behaviour. Where are the dogs? I can hear them barking somewhere."

"I put them in the basement, save us the chaos."

"Ooh. Here they come, Ali. Brace yourself. Yep, Cuzzocrea's leading the way, egg-in-the-nest is following behind and rust bucket is taking up the rear."

Ali felt a flutter of nerves in her belly. She wasn't easily intimidated but couldn't deny her discomfort at the prospect of being questioned in her own home. Her thoughts turned to David again. This would be a lot easier if he were here too, to support her like a husband is supposed to. She hit redial once more then 'end' when she heard his recorded voice.

Marlene scurried from the front door, leaving it open, ready for the arrival of the police officers. Her cheeks were flush with excitement and panic. She initially sat in the chair next to Ali then decided that she should be standing.

Cuzzocrea entered first and nodded to Ali before making the necessary introductions. "Ladies, this is Superintendent Shaw and my partner, Detective Munro."

"How do you do?" said Marlene in a high-pitched, falsely posh voice. Ali looked at her with a question. Marlene shrugged and shook her head, as shocked by her affected manner as Ali had been.

Cuzzocrea held his hand towards Marlene. "Mrs McKean, Marlene," he then pointed his hand toward Ali, "Mrs Dalglish, Ali."

"Good morning, ladies," said Superintendent Shaw.

"Feel free to take a seat." Ali said.

Cuzzocrea took the seat at the head of the table, seating himself between Ali and Superintendent Shaw who chose the seat directly opposite to her, with his back to the wall plastered with details of the investigation. Munro closed the front door and sat next to Shaw. Marlene was the last to take her place at the table, next to Ali. Her chair made an unfortunate farting sound as she sat and when Marlene pressed her elbow into Ali's ribs in acknowledgement of the embarrassing noise, Ali had to rub her lips together to stifle a poorly timed laugh which would have only served to make her look like a crazy woman.

Cuzzocrea began, "We have identified the animal found this morning."

"It's Oscar. Why else would you all be here?" said Ali.

"We also found evidence directly linking today's crime scene with the Giesbrecht case," Cuzzocrea added.

"Same perpetrator?" asked Ali.

"Possibly," replied Cuzzocrea.

Ali huffed and crossed her arms.

"We are working under that assumption, Mrs Dalglish," said Superintendent Shaw.

"I prefer Ali."

"Ali," said Shaw, leaning forward on his elbows, indicating to all that he would conduct the remainder of the interview. "When was the last time that you saw your dog?"

Ali thought for a moment. "Saw him? Last night when I got home from the memorial service."

Across the table, Munro was taking notes in a small, leather-bound book.

"What time would that have been?" asked Shaw.

Ali looked at Marlene. "What time did we lock up?"

"It was ten fifty, maybe ten fifty-five? I was just getting in." She looked at Shaw. "I live next door. It was ten fifty-five or so when I heard Ali pull into her drive."

"And your dog was here then?"

"Yes, he was at the door with my other dogs when I let myself in."

"Good," said Shaw. "Now, when did you notice that he was missing?"

Ali frowned. "When they were barking in the dog run…no, actually it was when Marlene arrived this morning. I noticed that Oscar wasn't at the door to greet her."

"And what time would that have been?"

"Twenty after eight?" guessed Marlene.

"Now, Mrs Dalglish – sorry, Ali," Shaw corrected himself, "could you run through the events of last evening, as well as you can recall them, please. Between your arrival home and Mrs McKean's arrival this morning."

"Let's see, ah, I came in, I said hello to the dogs, I checked on the kids."

"You have two children, is that correct?"

"Yes. First I checked on my daughter, Sandy. She was on her iPad, in bed. I said hello, then goodnight. I went into my son's room, he was already asleep. I turned off his T.V. and then I went to the kitchen."

"So your daughter is Sandy? How old is she?"

"Sandy is eighteen, Kenny is thirteen, almost fourteen."

"Good. So, after you checked on them, you went to the kitchen? Were all of your dogs present at that time? How many do you have, incidentally?"

"Four. I *did* have four, that is."

"Yes. So you were in the kitchen?"

"Actually, first I contacted Inspector Cuzzocrea."

"I'm aware of that. And you also sent him an e-mail at that time, is that correct?"

"Yes, I did."

Shaw nodded. "Our records show that the e-mails and texts were received between eleven oh six and eleven fourteen."

"Okay. It would have been fine for you to tell me that in the first place. You trying to catch me in a lie, Superintendent Shaw?"

"Not at all. What then? After the e-mail?"

"I fixed myself a drink, I sent the e-mail and then I decided to have a bath."

"Okay."

"I went into the master bedroom. David was asleep in there."

"David being your husband?"

"No, David being my manservant. Yes, David my husband, but I'm sure your records already show that too." Ali took a breath to calm her temper. "Yes. I took my bathrobe from our en suite. I decided to use the tub in the kid's bathroom so I didn't disturb David – my husband."

Shaw nodded. "How long were you in the bath?"

"I have no idea, as long as it took me to finish my gin and tonic. Forty minutes, maybe. Less than an hour."

"So let's guess that you got out of the bath at midnight, thereabouts. Fair?"

"Probably. The dogs were barking and I didn't want them

to wake the kids."

"They were barking?"

"Yes, but it was because David's pager had gone off and so he'd left."

"He's a firefighter at the local hall, correct? So when you say, his pager 'had gone off', what you mean is that he was responding to a fire call?"

"I suppose so, yes."

"Now, when David leaves on a fire call, does he leave the door open?"

"Not open but unlocked, yes. Time is of the essence for first responders."

Shaw grinned at her. "And this would be the *front* door, the one we just used to enter the residence, correct?"

"Yes."

"And the dogs, they always bark when David leaves?"

"They bark when anyone leaves or when anyone comes in. I got out of the bath, reassured them and then I went to bed."

"And at that time, the Newfoundland was present?"

"Oscar was indeed present at that time, yes."

"You went to bed. Do you remember anything else before this morning?"

"I was asleep but obviously I was aware of the dogs barking when David came home."

"And what time was that?"

"I have no idea, once I get to sleep, I try to stay that way."

"And that's all?"

"Basically. David came into the room, I was dropping back off to sleep, he sat down for a moment, he may even have lay down but then he got up again and left the room."

"Oh?"

Ali shrugged. "He left the room. He must have slept on the couch."

"Is that usual for him?"

"No, not really."

"So why did he sleep on the couch last night do you think?"

"You'd have to ask *him* that, anyway, he didn't get a chance to sleep anywhere because he left the house again shortly after. And yes, the dogs barked then too."

"Another fire call?"

"I assume so."

"That's interesting because we only have a record of one District of Mochetsin fire call last night. The one at eleven fifty-eight, when you were in the bath."

Ali looked at Cuzzocrea, who seemed to beg her silently to play nice, "And your point?"

"If he left again, it wasn't for another fire call. Do you remember the pager going off that time?"

"No. But he left so…"

"Okay, That's fine. So, the dogs barked when David left that second time?"

"Yes. I was asleep, though. Yes, they would have barked."

"And what time did your husband return from that second outing of the night?"

"I have no idea. Actually, you know. He didn't. No, he left a message to say that he stayed over at the hall to get an early run in then to get a head start on preparing for the Salt Spring Island trip."

"The Salt Spring Island trip?"

"Yes, he's on Salt Spring Island this weekend, until Sunday. It's a course. I'm not one hundred per cent sure what the course is, but he's there."

"So this message? He left a note for you? Because, as you said, time is of the essence for first responders. Would he have had time to write a note if he was heading for a fire call?"

"He sent a text to our daughter to explain, she wrote the note on his behalf."

"I see. Is it usual for your husband to communicate with you via your daughter?"

"Not really. He's being a bit of a cunt at the moment, if you must know. If you don't mind, I'd like you to keep your snide assertions regarding my marriage to yourself."

Ali felt Cuzzocrea and Munro both stiffen but she didn't give a fuck. Shaw wasn't her boss so she wasn't about to kiss his arse.

"I apologize. Obviously we need as clear an account of events as possible."

"That may be, Superintendent, but you better keep that nose of yours out of my personal business otherwise this informal chat we're having is going to take a turn."

Shaw looked at Ali, barely able to hide his distaste for her. Ali felt the angry troll inside her stirring and clenched her fists.

Shaw cleared his throat and continued, "Have you spoken to your husband regarding what happened to your dog?"

"I have not. I can't get hold of him. His mobile…his cell phone is dead."

"Any other means of contacting him at this time?"

"No."

"Okay, we'll look into that. So, when you woke this morning?"

"I showered, I dressed, I ate, I smoked, Marlene came, Cuzzocrea came. I went to Victoria, I received Cuzzocrea's text, I came back, Cuzzocrea told me about Oscar, he left. We waited here, Marlene arranged her sandwiches, you arrived, grilled me like I'm a criminal rather than a victim and…well, here we find ourselves."

Shaw nodded and briefly smiled before standing. "Munro and I are going to go and see if we can remedy the communication hurdle you're facing with your spouse. It would be advisable for you to remain here in the interim. Are your children at school?"

"My son is home schooled, he's in his room. My daughter is at work."

"Okay. Cuzzocrea will stay here and he'll run through a few things with you. Thank you for your time Mrs Dalglish."

Shaw looked at the investigation wall behind him before glancing back at Ali then left, followed by Munro.

Cuzzocrea sighed and seemed to relax back to the version of himself Ali was more familiar with.

"Someone needs to pull that stick out of his arse before I ram it all the way in," said Ali.

"He's just...that's his way, he's really a lot nicer when you get to know him."

"Don't you guys get sensitivity training?"

"Of course we do."

"Evidence to the contrary, Inspector."

"Your daughter," said Cuzzocrea, changing the subject. "You said she's at work?"

"Yes."

"Does she know what happened?"

"No, I haven't told the kids."

"I could get a uni to pick her up."

"She has a car, she's fine, doesn't finish her shift till two."

"Okay." Cuzzocrea nodded. "Where does she work?"

"The diner on Glandford Parkway. Lloyd's. Lloyd's Diner."

"Listen, I'm just going to see if we have any unis in the area, maybe get them to do a drive by, check on her car? They could escort her home, low profile? She wouldn't even know they were there."

"No. God, that's complete overkill," said Ali.

Cuzzocrea reluctantly acknowledged her wishes. "Fine, but I'm still going to have them do a drive by." Cuzzocrea stepped out to make his call.

Marlene looked at Ali. "Sandy's not in danger is she?"

"No, why would she be? Marlene, we have to look on what has happened as a positive, not Oscar dying obviously, but if Samantha's killer was the one to do it and then kill the Patterson guy? Well then, he's in crisis. He's unravelling. He's making mistakes. That's how you catch them, the *only* way you catch them. When they remain in control and focused they're elusive but when they start getting cocky or behaving impulsively, they lead you right to them."

"How?" asked Marlene.

"What happened to Oscar – or at least what they suspect happened to him – means one thing."

"What's that?"

"You and I pissed someone off, Marlene, actually, *I* pissed someone off, enough for them to want to send a direct message to me, or maybe it was an attempt to scare me off or distract me. Either way, we encountered the killer and we pissed him off. Which means…"

Marlene sat upright, understanding Ali's train of thought. "It's one of our suspects."

"Yep. Now all we have to do is work out which one of them it was."

Marlene looked at Ali with a serious expression. "Aren't you scared?"

"I'll be glad when Sandy and David are home. But I'm not scared, no."

"Why not?"

Ali put her mug down and looked at Marlene. "I'm a forensic pathologist, Marlene. I know all of the body's weaknesses. I know all of the ways to kill someone."

Ali smiled and sipped her tea.

CHAPTER 59 - THE ELIXIR

He watches her. She comes and she goes. Flitting in and out of view beyond the garish neon sign that hangs in the grease-hazed picture window of Lloyd's Diner.

One so elegant, one so gifted and bright should put herself above such lowly acts of self-degradation.

Servitude is only honourable when it is in the service of the elevated, the worthy, not the lowly masses.

However menial her responsibilities, however below her station they are, she conducts herself with grace, floating effortlessly around the shovelling pigs. Twisting and turning in her solo dance to avoid near collisions with her bussed tables, her ignorant co-workers and the snorting patrons in her path.

There she is: a ready-made specimen. Her existence was unknown to him and if he'd have found her earlier he would not have wasted his time on the dregs of the populous. She would need no cleaning – the cleansing of previous filth is negated by the fact that never has she allowed herself to be polluted. She is pure and she is willing.

It would be an honourable servitude for her. Servitude is in her nature. It is in her nature to do as she is told, not for the promise of freedom or escape but for the simple pleasure of fulfilling her duty. She lacks the ego and the petulance of the spoiled ones.

She is his gift.

In her, he has found what it has taken so long to find,

something that has eluded him. The elixir of his fantasies, something so unbelievable he'd had to try to create it for himself. She is already compliant, she has already drank of him. She allowed herself to be swaddled by him and she welcomed his lips upon her head. Sighing to him a sleepy thank you.

Now she would drink again. And then she would see him. The real him.

CHAPTER 60 - NO SALT SPRING

Ali checked her phone. No messages. Nothing from David. Sandy hadn't replied either.

"Thank you, Marlene," said Cuzzocrea as Marlene slid a sandwich between him and his laptop. Marlene had presented it beautifully, sliced in two down the middle, separated to show off its brimming filling and placed on a small china platter – the ones Ali kept at the very back of her plate cupboard due to their fragility and garish rose themed design (bought for them by her bitch of a mother in law as a wedding present). Ali wondered what other forgotten wonders Marlene had managed to find in her kitchen, hopefully the Minnie Mouse mug Ali'd been looking for since they moved.

"It's aged brie from Red Barn on a bed of arugula with a red wine, shallot dressing," said Marlene proudly as she sat and took a bite of her own prawn with thousand island dressing sandwich.

"Wow. Very nice. Thanks." Cuzzocrea raised his eyebrows to Ali.

"Not my doing, that's the fanciest food this house has witnessed in a while, Marlene made them for the homeless people downtown."

"Well, the great unwashed of Victoria are missing out on something here," said Cuzzocrea with a mouthful in his cheek.

Ali watched them chew and heard her stomach growl.

Having heard it too, Marlene asked, "Are you sure you don't want one, hon?"

Ali shook her head, "Maybe later."

Marlene nodded in reluctant acceptance of Ali's nervous fast.

"So, Ed Dunlop, the mayor, he was the first on your list," said Cuzzocrea. He pushed his plate to one side and rubbed his fingers free of crumbs then placed them over the letter keys of his laptop, ready to type. "Describe your interaction with him."

Distracted, Ali had been looking at her phone, willing a message to ping into existence.

"Ali?" Cuzzocrea gently touched her arm and sent a shiver of gooseflesh up her arm.

"Sorry. I wish Sandy would reply."

"I'll check on the unis, they were just clearing a scene, nothing major just a dispute outside Royal Roads University then they were going to head over to Lloyd's to check on her car."

"Good. Okay. Let's get on."

"Ed Dunlop."

"Yes," said Ali. "He was skinning a deer when we arrived to speak to him. His wife…"

"Theresa," Marlene added.

"She was present although I didn't witness any interaction between them. She was in the house and he was out back, like I said, skinning a deer. He spoke about his grandkids visiting the house. The house, very grandiose bordering on pompous. Ed Dunlop is all about the show. He was patronizing, condescending, sexist if not misogynistic. His passion is hunting, he likes to 'put lead in those suckers', I think that's an accurate quote."

Marlene nodded.

"Last night he was on a night stalk, as a matter of fact, according to his wife," Ali concluded.

"Ali probably ticked him off," said Marlene.

Cuzzocrea looked to Ali for her confirmation or denial.

Ali shrugged and nodded. "Probably. It's not like we hit it off and want to braid each other's hair, put it that way."

"Did you argue? Was his dislike made clear to you?" asked Cuzzocrea.

"No, it was strictly subtextual."

"Okay. Who was the next suspect that you visited yesterday?"

"After leaving Dunlop's house we drove up to McIvor Road, to whatshisname's place?"

Marlene interjected, "Charlie Chaud."

"Charlie Chaud," Cuzzocrea said as he typed.

"She definitely ticked him off. We both did. My fault actually, Inspector," said Marlene.

"Go on."

"Well he wasn't in, or so we thought. So we went round back and had a little look-see," admitted Marlene.

Cuzzocrea sighed disapprovingly and typed Marlene's account.

"We were snooping," said Ali. "We wanted to look in what we thought was his bedroom but the sill was too high so I went in this crawlspace thingy and I was getting a bucket for us to stand on…"

"…to cut a long story short," Marlene interrupted, "she had a nasty encounter with a giant spider so she somehow ended up topless which was funny until we saw Charlie Chaud standing there watching us, getting a good eyeful of Ali in all her glory."

Cuzzocrea stopped typing and looked at the women, "You're not kidding, are you. You two really know how to ask for trouble, you know that?"

"I had a bra on," said Ali, defensively.

"So, you're undressed. Only from the waist up presumably?"

"Obviously," said Ali.

"Continue," said Cuzzocrea with a disbelieving shake of his head.

Marlene jumped in, happy to continue the story, "Well

Charlie, he was a bit offish – can't blame him really, finding us back there and Ali, well, you know being half naked and all, but I managed to talk him round a bit. I gave him some excuse about sky lanterns but he – he's a strange one anyway, Charlie, only a mother could love him and even *she* struggles."

"Did he say anything to you? Was he aggressive or threatening in any way?" asked Cuzzocrea.

"If you call drowning two rats in front of us aggressive or threatening, yes," said Ali.

"He what?"

"He had these two rats in humane traps. He has this gunky bath tub out front, on his lawn, anyway, as we were leaving, he dunked them. Drowned them. Without a word and with no compunction, actually he did it with absolute cold indifference," Ali explained.

"Okay." Cuzzocrea's phone vibrated, he stood, swiped the screen and put it to his ear. He stepped away from the table.

Marlene pushed her empty plate away. "Thinking about it now, perhaps we were a little over zealous in our pursuits yesterday. If I could go back and do it over again, all things being said, I doubt I'd even go up to Charlie Chaud's house."

"I know but you do what you have to do, what you're compelled to do. We might have been a tad reckless. Hearing it back, we do come across like a pair of lunatics."

"I know," said Marlene. "I blame you. You're a bad influence."

"You're the one who wanted to snoop, Marlene."

"I'd still rather blame you, if it's all the same."

Ali smiled. "Let's secretly blame each other. That's how most relationships work."

Marlene smiled too. "Agreed."

"Hey," said Cuzzocrea, sitting back at the table, "Sandy, she drives a blue Bug, right?"

"Yes?"

"The officers I sent have confirmed that her VW Bug is parked up outside Lloyd's so we know she's safe. She finishes in just under half an hour, right? Does she usually come straight home?"

"Sometimes she'll pop to the shops but I texted her and told her to come straight back today. I doubt she'll go anywhere, she's usually tired after the Lloyd's shift. Thanks for getting them to check on her. Okay, after Chaud's house we went to that Hammond's house, the prison guard. Well, you know that because we saw you there."

"Good. Okay." Cuzzocrea looked at his laptop screen, "That's right. Then where did you go?"

"We went to Christine Labreque's house. Her husband is Dr Labreque." said Marlene.

"No. First we stopped for lunch, remember?"

"That's right, we ate at the cafe. I had the red snapper wrap," said Marlene.

"That's when we saw Carter," Ali said, feeling uncomfortable about it in Marlene's presence.

"Ah, yes. We did. *Then* we went to the Labreques," said Marlene.

"Carter Burrows, the letter carrier who was at the memorial last night?" Cuzzocrea asked.

"Everyone was at the memorial." Marlene was in protective mode. "They all were. Carter isn't a suspect. We agreed on that, Ali."

"Yes, we did."

Cuzzocrea looked at Ali reassuringly then turned to Marlene to explain, "For the purposes of the investigation it's best if you don't leave anything out. Carter may not be one of your suspects but I'll be in deep with Shaw if I don't account for even the most mundane detail."

"Oh. Oh dear, you don't want that. I understand." Marlene visibly relaxed.

"Was Carter in the café with you both?" asked Cuzzocrea.

"No, he was across the street. We were eating out under

the umbrellas. Marlene called him over, she wanted to introduce us."

"Because, it's actually quite funny, originally Ali had put him on the suspect list because he was there, at the site and then at the meeting later but obviously that's just silly. I didn't tell her, you see, about his problems, I thought she should see for herself, you know, that he's just Carter, he's a kitten."

Cuzzocrea paused typing and looked at Marlene. "He's special to you, to a lot of people in Mochetsin, yes?"

Marlene leaned toward Cuzzocrea. "Have you heard the saying, 'it takes a village'?"

"I'm familiar with it."

"Well, Carter's living proof of that. It was this village that raised him. We took care of him when his good-for-nothing stepfather beat the poor boy half to death and trampled his little skull while his junkie mother watched. And that wasn't even the worst of that boy's hell, but I won't go into all of that. We took him under our collective wings, we interceded on his behalf and worked alongside Child Protective Services to see that he was placed here. Barbara Cochrane fostered him, took him in and loved him as one of her own. Carter would be dead – or worse – if it weren't for us and it was a tough journey for all of us, especially him. But he came through, we got him there and look at him now?" Marlene's chin dimpled and quivered as she fought her emotions.

"That's very good of you Marlene, of all of you. Not many communities step up like that, take it from me," said Cuzzocrea.

Marlene raised her chin, folded her arms and nodded defiantly.

"Let's come back to Carter later," Cuzzocrea said, he smiled kindly at Marlene. "Dr Labreque's house."

"He wasn't in. Christine, his wife was – have you met her?" Ali asked Cuzzocrea.

"I saw her at the memorial last night, she's clearly a central figure in the community."

"She'd like to think so." Marlene snorted. "But she's just hot air and woollen knickers."

Cuzzocrea looked confused by Marlene's choice of words.

Ali continued where Marlene had left off, "I don't quite know what hot air and woollen knickers has to do with it but they're swingers, they have sex parties. Marlene and I got ourselves invited to one tonight because there's a basement, a storage area and we wanted to check it out."

"I take it we're not going tonight?" said Marlene.

"I'm not up for that, no." said Ali, she was beginning to feel on edge.

"Also, if I might be so bold to mention," Cuzzocrea suggested, "you may have poked at enough cages for the time being. Let us take it from here, you guys have certainly pointed us in the right direction but now it's important that we make sure everyone is safe," said Cuzzocrea, carefully navigating the issue he'd been dreading: telling Ali Dalglish what to do.

Ali checked the time on her phone again, it was one forty-seven. "That's okay so long as you know I, *we*, refuse to be excluded entirely. We're the ones who came up with the suspect list in the first place and yes, we may have been unorthodox in our practices but we still hit on something right otherwise we wouldn't be sitting here now."

"I agree," said Cuzzocrea. "Looking at your board, your wall, Labreque was the last on your list."

"Yes," said Ali.

"And you didn't interact with him at all?"

"No but he was very interested in Ali, not only could he not take his eyes off her last night once I'd negotiated our invitation to his party but Christine also mentioned it at the clean-up last night. She said something about Robert being thrilled that Ali was coming and, you know, when she said it her face looked like she was chewing a wasp."

"The clean-up?" asked Cuzzocrea.

"Some of us stayed behind last night to clean up the hall,

that's how we found out that Ed Dunlop was on a night stalk," said Ali.

"Who was present?"

"Let's see. There was me, Marlene, Carter Burrows, Christine Labreque, Theresa Dunlop and Annie Chaud."

Cuzzocrea frowned. "Who organized the clean-up crew?"

"I did," said Marlene proudly.

"So it was a deliberate manoeuvre on your part to have the clean-up crew consisting only of women connected to all of your suspects?"

"I didn't notice that, how dumb am I?" said Ali.

"Really? I thought it was obvious. Except for the two of us and Carter, of course," said Marlene.

"Cuzzocrea." Ali sat upright. "All of them were away last night. *All* of the suspects were M.I.A."

"Yes," said Marlene. "Yes, you're right."

"Go on."

Ali frowned, recalling last night's conversation. "Ed Dunlop was on a night stalk. Robert Labreque was…"

"…at a poker game," said Marlene.

"And Charlie Chaud?" asked Cuzzocrea.

"He'd gone off in some sort of huff, left Annie to find herself another ride home," said Marlene.

"That's good. Good information, we can use that. Thank you," said Cuzzocrea. His phone rang; he stood to answer it and stepped out of the room.

"Sandy should be home soon." Ali checked her phone again.

"Now don't you start worrying if she's a little late. Lots of traffic around the superstore at this time on a Friday *and* they're always digging up some road or another out of Glandford. You know what those flaggers are like, they never let more than four cars through at a time."

"Yeah," said Ali as she checked the time on her phone again.

"Shall I take a sandwich down to your little guy?" said Marlene.

"No. Kenny wouldn't eat anything like that. I'll call him up when Sandy gets home and he can have a Coke and make one of his sandwiches. He does these big, layered things, like three pieces…" Ali stopped talking when she saw Cuzzocrea's expression of concern as he re-entered the room. Ali's blood thickened and her heart pumped hard to circulate it yet it felt like it was coagulating in her carotid artery. "What? Oh God. Is it Sandy?"

"No."

Ali's temples throbbed with a mixture of relief and utter apprehension. "What then?"

"That was Shaw. He's at the fire hall. Ali, there is no course on Salt Spring Island this weekend."

CHAPTER 61 - A NEW PRIME SUSPECT

"What are you talking about?" asked Ali.

"Shaw just met with Chief Humphries and it seems David lied to you about the Salt Spring Island course. There is no course this weekend."

Ali rested her elbows on the table and steepled her fingers, taking a deep breath and hoping to maintain her detachment.

"Can you think of anywhere he might have gone?" Cuzzocrea asked.

Ali shook her head. She closed her eyes and imagined that she was back in a squad room in New Scotland Yard working a case, the case of a dead girl but in her imagination she stepped out of herself and looked back at Ali Dalglish as an outsider, as an investigator looking at a woman who had put a target on her own back, whose dog had been taken and killed, and worst of all, at a wife who has just been told that her husband has been lying to her. Ali looked back at herself and saw an idiot, a gullible, dumb housewife, the kind of woman she has always looked down upon scornfully and with contempt.

Ali opened her eyes and met Cuzzocrea's. "Go ahead. Ask me."

Cuzzocrea nodded and sat down opposite Ali. "Ali, where was David on the night of Sunday the eighth of April and during the early morning hours of Monday the ninth?"

Whenever, in the past, Ali had heard similar questions

being asked of spouses, she'd always had the same tendentious monologue running through her mind, *She knows. She has to know. She's covering for him.*

"We went to bed together at around ten thirty on Sunday night, David was asleep before me. I was reading for a while, maybe until midnight. I fell asleep and when I woke up the next morning – at seven or perhaps seven thirty – David had already left for work."

"What time did he leave? Do you remember?"

"I know how this looks but David didn't do it, yeah the fucker lied about Salt Spring but I'm telling you, he's not our man."

"We've issued a province-wide A.P.B. on David and his car, a black Range Rover, plate number AB8 STM, is that correct?"

Ali nodded.

"What does that mean?" asked Marlene.

"An all points bulletin, it means that David just lied his way into prime suspect territory," said Ali.

CHAPTER 62 - A CREAMY FRENCH VANILLA

Lloyd's Diner was the most popular eatery in Glandford. Not only because of its famous Super-Tall-All-In-One (a full breakfast of bacon, sausage, eggs, onions and mushrooms piled inside a toasted kaiser bun) but also because it was only open between nine a.m. and two p.m. every day.

Although it only paid minimum wage, Sandy liked the job for three reasons: one, the place was always packed with customers queuing out of the door so the tip share was awesome and boosted her shitty wage enough to pay her iPhone bill every month with plenty left over just in the three shift she worked per week; two, her duties were so mindlessly simple she felt zero pressure, unlike at her other part-time job as an unofficial children's liaison at Transformation House, the women's shelter in Esquimalt; three, the head chef, Danté, was a total dish – maybe a little too old for her at twenty-four but a dish nonetheless *and* he had made no secret of his attraction to her since the Christmas party, in fact, not only had he bought her the scarf she now wore (printed with little pictures of her favourite animated character) but he'd also just agreed to introduce her to his tattoo artist – some guy downtown called Felch who works at Let it Burn on Douglas.

Sandy knew that her mother would probably, *definitely* string her up for getting a tattoo, especially one on her upper arm, but she'd just have to get used to it because eventually Sandy wanted at least one full sleeve of them. Danté had made an appointment for them both on Tuesday night.

Sandy had had a close call on the tattoo front just last

night when her mum had walked in to say goodnight as she'd been scrolling through some designs that Danté had sent links to via Tumblr. Sandy hated it when her parents decided to make an effort with her and over-parent. Her dad had even tucked her in last night, like she was a little kid again when he used to make a sausage roll of her with the quilt. All fun when you're five but totally cheesy when your eighteen, especially if you fell asleep with God-knows-what on your iPad screen.

Still, Sandy didn't want them on her case too much, especially with her Tuesday night date with Danté on the horizon. She'd have to keep her head down and play the good little girl act this weekend. What they don't know won't kill them and besides, once that serpent was on her arm there was nothing that they or anyone else could do to erase it.

Sandy was beaming to herself as she waved bye to Danté and stuffed her apron in her bag. She opened her car door, it groaned in the process. She made a mental note to get some WD40 on the hinges later, the car was a bit of a banger but it was her pride and joy, a classic VW Beetle – or a 'Bug' as Danté would say – baby blue, a fixer-upper for sure but had still cost her almost three grand of her life savings to buy.

"Hello Sandy."

Sandy, who was just leaning in to her car to throw her bag over into the passenger footwell, jumped at the sound of the voice behind her and banged her head on her way out to see who had spoken her name.

"Hey! Carter. What are you doing here?"

"I brought you this."

Carter held a Tim Hortons cup out to her.

"Oh." Sandy was unsure of whether it was appropriate for her to accept the drink. It was weird that Carter, the postie who'd helped her to set up the sky-lantern table last night, was here. And to have brought her a drink too? *Shit*, thought Sandy, *maybe he was a weirdo like her mum had said – he is a few sandwiches short of a picnic basket.*

"I'm okay thanks, Carter. I'm actually just heading home."

"But it's French vanilla, you said that was your favourite when I bought you a double double last night."

Sandy saw the look of disappointment on his face and felt bad. "It is my favourite. Thanks for remembering." Sandy took the drink from him and tore back the plastic perforated flap that revealed the drinking hole. She clipped the flap back into place in a slot on the lid which made Carter smile and Sandy feel better. She took a long sip to demonstrate just how grateful she was, it could be her good deed for the day.

"Yum. Delicious," she said. "So, were you just in Lloyd's?" Sandy knew he hadn't been but felt that the responsibility to make conversation with someone like Carter lay with the more…educated? No, that felt elitist…more socially skilled.

"No. Your mum and Mrs McKean sent me to get you."

"To get me?"

Carter made a show of rolling his eyes. "They need us to help them. AGAIN," he said it like a disgruntled child and reminded Sandy of some of the kids she worked with at Transformation House.

"Are you kidding me? Again? What do they want now?" Sandy scrambled in her hoodie pocket and found her phone. "Is that why mum's been texting me?"

"She's up on Blinkhorn, on Lindholm Road. She can't get a signal up there so she asked me to come and get you. They need us to meet them up there."

"Shit." Sandy threw her phone onto the passenger seat. "I'm knackered, I just finished work."

She drank a gulp of her French vanilla, glad that Carter had thought to buy it for her after all.

"You want me to go up there and tell them that you went home?"

"Yes!"

"Okay then. Bye Sandy."

Carter smiled sheepishly and walked in the funny way that

Carter walks, like Dustin Hoffman in that movie about the autistic guy, to his Canada Post van which was parked next to Sandy's Beetle. Sandy thought about Tuesday, her tattoo date with Danté and how she wanted to keep herself free of suspicion this weekend.

"You know what, Carter? I will come. God, those two are driving me crazy. Look, I'll follow you 'cause I don't exactly know where Lindholm is but if that Marlene sends me out shopping for shit again, I'm going home."

"Okay." Carter nodded and opened his driver door.

"Don't go fast, this thing isn't so hot on hills, okay?"

"Okay Sandy. I'll go as slow as you want."

Sandy got into her car and buckled up. She picked up her phone, there was a text message from her mum:

<Have you finished work yet? Important. Get here ASAP>

"God! Woman! I'm coming!"

Sandy stuffed her phone deep into her bag just as her safety-conscious dad insisted upon so that she couldn't be distracted by incoming texts whilst driving.

Carter pulled out of his stall and waited ahead for her to pull up behind him. Sandy saw him dip his head enough to see her through his driver's wing mirror. She gave him a cheerful wave and he set off. She followed him closely as they entered Veteran's Memorial Parkway.

She depressed the play button on the centre console. Fleetwood Mac started slow and then wound itself up to the proper speed. Sourcing old tapes for her antiquated music system had become one of her favourite pastimes. Sandy sipped her creamy French vanilla, feeling altogether chilled. Actually, she was feeling super chilled all of a sudden. Mellow and fucking chilled, like she'd just smoked a spliff and it was a feeling that Sandy Dalglish did not mind one bit.

CHAPTER 63 – FIND SANDY

"Oh dear God," said Marlene. "David? Ali, you don't think?"

"No, no I don't but clearly the police do. Cuzzocrea, I need you to promise something, I know how this looks and I know you are obliged to follow up on this line of enquiry but I need you to stay open because if you blinker yourselves and you focus solely on David, the real killer is going to slip through your fingers."

Cuzzocrea nodded. "Ali, I have to do my job, I have to follow orders but I hope you can trust me enough to know that I'm considering everything and I'll rule nothing out until I know for sure. Hopefully we can track your husband down and clear this up as quickly as possible."

Ali balle d her fists. "There's something else."

"Yes?" said Cuzzocrea.

"Maybe I'm just in shock, with the whole Oscar thing and now David but I have a really bad feeling about Sandy. I just want her home with me and I know your focus is going to be David but can I take you up on that offer of an escort home? Low profile, like you said? She should be done now."

"Although we have no reason to be concerned about your daughter I think it would be prudent, if only for your peace of mind."

Ali nodded. "Thank you."

"I'll be right back," said Cuzzocrea.

Marlene turned to Ali as Cuzzocrea left. "Ali, let me go out and see if I can find her? I'll go to Lloyd's Diner, I'll drive through Goldstream Village then go over to the

Westshore Mall. I bet I can find her before the police do."

"Would you?" Ali was not only grateful to Marlene, she could also do with her being out of the house for a while since there was something that she was suddenly itching to do, something she couldn't do with Marlene hovering over her.

"Of course." Marlene grabbed her handbag and headed for the front door. "I'll find her, hon. Don't you worry, just sit tight."

Ali tried to smile but as Marlene left she felt a dark emptiness overtake her soul. And no matter how hard she tried to convince herself that Sandy was fine, that she was just finishing her usual shift and probably already on her way home, hell, maybe David even had a good reason for lying to her, still, Ali couldn't shake her sense of doom.

Ali picked up her phone and sent another text to Sandy then she dialled David's number, waited for the tone and decided that it was necessary to leave the stupid shit a message. "Where the fuck are you, David? I know you're not on Salt Spring. Look, you're in trouble, something bad happened and the police needed to speak to you so they went to the chief and now they know you've been lying so they're looking for you. David, this is bad, it's all bad and Sandy didn't come home yet…fuck. David. You need to come home. Just please, come home."

Ali pressed end, her home screen blurred before her eyes as they filled with tears before she angrily blinked them away and pulled herself together again.

"Keep it together Ali, keep it together."

The manila envelope in the middle of the table caught her eye; it was the reason she'd needed Marlene to leave. Ali reached over and slid Carter Burrow's file to her, opened it, pulled out the contents and began to read.

CHAPTER 64 - RHIANNON

Cathump. Cathump. Cathump. Cathump. Cathump.

At first the rhythm had been soothing to her, pounding in perfect time along with Mick Fleetwood on drums as Stevie Nicks's sandpapery voice told the story of the itinerant Welsh goddess but as she'd followed Carter taking a right onto Lindholm – just down from the cute sheepy-weepy farm (she imagined the flock being herded in the sunny meadow by Rhiannon on her majestic white steed, guided by her three magical birds) the gentle cathump had metamorphosed into a duller, more depressing noise altogether.

If her seat had been equipped with a headrest she'd have happily rested back against it. Her eyelids were not so much blinking but lazily curtaining out the intermittent strobing of the sunlight through the pines *and* her teeth felt funny, slack, like she could reach right into her mouth and start plucking them out of her gums one by one.

"Dunga-dunga-dunga-dunga-dunga-dung," Sandy mumbled, mimicking the cathumping's new timbre.

Sucking back a dribble of saliva from her lips, Sandy pulled over after the bend into the gravel mart. She forgot how to turn the car off; it should have been easy but it wasn't. She eventually realized that she couldn't turn the engine off with any of the buttons on the stereo and so she yanked up the handbrake. The sound of it made her giggle, she imagined it to be the noise a timpani percussion mallet would make if it was rattled over a glockenspiel made of her own vertebrae.

"Glockenspiel?" said Sandy, savouring the *shh* of the 's' as she opened her door. It was so heavy she decided she'd have to push it the rest of the way open with her foot.

...

He'd punctured the rubber with his Havalon knife, one swift stab, not too deep or wide a fissure because that would have caused the tyre to flatten too early, perhaps in a densely populated area but just enough so that the flat was a guarantee. It was important that her journey be limited otherwise she'd be in danger as the morphine took hold.

She'd driven on the flat for longer than he'd expected though, at least three kilometres past the school on Daisy Farm and through the triple bends, riding the tide of her high but now she pulled over into the nearest place that she could, the perfect place, the deserted gravel mart.

Carter reversed his van back down the hill then pulled into the carpark just in time to hear her engine give a death rattle as it stalled. He did a three-point turn and reversed back so that the double doors of his van could open up at the sloped rear of her VW Bug. Her driver's door was open and her foot dangled free of the car and he knew then that her virginal blood had bent itself penitent to the power of the narcotic in her drink.

She was light and floppy, easy to carry and he was able to lay her in the carpeted cargo space swiftly. Safely secreted in his van, she gurgled like an infant put down for a nap, a bubble of spit popped on her lips and Carter felt the spawn of his arousal as his excitement throbbed and pushed against his zipper.

CHAPTER 65 - THE BLUEPRINT

The fuchsia roses were no more as the crumb-covered china plates crashed to the floor and smashed into myriad irregular shards, big and small, as Ali swept her forearm across the table. Cuzzocrea's laptop was the only item spared the fate as Ali's anxiety twisted itself into something darkly dangerous and brutally productive. Ali Dalglish had sniffed out her prey and the hunt was underway.

She hurriedly laid each individual portion of the file she had been reading out on the cleared table. The file was a comprehensive record, a detailed report on a young boy, a damaged young boy. He was a boy who had managed to survive an existence as hellish as any she'd encountered during her extensive research into the effect that a negative environment can have upon an individual born with a dysfunctional prefrontal cortex and amygdala – the regions of the brain associated with social and moral reasoning, things like empathy and remorse and the regions in charge of inhibiting destructive boldness.

The theoretical notion is controversially adopted by those who believe that specific environmental factors lead to psychopathy, narcissism, Machiavellianism and sadism, known to psychiatrists and neuropsychologists as the dark tetrad.

The various reports that lay before her were punctuated with photographs of the boy. One of them was a typical school photograph. In it he was aged around six, young enough to have not yet grown out of the narrow, elongated skull common in children who were born severely premature. A gummy void where two front teeth should have been grinned beneath innocent eyes, one of which was marked with the yellow-green of a healing bruise shadowed by a floppy, uncombed fringe which had been hacked at with scissors in an attempt to make the scruffy boy more presentable. The grimy collar of his blue polo shirt poked up on one side where his pilled maroon sweater, several sizes too big, drooped from his bony shoulder, hinting at a near skeletal physique.

Later pictures were an illustration of a bleak narrative, the story of a boy who suffered far worse than mere neglect and deprivation, a boy whose narrow head had been stamped upon repeatedly with such ferocity that the skull had split along the squamosal suture of the neurocranium (the bony ossification that lies between the temporal bone below and the parietal bone above it). Ali estimated, given his age at the time (nine years and three months) as well as factoring in his prematurity and malnutrition, that a force of at least two thousand Newtons had to have been applied swiftly in a downward, stamping motion while the child's head lay on an unyielding surface to split the skull along the fused fissure.

His recovery was documented in a series of photographs too but regardless of the boy's swollen and battered visage, regardless of the feeding and breathing tubes, of the drains and the staples, Ali felt no compassion, no empathy – not because she suffered from a dysfunctional prefrontal cortex, but because she could see past the images of a healing child. To her the photographs were a progressive visual record that tracked the birth of a monster.

Carter Burrows was born with a damaged brain, of that she had no doubt, and the atrocities he had witnessed and suffered during his formative years drip-fed his genetic predisposition – his birth defects – allowing them to blossom and bloom. The viciousness meted out by his stepfather, his drug-addled mother and a series of violent and abusive stepfather figures sculpted his diabolical potential.

The file was also laden with court transcripts. The first trial was that of Gord McAllister, the mother's partner who had squashed the boy's skull beneath his steel-toe-cap workbooks one snowy Christmas Eve. The others were all proceedings *against* Carter Burrows for crimes ranging from arson through to the final case, the one which had landed him in a secure mental institute for three and a half years. Ali was shocked, not only by the details of the crime he had committed and that he now walked free but because he had served his sentence in a facility that Ali was very familiar with: St. Fillan's Hospital for Forensic Mental Health Care.

Ali snapped her head up as she felt fresh air rush in from the front door. Cuzzocrea had a look of concern on his face as he noticed the broken plates and looked at Ali, hunched over the paperwork on the table.

"Sandy?"

Cuzzocrea shook his head. "She'd already left by the time they got over there."

"Are you kidding me? Can't you fuckers do anything right? Did you read this file?"

"Briefly, why?" answered Cuzzocrea.

"This is him. This is the guy, I fucking knew it." Ali pointed at the various reports. "This shit is a blueprint – a...a recipe sheet for a psychopathic predator and he's been right there, in our faces, the whole fucking time."

Cuzzocrea stepped to the table and scanned the documents.

Ali continued, "He's not a victim. Sure, to the untrained eye he might look that way, which is probably why some thick as fuck judge with chronic fucking hero syndrome sealed his file and let him walk!" Ali slammed her fist onto the school photograph of Carter.

"Hey, calm down, Ali." Cuzzocrea put his hand on her shoulder but Ali shrugged it away.

"Don't tell me to calm down! Carter Burrows! That's who

you need to be looking for. And you better hope that my daughter walks through that door in the next ten minutes because if she doesn't then you need to get out there and look for her because this bastard, he hold grudges, he makes it personal not because he's angry because he's incapable of emotion. He makes it personal because he can, because he's a cold, heartless, sadistic fuck and I think he's making it personal with me. I think he killed Oscar and I think he's going after Sandy. He asked about her last night. Jesus! Cuzzocrea, what if he's following her, what if he's watching her?"

Cuzzocrea held his hands up. "Ali, I'm listening, okay. Just stop. You have to calm down because if you are onto something then you acting like this —"

"Like what? What am I acting like? A crazy woman? Well, guess what? I am a bit fucking crazy but I'm also really good at sniffing out sick fuckers like this and so you better listen."

"I am!"

Cuzzocrea raised his voice so uncharacteristically that Ali was struck by his honesty, how engaged he was, how his eyes lacked a question or any judgement towards her. She could see that he was open to her suggestions.

Ali took a deep breath and nodded.

Cuzzocrea put his hands on his hips, his handgun poked out from under his jacket. "I want to hear it. Tell me. Tell me everything."

CHAPTER 66 - KATY'S LOVER

At the moment her lover's world began to crumble, Katy had been intent upon flicking free then peeling off the ingrowing section of her big toenail. She wriggled a sewing needle carefully underneath it and along to the place where its intrusion was making the skin swell and redden to almost the exact shade of her nail polish. It was really beginning to bug her, especially in her new Jimmy Choos.

Katy gave up on the toenail and relit her joint as David stepped out onto the balcony, his phone to his ear, his face the colour of the lightest piece of ash that snowed down onto her tanned thigh. She knew he was checking messages from *her*, his attention-seeking bitch of a wife. She'd been calling him relentlessly all morning until, that was, Katy had finally taken the phone and powered it off so that they could continue their lovemaking in peace. Now, it seemed, the peace of their long-awaited weekend together was about to be ruined.

"What is it with that woman?" said Katy. "What? Has she finally decided to notice you? This weekend? *Really?*"

When he didn't answer, Katy felt a flash of the jealousy that was the undercurrent of their passion. There was no way she was coming in second.

"David! What the fuck?"

David turned to her at last, lowering his phone to his pocket as he did. His face was even paler than it had been. "I have to go."

Katy was having none of that crap, no way she would allow him to treat her like a piece of shit. "Oh no you don't. We've been planning this weekend for months. No way are you running off to her."

"It's serious, Kat. This is bad."

Katy pouted and went back to peeling her toenail.

"Look," said David, "I'm sorry, okay. She knows I lied about Salt Spring. The police are looking for me."

Katy laughed. "Oh, please! Really? *Really*? Yeah right, like the police are going to arrest you for lying to your wife."

"No, it's something else. I have to go."

"David? We agreed, no lies. You know I've been patient, I've given you all the space you need and I haven't complained even once about only getting to see you for a couple of hours every morning and on practice nights but this is my time now. My weekend with you." Katy put her joint in the ashtray and moved to David, crossing her wrists behind his neck she tiptoed and teasingly wriggled her butt – barely covered by the new Victoria's Secret panties she'd bought just for him. "Are you seriously telling me that you'd rather go running off to her when you could stay here and let me suck your dick?"

David peeled Katy's arms from his neck and held her away from him. "I *need* to go, I think I'm in trouble. It's not even about Ali."

"Don't! Don't say her stupid name, okay." Katy slumped into the chair again.

"I'll come back okay. I'll sort it out and I'll come back, we can still have our weekend."

"Just fuck off, David. You shit," said Katy, studying her new gel manicure. "You think I can't do better than you? Because I can. You go, I might just call some friends, go out and party, have a real weekend. Suck some real dick."

"Katy, don't be like that."

Katy sat forward, leaning aggressively towards him. "Go, David. Go back to your crazy-ass wife, see if I care."

David sighed and stepped into the condo. As he put his

coat on and was opening the front door, Katy called to him from the balcony, "If this is because she's tried to kill herself again, tell her to do a better job of it this time – do us all a favour."

David halted in the doorway, hypocritically compelled to defend Ali's honour and admonish Katy for her unkind words but how could he justifiably scold the twenty-six-year-old he enjoyed fucking every chance he got behind the back of the wife he wished to defend? Also, since Ali knew something – the extent of her knowledge he was yet to learn but someone had blabbed – he might just need to crash at Katy's for longer than a weekend. Like his dad used to say, 'Don't shit where you eat, son' and so David said nothing to Katy as he pulled the door closed behind him.

CHAPTER 67 - FAILURE TO PREPARE

Regardless that he has been forced to improvise, he could not bring himself to share his most intimate of spaces, his private sanctuary, his sacristy. It is in a shambolic state and was tainted once already by last night's intruder and so he will have to leave her in the van for now. Her system is pure, she will have no tolerance for the powerful sedative and he is therefore buoyed by the knowledge that she sleeps deeply. The inconvenience of it all is salved as he climbs into the cargo space with her, to check on her before heading down into the lair, her very presence and the graceful bend of her proffered neck sends a wave of excitement through him.

She is still cloaked in the stale buttery stench of the diner, her clothing thick with the cloying atmosphere of grease. He pulls the ugly chiffon scarf of animated characters from around her neck and discards it on some boxes. He lowers himself onto her and sniffs at her, below the oil and vinegar and the carcinogens of burnt bacon rind and toast resides the delicate nuances of her natural musk to which his olfactory sense is inseparably adhered. He breathes her in, her enticing odour intoxicates him, her hair tickles the end of his nose as he nuzzles into the crease at the back of her ear and traces the elegant slope of her nape.

He will soon be deft in his slicing, he can barely resist the need to dispose of her stinking clothes but resist he must, he must deny the temptation to explore further, to seek out other musks because he must clear the chamber of what had once filled him with pride but now seemed nothing more than an unworthy, lesser specimen, an embarrassment to him.

He walks himself back to a kneeling position over her, trailing a finger between her breasts and down to her private place. "Wait, Carter, wait." To fail to prepare is to prepare to fail and steps must now be taken to assemble components for a ritual that will surely promise to be beyond even his own ability to envisage. What lay ahead for him would be undeniably splendid and delectable but he must first clear the chamber. Out with old and in with the superior new. Only then can he explore the delightful gift that has floated to him amongst the chaotic flotsam and jetsam of the troublesome, unprecedented happenings of the past twenty-four hours.

He must clear the rubbish, feed the fire and prepare.

...

Before she was able to open her eyes, Sandy sensed that she was trapped. She felt trapped inside her own body. Her mind was as alert as ever but for some reason her body would not comply with the orders she was sending it. From outside she must have looked like she was sleeping but inside her skull her brain had kicked into survival mode. It was needling at her to wake up, to move her body, to pry open her eyes yet all she could do was lie there, her mouth agape. Her tongue had spread itself flat across the opening of her throat, her spit and phlegm had pooled in the cup created by the obstruction and kept dislodging itself with a snorting gurgle which would otherwise have caused in her a sense of embarrassment, but now, as a more urgent sense was settling upon her, a sense of danger, embarrassment was far from her mind.

Sandy felt a tear pile out of the corner of her eye and speed down her cheek, wetting her ear and she wondered if she was crying. She could feel that she was rocking, a gentle bounce accompanied by a low, comforting humbly-rumbly noise; it was nice, womb-like and cosy but Sandy knew there was nothing truly nice about it. She was in a vehicle, a moving vehicle. She knew she was lying down. She was lying down in a vehicle, a moving vehicle and she knew that she was unable to move, unable even to open her eyes.

It occurred to Sandy that she might have been involved in an accident. Had she crashed her car? Yes, that seemed to fit because she remembered now. She'd been feeling woozy when they'd passed the sheep farm – yes, the sheep farm where she'd seen the white horse and the goddess and the birds. There was a bad noise, the Beetle was difficult to steer…wow, maybe she'd crashed and now she was in an ambulance. She'd crashed and she was hurt and she was in the back of an ambulance and maybe she was in a coma and that's why she couldn't move or open her eyes.

Sandy tried to make sense of it, to remember the events leading up to the accident. She remembered the wooziness, like she was high and then she must have…no, wait, there wasn't a crash, she'd pulled up after the bend, into the place where mum got soil last year for the garden, the gravel what's-it's-name?…market or something. There'd been a noise and the steering was pulling and her head was swimming and they'd been going up the hill…they? Who was it? Someone was there, she'd been following someone up to find something…mum and Marlene…Carter, she'd been following that Carter guy.

Carter.

The rocking and swaying had stopped, she wasn't sure when, just that now everything was quiet and that nice noise was gone. There's cold air. Pink light through her eyelids.

Someone's on top of her, Sandy can feel them, their weight upon her. She feels the scarf Danté gave her being pulled from around her neck. And then he's sniffing, like a dog, first her hair, then in at her tear-wet ear and now behind it, bending it forward and then the sniffing moves down her neck; it tickles but not in a nice way.

The weight shifts and now it's only across her pelvis.

Touch. Fingers touching, down her chest. His fingers are on her, *down there* and now she wants to scream, to kick and to scream and to cry and run. Run! Run!

But Sandy cannot kick or scream or run. Sandy lies still, her body is in a state of absolute nothingness, complete relaxation. Except, that is, for the tear which chases its predecessor to add to the puddle in her ear.

CHAPTER 68 - IT'S HIM

It was vital that Cuzzocrea maintain control of the situation, Ali was tightly wound and rightly so.

When she'd described the Carter file as a blueprint, a recipe sheet of psychopathy he'd initially thought that she was desperately grasping at straws, trying to convince herself of something that wasn't there – spiralling into a delusional state of panic but now, as he picked through the pages and the photographs, the transcripts and witness statements, Cuzzocrea could think of no clearer analogy than that of a recipe for disaster: add a pinch of neglect, a tablespoon of sexual abuse, a hundred grams of violence, then combine the ingredients with a brain defect caused by in-utero exposure to hypoxia, stress, malnutrition; finish with a dusting of substance abuse for the all-important layer of kindling mechanism and you have exactly what she said, the ultimate psychotic predator. You have Carter Burrows.

For the second time during the course of the investigation, Cuzzocrea was at odds with his directives. What needed to take priority was not the search for David Dalglish – he may be up to something worth lying to Ali about but it wasn't murder. Two other searches needed to take priority: the first for Carter Burrows; the second, possibly more urgent than the first, was for Sandy Dalglish. His foreboding gut instinct made him dread the possibility that the two searches would become one.

Cuzzocrea now faced the problem of convincing

Superintendent Shaw that the search for either of them was justified, that it wasn't just a response to the demands of a panicked mother.

"We need something," he said. "Something to tie Carter to the profile. Shaw's never going to get onboard otherwise."

"Everything about the profile fits," Ali said.

"No it doesn't."

"Yes! Gender, age, race…vehicle, job, history of mental illness, rejection, abuse, neglect, sexual dysfunction. He involved himself in the case,"

"No, you and Marlene involved him in the case…" Cuzzocrea corrected.

"Damn it Cuzzocrea, you said yourself he's a regular at the station, he's obsessed with the firefighters too. He was at the crime scene and the meeting *and* the memorial."

"Ali, he's unmarried and, for want of a better term, handicapped."

Ali balled her fists in frustration, she pressed them hard against her forehead. "No! You're missing the point, Cuzzocrea."

"Then explain it to me!" Cuzzocrea matched Ali's frustration. "I'm not a mind reader."

"Okay, look. Why do psychopaths get married? Not because they fall in love – they lack emotion, right? They can't feel love, they see other human beings as things, objects, disposable, worthless, amusing at best but otherwise an utter nuisance, a blot on the earth. So then, why would a psychopath marry? Why procreate?"

Cuzzocrea felt condescended by Ali's question, it was basic but he played along. "Narcissism – with the children. They get married because they are compelled to appear normal, to pass as a regular person, it's a façade of normative behaviour, a manipulation so that their true self remains their secret."

Ali's eyes sparkled. "Yes but Carter built a different kind of façade, if other psychopaths are the pigs with the houses made of sticks then he's the one with the house of bricks.

He found an even better way to fly under the radar, a way to manipulate everyone around him, a way to get them to do everything for him, to protect him and even to help him."

"Are you suggesting that his disabilities are a sham?"

"Yes. They probably started out as a survival mechanism. Maybe he learnt that if he played dumb he could inspire the people around him, his abusers, to feel sympathy or even – and more likely – he wanted them to feel embarrassed, repulsed, sickened, disgusted. Like sexually abused girls who become anorexic, subconsciously attempting to reverse puberty in the belief that they would therefore be less attractive to men, to sexual predators."

"It's thin Ali, no pun intended, and you have nothing tangible to go on, you don't even know this for sure."

"I do, I saw the intellect in his eyes. His eyes are anything but vacant, it's what set me on edge about him in the first place and then the other night, after the memorial he did something weird. I couldn't put my finger on it at the time but I knew, *I knew*. When he walks, he drags his right leg, not like some pantomime, peg-leg pirate, he does it really well just like someone who has suffered a massive head injury…"

"Which he did…"

"Okay, and maybe he was like that at first, maybe that's when he realized that it was a powerful tool? Listen, he moves like someone who has worked through physiotherapy, he stalls, like brain injury survivors do, like he has to work to get his leg to move and at the same time, his head, it leans to the left…well, the other night, the fucker mixed it up. His head was tilted to the right, it was his left leg that was slow. He's faking. Faking like Robert-fucking-De-Niro might, but he *is* faking. Carter Burrows disguises his psychopathy, not in the typical way – by building a life of normalcy, of the two-point-four children and the vocational success – but by pretending that he's not all there, that he's broken, damaged, fragile. But Carter Burrows *is* all there, he's more *there* than the rest of us. He's highly skilled, he's diligent and committed, he's extremely manipulative and I'd put money on him being as far from retarded as you can get. I'd put money on him being an I.Q. superior."

Cuzzocrea considered Ali's case. "I can argue that, *we* can argue that but it's theory, it's mere conjecture. There's no way we'd be issued a warrant on that basis."

"No? Well maybe on the fact that he has a previous conviction with the same M.O.!" Ali shuffled through the papers and found the stapled report she was referring to, she slammed the document against Cuzzocrea's chest. "He has previous, Cuzzocrea. The biting? The cutting? It's all there."

Cuzzocrea looked through the report. It was a summary of the charges brought against Carter at the age of fifteen. Amongst the pages was a group of ten-by-eight photographs taken in an examination room of a hospital. The little girl in the picture was alive but she had been brutalized, her face and body was littered with deep bites and bruises, a section of the skin on her neck seemed to have been torn away.

Ali paced as Cuzzocrea read.

"The little girl in those photos was nine at the time of the attack," Ali explained. "When Carter was nine years old, his skull was crushed under Gord McAllister's foot. During his recovery and as a temporary ward of Child Protective Services, Carter had to see a great many specialists, his least favourite of all of them was a dentist called Edward Colling. Despite his protests, Carter was forced to continue with Colling's reconstruction of his teeth as well as basic work like fillings and extractions since the boy had never been to the dentist prior to McAllister's assault. Fast forward six years – *six years*, Cuzzocrea – Colling's daughter, Christa, turned nine and that's when Carter Burrows starts to follow her home from school, he befriends her, he stalks her. He works on her for seven months until finally she trusts him, maybe like a big brother? One day Carter takes her up to the top of Mount Blinkhorn and he does that to her. He bites her with the very teeth that her father had fixed. She was exactly nine and seven months. It was the same age as Carter had been on the first day that he'd found himself in Colling's chair."

"There's something else," said Cuzzocrea. "The sexual assault on Christa Colling, it was carried out with the use of a foreign object. That fits too, Ali."

"Is it enough?"

"It might be."

Ali let out a shaky breath, her cheeks were burning and her eyes felt sticky and dry. "It's him. We've got him."

Before Cuzzocrea could respond, the front door opened and in walked David.

CHAPTER 69 - DETAINED

Before Ali could speak, Cuzzocrea held his hand out as a warning to her. "I need you to step away, Ali. It's very important that I am able to speak to David and ask him a few questions."

Ali looked at David. She wanted to help him but any attempt on her part to guide him could look like coercion and worsen his predicament. Ali, in need of support herself, stepped back and leaned against her housewife's hatch. The Carter file had caused a cyclone of brain chemicals to whirl in her skull like a mad dervish and her equilibrium was on the verge of failing her. She was sure that if she pulled herself away from the ledge on which she rested, she would pass out.

"What's going on, Ali?" said David, stepping to the table.

Cuzzocrea held out his palm to Ali once more and once he was satisfied that she intended to remain compliant, he simultaneously placed his hand over his service revolver, his thumb poised under the leather press-studded latch while he retrieved his phone and slid his other thumb across it to illuminate its lock screen.

Cuzzocrea angled himself so that his back was favouring the corner of the dining room adjacent to the outside wall. He was suddenly in absolute command of the room.

Cuzzocrea spoke while he sent a text using his phone – Ali assumed the text was for either his partner, Munro, or his superior, Shaw, or maybe it was to alert the uniformed police officers he had been communicating with – alerting the recipient to David's presence in the house. She hoped the text hadn't been to the 'unis' (as Cuzzocrea called them) since they were the officers who were supposed to be looking for Sandy.

"Take a seat, if you will, Mr Dalglish."

"Do you mind telling me what this drama is about?" said David, sitting in the chair that Shaw had earlier vacated.

"I need to ask you a few questions about your whereabouts over recent days," said Cuzzocrea.

"What the hell?" David looked at Ali. "What's going on here?"

"David, just answer the questions," Ali blurted, almost unaware of the fact that she had.

"Mrs Dalglish, if you don't mind stepping out of the room," said Cuzzocrea.

Ali looked at him. "Not a fucking chance. But I will be quiet."

Cuzzocrea's face tightened; he turned to David, placing his phone on the table between himself and David and stepping seamlessly into a dominant role. "Mr Dalglish. David. I'm going to record the following conversation. Do you understand that you are not under arrest at this time and no charges have been brought against you?"

David nodded and shrugged.

"For the benefit of the recording could you please state your response?" Cuzzocrea readjusted the iPhone's proximity to David.

"Yes," David said with a petulant air.

"Mr Dalglish, can you tell me where you were on the night of Sunday the eighth of April and during the early morning hours of Monday the ninth?"

David frowned and thought back to the beginning of the week. "Here. In my house. I was sleeping. In bed."

"Can anyone confirm that on your behalf?"

"My wife, Ali Dalglish."

"And did you leave at any point prior to seven a.m. on

the morning of Monday the ninth?"

"Yes. I went to work."

"At what time?"

"I get up around five, I go to the gym at the fire hall then I shower and then I start work."

"That would be the fire hall here in Mochetsin, correct? Can anyone corroborate your presence in the fire hall at that time?"

"No. I'm always the first in. The Chief gets in around seven. Why?"

Ali closed her eyes. Her brain swam again and a feeling of nausea overcame her.

"Can you confirm your whereabouts last night?"

"I was here. I was in bed. Ali came home from her thing. She was in the bedroom for a while, I remember that. Then there was a call, a fire call at…I think it was around quarter to twelve."

"And what was the nature of the call?"

David ran his tongue across the inside of his cheek. "This is ridiculous."

"Just answer the question please, Mr Dalglish."

"It was a report of smoke in an apartment building. A false alarm. We evacuated the block and checked all the apartments. Nothing. It was a prank, it happens."

"What time, approximately, did you clear the scene?"

"It took about thirty minutes all in; we were back at the hall by ten to one."

"And then what happened?"

"Then…we cleaned up."

"How long did that take?"

"Not really a clean-up, there was no incident so we just checked the trucks and then secured the building."

"And what time did your truck check and securing of the building conclude?"

"All done by one fifteen, probably."

"And then?"

"Then nothing."

"Nothing? What happened once the building was secure?"

"Then…I decided to…I stayed at the fire hall. I slept there last night."

Ali blinked her eyes open and frowned.

"You didn't return home at that time?"

"No. I stayed at the hall. Ali knows that, I texted Sandy to tell her. Look, if this is about Salt Spring, I got my dates mixed up, that's all. I've been at the hall all day, my phone was on silent and I just got Ali's messages so I came home."

"Mr Dalglish. David. It's in your interests to tell me the truth at this point. I do have to advise you that my colleagues have interviewed others present at the fire hall during and after the call last night. Now, I'm going to ask you again, once clean-up was done, once the truck checks and the securing of the building was complete, at approximately one fifteen a.m., you left the fire hall. Where did you go?"

David looked at Ali, he swallowed nervously then looked at Cuzzocrea. "I didn't come home. I didn't stay at the fire hall but I didn't come home either."

Ali pulled herself away from the wall. She shared a look of concern with Cuzzocrea.

"You're absolutely sure that you did not come home to this house after you left the fire hall? You did not return home, you went somewhere else, is that correct?"

"Yes."

Cuzzocrea paused. Ali wanted desperately to interject but knew that she mustn't interrupt the interview, the sooner it was over, the better.

"Where did you go, Mr Dalglish?" asked Cuzzocrea.

David looked at his hands, the same gesture of guilt she'd read in her own son when he was little and had been caught putting crayons down radiators or scraping his plate for a dog before his meal was finished.

"Mr Dalglish?"

"I want to speak to a lawyer."

Ali couldn't believe what she was hearing, "David! Just

answer the fucking question. I know you came home, I heard you, I felt you."

David stared at his wife, "I didn't come home, Ali. I was somewhere else. Monday morning too, I wasn't in the gym."

Cuzzocrea stepped up to David, releasing a pair of handcuffs from the back of his belt as he did. "David Dalglish, I am detaining you for further questioning in connection with the murder of Samantha Giesbrecht. It is my duty to inform you that you have the right to retain and instruct counsel of your choice in private and without delay…"

Ali stared incredulously. She knew David well enough to know that he was telling the truth but that truth had huge ramifications.

"Before you decide to answer any question concerning this investigation you may call a lawyer of your choice or get free advice from duty counsel. If you wish to contact legal aid duty counsel I can provide you with a telephone number and a telephone will be made available to you. Do you understand?"

Ali's ears buzzed and then fogged over all the sounds from the world around her. She saw David say yes but she didn't hear it. She saw Cuzzocrea ask another question, but she didn't hear it. She saw the red and blue flashing lights lick at the white ceiling of the dining room but she didn't hear the sirens.

CHAPTER 70 - DENIAL IN THE RCMP

Although he was putting on his bravest face, Ali could see that Kenny was close to crying and so, regardless of his height in comparison to her and that he probably thought it was totally un-cool, she held her son's hand as they crossed the carpark and entered the Glandford R.C.M.P. building.

Across the foyer, shielded by her plexiglass barrier, the same receptionist Ali had encountered earlier in the week (the one she'd named Ginger Vitus due to the woman's wretched halitosis) was already trying to appear far too busy to deal with mere peasants.

As she crossed the foyer, Ali wished that Marlene was with her right now. Not only did Marlene know the receptionist, Ali had no doubt she'd know exactly what strings to pull to inspire her cooperation.

"You sit right there baby." Ali pointed Kenny toward the bank of seating along the brick wall, under the R.C.M.P. crest. "I'm going to find out what's going on."

"'kay." said Kenny as he pulled his headphones up onto his head and folded back the cover of his tablet, only too happy to escape into some alternate reality, one where his dad wasn't in police custody.

"Excuse me?" Ali spoke to the receptionist's back as she was fussing over the sheets of paper spewing out of the photocopier.

The plexiglass may have been bulletproof but it certainly was not soundproof, Ali mustered patience in the face of the woman's obvious and deliberate attempt to snub her.

"Hey! Oi! Excuse me!" Ali shouted too loud to be believably ignored. The receptionist turned, stony faced and took her time to approach Ali. Ginger Vitus was already reaching into the tray where she kept her petty request forms.

"No. Don't bother with that crap. My husband was detained for questioning." The receptionist gave Ali a satisfied smirk. "I'd like to speak to the arresting officer. Inspector Cuzzocrea."

Ginger Vitus predictably slid a form into the steel basin between Ali and herself. Ali toyed with the idea of finding a way to access the plexiglass and shove the form down the woman's gullet but decided instead that she would rise above the provocation. She had to remain focused on David but, more importantly, on Sandy who had yet to reply to a single message.

Ali turned to look at Kenny as she assessed the situation as objectively as she could. Sandy would be fine, odds were that she had probably gotten home, maybe her phone was out of battery life and she was finding a charger right now. Ali tried to reassure herself that her phone would peep with an incoming text any second from Sandy but, God, she'd love to know, know for sure that she was home and safe, even if not home, just anywhere safe. It would help too if Marlene had a cell phone, at least then she'd know whether she'd seen Sandy around Glandford.

As if it were the days before mobile devices, whenever that had been, Ali had resorted to taping a written note to her front door for Marlene, telling her that she and Kenny had gone to R.C.M.P. and that Marlene should meet them here.

Whether it was the product of her imagination or not, Ali could smell Ginger's rank breath and so stepped away from the barrier. Her phone told her that it was two fifty-five. Sandy had finished work over three quarters of an hour ago.

"Ma'am, you have to fill out a request form."

Ali played Ginger at her own game and allowed the twat to speak to her back while she went directly to the organ grinder and sent a text to Cuzzocrea:

<In reception. Need to speak to you. if you don't come soon you're going to have to arrest me for grievous bodily harm against your power-pissed receptionist with the furry gums>

Ali took the seat next to Kenny and rubbed his shoulders. He slipped his headphones back. "Can we see dad now?" he asked.
"Soon, baby. Someone's coming to talk to us now."
Kenny nodded. He seemed to trust Ali's false confidence so she smiled and let him get back to his game. She envied her son's capacity for denial as she checked to see if Sandy had contacted her.

...

Cuzzocrea replied to the text message Ali had sent from downstairs in the reception area:

<give me five. don't leave>

"If his alibi checks out, he's free to go," said Shaw as he watched David Dalglish from their side of the transparent mirror located in the brightly lit interview room Munro had just stepped out of.
"And the Burrows warrant?" asked Cuzzocrea.
"If Dalglish's alibi is confirmed by Miss Massey then I'll move forward on it – but *only* then." Shaw turned to Dalglish who was leaning against the wall in the darkened observation room. "The woman, Ali Dalglish, officially speaking she's a witness, a possible victim *and* the wife of a suspect, if we refer to her on the application, the whole case could be dismissed on those grounds later."

"She's an expert. She profiled Carter Burrows *before* her husband was detained and if she's right, she was only a victim because the unsub – *Burrows* – knew that she was closing in on him."

"Muddy waters, Rey. The Burrows line has teeth because of his previous convictions, because of the consistencies with regards to the sexual assault and the fact that the trace narcotic present in our victim's system happens to be one repeatedly prescribed to Burrows for his chronic pain. That being said, I'm going to push for a warrant granting investigation by the special I techs. Our best bet at anything other than circumstantial evidence is to catch him in the act or even in the planning of the act. Moving forward that is going to strengthen the case against him and failing a certain result we might just gather enough additional evidence to warrant a search and arrest. I have to tread carefully, a judge restricted his youth record for a reason – to protect him as a vulnerable member of society."

"*Restricted* the record. It wasn't expunged or sealed. There's a reason for that too, sir."

Shaw nodded. "I'm keeping that in mind, Rey. Munro's going to take Katherine Massey's statement, see what this guy's mistress has to say. If Dalglish was with her on the morning of the ninth and then again last night, we can cut him loose and recalibrate our efforts."

Shaw made to leave, his hand was already on the door handle as Cuzzocrea spoke, "Sir, the Dalglish girl? The daughter?"

"An eighteen-year-old girl – woman, actually – who, by my watch, is less than an hour late home from work? Rey, that doesn't have teeth and I expect more of you than to be swept along with a victim's paranoia. Don't let whatever spell she seems to have cast upon you affect your decision making." Shaw turned the handle, opened the door a crack then turned to Cuzzocrea once more. "Incidentally, if her husband's alibi does check out, then I'm giving Trina the nod to declare 555 Alder Beach Road an official crime scene

393

so you might want to let Mrs Dalglish know that she won't have access to her home until we are satisfied that we've gathered all of the relevant evidence. If she needs anything from the house I expect you to accompany her in a supervisory capacity. Ordinarily I'd task a family liaison with that but, since you seem to have connected with her and to have built a rapport *and* because, well, I just don't trust her, I'd prefer you to assist."

"Sir. I'll let her know, she's downstairs."

Shaw left the observation room. Cuzzocrea looked through to David Dalglish who had his head in his hands and was scratching his scalp. A guilty tell, not of murder in this particular case, but of really poor choices.

"Stupid prick," said Cuzzocrea as he left to find Ali Dalglish.

...

Ali had begun to pace the length of the foyer, she'd read every pamphlet and pinned notice all of which had only served to worry her more.

By the time Cuzzocrea was buzzed through the door of Ginger Vitus's glass box, Ali had bitten down every fingernail, discarding her D.N.A. in the shape of tiny crescent moons all over the tiled floor.

Ali approached Cuzzocrea. She wanted to hug him and throttle him in equal measure but resorted to neither measure and instead pulled him across to the wall farthest from her son and out of earshot of the receptionist.

"Well?" Ali asked, searching his eyes.

"We're just about to check his alibi now."

"So he told you where he was then?" asked Ali. She noticed that Cuzzocrea's attention had been pulled from her and to a young blonde woman in ridiculous heels with criss-crossing feathered straps, who was click-clacking her way to the reception desk.

"Are you fucking serious right now?" said Ali, demanding

that Cuzzocrea focus on her. "Really? Any chance you can roll your tongue back into your mouth for a minute and talk to me?"

"What?" said Cuzzocrea before realizing what Ali was implying, "No, you misunderstand, I think she's…I'll be right back."

Ali watched incredulously as Cuzzocrea approached the woman, spoke to her briefly then to the receptionist who promptly made a phone call. Cuzzocrea returned to Ali.

"I see you get better service here if you're wearing a wonder bra and hooker heels, I'll remember that next time my fucking daughter goes missing."

Ali checked over her shoulder to ensure that Kenny wasn't listening. He was lost in concentration, staring intently at his tablet screen.

"It looks like we'll be releasing David."

"Good. So? Where was he?"

"Maybe that's something the two of you might want to discuss in private."

Ali took a deep breath and held it before blowing it out slowly and readying herself for a truth she'd already accepted. "An affair?" Ali nodded and raised her chin in defiance of the hurt she was feeling. "It's all it can be."

Cuzzocrea said nothing but maintained his eye contact with Ali, something she was grateful for. She'd have hated him to pity her or feel embarrassed on her behalf.

Ali shrugged, her defiance was surprisingly hard to maintain. "Fucker. I can't go there just now." Ali waved her hand as if to bat away the pestering fly that was her husband's infidelity. "Whatever…fuck him." Ali tried to smile. "It's funny really, isn't it?"

"No, I don't think it is," said Cuzzocrea.

"I'm so fucking arrogant, you know? Always have been." Ali's eyes filled with tears which she rushed to blink away and Cuzzocrea almost moved to touch her but decided against it when Ali predicted his offer of comfort and pulled away from it. "Here I was thinking that I had more to offer, that my husband would never do that to me, you know, I'm *me*, I'm amazing and I trump that shit," Ali said, mocking herself.

"You do trump that, Ali. Trust me, you trump it." Cuzzocrea paused for a moment, wanting to say more but unable to find the words. "Have you heard from Sandy?"

"No. Marlene went out to look for her. Did your officers come up with anything?"

Cuzzocrea shook his head, he wanted to avoid having to admit that there were no officers tasked with a search for Sandy Dalglish, and neither would there be. "No. Marlene?"

Ali shook her head. "She doesn't have a cell phone so I have no idea. I left a message, a note on my front door for her to meet me here."

Ali heard the clunk and scrape of the lock uncoupling and saw Munro step out from the vestibule. He held it open behind him and allowed the young blonde to step through. Munro nodded at Cuzzocrea who retuned the gesture and nervously cleared his throat as he met Ali's eyes.

Ali studied Cuzzocrea's eyes for a second then glanced back at Munro and the blonde as they disappeared through the inner door to the station. Realization dawned on Ali.

"Holy shit. You must be on glue." Ali read Cuzzocrea's nervousness accurately. "That's who David was with? Oh my God, what a fucking cliché. Who is she?"

Cuzzocrea was clearly unwilling to provide Ali with that information.

"Jesus! Fuck!" Ali paced away from Cuzzocrea. "Fucker!" This time Kenny had heard her and was looking concerned so Ali faked a reassuring smile long enough for her son to relax again and return to his game.

Ali stepped back to Cuzzocrea. "My God, if I'd have known who she was when she'd walked in like that, I'd have ripped her tits off."

"How do you think I got lazy Munro down here so fast?" Cuzzocrea smiled.

"Was he with her last night?" Ali asked.

396

"Don't do that to yourself, Ali."

Ali tutted impatiently. "I'm not asking because I'm some shattered cuckold, you prick, I'm asking because David was in my room last night, on my bed. David tucked Sandy in, remember? But if David was with slut-bag last night, then who the fuck was in my house?"

Cuzzocrea nodded. Ali put her hands on her hips, fighting panic and battling a sinking feeling in her abdomen. "Carter Burrows. He was in my house. My bed. That's when he took Oscar, just waltzed right in, made himself at home and took my fucking dog for his last walk." Ali visualized the intruder in her home, her eyes dream-like and glassy. "And Sandy, he was in Sandy's room."

CHAPTER 71 - THE IMPROVISER

As he crumpled it to the floor he was faced with the remnants of his pathetic attempt at perfection. How he thought he had mastered it all, how he'd thought he was ready to display his work but it was child's play. Defunct. Obsolete. As far from his ideal as a thing could be. There are two others remaining besides her and they too inspire in him feelings of embarrassment and shame.

He berates himself for his shortcomings. So much time, months, years, his eager attempts culminated in nothing but a symbol of his own failings. He had thought he was creating something unique, dazzling and spectacular but as he looked at them now, they had transmutated into their true worth: puddles of vomitus pointlessness.

He pushed it deeper into the darkness under the bench and as he did, he felt its bony spine beneath the sole of his boot. How pathetic he was to have feasted on the filthy debris of the streets. They had been forsaken by the people they were born to and it was beyond him now to comprehend what had compelled him to sift them out of the slurry and attempt to cocoon them here, hoping for something better to emerge.

He wished he could purge himself of his previous delight in them, eradicate them not only from view but from existence entirely. However, it would pose too great a risk to venture out with them now that he had been forced into a state of overexposure by the intruder right off the back of his unusually rash decision to punish the Dalglish woman.

Carter ran his fingertips along the deep and gnarled scar on his skull and was heartened by its message: he will rise again and he will triumph and then he may reap the true fruits of his labour.

It was coming to the hour when he would place Sandy in the chamber and then he would indulge in the cleansing and purification, the necessary sanitization required for greatness and true delectation. Only then can the ritual proper commence.

He was Tenzing Norgay on the precipice of greatness with the clouds atop Mount Everest brushing his cheeks and there was no way he would step aside for a lesser to summit before him.

CHAPTER 72 - LINDHOLM

Marlene had exhausted her search of Glandford and of Goldstream Village. Sandy's car wasn't parked anywhere around the Westshore Mall either and now, as Marlene passed through the school zone on Daisy Farm Road, she decided she might as well take the extra few minutes to bypass the direct route to the café by heading up Lindholm and looping back around via Kangaroo Road. That way she could at least let Ali know she'd helped to narrow down the search area. Besides, Marlene had a feeling that she'd pull into Alder Beach Road to find Sandy's cute little Bug parked up right next to Ali's car.

As Marlene headed up Lindholm, passing the sheep farm on the first bend, she crossed her fingers, saluted and spat out of the window – it was a little superstition of hers and thus far had only steered her wrong on a couple of occasions.

Marlene slowed down, yes she was eager to make headway but the bends on Lindholm were very tricky to manoeuvre over twenty-five kilometres an hour especially with the possibility of trucks reversing out onto the road from the gravel mart just ahead. Then Marlene remembered, the gravel mart is closed on Friday's and so she allowed herself a comfortable twenty-seven…and a half.

CHAPTER 73 - FINGERTIPS

Sandy felt a patch of lovely heat diffuse across her crotch and down her thighs. It felt soothing and comforting until its warmth quickly cooled leaving her feeling itchy and sticky and she realized that she'd peed herself.

She wasn't in an ambulance or a coma because she'd have a catheter in and paramedics don't usually feel you up like a sleazy perv.

She had to move, somehow she had to get herself out of this state and she begged herself, silently screaming at her lifeless limbs. She tried her toes, no use. She imagined she was raising her eyebrows, higher and higher although she wasn't even sure how that would feel, let alone being able to scrunch her forehead enough to force her eyelids apart. Nothing.

Carpet.

Under her fingertips, she could feel it, the nylony scratch of cheap carpet. She was suddenly in command of her left hand and that was all the encouragement Sandy needed because if she could now move her fingertips when only minutes ago she could not, then soon she would be able to move everything.

"Come on, Sandy! Move your arse!" she silently shouted from within her own useless body.

CHAPTER 74 - ARE THEY EVEN LOOKING?

"He has her. I *know* it," said Ali.

"Once David is released, VIIMIS's official prime suspect becomes Carter Burrows," said Cuzzocrea.

"And that means what? What? You apply for a warrant? You arrest him?"

"Yes, that's the idea," Cuzzocrea lied, all too aware that Shaw had no intention of arresting Burrows yet.

"And how long is that going to take?"

"I don't know but at least Shaw's listening. He pulled Carter's file – his previous assault is ample grounds for suspicion…but…"

"But what?" Ali stepped closer to Cuzzocrea.

"There's always a chance that things could get held up."

"Oh, for bastarding, fucking-cunting sake, Cuzzocrea! Don't give me that shit."

"Ali, we have procedures, we can't just storm in there and arrest him. We need a judge to look into the case first, all of the evidence, you know that."

"There are ways around that shit, *you* know *that*. Are they even looking for Sandy?"

Ali searched Cuzzocrea's eyes and didn't like what she saw in them.

CHAPTER 75 - THE BLUE BUG

Marlene almost missed it. The bend after the sheep farm sweeps past the gravel mart as Lindholm straightens out and heads up to Mount Blinkhorn – it was just the briefest flash of blue, glinting in the sunlight which caught her attention and it was her unconscious mind one hundred yards later that told her to turn around.

Marlene pulled into 6929 – tutting at the mess of empty recycling bins strewn across the grass verge next to it, a full day after the trucks had been and gone. She reversed back out onto Lindholm and headed back down the hill.

Marlene checked her rear view as she slowed on her approach to the gravel mart. Yes, there was a car in the empty lot, a baby-blue Volkswagen Bug.

Marlene felt a thrill of relief, thanking God that she'd found the little car. As she pulled up alongside it, it occurred to her that it was a strange place for a young girl like Sandy to have parked, especially since it was closed. To Marlene, it made absolutely no sense.

CHAPTER 76 - THE AWAKENING

Sandy wiggled her feet and moved her head a little too; it caused her brain to swoon but it did dislodge her slack tongue. Almost drowning on her own spit, Sandy spluttered, her body rejecting the sudden influx of moisture that raped her airway and the reaction made her eyes flicker open. Sandy knew at once that she was *not* in the back of an ambulance *or* in a coma. She was in the cargo space of a mail van, surrounded by packages.

There was a small window above her head, cut into the wood. Sandy guessed that it must separate the cargo space from the driver's cab. The rectangular hole was caged but light filtered through it and painted a shadowed mesh upon the white metal doors that were closed just beyond her feet.

CHAPTER 77 - HIGGLEDY

He shook the blue blanket and turned it, smoothing it out as much as possible upon the dirt floor of the chamber. He'd stoked the stove with slow-burning pellets to ensure adequate warmth and comfort.

Everything's perfect.
Everything should be perfect.
Everything has to be perfect.
But it isn't.

Carter pressed his fingertips hard against his closed eyelids, watching the black dot disappear when he released the pressure. Sometimes that helped him to focus but today it was hard. There was so much to do but it was the order in which to do it all that was causing him distress and making his brain nip…what first? Then after that, and that, and that, and that? Have to be careful, it has to be perfect.

Carter balled his fists and screamed, curving his spine so that his tailbone tucked under his pelvis forcing the muscles on his abdomen into a rigid shield, a shield that he punched. Hard. Repeatedly. Until at last he screamed again, a deep, guttural, bellowing yell.

Panting and breathing heavily, spittle spraying out from his thin lips. Every sinew in his body clenched, his dick hardened and he scratched against it with his knuckles. It was all that bitch's fault, fucking newcomers sticking their foreign fucking noses into other folks' business. He'd show her. He'd watch her break. What will her face look like when she sees it, eh? When she has to identify the putrid remains of her spunk-filled daughter – because Carter knew that this time had to be for keeps and he was going to fill the little one up, every fucking hole, she'd be swimming in his cream, he'd push out her eyeballs and fill the glistening, scarlet sockets with it too.

Now.

It had to be now, before things got too higgledy-piggledy because Carter knows that when things start to get higgledy-piggledy, he gets in trouble just like on the higgledy-piggledy Christmas Eve.

Carter left the chamber and was about to pass all the way through to the sacristy when he heard it moan, the one under the bench. He grunted angrily as he turned to it, already smelling it then he saw that the dirty fuck had shit herself.

"Fuuuuuuck!" Carter screamed as he dived onto his knees and grabbed a fistful of her loose skin, dragging her to him. How fucking dare she taint this day with her noise and her stink.

Her back was curved towards him, he reached down and wiped the wet shit from her arse. He pushed his shit-covered fingers into its mouth, scraping them on her teeth on their way back out. He planted his feet on the ground, crouching powerfully above her. He took her head in his hands, squeezing it between them and in one swift movement he stood and pulled her up and snapped her head almost all the way around. Her arms windmilled and the stupid bitch chirped like a strangled bird. He dropped the dead, filthy body to the ground once more where he shoved it back under the bench with his boot.

"Now you'll shut up, won't you?"

Suddenly calm, measured and in control again, Carter passed through the sacristy and into the tunnel.

It was time for Sandy to take her place.

No more higgledy-piggledy.

CHAPTER 78 - THE KEYS

Marlene pressed her nose up against the glass, looking into the interior of Sandy's blue Bug. A Tim Horton's cup lay on the passenger seat, the contents had spilled leaving a dark patch of wetness on the upholstery. Then she noticed a handbag in the passenger footwell.

Marlene looked around the deserted parking lot. "Sandy? Sandy, hon? Are you here? It's Marlene, sweety."

A blue jay pleeked the only response to Marlene's cry.

Marlene tried the driver's door handle and much to her surprise the car was open. The hinges gave a high-pitched groan as she pulled open the door and sat in the seat. The car shifted with her weight and a bright flash of azure blue glinted as a glass keyring – a pretty dolphin – swung through a shaft of sunlight.

Why would Sandy leave her keys in the ignition?

CHAPTER 79 - A SATISFYING CLICK

Sandy kicked at the doors. They rattled but didn't budge. She rolled onto her tummy and pulled her knees up under her stomach. The movement exhausted her and for a moment she could only rest there, her forehead pressed heavily into the prickly carpet fibres. Once she regained energy enough she pushed up into a kneeling position. She felt the immediate rush of vomit and puked over the parcels in front of her and the sight of the curdled French vanilla made her retch again.

Her stomach tightened again and again but all that left her then was a thick trail of snot from her nose. She wiped it onto her sleeve and reached out, clasping her fingers through the caged window and pulled herself up. She saw a house; the van she was in was parked in front of it. It was little, a brown house with a grey roof and beyond it she could see the edge of what looked like an old barn. There were trees to the right of the barn, lots of trees. Maybe a forest. Sandy blinked, the forest looked smoky, like it was on fire or a thick mist was crawling its way between the trunks.

Sandy shuffled herself around to face the doors, caring not that she had crawled through her own sick. She pushed against the doors, then thumped at them but was quickly overcome with exhaustion and desperation. She puffed, her eyes watered. Sandy understood that she had to get out of this vehicle, that maybe her life depended on it. She pressed her head to the cold metal of the doors and cried but through the shimmering haze of her hot tears she noticed the latch, the handle for opening the door from inside. She wiped her tears away and clasped it.

Hoping like she'd never needed to hope before, Sandy pulled the latch upwards and heard a satisfying click.

CHAPTER 80 - TRUST

"Where is David right now?" Ali demanded.

"He's in an interview room," replied Cuzzocrea.

"Can I see him?"

"No."

Ali took a breath. "Well, when are you releasing him? He needs to take Kenny home."

"Why? Where are you going?"

Cuzzocrea knew with absolute certainty that Ali Dalglish was planning to do something dangerous. Frankly, he didn't blame her and understood the impulse. "He can't take Kenny home. Your house is a crime scene. If Carter was in there and we can prove it, we can arrest him on those grounds."

"And what happens in the meantime? What happens to Sandy?"

Cuzzocrea cast a look at the receptionist who was busy with a jammed photocopier, then he ensured that Kenny was engrossed in his game. Cuzzocrea took a firm hold of her elbow and pulled her to him. He lowered his face to hers, hunching so that his lips brushed against her ear.

"Ali, I want you to trust me, do you think you can do that?" He maintained his grip on Ali until he felt her succumb and allow herself to trust him, her body relaxing, she turned her cheek close to his; she was willing to listen. "I know what you need to do, Ali. I know it too and I'm coming with you, do you understand that? I'm going to be right there with you and we're going to find Sandy together but I need you to trust me because we have to be careful. There *are* ways around things like warrants but those ways have to appear to have been spontaneous."

Ali's heart had slowed but was pumping hard. Cuzzocrea's sudden shift in power was intoxicating and for a reason beyond her ability to comprehend, she found herself willing to trust anything the man said.

CHAPTER 81 - NO DEER

Higgledy-piggledy.

One of the bulbs in the tunnel was out. Carter screwed it tighter; it remained dark. Bulbs. Bulbs are in the kitchen. What first? No, no...*her* first, the van. Her *then* everything else.

He slammed the hatch closed behind him, his wrath seethed. He covered the hatch over. First the van...then the bulbs...no, not with her...the van then back down with her, then maybe bulbs. Carter ran through the field, his keys bounced on his thigh from the chain attached to his belt.

He muttered to himself. "No higgledy-piggledy, order, routine, ritual."

Something caught his eye, movement to his right, amongst the broom. He stilled, studying the yellow bushes. There was hardly a breeze, nothing moved, yet still he watched. Must have been a deer. The van. The van first.

Carter broke into a sprint once again, pounding his limbs, adrenaline driving him faster and faster.

On the gravel drive, he skidded to a halt. The van doors were open.

...

She hadn't gotten far, just to the house but Sandy knew better than to assume it was a safe destination. It was clear to her now that someone meant her harm, someone had put her in that van and had given her something to knock her out, it had to have been Carter – that fucking freak. This was probably his house so there was no way she was going to knock on the door.

She had to get as far away from him as she could but the obvious way would be stupid. If she were to go down that drive and onto the road she wasn't likely to find a passerby for ages, up here in the hills, the boonies (as Danté would say) you were more likely to cross paths with a cougar than a human.

Sandy rounded the little brown house, ducking under window ledges as she went. So enervated was she, she'd had to rest against the siding twice already. At the rear of the house she could see the expanse of field that lay between her and the forest. Sandy decided that her best bet would be to get to the barn, hide in and around that until she was sure the way was clear enough for her to make it to the woods. Maybe then she could find her way through it to the nearest house and call the police.

She dreaded risking exposure by venturing into the field, she would be a target all the way to the barn. The field was overgrown and shabby but the weeds only looked to be waist height at the most.

Sandy was sure that running wasn't an option. She could barely stand on her shaky legs and she was pretty sure she was close to vomiting again. She pushed up from her knees and stood against the wall. She pulled her hood up over her head and began her journey over the field.

Checking behind her every so often to ensure that the nutcase wasn't watching from one of the windows of his house, Sandy kept up a steady pace but when she was almost halfway through the yellow bushes she heard a loud bang to her right. She froze and instinctively dropped down to her knees, keeping her head lower than the surrounding weeds. It had sounded like a door banging but it hadn't come from the direction of the barn straight ahead or even the house directly behind her – it had emanated from the right, in the field, near the trees.

Sandy gingerly raised her head and peeked over the bushes. It was a man, running fast through the field, in the opposite direction to her, towards the house. Sandy threw herself back to the ground, praying that he hadn't seen her and yet she knew that he had, he wasn't running anymore, she could hear his panting, he had stopped and he was looking for her. Sandy covered her mouth to muffle the sound of her own breath – if she could hear him then it was likely he was listening out for her.

Sandy thought about the man, replayed how he was running so quickly, so powerfully. Carter can barely walk, he's a gimpy shit. So who the hell is out there? Not knowing was too much to bear so Sandy picked her head up slowly and pushed herself to her knees. Raising her head, she dared to peek over the bushes again. The man was running again, towards the house but even faster than before, fast and strong and sure and he was most definitely Carter Burrows.

Sandy waited until she lost sight of him as he rounded the house before she got to her feet and began to cross the field as quickly as she could.

When she heard Carter Burrows scream, Sandy decided that running was an option, after all.

...

The cargo space was empty except for puke. Carter slammed the doors shut and thumped at the scar on his head, he screamed as loud as he could, "Bitch!"

He pulled at his keys and threw himself into the driver's seat, she'd be on the road, heading back down probably and if she found her car, she'd make a run for it. Why had he left her keys in it? Stupid! Stupid!

Carter reversed his van and stamped on the brake, the rear doors flew open as he turned and shot forward towards the drive. Everything was bad now.

Higgledy-piggledy.

He put the van in park and ran around to the rear, slamming the doors again but this time checking that they were secure. He heard a beep. At first he thought it was in his head but then a second, longer beep sounded. He peeked around the van and saw a green Subaru pulling up to his van. Mrs McKean's green Subaru.

Carter leaned his head against the rear doors of his van. He closed his eyes and aimed to centre himself. Carter – the Carter that Mrs McKean knew – was very different from the one she would encounter if he didn't find a way to pull himself back.

"Carter? Oh, thank God, Carter."

The McKean bitch was out of her car, she'd seen him.

"Carter?"

Carter was ready, he stepped around the van, careful to walk just like she'd expect him to – like the pitiful fucking retard she liked him to be.

Carter smiled and waved. "Hello, Mrs McKean."

"Oh, Carter." Her jangling jowls were purple and she was short of breath. "Oh, Carter, hon. I need your help, can I use your phone?"

"What's wrong Mrs McKean?"

"It's Sandy, Ali's daughter."

The wobbly bitch had to lean her weight on her knees to catch her breath. Carter wanted to kick her head like it was a soccer ball.

"Sandy? Did she get hurt?"

"I don't know, hon."

McKean stood straight and reached out her hand. Sweaty, clammy fingers like uncooked sausages, gripped his wrist.

"I think something terrible might have happened and I need to call the police."

"Oh no."

"Her car is down at the gravel mart,"

Carter nodded. "The gravel mart?"

"Yes, there. She didn't come home from work and David's been arrested but Ali said he didn't do it – Ali says that the killer, whoever that is, the one that killed the girl…that he's after Sandy and the police were looking for her, I was too…and then I saw the car so I have to call them, you see? I need to tell them to get up here."

Carter was shaking, his fury multiplying exponentially beyond his control, just like the events of the day.

"Oh, hon," said Marlene, taking both of Carter's hands in her own. "You're shaking. It's okay, we'll…" Marlene looked at Carter's hands and suddenly let them drop from her own. "Oh, oh dear, I think…"

The shit. She'd seen the shit. Retards were probably covered with their own shit all the time, so what difference did it make? "No reception up here Mrs McKean, never has been."

Marlene was trying to pretend she wasn't wiping her hands on the back of her trousers. "What about a landline?" She looked above her, tracing the thick, black cables that led from the telegraph pole at the top of the drive to the apex of the roof with her eyes.

"Disconnected a long time ago. Sorry," said Carter.

McKean was looking at him like she knew he was lying but still with that *I feel so sorry for you* look in her eyes. Carter wanted to rip her throat out.

"She wasn't on the road then?"

"Pardon me?"

"Only downhill from here, Mrs McKean. Up there is Blinkhorn, no other houses after mine, so you might have passed her on the road between here and the gravel mart."

"No…no, just her car but all her things were in it…then I remembered you live here so…I'm going now, I think."

McKean moved faster than her jiggles wanted her to as she stuffed herself back into her car but Carter didn't care anymore – he was feeling much better. He smiled at Mrs McKean but she didn't smile back, only drove away. But she watched him all the way then even in the rear-view mirror.

Time's up.

Carter waved and smiled until the sound of the Subaru's

engine was safely in the distance and then he turned to look at the field of Scotch broom.

That wasn't a deer.

CHAPTER 82 - EXQUISITELY GROUNDING PUNISHMENT

Ali pressed her skull against the brick wall behind her. She pushed it hard then harder still, feeling the little spikes and miniature promontory juts of masonry digging into her flesh and the pain was exquisite, far easier to process than the emotional displacement she had been treading water in for the past thirty minutes since Cuzzocrea had asked her to put her trust in him.

The nothingness was eroding her resolve. To know nothing, to be doing nothing, for nothing to be happening as she existed in time and space battling her own atavism – her absolute knowledge that Sandy was in the hands of a savage, beastly, sadistic predator bent on cruel and vicious vengeance.

But dark exists only because of light and so nothing exists alongside everything. Suddenly nothing became everything in the sweep of one vast cyclone of events that started when she felt a thorn of misplaced mortar genuflect its tenuous grip under the persistent push of her scalp, forsaking its determined hubris to crumble in her hair causing recognition to snap in her brain: Ali had met her husband's click-clacking, feather-ankled mistress before. At the fire hall's Christmas party last year and while Ali was unable to conjure a name to go with the blonde hair, she was positive that she had encountered the woman – *girl* – in passing at the event…a dispatcher. Yes, she worked in dispatch. Ali had heard her voice a thousand times summoning all the wannabe heroes of Mochetsin Fire Rescue Service to incidents both major and minor throughout their little municipality. A double cliché – firemen often have affairs but rarely with a regular human being. They historically revert to a stereotype that navigates them towards nurses, emergency room staff, paramedics or…911 dispatchers. They invariably allow their tired relationships to be put asunder by younger, tighter lovers who understand them better, able to empathize with their needs and stresses. Perhaps it is the intense nature of their heroic, adrenaline-fuelled vocation that allows for their boredom, perhaps a need to replicate the rush, their heightened state in the face of a tragedy or a death or the saving of a life, to recreate that in their private lives – a need that fuels their inclination to put their dicks in other holes.

Just as Ali was feeling dull and droopy a gust of fresh air tickled a rash of gooseflesh on her arm. She turned to the open door to see Marlene entering the building. Marlene's eyes were already intent upon Ali but the strings at the end of her purple pashmina snagged on the handle of the door and garrotted her backwards. Marlene struggled to free herself as Ali heard the door to the receptionist's partition open and Cuzzocrea hurried out.

Seeing that Marlene had tethered herself to the door handle, her splenetic efforts to free herself only managing to ravel the strands of cloth further, Cuzzocrea passed Ali to assist Marlene.

Marlene had managed to pull herself free and was up the three tiled steps that separated the entranceway from the foyer by the time Cuzzocrea reached them. And that's when nothing became everything.

Marlene's lips quivered thinly and her cheeks were more rubescent than ever. "I found her car…"

"Oh my God." Ali covered her mouth, suppressing premature relief. "Where?"

"The gravel mart."

"What?" asked Ali.

Marlene nodded and swallowed. "Her keys and her bag were in it but she's not there…why would she be? Anyway, it's closed."

"Where is this gravel mart?" Cuzzocrea asked.

"Lindholm," replied Ali and Marlene in unison.

Cuzzocrea made to step away but Marlene grabbed at his sleeve and yanked him back. "Wait. I saw Carter…"

Ali and Cuzzocrea glanced at one another and back at Marlene.

"At the car?" asked Cuzzocrea.

"No. His house. He lives at the top of Lindholm, just before it becomes Mount Blinkhorn."

"And?" Ali pressed, her forehead vein pulsing.

"Ali, hon, he was…he was different, he had…his hands…I just got a *feeling* and there was this look in his eyes. He scared me."

Ali looked at Cuzzocrea and without a word they made a decision.

"Marlene, thank you." Ali hugged Marlene tightly.

Marlene, hugging Ali back just as firmly, said, "I think maybe you were right about him…I should have listened because he did something once, when he was young…" Marlene pulled out of the hug and regarded Ali with a serious expression. "Nobody ever talks about it but…"

"I know, Marlene. It's okay, we know about the little girl, the dentist's daughter."

"I'm so sorry, hon. What can I do? What if she's up there? Oh God…we have to get, I don't know, SWAT or something, right?" Marlene looked at Cuzzocrea.

"E.R.T., actually, Emergency Response Team." Cuzzocrea realized his correction was ill-timed. "Sorry, go on." He nodded to Ali.

Ali stepped to Marlene and spoke to her. "Marlene, I need you to do one last thing for me."

Marlene nodded. "Anything. What?"

"Kenny. Can you look after him for me? Take him to your place because the police are going to lock my house down."

"Yes. Yes, of course…but David, he isn't…"

"No. David's off the hook, at least from a legal standpoint but they think that Carter was in my house last night, that he came in and that's when he took Oscar."

Marlene was nonplussed.

"It's okay," Ali reassured her. "It's going to be okay." Ali headed over to Kenny.

Marlene looked at Cuzzocrea. "Aren't you going to get your men? Get up there and do something?"

"No. And you can't tell anyone about the car just yet. Ali and I are going to pick up some things from her house before they lock it down and we'll be right back."

Marlene eyed him with suspicion. "Wait a minute, what are you doing?" She thought for a moment. "That's insane, you can't go up there."

Ali returned to Cuzzocrea's side and tugged at his sleeve, urging them to leave.

"Ali, you two can't be serious, are you going up there by yourselves?" said Marlene, her cheeks flushing even more than before.

"These guys have to follow procedure, apply for warrants – there might not be enough time for that." said Ali.

"Yes there is, you said he keeps them for years, he does that thing to their necks and he keeps them…"

"Not now. He's in crisis, he's unravelling, remember? We have to find her now," said Ali, her own words sickening her.

Marlene nodded reluctantly and watched Ali and Cuzzocrea leave before her focus switched to her new responsibility: Kenny.

Kenny didn't notice Marlene as she stepped up to him and took a seat. She gently tapped on the boy's arm. Kenny paused his game and slid his headphones back.

Marlene, pushed her shoulder against his. "What's your poison kid?"

"Poison?" said Kenny.

"McDonald's or Burger King? My treat."

"I'm not allowed junk food in the week, mum says."

Marlene whispered conspiratorially to him, "Screw Mama, I've got some serious dollar baby and I'm willing to throw a little your way because, by my recollection, E.B. Games is right across the street from McDonald's and I just might know a young man who needs a new game, am I right?"

And at that, Kenny brightened.

...

Ali was opening her car door as she watched Cuzzocrea head around the building to his car, the blonde in the silly shoes passed him and simpered a flirty smile his way.

Ali's heart pumped, the sight of the woman and the wrath it inspired in her evoked a similar respite from her panic as had pressing her head against the bricks.

Ali slammed her car door shut and crossed to the blissfully ignorant dispatcher. Beyond her, Ali noticed Cuzzocrea registering the potential encounter, he too was heading toward the woman. Ali knew she would get to her before he did.

"Hey," said Ali, smiling.

The girl looked at Ali and her eyes immediately widened like a rabbit finding itself inches from a slobbering wolf. She attempted to communicate. "Listen…"

But one word does not a conversation make. Ali introduced David's lover to her right fist. Ali enjoyed how the slag had cried out in pain and how she'd crumpled pathetically to the concrete, her heel twisting painfully out of her strapped sandals as she'd held her damaged jaw.

Cuzzocrea stopped walking and held his hands up in helpless acceptance. Ali bent down to her foe. "You're welcome to the sad cunt, bitch."

Ali returned to her Porsche, got in, started the engine and put it in reverse before speeding back so that she was facing the girl, she left it in neutral and revved the engine, almost laughing as the woman scurried to her car, afraid that Ali intended to run her over. Ali looked in her rear view and watched the bitch blink away dust as Ali accelerated away from the R.C.M.P. building.

She was heading back to Alder Beach Road to rendezvous once more with Cuzzocrea for them to prepare for their final destination.

CHAPTER 83 - CIRCUMVENTING THE BARN

Cowering around the rear corner of the barn, Sandy had first shed tears of hope when Marlene pulled into the drive beyond the house. She'd watched her speak to Carter and Sandy had considered running out from behind the barn to scream for help but then the visual had stopped her – the sight of Marlene next to Carter. Knowing now that he isn't handicapped, he doesn't have a gimpy leg and he's actually strong and fast and mean, he could easily outrun and overpower Marlene. By the time the last of her hope had dripped from her chin, fresh tears of terror sprang from Sandy's eyes as she'd watched Marlene get back into her car and drive away. In a last ditch bid for salvation Sandy had stood, waving her arms in a futile attempt to catch the woman's eye but Marlene had been in a rush to leave and she'd kept her eyes glued on her rear-view mirror, on Carter, as she'd left.

Once Marlene had gone Sandy had just enough time to see Carter turn and look in the direction of the barn before she darted behind it. Directly behind the barn was a steep drop-off that eventually led to the forest, it was a steep embankment and regardless of her terrifying predicament Sandy decided against slip-sliding down its rocky face because she was doubtful that she'd reach the woods at the bottom before Carter saw her.

Sandy side-stepped along the barn's rear wall, past two brick buttresses and around the far corner. She carefully felt her way down to the front corner of the building, listening all the time for any noise that may betray the fiend's location. She could hear the swashing noise of his sleeves against the body of his jacket, a paced, rhythmic swiping motion. He was walking towards the barn but he wasn't running and so Sandy dared to deduce that he might not be entirely convinced of her presence. It sounded like he was investigating the field, maybe he had caught sight of her head before she'd dipped in amongst the broom earlier, when he'd stopped running on his way to the house?

Sandy waited short of the corner at the front of the barn and listened carefully. The swash ceased and she imagined Carter to be watching the very corner she was about to round so that if she did, he would pounce at her. Sandy baited her breath and held in her wimpish whimper with her palm tight against her lips.

Across from her the forest still smoked and she wondered if there could be a cabin nestled in there, amongst the trees, somewhere she could hide and call for help. It was a distance from her and she'd be taking a risk in dashing for it and she had no actual guarantee of any help therein. She guessed Carter would surely see her and chase her down if she were to brave the crossing.

The swoosh of his jacket began again, at first growing louder, nearer. Carter was approaching her. Sandy's eyes darted to the rear of the barn – if he rounded the front corner her only option would be to make for the precipice and launch herself down the slope.

There was a loud bang that seemed to shudder the entire structure of the barn and then Sandy heard the shuffle of his boots behind her, at the other side of the planked wall upon which she was leaning. He was inside the barn.

CHAPTER 84 - THE PLAN

Ali pulled up to her house and wasted no time. She took the outer steps two at a time and when her key refused to turn in the lock she cursed it.

"Fuck you, you piece of fucking…"

The lock relented under the weight of her honed profanity. She left the key in the lock and the door open in anticipation of Cuzzocrea's imminent arrival. In the master suite, removing and discarding her clothes as she went, she sat heavily on the bed and pulled off her boots. The zip on her jeans was playing the same game as the lock on the front door and so she simply yanked her jeans down over her hips and walked herself out of them as she reached the closet.

Ali was naked except for her underwear and socks when she heard Cuzzocrea's car pull up outside. Ali dragged a pair of black combat trousers from their hanger with such force that the coat hanger slapped against the shelf above it and pinged free of the rail, stinging her with sharp slap to her cheek before falling to the carpeted floor.

Ali stepped into the combats and zipped them then tucked the bottoms into her socks.

"Ali?" called Cuzzocrea from the front doorway.

"In here, in the master, come through," said Ali as she pulled a black t-shirt down from a shelf. As she stuffed her head and arms into it Cuzzocrea entered, he threw two black items on the bed and turned to her, immediately apologizing for finding her in a state of undress.

"It's okay." Ali noticed that he'd picked up her trail of discarded clothes on his way in. "Tidying up for me?"

"My super already thinks I'm under your spell, last thing we need is Trina reporting back that I undressed you while we were here."

Ali pointed to a wicker basket in the corner of the closet. "Stick them in there. So, what's the plan?" Ali tucked her t-shirt into the waistband of her trousers. She dropped to the floor and rummaged through a messy pile of shoes beneath the hanging clothes, she found her favourite pair of Gortex walking boots and put them on.

"Our priority is Sandy and getting her to safety. Our secondary objective is to keep ourselves out of jail. We have to ensure that we can justifiably argue spontaneity, in that events beyond our control dictated action."

Ali stood. "I know. I'm thinking this: you brought me here, you followed me round while I packed a bag and then we were going to head straight back…"

"You'd better actually pack a bag, you know."

Ali nodded. "*Then*, on the way back we happened upon Sandy's car…"

"Nope. Doesn't fit. We wouldn't take Lindholm back…come here." Cuzzocrea retrieved one of the two items he had placed on the bed. It was a heavy body-armoured vest with several pockets.

"I tell you what won't fit, is me wearing a bulletproof vest."

"Obviously you'll be taking it off before I make the call."

"I don't like it…" despite her opposition, Cuzzocrea placed the vest on her and fastened it around her. "Cuzzocrea? Why are you doing this? Risking your job for me?"

Cuzzocrea examined the fit of the vest, "You're the brains of the operation, you tell me."

"You seem to have a lot of confidence in my capabilities, maybe I'll be a hindrance, a liability to you. Maybe I'll make everything go tits up."

Satisfied that the vest was secure, Cuzzocrea removed his waterproof VIIMIS jacket and donned his own vest. "Research. I'm not driven by guess work here, I'm aware of your experience in the field. There is one problem though."

"What's that?"

Cuzzocrea took his service pistol from its holster and discharged the clip, checked it and snapped it back in place, as he turned the gun to check the safety button Ali noticed an engraved insignia on the stainless barrel. It was an image of a lance-equipped Mountie on horseback with the letters R.C.M.P. to the left and G.R.C. to the right.

"G.R.C.?" asked Ali.

"Huh? Oh, Gendarmie Royale du Canada. French equivalent or translation. I can't give you a firearm."

"I don't want one. I don't need one," Ali replied.

"You need one if he's armed…you're not in Kansas anymore Dorothy…there's a big difference between entering a domicile in the U.K. and going in for an unwarranted raid on a redneck's house in Mochetsin."

"You're armed, I'll stay behind you."

"You can't have any weapon, you know that – no knives, nothing."

"That's where you're wrong Cuzzocrea."

"Trust me, Ali, if this does go *tits up* and you're found in possession of body armour and a weapon, you'll do serious time and I'll be looking at more than a dismissal."

Ali untethered herself from the vest and dropped it onto the bed as she spoke. "When I was a student I used to carry a variety of weapons in my handbag. Now, in Britain you get a nine-month sentence – *minimum* – just for carrying a weapon, you can't even have rape spray and if you were to use a weapon, even on someone who broke into your house, you'd feel the full weight of the law, regardless of the circumstances. But I made sure that my weapons were lethal but not illegal…because I'm a D.I.Y. enthusiast."

"You need to wear the vest, Ali."

"No, I don't, Cuzzocrea."

"You are so annoying, you're wearing the vest, I'm not letting anything happen to you, that's bigger than jail time or unemployment."

"Cuzzocrea, I know enough to know that body armour is as serious an offence as an unlicensed weapon here. I'm going to pack that bag and you're going to follow me just like you have been ordered to. You need plausible deniability, you can swear to the fact that I didn't take anything else, I didn't pack weapons, no kitchen knives or razor blades…nothing that could make you suspect what I was planning all along."

Ali pulled a burgundy bomber jacket from a hanger, put it on and zipped it up. She tip-toed, trying to reach the strap of a black hold-all bag on the highest shelf. Cuzzocrea stepped up behind her and effortlessly pulled the bag down for her.

"Thanks," said Ali as she began throwing random items of clothing into it.

"So…I follow you round, you pack the bag…"

"Yes," Ali said as Cuzzocrea followed her to Kenny's room where she packed items of his clothing into the bag. "We leave here – you put that armoured vest back in the boot of your car – I agree to follow you back to the R.C.M.P. building, except I peel off and head up to…"

Cuzzocrea picked up on her plan. "…Lindholm, because Marlene told you…"

"…that she'd seen Sandy's car on Lindholm, you turned and followed, hoping to catch up with me, finally you do but only in time to see me pulling away from the gravel mart."

Cuzzocrea nodded, "You were the one who declared Carter Burrows a prime suspect – you know where he lives."

"Because everyone in Mochetsin knows Carter Burrows. You head up to the top of Lindholm, you find my car parked near his driveway…and the rest is therefore lawful, especially if you were to hear me scream."

"These weapons you armed yourself with as a student? The D.I.Y. enthusiast stuff?" Cuzzocrea asked.

Ali left Kenny's room and opened the door to her

daughter's room. Cuzzocrea caught up to find Ali standing still in the doorway. Sensitive to the impact the sight of Sandy's room must have had on Ali, Cuzzocrea gently took the bag from her hand and slipped past her into the pink and lilac room.

"Here let me," he said.

Ali's eyes shimmered. She stepped next to the bed and ran her fingertips over the cerise fur comforter as she spoke, "I used to carry a hammer and a screwdriver – new, with the plastic tags still around the handle – and a little box of picture hanging pins and hooks and wire."

Cuzzocrea pointed to the drawers of a purple dresser, Ali nodded her consent as she continued, all the while watching Cuzzocrea gather items of Sandy's clothing and place them in the bag.

"I have a tire iron and lots of tools in my car. I'll say that I'd assumed that Sandy must have gotten a flat or broken down and then I'll say that when I saw she wasn't with her car, I panicked, I put two and two together and became so fixated on the idea that Burrows had taken her I was overcome and found myself in a fugue state. I had no recollection of arming myself with the nearest things I could get my hands on." Ali sat on the bed, overwhelmed by her racing mind and the scent of Sandy's perfume hanging in the air. "There's history to back that up, unfortunately. Any psychiatrist would attest to it's validity, especially under the circumstances."

Cuzzocrea zipped up the bag and sat next to Ali on the bed. He tentatively reached for her fingers and when she didn't pull away, he slipped his hand around hers.

"I know about that history, Ali."

Ali tightened her grip on his hand, she turned from him, feeling unmasked somehow by his knowledge. "That's some intensive investigation, Inspector. You didn't find that out through a Google search or by chin-wagging with a former colleague of mine."

"Actually, it's right up there on PRIME, alongside a

traffic violation in two thousand ten."

"What?" Ali looked at him, her curiosity outweighing her embarrassment. His eyes were kind, and so was the way he had dipped his head to meet her gaze, the crow's-feet wrinkles at the edges of his eyes told a story of a man who often laughed and Ali suddenly craved a time when she might witness that.

"Every time a citizen – or a resident, in your case – interacts with an R.C.M.P. officer, it goes into our database. It's comprehensive. The R.C.M.P. were in attendance the night you tried to kill yourself."

"Oh, I don't remember."

"You wouldn't."

A silence followed, a silence that lasted long enough for Ali to lick her wounds and find strength again to build up her inner fortress after Cuzzocrea's accidental yet wholly decimating attack upon it. Ali watched his fingertips caress her own. It was a simple, relatively innocent gesture but Ali found it to be intensely intimate and it moved her near to tears, his unwavering caress in the wake of the revelation of her most guarded flaw communicated an element of acceptance, if not understanding. Those closest to her had left her bereft of anything but quiet loathing, mistrust and resentment since the events of that particular night, to the point that Ali herself had begun to accept that their reactions were justified and that she deserved nothing but negativity, that she was no longer worthy of love or respect.

"I bet you're wondering how a pathologist could fuck up her own suicide, huh?"

Cuzzocrea cleared his throat. "Actually, no. That's easy to figure out."

Ai looked quizzically at him.

"You're not the only one with an education, Ali. Hysterical strength phenomenon. Whatever took you to that place, it wasn't strong enough to keep you there. You're a survivor and if that punch you laid on that girl earlier is anything to go by, your survival instinct is one stubborn, kick-ass bitch."

Ali smiled and squeezed his hand then she set it on his own thigh. Ali stood and left the bedroom. She turned in the doorway to face Cuzzocrea, "If he does have Sandy up there, let's hope that she takes after her mother and that hysterical strength thing is genetic."

CHAPTER 85 - CORNERED

"Saaandy? Are you hiding?"

Sandy squeezed her eyes tightly shut as his voice moved through her marrow, deeper and less sweet than the voice he had spoken with outside Lloyd's diner. His voice changed again and took on a playful quality, a sickening sing-songy monotone.

"Here I come, ready or not…"

Carter was pacing now, maybe walking in circles, searching the interior of the barn. The sound of the fabric of his jacket returned, he was outside the barn again, just feet from Sandy. She heard him sniff and remembered his nose against her ear. Sandy's thighs quivered and she prayed that she wouldn't pass out. The noise of his motion started up again but this time the swash moved away from her. Carter had been faced with a fifty-fifty choice, luckily for Sandy he'd decided to go around the other side of the barn.

She exhaled as quietly as she could. He was heading in a clockwise direction around the barn – maybe he'd stop to glance down the slope but then he'd be around the rear corner and on top of her fast if she didn't move. The house was too far away and so were the smoky woods.

Sandy moved, taking each dreadful step more carefully than the last so that she didn't cause any noise by dragging a foot or turning a pebble. Sandy slipped silently into the barn, dust motes danced lazily in the light filtering through the gaps between the planks of the walls. She looked for somewhere to hide; there was a ledge up high, a hayloft with its open door on the right-side wall. A ladder was positioned in the centre of the upper platform. It was as good a place to hide as any.

Sandy listened and stepped, listened and stepped. Between the planks of the rear wall, right in the centre of it, the light was disturbed as Carter moved along the outer side of the barn. He was between the buttresses.

Sandy froze – what would happen in a few seconds when he had finally circumvented the perimeter? He'd probably start up his game of hide and seek again, this time more thoroughly than before because Sandy was now sure that he'd seen her in the field. Why else would he spend so long looking for her here?

Sandy put her foot tentatively on the first rung of the ladder, allowing only a portion of her true weight upon it to ensure that it wasn't liable to creak or groan under the pressure. The ladder seemed sturdy and didn't respond to her weight but as she reached to hold onto the sides she noticed an object in a mound of hay at its foot. Sandy retrieved the item; it was a large hook, sharp and rusted with a perpendicular wooden handle. She dropped it down the front of her hooded top and tucked the waistband firmly into her jeans so that it couldn't slip out of the bottom.

Carter's silhouette slipped around the corner of the barn – it would be clear to him now that she wasn't hiding outside the barn, she'd have to move and hide and do it fast because Carter was on the move and he was fast – so much so that by the time Sandy reached the top rung and scuttled on all fours across the platform to where an orange blanket had been laid out on the straw, Carter's shadow had disappeared from the slatted side of the building.

Sandy caught her breath, resting down on her elbows, she was briefly only barely mindful of Carter's existence until she heard him scream,

"You fucking bitch! I'll find you! You think I can't find you?"

Sandy's eyes widened, disoriented by the bounce of his echoing voice, where was he? She crawled forward to see if she would be able to see him through the open hayloft doors. Her fingertips struck something, something that then rolled away from her. It was a bottle of water, Sandy reached for it as it neared the opening, hoping to thwart its journey but, as her fingertips jabbed against it, she only managed to project it faster.

"Shit," whispered Sandy, she crawled after the bottle and dived at it just as it rolled out of sight and disappeared over the edge of the opening. Her hand was still outstretched as she saw Carter in the field, his body was facing the forest and his head was turned to the house. Sandy sighed an, "Oh God," as she heard the plastic of the bottle buckle and its top pop free of the threads upon which it had been screwed as its gathered mass met with the hard ground. Carter's head snapped around like a hawk on the hunt and Sandy found herself in his sights.

That Carter had seen her was less terrifying than the instantaneous hunching of his shoulders as if he were drawing dark energy up through the ground beneath him. His eyes shimmered as yellow as his stubby teeth, a chilling grin of satisfaction that contained within it all his wicked potential.

A sound left Sandy, one she'd never made before – an honest sound, the dreadful sound of her higher self in recognition of her inevitable end.

Carter, his arms longer and stronger than before, projected forth with the power of a jaguar at the denouement of a patient stalk, teeth bared, every muscle in his lithe body synchronized perfectly, catapulting him at a vicious velocity.

He was inside the barn before Sandy could scramble to her feet. The hayloft may have been a reliable hiding place but, finding herself cornered upon it, it was the very worst place she could imagine finding herself face to face with the real Carter.

Her only means of escape was the ladder that Carter stood less than five feet away from, grunting gleeful, excited breaths.

"Found you." He growled through his teeth, a string of elastic white spittle sprang from between them and slapped itself stuck to his cheek.

Sandy began to cry, "Please don't. Please don't hurt me, Carter, please." Sandy held her palms up to him, half begging, half defensive. She quickly observed every corner of the hayloft in the unavailing hope that either a hidden egress or a useful weapon should magically appear.

Sandy was defenceless then it occurred to her that one means of escape meant that there was only one means of entry. The ladder. If she could remove it then…well, she didn't know what then but at least she'd have bought herself more time to think. Carter was no invalid but neither was he Spiderman – he'd need a ladder to get to her so he'd have to fetch another and that could allow her enough time to run away, anywhere, right now she'd happily tumble down that rocky slope out back.

Sandy gripped the thick wooden stringers that were the vertical sides of the ladder, she crouched down and summoned her own dark energy, pulling up with all her might, lifting from her thighs intending to pull the ladder up to the platform with her.

She heaved the heavy ladder three feet or so from the ground with one loud grunt but her satisfaction was eradicated as Carter pounced at one of the rungs, he snatched the ladder back and as it rushed from Sandy's grip she felt a thick splinter from a split in the wood embed itself deeply in her palm. As the ladder was yanked again the shard moved with it and turned in her hand before snapping off in the flesh. Sandy grasped her wrist, her breath caught by the pain as the sliver stabbed sharply into the already blueing flesh of her palm. Sandy tugged the wood free and felt its unwilling relent from the deep fissure, expelling tiny, thorny flinders from its larger body into the deep and stinging banks of the wound.

Sandy let out a constipated moan, loathe to exhibit such weakness. Carter's eyes were on her as he slammed the ladder back in place, panting curdled slaver out of his teeth, he started up the ladder.

Sandy remembered the hook she'd hidden in her top, she stuffed her hand down the neck of her sweater. Unable to reach it, she lost vital seconds before she released the zip enough to find the smooth handle. Carter was further than half way up the ladder. With no choice but to put herself within reach of the man, Sandy dropped to her knees and swung the hook at Carter, he dodged it like a boxer dipping away from a jab and he laughed at her. A loud, high-pitched, mocking laugh, his eyes fiery with madness.

As if it were something to be found on the table of elements, Carters madness floated up to her through the dusty air and Sandy felt his lunacy engulf her like a grim mist. She screamed and swung again and again and again. Carter laughed harder even as the hook whistled close to his nose.

"Come on, you fucker, come on!" Sandy sobbed bravely, ejaculating her own spittle. The handle of the hook was slippy with the blood spewing from the gash on her hand as the tiny splinters burrowed and mined themselves deeper into the meat of her with every swing.

The hook struck the wood of the ladder and hot pain speared through her hand, she pulled back, instinctively clutching her agony to her soothing breast. Carter seized the opportunity at once and scrambled madly up the last third of the ladder. Sandy squealed and dropped back from him as a blast of his putrid, chickeny breath plumed in her face.

She kicked out at him and missed his head but struck the top rung of the ladder. Sandy's eyes mirrored Carter's as they both realized what had happened. The ladder pulled away from the ledge, slowly at first but somehow gaining momentum as it moved despite his weight upon it and his wild thrashing at the void of nothingness now between them. This time Sandy seized the opportunity and slid herself closer to the edge, kicking out her foot again and managing to toe-poke the ladder. Carter reached for her foot, she pulled it back to her and curled her legs up to her chest. The ladder was intent in its pursuit of the opposite direction and it moved languidly through its most upright position then began to speed all the way to the floor. Carter wrapped his arms around the top of the ladder and Sandy wondered if she'd seen fear in his eyes.

CHAPTER 86 - FUCK SIXTY

Despite his height, Cuzzocrea was remarkably stealthy as he moved ahead of Ali, pointing out to her possible pitfalls amongst the wildly viny vegetation underfoot. The tire iron in her right hand was a pathetic understudy to Cuzzocrea's Smith and Wesson which he left sheathed in its holster but with his hand resting atop the handle in readiness.

Cuzzocrea had insisted that they approach the property in a diagonal line through the thick woods that bordered the steep drive to Carter's house in order for them to remain unseen upon their arrival.

As the thicket thinned Ali could see the tinge of pink from the westering sun as it kissed the apex of an asphalt roof. Cuzzocrea dipped to a crouch and held up his closed left fist, instructing Ali to stop.

Ali crouched but covered the distance between herself and Cuzzocrea then squatted next to him. Through the trees she could see a brown bungalow-style house to the left and Carter's Canada Post van to the right. In what she guessed to be a southerly direction, between and far beyond the house and the van, was a forest of tall pines; the pasture between was overgrown and unkempt.

Cuzzocrea whispered, "I'm going to check out the house, you wait here for my nod and then you go and check the van, okay?"

Ali nodded. She watched Cuzzocrea crouch cautiously out from the trees. His hand on the butt of his sidearm and his senses keen, he criss-crossed his way over to a shabby open vestibule where he waited for a moment before progressing along the front of the house and stopping next to the first of three windows.

Cuzzocrea slowly raised himself up and took a careful look through the window before dipping down again and moving along to the next. His investigation of the second window was swift and efficient and he crouched along the remainder of the front elevation to the final window. Carefully standing and looking through he then crossed to the other edge of the window presumably to check the room from another vantage point.

Cuzzocrea dropped to a squat again and looked at Ali, he gave her a clear nod, permitting her to investigate the van.

Ali kept herself as low as she could but covered the distance between the trees and the van quickly. It had already been clear that the cab was empty although she glanced inside to make sure there wasn't someone hiding low behind the dash. She moved to the rear of the van, momentarily losing sight of Cuzzocrea in her peripheral vision as she did.

Ali scanned the field and the tree line beyond. Now she could see more of it, the forest continued around the property, heading east where it looked like the trees were smoky. Satisfied that there was no movement but for the intermittent bustle of a breeze, Ali stepped to the back of the van and tried the handle. It clicked loudly enough for her shoulders to tighten as her flight or fight instinct kicked in. She scanned the tree line once more. Nothing.

Ali pulled open the door to the van, keeping herself shielded behind it. She readjusted her grip on the tire iron and glanced around the door and back again. The glance was enough to ensure that nobody lay in wait, ready to attack and that the van was empty. With slight caution Ali stepped around the door, peripherally aware of Cuzzocrea once more and sensitive to the care with which he watched her.

The cargo space was what one would expect of a postal worker's van, empty but for packages and yet there was something else. It was the unmistakable sting of spent vomit. Ali's nostrils flared, a mother picking up on the scent of her own desperate child. Something caught her eye – a piece of black fabric lying across one of the boxes. Ali leaned closer to it, studying the print on the fabric. Jack Skeleton's stitched grin goaded her and Ali vowed that she would kill Carter Burrows regardless of the consequences.

...

For one horrible moment, as he watched Ali look into the rear of the van and the colour drain from her face, Cuzzocrea thought that he'd exposed her to the worst thing a mother could see – the body of her own child. But when she set off from the van, crouching low with a determined look upon her face he was relieved to realize that the search was still on. Ali reached him and squatted alongside him, her back against the brown siding of the house,

"He had her in there, her scarf's in there and she'd been sick."

Cuzzocrea said nothing and batted away a possibility he would otherwise take to be a given in any other case: the possibility that they were too late. He gestured for Ali to follow him as he made his way around the front corner of the house, managing to avoid an ankle-turning hole probably left following the removal of a tree stump. Cuzzocrea stilled.

Coming into view around the corner of the house, looming ominously in the field beyond was an old barn. Squinting and skewed, deformed and neglected, the broken building struck him as the structural equivalent of Carter himself. Although the sunburst of the day spilled through the trees behind them, giving a rose-tinted hue to all it touched, the barn seemed to remain adamantly encased in a shadow of its own.

Cuzzocrea backed up forcing Ali to retreat with him, back around the corner of the house.

"Let's go," she urged.

"I need to check the rear of this house first. It's open space between this house and that barn. We need to split up and approach wide and from opposite angles."

"Fuck," Ali said through clenched teeth.

"There are no windows on this side so, when it's time, you'll progress via this elevation. I'm going around the other side, I'll clear any windows at that side or on the back and then I'll take the barn from the left, you from the right. When you see me disappear around that corner," he pointed to the corner at the front of the house where he had first begun his investigation of it, "you give me a count of sixty before you go around this corner again. Understand?"

"Sixty, got it." Ali nodded.

...

Cuzzocrea bent low and found his way back along the house. Ali watched him slip around the corner and began her count – probably too fast, she knew, but what the hell. She only made it to twelve before a heavy thud came from the barn. Ali looked around the corner and saw a cloud of dry straw puff from the open front doors.

Ali ran. *Fuck sixty*, she thought. At the back of the house she was barely aware of Cuzzocrea at the other end of it. Ali considered the situation for a moment then she heard a blood-curdling scream from within the barn and she darted out towards the field. Cuzzocrea may have called to her but it didn't matter because nothing was stopping Ali Dalglish now.

CHAPTER 87 - MONSTERS, GODDESSES AND WILL O' THE WISPS

Sandy was momentarily mesmerized by the sight of her attacker's body crashing to the floor, sending a plume of debris out of the doorway. Was he dead? Please let him be dead.

The ladder bounced up from his chest and slapped back down upon him. Sandy stepped to the edge of the platform and stared down. His eyes flashed open and met hers, he screamed a maniacal scream, pulling himself up with monster strength.

Sandy scanned the hayloft, desperate, desperate now, backing into a corner near the open hayloft doors, she saw that the ladder was up again and it shook with Carter's weight as he ran up it and tipped himself over the top. He seemed to have tripled in size as he slavered his horrible grunt, almost silhouetted against a gaping hole in the roof behind him.

Sandy gripped the hook and Carter smiled. He kicked the ladder away from the platform and it clattered uselessly to the ground. Sandy saw her only hope: the open hayloft doors – a fall far enough to make a bottle explode but surely not a fatal fall for a human.

Carter darted to her as Sandy sprang for the opening but he was too fast and she felt her breath gush from her lungs as he slammed into her legs, taking her heavily to the planked floor and sending a rush of lucky blades of old hay out into the evening sun.

Sandy gripped the handle of the hook, something had changed within her and now she relished the pain it brought. She turned herself enough, pivoting at the waist and swung the hook fiercely, slamming it into a section of exposed skin, the flesh between his shoulder and his neck. Sandy pushed the hook deeper and, as if his body was sucking it from her, the hook curled out of her grip. Sandy could see the sharp tip of it, having hooked itself around his collarbone, poking against the thin material of his t-shirt.

Carter yelped and released her. Grasping the hook in both hands, trying to pull it out of him but only serving to drive it deeper, suddenly the rusted point broke through the skin at the front of his chest and curled upwards out of his shirt collar.

Sandy peeled her legs out from under him and scrambled to her feet. Neither caring nor thinking, she launched herself through the open hayloft doors.

Time slowed. Time was drunk or doped up like she had been earlier that day and now Sandy thought of the goddess on the white horse again.

The impact was sudden and horrendous as her leg snapped loudly and sent a searing pain through her that would otherwise have been unimaginable. Her head smashed against something sharp and the smoky trees sparkled with a thousand will o' the wisps.

As Sandy sank into a gloriously peaceful twilight she thought she imagined something else too: the sound of her mother calling her name and that made her smile.

CHAPTER 88 - THE RETURN

Halfway across the field – her trousers seeming to snag on every fucking bush – Ali caught sight of movement within the barn then there was another clattering sound and just as she thought she'd get there in time, Ali saw her daughter.

Relief at the sight of Sandy was but a whisper of a thrill as Ali watched her child fall from the side of the barn. Ali was frozen to the spot.

Ali cringed as she saw Sandy hit the ground, her leg crumpled and audibly snapped then her head hit the ground and bounced off the unrelenting surface of a jagged rock.

Dropping the tire iron, Ali screamed her daughter's name and ran to her still body.

...

Cuzzocrea decided that he had chosen the wrong side of the house to circumvent as he sprinted after Ali, having to cover almost double the distance she did.

Cuzzocrea snapped up the strap of his holster and clicked off the safety as he snatched up his Hogue grip in one fluid motion without slowing.

He saw Ali stop and was dismayed to think that she may have found herself at the wrong end of a gun. Ali had screamed her daughter's name and started running again. Cuzzocrea felt just a touch of relief because not even Ali would run headlong into a bullet.

Now only feet behind her, Cuzzocrea rounded the corner of the barn and skidded to a stop. Ali was kneeling over her daughter's body. She was checking for vital signs and calling her name over and over again. Cuzzocrea watched as Ali rubbed her knuckles harshly on Sandy's sternum then he knew that the girl was unconscious but not dead.

Cuzzocrea gripped his pistol, he looked up at the opening from where Sandy must have fallen, he saw the figure of a man, Carter, sliding up the wall from a seated, to a standing position. Cuzzocrea slid around the front corner of the barn, heading for the open front doors.

He looked into the section of the barn visible to him. It was clear and so he stepped out from the wall enough to allow him a view deeper into the barn.

Taking careful steps he scanned the lower area and the section of the upper mezzanine before he readied himself to switch to the other side, giving him a view of the interior where he already knew at least one male was present.

He swiftly crossed, kitty-corner, to the other side of the doorway and inside it, training his gun with hawk-like precision at various points within the structure, then finally bringing it to rest on Carter Burrows.

Blood had saturated the front right of Carter's shirt and was dripping from his fingertips. He was leaning against the doorway of the open hayloft doors from which Cuzzocrea assumed Sandy had either fallen or had been pushed. His nylon-looking jacket hung from his right shoulder exposing the site of his bloody injury. Cuzzocrea couldn't quite make out what it was, but something was protruding from the man's shoulder.

Carter watched Cuzzocrea. He appeared unfazed, his face a picture of empty vacuity.

"Let me see your hands." Cuzzocrea demanded, moving his index finger from the trigger guard to the trigger itself.

Carter made no movement but smiled at Cuzzocrea. He looked briefly out of the doorway next to him and down to the ground beneath.

"Carter," Cuzzocrea warned, "hands!"

Carter assumed the blank expression once more and Cuzzocrea took careful aim, blowing out the last of his breath. Cuzzocrea's intense focus allowed him to perceive a shift in Carter's expression, a subtle shadow of something demonic flitting over his face. Cuzzocrea began to depress the trigger when Carter suddenly, without even a blink, launched himself out of the hayloft doors.

...

Sandy's cheeks pinked up. Ali expertly applied a trapezius squeeze (gripping and twisting Sandy's shoulder in a deliberate effort to inflict excruciating pain). Sandy reacted by squeezing her eyes even more tightly shut and furrowing her brow. Ali felt a wave of relief.

Ali was unaware of Cuzzocrea's communication within the barn and so was caught entirely off guard when her first contact with Carter Burrows that day was as the full weight of his body slammed on top of her.

Ali was winded, crushed and trying desperately to act as a bridge over her daughter's already broken body. Her eyes bulged under the pressure and she grunted gutturally when she felt the agonizing clench of Carter's teeth at the back of her neck, she screamed in pain as he grunted and growled like a rabid dog above her.

Ali flailed her hands behind her own head and felt the stubbly scratch of his buzz cut hair. Ali scratched and dug, she felt the contour of his eye socket and drove her thumb as viciously and as deeply as she could – happy to find brain if she had to.

Carter's jaws relented and Ali spun herself under him enough to see that a large hook had penetrated the flesh above and below his clavicle. Ali grabbed the hook and twisted it with as much force as she could muster. Carter screamed, recoiling back from the pain and Ali flew onto him, straddling him. She grabbed the skin on either side of his neck, dug her fingers into the right places and pinched shut the passage of blood to his brain. Carter grimaced a sardonic grin as Ali rendered him helpless with a swift and efficient blood choke.

Cuzzocrea called from behind her. "Off him, Ali. I've got this."

She saw Carter's eyes swim back in their sockets and so she released her grip, denying him the luxury of unconsciousness.

Ali rolled off Carter and instinctively used her own body to shield her daughter as she heard the thick, sharp snap of two bullets and felt the power of them obliterate the air particles around her, sending them into a momentary, cowering submission.

Behind her, Carter lay flat, the veins in his neck and skull pumping thickly was the only indication of his pain. He was immobilized by a gunshot to the upper left shoulder and one through his right calf.

Cuzzocrea stood above him, training his gun to Carter's head, if he dared to move, the next bullet would penetrate skull.

Cuzzocrea made the call.

Ali shifted to the other side of Sandy, this time ensuring she didn't turn her back on Burrows. Sandy was quietly moaning, softly sobbing and as Ali comforted her, Carter gazed at them both. Despite the circumstances, something evil danced behind his eyes as his lips curled up into a cold, unnatural smile before Ali watched him don his former persona, affecting a look of innocence, of intellectual retardation, blinking slowly, making a mime of utter confusion in a vile and wicked display of his conniving skill.

CHAPTER 89 - HOPE

As it turned out, Carter Burrows was a man of means – both financial and in terms of his diabolical resourcefulness.

During his transportation from the house he inherited following the death of his foster mother to Victoria General Hospital, Carter told the accompanying officers – Sergeant Hewer and Constable Burton – that there were two other girls who would surely die if he didn't meet with his lawyer upon his arrival at the hospital. His lawyer consulted with him prior to surgery to remove the hook buried behind his clavicle as well as Cuzzocrea's slugs in his leg and shoulder. Together they fashioned a deal.

It was a deal that was agreed upon and signed just moments before Carter Burrows counted back from ten all the way to seven, succumbing to the velveteen escape of his general anaesthetic.

At that very moment, six miles from Victoria General, a line of R.C.M.P. officers were conducting a grid search of Burrows's property and happened upon a strange patch of earth in the field at the rear of it. Had those officers uncovered the subterranean oubliette mere minutes earlier, Carter Burrows would have been transferred, following his post-operative care, to a high-security facility where he would await his trial.

However, as a result of his deal, a binding agreement granted in return for his confession stating that he was responsible for the kidnap, torture and murder of not only

Samantha Giesbrecht but many other girls too – girls he had disposed of in a variety of ways including one girl who he had decapitated and sent into the frigid waters off the Sooke Peninsula just two years ago – he would instead be transferred to another type of room, a private room in a place he referred to as 'home': St. Fillan's Hospital for Forensic Mental Health Care.

At Victoria's Royal Jubilee Hospital, after all statements had been made and photographs had been taken, when Sandy's leg had been operated upon and reset and when the bite on Ali's neck had been cleaned and stitched, Ali stroked her daughter's head as she watched her drift into a sedative-touched slumber.

Cuzzocrea had stopped by with the offer of coffee and to fill Ali in on the aftermath of their terrible afternoon. He took care to emphasize the positives: Carter's capture and incarceration; his subsequent confession – which had led to the rescue of two live victims from an old, underground moonshine still on his property; and, Sandy's escape – the credit for which he was at pains to express, lay firmly with Ali.

Ali listened but took no time in sniffing out Cuzzocrea's bullshit. She demanded to know what they'd given Carter in return for his confession, since Ali knew the twisted fuck wouldn't give up the game easily.

Ali had seen the system manipulated a thousand times. She'd seen solicitors, lawyers and Crown Court barristers argue the insanity plea; she'd seen them fail but she'd also seen them succeed. It defied logic that Carter Burrows should have intellectual capacity enough to give precise locations of burial sites and details of victims, even the dates of their kidnaps and deaths, and yet hope to secure a reduced sentence on the grounds of diminished responsibility.

As a criminal psychologist Ali picked up on many key statements used in the wording of the deal as she heard it from Cuzzocrea, things like 'higgledy piggledy thoughts'; 'the higgledy piggledy man'; that maybe he'd remember more once he was back on his medication because the 'higgledy had gotten him all muddled inside his head'; he 'didn't know nothing about no neck things 'cause of the piggledy'.

Ali could see through the crap, the manipulation and the game playing. Carter knew all the tricks – he'd confessed enough to warrant a negotiation and his resulting cushy pre-trial surroundings yet all the confessions bounced on a pillow of insanity and incapacitation due to mental illness. He had side-stepped any element that could potentially support a prosecution based on pre-meditation and his grasp of right versus wrong.

Sandy's tibia had snapped upon impact with the ground. It was a compound fracture – the lower half of the broken tibia had pushed up alongside its other half and had then journeyed its way through the skin of her lower leg. The injury was significant enough to warrant surgery to remove bone fragments and to insert a series of supporting rods and screws but did not require skeletal traction – a lengthy and painful ordeal which would have required a depressingly long stay in hospital. After only five days Ali and David were able to take their daughter home to complete her recuperation in the comfort of her own bedroom.

On that same day Carter Burrows claimed another life when one of the two girls rescued from his abandoned still, his dungeon of horrors, passed away during a sedated detox. Ali imagined that the girl's body had simply decided that it had suffered enough and although that was inarguably tragic, Ali felt more pity for the girl who was still alive for she would one day wake up and begin to remember. Sandy had only suffered a fraction of the hell that Carter's other victims had gone through yet night after night she woke, sweating and screaming. Her nightmares, a freshly torturous ordeal.

The house was unusually quiet since Ali found herself one dog and one husband short. It was in that new quiet that Ali often caught herself drifting off into the thoughts that had begun to take root in her brain like a malevolent cancer, a new type of madness. Ali never claimed to be any sort of saint, she was comfortable with her flaws and imperfections and was even beginning to nudge towards a sort of acceptance of her truest, most authentic self, flaws and all. But Ali's fresh struggle was with her own morality, her sense of right and wrong because what Ali craved more and more every day was the brutal demise of Carter Burrows and her craving for that was almost intolerably insatiable. Ali would find herself enraptured by her fantasies, playing like a silent movie across the cinema screen of her tainted mind, images of her brutalizing, torturing and killing the man who she knew would evade any sort of proportionate justice.

What Ali needed was a distraction, something tangible and real, something she could turn her focus on and disappear within. As she poured a large glass of cheap red wine, so far the only sufficient means of distraction at her disposal, her phone chirped from its place on the kitchen countertop. Ali saw that the message was from Cuzzocrea:

<hi ali. hope you're well. wondering if you're free tomorrow?>

Ali started to brush her fingers through her messy hair then tutted in defiance. It was pathetic that, since Cuzzocrea was communicating with her via text message, she should care about her appearance suddenly. She replied:

<Sure. What's up?>

And then came the distraction Ali had been hoping for. She found herself holding her breath as she read then reread Cuzzocrea's response:

<a case we're working on. shaw was hoping for a fresh perspective on a couple of elements regarding a profile, he'd like you to come downtown tomorrow about noon to discuss?>

Ali forced two gulps of wine down without daring to savour its flavour in an attempt to fray the edges of something that had wound too tight within her. What was it she was feeling? Then, after another swallow of the claret, Ali recognized the near-alien emotion she'd been teased briefly by not so long ago.

It was hope.

THE END

Ali Dalglish will return very soon in

BRIEFLY MAIDEN

Also published by Fahrenheit Press

About the author

Jacqueline Chadwick is probably best known for her roles in the British soap operas *Emmerdale* (1994–96) and *Coronation Street* (1998–2001).

These days she lives happily ever after on a small Canadian island with her husband, two kids and too many dogs, joyously penning her twisted wickedness.

In The Still is her first novel.

More books from Fahrenheit Press

If you enjoyed In The Still by Jacqueline Chadwick you may also enjoy these other books published by Fahrenheit Press;

A Savage Art by AE Rawson

Hidden Depths by Ally Rose

On A Small Island by Grant Nicol

Printed in Great Britain
by Amazon